P.J. PARRISH

HEART OF ICE

Pocket Books

New York   London   Toronto   Sydney   New Delhi

Pocket Books
A Division of Simon & Schuster, Inc.
1230 Avenue of the Americas
New York, NY 10020

This book is a work of fiction. Names, characters, places, and incidents either are products of the author's imagination or are used fictitiously. Any resemblance to actual events or locales or persons, living or dead, is entirely coincidental.

First Pocket Books paperback edition March 2013

POCKET and colophon are registered trademarks of Simon & Schuster, Inc.

For information about special discounts for bulk purchases, please contact Simon & Schuster Special Sales at 1-866-506-1949 or business@simonandschuster.com.

The Simon & Schuster Speakers Bureau can bring authors to your live event. For more information or to book an event contact the Simon & Schuster Speakers Bureau at 1-866-248-3049 or visit our website at www.simonspeakers.com.

Manufactured in the United States of America

10   9   8   7   6   5   4   3   2   1

ISBN 978-1-4391-8937-5
ISBN 978-1-4391-8939-9 (ebook)

To first loves and Michigan summers

"Intense. . . . The frenetic pace barely gives the reader time to breathe."

—*Orlando Sentinel*

"If you enjoy a good travelogue with your thrills and chills, this is one you won't want to miss."

—*Criminal Element*

More praise for the spellbinding crime fiction of P. J. Parrish

"If you haven't discovered the fast-paced action, terrifying suspense, and hairpin twists of P. J. Parrish yet, now's the time."

—Mystery Guild

"An invigorating ride."

—*Baltimore Sun*

"Her ability to raise goose bumps puts her in the front rank of thriller writers."

—*Publishers Weekly* (starred review)

"Wonderfully tense and atmospheric . . . keeps the reader guessing."

—*Miami Herald*

"A really fine writer."

—John Sandford

"A masterpiece of shock and surprise . . . startling, stunning."

—Ed Gorman, *Mystery Scene*

"Parrish is an author to read, collect, and root for."

—James W. Hall

"Opens like a hurricane and blows you away through the final page. . . . A major-league thriller that is hard to stop reading."

—Robert B. Parker

Also by P. J. Parrish

ACKNOWLEDGMENTS

Like Louis's daughter, Lily, when we were little all we wanted to do was go to Mackinac Island. We lived in Detroit and although our dad took us up north many times, most of our trips ended halfway up the state at Houghton Lake, where we swam in warm brown water, played miniature golf, and cooked marshmallows over a campfire. Sometimes, if we were lucky, we took day trips to the Sleeping Bear Dunes, Tahquamenon Falls, Holland, and Frankenmuth—all places where we could see everything for free.

But the island . . . well, it was expensive for us, what with the ferry ride, bike rentals, Fort Mackinac admission tickets, and, of course, lunch and souvenirs. And the decision between one day on the island and two nights at Houghton Lake was not one to be taken lightly by a single father raising three girls. But finally, one summer, we made it. We didn't have lunch on the veranda of the Grand Hotel but at a curbside shack that served the best greasy burgers in the state. We didn't rent a horse with a guide but we did rent rusty bicycles. And with the wind in our faces and the smell of the gardens in our noses, we rode past Fort Mackinac just as the cannons were booming over our heads. We pedaled past a stable where a man was

Acknowledgments

making horseshoes, past the gracious old homes on the bluffs, and beneath the shadow of Arch Rock with the blue expanse of Lake Huron never out of our sight. We climbed a steep staircase to the top where we could see both the upper and lower peninsulas in one glance. And when we were breathless, we laid down our bikes in the shade and talked about how when we were older we would bring our kids here. We returned many times as adults, even bringing our kids. The island never changes. And that is a good thing, we think.

We get by with a little help from our friends. So a big thank-you goes out to:

Jill Sawatzki of the Island Bookstore on Mackinac Island, who came up with the idea of finding a dead body in the lodge. Also thanks to her fellow booksellers on the island and in the Mackinaw City store: Jane, Kathy, Tam, Cass, and Jeremy.

Sharon Plotkin, certified crime scene investigator for the North Miami Police, whose assistance on explaining fingerprint analysis was invaluable.

Brenda "Bree" Horton, who writes a terrific blog, "Bree's Mackinac Island Blog," about life on the island.

Dr. Doug Lyle, who never fails to keep us honest on all the medical mysteries, and to Peter Lent, who's an okay guy for a lawyer.

And Daniel, as always, for his love, patience, and eagle eye editing our manuscript.

PART I

What love is now I know not; but I know
I once loved much, and then there was no snow.
—Augusta Webster, "The Snow Waste"

1

Wednesday, December 31, 1969

He was staring at the frozen lake and thinking about his mother lying on a table somewhere, screaming in pain.

He was remembering what she had told him, how they had kept her in that little room and held her down, how it felt like her insides were being torn in half, and how it went on and on and on for two days until she begged to die.

He was thinking about her and how much he had loved her. But he was also thinking that if she had been able to stand the pain for two more minutes—*two damn minutes*—his life would have been so very different.

But she couldn't. So he was pulled from her womb at two minutes before midnight on September 14, and because of that everything now had changed.

The ferry was coming in. He heard its horn before he saw it, a white smudge emerging slowly from the gray afternoon fog. It was running late. The straits had frozen over early this year because of the long, bitter cold snap. He pulled up the hood of his parka and looked down at the duffel at his feet. Had he remembered his gloves? Everything had happened so fast he hadn't given much thought to packing. Now he was so cold he didn't even want to open the duffel to look, so he stuffed his red hands into his armpits and watched the ferry.

The ferry was taking a long time to get to the dock, like it was moving in slow motion. But everything was like this now, moving as if time no longer existed. It didn't really, he thought. Not anymore. Time was nothing to him now. By tomorrow he would have all the time in the world.

He looked around. At the clapboard ticket house of the Arnold Line ferry, at the docks, at the empty parking lot and the boarded-up pastie shack. He looked past the park benches and the bare black trees still wearing their neck-laces from last night's ice storm. He looked back toward town where the fog blurred all the places he had known during his nineteen years here, and he tried hard to burn everything into his memory because he knew that once he got on the ferry there would be no way to come back and he would forget all of this and the person he had been here.

He looked to his left.

Canada. It was just fifty miles away, less than an hour's drive up I-75. He had never been there before.

Until now he had never had a reason to.

The ferry docked. No one came out to take his ticket, so he picked up his duffel, sprinted up the gangplank, and boarded. The cabin was empty and dingy but at least it was warmer. He set his duffel on one of the wooden benches and sat down. He wanted a hot cup of coffee but there was no one at the snack bar. The clouded glass pots sat empty on the coffee machines. There wasn't a soul to be seen any-where, and he had the weird feeling that he was the only human being left on earth.

But then the metal floor began to vibrate beneath his feet and the ferry pulled away from the dock. He leaned his head against the cold glass of the window and closed his eyes.

He slept. And for the first time in weeks, he dreamed.

Dreamed of a bald man in horn-rimmed glasses and a blue suit. Dreamed of shooting a rifle that looked nothing like the one he used to hunt deer with his dad. Dreamed of lying naked on a cold steel table in a white room with his intestines pouring out of his gut. And then the bald man was holding up a big bright blue capsule and smiling and telling him that if he just took it all the pain would go away.

He was jerked awake by a jabbing on his shoulder.

He looked up into the red face of an old man wearing a navy peacoat with the ferry line emblem on the pocket.

"Time to get off, son."

The window had fogged over. He rubbed it with the sleeve of his parka and saw something in the mist. It was the boarded-up pastie shack. They were back in St. Ignace.

"Hey!" he called out to the old man who was heading toward the door. "What happened? Why did we turn back?"

"No choice," the old man said. "Got out a ways but it was frozen solid. Got a call in to the cutter but she's working the shipping lines and can't get here until tomorrow morning." He turned and started away.

"But I have to get to the island tonight!"

The old man stared at him, then shook his head. "No one's getting over there tonight, son."

The old man shuffled off, the metal door banging behind him. The young man's eyes went again to the window. His mind was spinning, trying to figure out his options. Stay here and wait? No, because tomorrow would be too late. Go home and try to explain? No, because he couldn't look his father in the eye and tell him one more lie. Leave and try to start over somewhere new? No, because she wouldn't be there.

And this was all about her.

Cooper Lange reached for the duffel at his feet but paused. The name stenciled on the green canvas was so faded it could barely be read: CHARLES S. LANGE. It had belonged to his father, and U.S. Army sergeant Charles Lange had put in it everything he needed to survive—heating tablets, rations, mittens, compass, bullets, and a picture of his wife and baby son. When he came home from Korea Charles packed it away, emptying it and himself as best he could. Even his wife couldn't get him to talk about what had happened over there, and when she died three years later Charles Lange withdrew into himself even more. When his son turned sixteen he brought out the duffel and gave it to him.

Cooper had never used the duffel until last night, when he hurriedly packed it with the things he guessed he might need to survive. A change of clothes, matches, some Mounds bars, the three hundred and two dollars from his bank account, his father's old army compass.

He grabbed the bag and hurried from the ferry. The temperature had dropped since boarding and the cold was a hard slap against his face. He glanced at his watch. Almost four. It would be dark soon. He had to figure out something fast. The dock was deserted and there were no cars in the lot. Chartering a plane in this weather was out of the question, not that he could afford it.

The weather was getting bad fast, a bank of heavy pewter clouds building on the horizon of Lake Huron. His eyes caught a spot of something dark on the frozen lake just offshore. Then he spotted another dark spot beyond the first.

Trees. The dark spots were trees. That meant someone had started laying out the ice bridge. But was it finished?

There was no time to check. If he was going, he had to go now. He unzipped the duffel and found his gloves. He cursed himself for not bringing a flashlight and screwdrivers—it was crazy to cross the bridge without them—but he hadn't planned on having to do this.

He hadn't planned on doing any of this. But she . . .

God, had he forgotten it? Digging beneath the clothes, he found her picture. It was her senior class portrait. Perfect oval face framed by long black hair, somber dark eyes, and not even a hint of a smile. He turned it over to read what she had written even though he knew it by heart.

When love beckons to you follow him, though his ways are hard and steep. And when he speaks to you believe in him, though his voice may shatter your dreams as the north wind lays waste the garden.

—Julie.

He started to put it back in the duffel but instead slipped it into the chest pocket of his parka and zipped it shut.

He put on his gloves, slung the duffel strap over his

shoulder, and headed across the parking lot. At the snow-covered beach he stopped. Someone had tamped down a path that led to the shoreline, creating a crude entry to the ice bridge beyond.

The huge gray expanse of Lake Huron lay before him. And somewhere out there in the fog was Mackinac Island.

The channel was only four miles across, but he knew what he was up against. He had grown up in St. Ignace and spent the last five summers on the island making good money slapping fudge in the shops on Main Street and cleaning stalls at the stables. When the tourists left in October, the island closed down and the hard winters left the couple hundred residents there isolated and dependent on the coast guard icebreakers. But when it was cold enough the straits between the island and St. Ignace would freeze over. Someone on the island would venture out onto the lake with spud bars to test the ice's thickness. If he made it to St. Ignace he'd call back with the news that it was safe. The townspeople would take discarded Christmas trees and plant them in the ice to mark the safe path across.

He glanced back over his shoulder at the redbrick coast guard building on Huron Street. There was a light on inside. The coast guard guys didn't want people out on the ice bridge but they couldn't stop them, so every year they sent out the same warning—tell someone if you go out on the ice bridge. For a second he thought about going up to the station.

But he couldn't. He couldn't tell anyone where he was going. That was what they had decided. She wouldn't tell her parents and he wouldn't tell his father. No one could know.

He hoisted the duffel and stepped onto the ice. It groaned but held firm. He pulled in a deep breath and headed toward the first tree, just a dark shape in the mist.

At the tree, he stopped and looked back. The lights of St. Ignace were just yellow blurs in the fog. Looking ahead again, he spotted the next tree and started toward it.

The sun was now just a pale pink glow above the gray horizon, and out on the exposed lake the wind hit his face like needles. But he kept moving in a tentative shuffle, trying not to think about the deep cold water beneath his feet.

His head was throbbing by the time he reached the fifth tree. Its web of fake silver icicles danced in the wind. One small blue Christmas ornament clung to a branch.

Seeing it brought back the dream about the blue capsule and he realized now what it had meant. Just one month ago he had sat with his father in front of the TV watching a man pour hundreds of blue capsules into a huge jar. No *Mayberry R.F.D* tonight, just Roger Mudd staring back over his shoulder into the camera and whispering as a man in a suit and horn-rimmed glasses pulled out the first blue capsule.

September fourteenth, zero zero one.

His father, sitting in the shadows, had said nothing, just got up and went into the kitchen. Alone, Cooper watched as they put the little slip of white paper with his birthday on it up on a big board next to the American flag. He had never won anything in his life—except this. The luck of being among the first young men drafted into the Vietnam War.

His eyes drifted left again, toward Canada. He would

be there soon enough, but right now he had to get to the island. Julie was waiting for him.

A loud crack, like a rifle shot.

He froze. Afraid to look down, afraid to even take a breath. Another crack.

Suddenly the world dropped.

Blackness. Water. Cold.

His scream died to a gurgle as the water closed over him.

He groped but there was nothing but water. Everything was getting heavy and darker. He had to get some air. He pushed the duffel off and kicked upward. But his hands hit only a ceiling of ice. He couldn't find the hole; he couldn't see anything; he couldn't breathe.

He could almost feel his heart slowing in his chest, his blood growing colder.

Mom, I miss you.

Dad, I'm sorry.

Julie . . .

2

He stood at the railing of the ferry, the sun warm on his shoulders but the spray on his face cold.

Twenty-one years ago he had stood at the bow of a ferry much like this one. Then, the air had been filled with the smell of diesel, but now the ferry left nothing in its wake but a plume of white water and shimmering rainbows.

Then, it had all been about leaving behind the ugly memories of his foster homes in Detroit and going "up north" to the magic island just off the tip of the Michigan mitten. It had been about eating all the fudge his stomach could hold, seeing a real horse up close, and racing the other foster kids around the island on a rented Schwinn.

Now, it was all about her.

Louis Kincaid looked down at Lily. She was peering toward the island, so he couldn't see her face. But he didn't need to. He knew what this trip meant to her. He wondered if she had any idea what it meant to him.

Only seven months ago he had found out he was a father. It had been a shock, but from the moment he saw Lily he was grateful Kyla had not done what she'd threatened to do that night in his dorm room.

I'll get rid of it.

And his response: *Go ahead.*

He looked down again at Lily's crinkly curls.

Thank God . . .

The case seven months ago that had taken him back to Ann Arbor had left him no time to get to know Lily. And once he returned to Florida the twelve hundred miles between them had felt like a million. He spent the next six months trying to convince Kyla that he wanted to be a part of his daughter's life.

He sent Lily postcards from every place his work had taken him, from the glamorous mansions in Palm Beach to the dilapidated Gatorama in Panama City. At first Lily had sent nothing back, but then the letters began. Always short, always filled with drawings, always signed "Lily Brown."

What had he expected—Lily Kincaid?

What was he expecting now?

He had no idea, but he was just glad Kyla—and Lily— were finally giving him a chance.

He hesitated, then touched her hair. She looked up.

"Are you cold?" he asked.

She shook her head and looked back to the island. It was late October, weeks past prime tourist season for Mackinac Island. Weeks past the date he had promised her he would come for her tenth birthday. But there had been an important case to finish and testimony to give.

"I'm sorry I couldn't come up last month," Louis said.

"You already apologized," Lily said.

"I know. And I know how much you wanted to come to Mackinac Island. But we're here now."

Lily leaned her head back to look at him. Her caramel-colored skin was damp with mist, her ringlets frizzed around her forehead. She was a pretty girl, with Kyla's broad forehead and full pink lips. But it was her gray-felt eyes—his eyes—that brought a catch in his throat. He couldn't read the look in her eyes now but felt the need to explain one more time.

"I was testifying in a trial," Louis said. "Trials are important things, not just to the person in trouble but for the prosecutors, too. You can't just not show up if you're a witness."

"Was it a murder trial?"

This was the first interest she had shown in his work.

"No," he said, "it was insurance fraud. Do you know what that is?"

"Some kind of cheating?"

"Yes, it's when—"

"Daddy solved a murder this week."

She didn't wait for his reaction, just turned away and waved to the other ferry that was crossing their wake.

Louis sighed. Lily's stepfather, Eric Channing, the man who had raised her, was a police officer in Ann Arbor. He was a good man—no, he was more than a good man. He had been the one who convinced Kyla to tell Lily about Louis.

Louis and Lily hadn't discussed their relationship during the five-hour drive up north. She had talked about school and ballet classes, her mother's hat business. And about how Daddy had just been promoted to detective and how he now handled the important gross stuff like robberies and shootings and that she sometimes worried about him getting hurt. She'd also let it slip that her mother had told her that private eyes like Louis didn't have to worry about getting hurt.

Louis had been tempted at that moment to tell her about his plans.

He had taken the first steps to go back into uniform. Filled out the application for the Florida Department of Law Enforcement police academy to be recertified. Approached Sheriff Lance Mobley about a job with the county. Bought a second gun. Cleaned up his credit. He even joined a gym because he knew that going back in at thirty put him up against ex-marines and kids who had been pumping iron in their basements since they were twelve.

He hadn't planned to tell anyone until he had a badge on his chest. But he didn't like that Lily had turned away from him when he talked of his work.

"Look! Look!" Lily squealed. "I see the horses!"

They were close enough to the island now to see the sign for the old Chippewa Hotel. The engines cut off, and Lily broke away from him, heading toward the gangplank. He kept her bright yellow sweatshirt in view and finally caught up with her on the dock. As they walked up to Main Street, her eyes widened.

Victorian storefronts advertising fudge, souvenir T-shirts, fancy resort clothes, and oil paintings of Creamsicle-colored Lake Michigan sunsets. A horse and carriage clopped along the street right in front of them, and Lily watched as if it were Cinderella's coach.

"Where are the cars?" she asked.

"They don't allow any cars on Mackinac Island."

"We have to walk everywhere?"

He pointed to the bike-rental shack, and her eyes lit up. She took off again, and he followed her, watching as she wandered down the rows of bikes. She looked up at him.

"These are all old," she said softly.

"Well, we're not entering the Tour de France," Louis said.

His words were out before he thought about it and he didn't know her well enough yet to tell if he had hurt her feelings.

Those gray eyes slid up to him. "I bet you think I don't know what that is."

He sighed. "Knowing your mother, I bet you know exactly what it is. Now pick out a bike. Please."

She settled on a purple Huffy with a white basket. Louis chose the largest mountain bike, glad he had borrowed his landlord's bike last week to practice. Lily sped off ahead of him, the sun glinting off the silver barrettes in her hair as she wound her way through the pedestrians, bikers, and horses.

They kept to the eight-mile road that circled the island, biking past the ramparts of an old fort, ancient limestone formations, and steep hiking paths that led up into the dark pines. And always, there on their right, was the deep blue expanse of Lake Huron.

Suddenly Lily stopped her bike.

Louis pulled up behind her. They were about three-quarters around the island. There was no one else on the road, and the whisper of the surf was the only sound.

"Look at that," Lily said.

Louis looked to where she was pointing. Up on a bluff

was a huge log building. It looked like an old hunting lodge, with a high peaked roof, dormers, and verandas wrapping two of the three stories. A rusted iron fence rose from the weeds in front.

"It looks like a haunted house," Lily said.

"Could be," Louis said with a smile.

"Can we go up there?"

Louis remembered enough about Mackinac Island to know that most visitors kept to the lakeside road. Only the adventurous and well-muscled took their bikes into the hilly woods. He looked down at Lily, meeting her expectant eyes.

"It doesn't look like there's any way up," Louis said.

"Maybe there's a back way," Lily said.

She jumped back on the bike and was off, her skinny legs pumping. About fifty yards up the road she pointed left and turned.

Her sweatshirt was just a blur of yellow in the dark woods as Louis followed her up the dirt road. At the top he stopped to catch his breath. The trees were thick, the air at least ten degrees cooler here out of the sun.

There was no sign of her.

"Lily!" he called.

"Over here!"

But he couldn't see her. He rounded a curve and pulled up at a chain-link fence. There was a big red sign: NO TRESPASSING. He was at the back of the old lodge. Lily's purple bike was lying in the weeds near a gap in the fence.

Damn it.

"Lily!" he shouted.

Nothing.

He dropped his bike and ducked through the fence. As he trotted through the weeds, he caught sight of an empty swimming pool littered with leaves, but he was sure she had gone to the lodge.

He jumped onto the wide wooden veranda. All the windows were shuttered. He went to the front of the lodge. The heavy wood front door was boarded shut and padlocked. There was one window with no shutter but covered with two boards. He peered through the crack between them. He could make out a table with an old oil lamp but no sign of Lily.

Where the hell had she gone? His heart was racing. He had never felt this kind of fear before. He didn't even understand it.

He spun toward the yard but there was nothing to see except the iron fence and beyond that the lake.

"Lily!"

No sound except the buzz of insects.

He headed around the side of the lodge, going so fast he almost missed it—a small metal door about five feet from the ground. It was ajar and there was a cinder block beneath it. It was a milk chute.

He jerked the door open and stuck his head inside.

"Lily! Answer me!"

"I'm here."

Her voice was small and far away, but he let out a huge breath of relief.

"Come back to the milk chute. Now!"

"But there's a reindeer head."

"What?"

"Come in and look. There's a reindeer head over the fireplace. Come look, Louis!"

"I can't. Now get back here now!"

"Oh, all right."

Louis stayed at the chute, peering into the gloom for that spot of yellow sweatshirt.

A sharp crack, a muffled scream.

Louis tried to wedge into the chute.

"Lily!"

Nothing.

"Lily!" he screamed.

He frantically scanned the back of the house. No way in.

He ran back to the front, back to the one window that wasn't shuttered. He ripped the two boards off and used one to smash the glass. Inside, he took a second to get his bearings, then headed toward the back. The dark hallways were narrow and he kept calling Lily's name. But there was no answer.

Then he saw it—a ragged hole in the floorboards. He dropped to his knees, but it was pitch-black below.

"Lily!" he shouted. "Lily!"

A muffled, kitten-like cry from below.

"Lily! Are you okay?"

"I'm scared."

He let out a painful breath. "Are you okay?"

"My arm hurts."

He could hear her crying now.

"Don't cry," he said quickly. "I'm coming down to get you. Don't move!"

"Okay."

He jumped to his feet, scanning the dark room. It

looked like it was a kitchen but with no light he couldn't be sure. And because the shutters were on the outside, he couldn't even break the window. His mind raced and then suddenly he remembered the oil lamp he had seen through the window. He ran back to the front and grabbed the lamp. He shook it and let out a breath of relief when he heard a sloshing sound.

Matches . . . goddamn it, matches.

He took the lamp to the kitchen and started yanking open drawers. Nothing. He was about to give up when he spotted a small tin box on the wall near the stove. He thrust a hand in the bottom and pulled out a handful of wood matches.

"Louis?"

"I'm coming, honey!"

It took four strikes against the fireplace to finally light a match. The old kitchen shimmered pale gold, and he dropped to his knees at the hole in the floor.

He carefully lowered the oil lamp into the darkness.

A spot of yellow. Then Lily's tear-streaked face looking up at him.

Oh my God.

She was lying on a pile of bones.

3

It had been almost forty minutes since he had scooped Lily off that basement floor and carried her outside to the veranda. He tried to stay calm as he gently examined her. He could tell that her right arm was sprained. Going down to the iron fence facing the lake, he managed to flag down a bicyclist to go get help.

When he returned to Lily she was crying. He cupped her face in his hands and asked her if she was all right, even though he could tell by the blank look in her eyes she was nowhere near okay.

Louis heard the sound of a car engine and looked up, surprised to see an ambulance pull in behind the chain-link fence.

"I thought you said there were no cars here," Lily whispered.

"For kids who get hurt there are always cars. Come on, let me carry you over there."

She pulled away from his touch. "I can walk."

"Keep your arm tight to your chest," Louis said.

Lily walked with him to the ambulance to meet the young paramedic. It didn't take a genius to see Lily had fallen into something—she was dirty, her yellow sweatshirt was torn, and her face had some cuts. But the EMT's eyes went right to the arm she cradled against her body. When he began to examine it Lily started to cry again. Louis moved a little closer, trying to keep a reassuring smile on his face.

Louis had dealt with death many times, seen bodies floating in water, left in shallow graves, and laid out on the medical examiner's table. He had even held a baby's skull in his hand. But seeing Lily scared and in pain touched him in a way he never thought possible, in a place he didn't know he had.

He heard another voice and turned to see a man dismounting a bike. He wore a white shirt and dark pants dusty at the cuffs. As he ducked under the fence and started across the yard, Louis could see the gold badge on his chest and brown leather holster on his hip.

Louis had intended to get Lily settled somewhere and then visit the island police to tell them about the bones. He hadn't expected a cop to respond to an accident call. But on a small tourist island it was probably standard procedure.

The officer greeted the EMT by name and looked first at Lily, then at Louis. His badge read MACKINAC ISLAND CHIEF OF POLICE, the sleeve patch displayed an embroidered horse's head.

"Jack Flowers," he said, extending a hand. "Chief of Police."

"Louis Kincaid."

Flowers gave a slight nod, indicating Louis should follow him. They stopped a few yards away from the ambulance.

"Your little girl okay?" he asked.

"Scared mostly."

"Chuck says you were inside the lodge."

"Yes, sir. Lily—"

Flowers cut him off. "Guess you didn't notice the boarded-up windows and NO TRESPASSING signs?"

"Lily snuck in through a milk chute," Louis said. "When I heard her scream I broke a window to get to her. I'll pay for any repairs."

Flowers glanced at Lily, then looked back at Louis. "I'll need to see some ID for the accident report," he said.

Louis reached for his wallet and handed Flowers his Florida driver's license. He thought about telling Flowers he was a private eye but decided against it. The title brought him little respect with most police departments, less here in Michigan, where he had been told he was red-flagged in the state's law enforcement computer as a troublemaker.

Flowers's radio crackled, and the chief keyed it.

"I'm out at Twin Pines, Barbara," he said. "Just some overly curious tourists."

Louis used the moment to size up Flowers. He was about forty, with a rough-hewn face and short jet-black hair that sprang from his head like mondo grass.

Flowers handed Louis back his license. "I should give you a trespassing citation," he said. "But I won't. Looks like your little girl over there feels bad enough."

"You have no idea," Louis said.

"What do you mean?" Flowers asked.

"There's something inside the lodge you need to see," Louis said.

Flowers's thick black brows arched. "We got squatters?"

"I better show you," Louis said.

Louis went back to the ambulance, explained to Lily that he had to take the policeman back inside, and made sure she was comfortable staying with Chuck the EMT. She gave him a small nod.

When Louis got back to the chief, Flowers was just lowering his radio. From the curious expression on Flowers's face Louis knew the chief had run a quick background on him.

"So you're a PI out of Florida?" Flowers asked.

"Yes, sir."

"You carrying?"

"No, I'm on vacation."

Flowers considered him again for a moment, then gestured toward the lodge. "Okay, Mr. PI from Florida. Show me whatever it is in that lodge you think I need to see."

"You'd better get a flashlight."

Flowers gave him a quizzical look, then went back to get a flashlight from the bag on his bike.

Louis took Flowers through the broken window. He picked up the still-lit oil lamp from the fireplace mantel and led Flowers to a narrow hallway off the kitchen. The wood steps leading down to the basement were steep and worn. The air grew colder as they descended into the darkness.

"Over here," Louis said.

The beam of Flowers's flashlight skittered across the floor, finally stopping on a spot about ten feet from a giant boiler in the corner.

"There," Louis said.

Flowers's Maglite caught the white of the bones and for

a long time stayed steady before Flowers slowly began to move it again. The beam picked up the distinct shapes—from the large heart-shaped pelvis to the tiniest finger bones.

Flowers angled the light upward to the hole in the ceiling. "Sweet Mother of God," he whispered. "Your little girl fell from there?"

"Yeah," Louis said.

Flowers turned a slow circle, skipping the light over the stone walls, across the floor, and around the base of the boiler. Dust swarmed in the beam like a million gnats.

"You see any clothing?" Flowers asked.

"No," Louis said. He paused, moving the oil lamp slowly over the floor. "I don't see the skull, either."

Flowers swept the beam over the floor again, then he went behind the steps. He came out and looked behind the boiler before coming back to Louis.

"Maybe an animal got in here and took it," he said.

"They usually take the smaller bones," Louis said. "And from the looks of it I'm guessing most of the bones are still here."

"You touch anything?"

"Lily fell right on the bones. I wasn't thinking of preserving the scene when I was getting her out of here. But I didn't touch anything else."

Flowers turned the light back on the bones. Louis had seen detectives in big cities screw up crime scenes. Flowers looked like he knew enough not to stomp around down here in the dark. But he also looked like he didn't have any idea what his next step was.

"First homicide?" Louis asked.

Flowers looked to him quickly. "What?"

"I asked if this was your first homicide."

"Who said it was a homicide? Maybe someone just came down here and couldn't get out for some reason."

Louis hesitated. "There's no clothing. And the fact the skull is missing could be important."

Flowers just stared at him. Then he turned in a tight circle, running the flashlight beam again into the dark corners.

"Chief," Louis said. "I have to go. Lily's—"

"What's that?" Flowers asked.

"What?"

Flowers moved forward and his beam of light picked up a glint of metal on the floor near the bones. He squatted down, drew a pen from his pocket, and poked at the metal.

"It's a ring," Flowers said.

Louis squatted next to the chief. The gold ring was dusty, but he could see a red stone and what looked like embossing.

"I guess I should just leave it and go call in some techs," Flowers said. "They'll have to come over from St. Ignace."

Louis knew that once something was removed or disturbed it was impossible to restore the scene to its pristine condition. But Lily's fall onto the bones had already compromised the crime scene.

"Take the ring with you now," Louis said. "Get it to a lab or someplace so you can get started on an ID. That's always the first step. Then get some of your guys out here to secure the place and make sure no one gets in."

Flowers looked him square in the eye, and Louis waited

for some defensive comeback. But the chief let out a long breath and began swinging the flashlight slowly over the floor again. Louis realized he was looking for something to put the ring in.

Louis was about to offer to go upstairs and ask the EMT for a plastic bag when Flowers pulled something from his back pocket.

It was a small rolled-up Baggie. Flowers emptied what looked like three aspirin from the Baggie and swallowed them dry. Then he turned the Baggie inside out and used his pen to push the ring inside.

Louis followed Flowers up the stairs and out of the lodge.

Chuck had Lily wrapped in a blanket, and she was sitting in the back of the ambulance. She was licking a lollipop.

"You okay?" Louis asked her.

"It hurts," she said.

"I think it's a sprain," Chuck said. "But we need to get her to the clinic to be x-rayed to be sure."

Louis looked at his watch. "When's the last ferry?"

"At five o'clock," Flowers said.

"You're staying in Mackinaw City?" Flowers asked.

"Yeah, the Best Western."

Louis let out a hard breath. Their luggage was at the hotel, they were stuck here, and he still had to call Kyla.

"Look," Flowers said, "I'm going to have to call the state in on this, and the investigator is going to want to talk to you. Why don't you stay here on the island tonight?"

Louis hesitated.

"I'm going to need your little girl's prints for elimination," Flowers said.

Louis glanced back at Lily. She was hurt and scared, but he could also see the disappointment in her face that their trip was ruined. And that she had caused it.

"My cousin works at the Grand Hotel," Flowers said. "I can call and get you a room. It will be on the department's dime."

When Louis had planned this trip he had called the Grand Hotel, hoping the October rates might be more affordable than in peak season, but there had been no room for less than three hundred a night. A stay in the best hotel on the island might be just what Lily needed.

"Okay, I'll take you up on that," Louis said.

"Great," Flowers said. "You go get your little girl taken care of, and I'll send an officer over to Mackinaw City to get your things. I'll send someone back for your bikes."

"Thank you," Louis said.

Flowers pocketed the Baggie and headed off to retrieve his bike. Louis watched him pedal off as he made his way back to the ambulance.

"Did he give us a ticket?" Lily asked.

"What?"

"Did the policeman give us a ticket for transgressing?"

"Trespassing," Louis said. He smiled. "He let us off the hook."

She looked down at the splint on her arm, then wiped her nose with her good hand.

"How you doing?" Louis asked softly.

"Okay, I guess," she whispered, but didn't look up.

Chuck came over. "We should get her to the medical center, sir."

Lily looked at Chuck. "I've never been in an ambulance before. Can I work the siren?"

Chuck smiled. "We don't use the siren here. It scares the horses."

Lily considered this, then nodded gravely.

Chuck started to close the ambulance door, then paused. "Would you like to ride in the back with your daughter, sir?"

Louis met Lily's gaze. He wondered if she had felt the same strange tug that he had when she heard "your daughter." But he couldn't read a thing in those somber gray eyes.

4

The last time he had laid eyes on the Grand Hotel was when he was nine and on the trip up here with the other foster kids. He could remember looking up at the huge white hotel on the hill and thinking that it was called the "grand hotel" because it must have cost a grand to stay there.

He didn't know much about hotels then. His only exposure had come that very same weekend, when his foster father Phillip Lawrence checked them all into the Wonderland Motel back in Mackinaw City. That place had two hard double beds and a cot, a bathroom that smelled like Clorox, and a black-and-white TV that picked up only a Canadian station showing hockey games.

But this place . . .

Louis leaned forward to get a better view as their horse-drawn carriage approached the covered portico. It was as big as he remembered: a sprawling white wedding cake of a place, with soaring pillars, a veranda with bright yellow awnings, and a cupola topped with a huge American flag snapping against the cobalt sky.

He glanced over at Lily. Her face was somber but he could see something in her eyes that made him relax a little.

"Are we staying here?" she whispered.

"Yes. Is that okay?"

"I don't have any pajamas," she said, looking up at Louis.

"The police are sending someone over to our hotel to pick up our stuff," Louis said. "They'll bring it here."

"What about Lucy?"

Louis remembered the stuffed rabbit she had carefully positioned on her pillow before they left for the ferry. "They'll bring Lucy, too," he said.

The carriage stopped, and Lily's eyes locked on the man in the red livery coat, white britches, and black stovepipe hat.

"Welcome to the Grand Hotel, miss," he said, holding out his hand.

She glanced at Louis, and he gave her a nod. She let the man help her from the carriage and walked ahead of Louis up the stairs. She slowed as they entered the lobby. Even Louis had to stare. Green walls with white wainscoting, burnished antiques, and gilt-framed paintings. Pink and green upholstered wing chairs and tufted sofas dotted the flowered carpeting, and every corner glinted with mirrors and chandeliers.

At the front desk, Louis checked in and told the clerk their luggage would be coming later.

Lily was quiet on the elevator ride, and when he unlocked the door he let her go in first. He watched her as she went to the center of the room, turning slowly as she took in the pink flowered wallpaper, green carpet, and two white canopy beds.

"This is like for a princess," she whispered.

"Well, I don't know about princesses but President Bush stayed here once," Louis said.

"Who?"

"Never mind."

Lily went to the window and looked out at the lake and came back to perch gingerly on the edge of the bed. She stroked the comforter.

"How's your arm?" Louis asked.

She gave a small shrug. The doctor had given him some liquid acetaminophen and a mild sedative. But he wasn't sure if he should give her either—or both. Then he remembered they hadn't eaten since breakfast, which was more than seven hours ago.

"Are you hungry?" he asked.

"Kind of."

"Me, too. Let's go see if we can find something to eat."

She was picking at the mud on her pants. "I'm all dirty," she said.

"Me, too. No one will notice," Louis said.

The clerk at the front desk had told Louis that because it was the last weekend before the hotel closed for the winter and the pantries were being cleared, there would be a bounty of good food and wines at reduced prices. Louis said that all they needed was a couple of sandwiches for now.

The clerk directed them to a small tearoom, where they ordered sandwiches and orange pop. Lily ate only half of her egg salad as she watched the carriages come and go outside the window. Louis felt helpless as he tried to get her to talk.

"How about some ice cream?" he asked.

She perked up. "Can I have a hot fudge sundae?"

"I am pretty sure they have hot fudge here." He signaled to the waitress and ordered two sundaes and a coffee. Lily dug into hers eagerly, but Louis couldn't stop staring at the splint on her forearm. Couldn't stop thinking of the phone call he was going to have to make to Kyla. And more than anything, couldn't stop thinking about what Lily felt when she saw those bones.

He waited until she was finished, then decided to just plunge in. "Lily, I think we should talk," he said.

She took a sip of orange pop. "About what?"

"What happened today."

She didn't look up, just kept drinking.

"How do you feel about it?" Louis said. "I mean, what happened today.".

"I didn't mean it," she said.

"What?"

"I'm sorry I went inside the house," she said softly. "I'm sorry I broke the floor."

He touched her hand. "Oh God, Lily, that's not what I meant. I meant how do you feel about seeing those bones?"

She looked down at the place mat.

"It's okay to be scared," Louis said. When she didn't say anything he decided to press on. "I've seen a lot of bones before and I know it's scary."

She looked up at him. "Is that what I'm going to look like when I die?"

He tightened his hand around hers. He didn't have a clue about what to say but he knew instinctively that the wrong words right now could stay with her forever.

He was saved from saying anything because she spoke first.

"I saw a dead person once when I was little," she said. "When Grandpa Brown passed, Momma took me to say good-bye to him. He was in a really pretty wood bed with a lot of flowers. He looked okay, like he was asleep. But I knew he was dead."

"So you know we leave our bodies here when we . . ." He paused.

"When we go to heaven," she said, nodding her head.

She pulled her hand away and started playing with the straw in her drink. "What's going to happen to those bones?" she asked.

This one was easy at least. "The police will try to find out who they belong to," he said.

"And then what?" she asked.

"They will be sent home so the person's family can have a funeral, like you did for Grandpa Brown."

She considered this for a moment. "How will they figure out whose bones it is?"

"They have lots of ways of finding out," Louis said. When he realized she seemed okay with where this conversation was going he couldn't resist showing off a little. "They can match teeth. They can sometimes match hair or jewelry. They can check records to figure out if someone disappeared."

She was looking at him intently now. "Is that what you do in your job?"

"Sometimes," Louis said.

Lily sat back in her chair, thinking. "It's sad," she said softly.

"What is?" he asked.

"It's sad that the bones were down there in the dark for so long and no one knew it."

Strange that she should put it that way. It seemed that during most of his career he had been dealing with cold cases, cases where people had gone missing, leads had died, and detectives had lost interest. Even his first homicide had been unsolved for thirty-five years—a pile of bones found with a noose in a Mississippi swamp.

"Yes," he said. "It is sad."

They stopped off in the gift shop so Louis could buy toothbrushes and two Grand Hotel T-shirts. As soon as they got back to the room, Lily wanted to take a bath. Louis filled the tub halfway, throwing in some stuff that looked like bath salts at the last minute. He carefully positioned two big pink towels and a T-shirt on a stool by the tub's edge, then returned to the bedroom. Lily was struggling to take off her sweatshirt using her one good arm but finally just gave up and looked at him with big eyes. He wasn't sure who was more embarrassed. She allowed him to ease the sweatshirt up over her head, leaving her wearing just a white T-shirt and slacks. He took a step back, feeling helpless. She set her lips in a determined line.

"I can do the rest," she said.

"You sure?"

She nodded and walked off to the bath. He followed her and she turned, looking up at him.

"Be carefully not to get your splint wet," he said. "I'll leave the door open just a crack. You just holler if you need anything, okay?"

"Okay," she said. Standing in the big white bathroom, she looked very small—and very tired.

He left the door ajar and sat on the edge of the bed. He felt tired, too, as if the full weight of the day was suddenly bearing down on him. He pulled off his shoes and lay back against the headboard.

He was about to close his eyes when he focused in on the telephone.

Shit.

There was no way to avoid it a moment longer. He swung his legs over the bed, pulled out his wallet, and found the slip of paper with Kyla's phone number. The area code was for Chicago, where she was attending a conference for black career women.

He dialed the number, halfway hoping she wouldn't be in her room. But she picked up on the fifth ring.

"Kyla, it's Louis."

"Louis? What . . . ? Why are you calling? Where's Lily?"

God, was the woman psychic?

"She's right here with me. She's taking a bath."

There was a pause on Kyla's end. "Louis, is something wrong?"

He rubbed his face. "She . . . we had a little accident—"

"What? Oh God, what—?"

"Kyla, calm down, everything's fine. Lily's fine."

"Don't tell me to calm down. What's going on up there?"

"She fell down. She's fine, the doctor says it's just a sprain and that—"

"A sprain? Don't lie to me!"

Louis's eyes shot to the bathroom door and he turned

toward the wall so his voice wouldn't carry. "Kyla, god-damn it, calm down. Lily's fine. I wouldn't lie to you about her. Now, calm down and just listen."

He could hear Kyla breathing hard, and he pulled in a deep breath himself before he spoke. "We were riding bikes and we were doing a little exploring." He knew Lily would eventually tell her about the bones, but he also knew there was no way he could tell Kyla about them right now.

"She fell and sprained her arm," Louis said. "They took X-rays and the doctor said—"

"There's a doctor on the island?"

"There's a good medical center," he said. "Kyla, you have to believe me, Lily's fine." When Kyla didn't say any-thing for a long time he knew what she was thinking—that he wasn't competent enough to keep his own daughter safe on a tourist island for three days.

"I can be there tomorrow," Kyla said.

"No," Louis said quickly. He glanced at the bathroom door. "She's fine, Kyla, and she doesn't want to go home." He paused. "And I don't want her to. I need this time with her. Please don't cut it short."

There was a long silence on the other end. Then she said, "Are you going to Echo Bay after this weekend?"

Louis sat back against headboard. The last thing he needed right now was a lecture about Joe. "Yes, I am," he said.

Another silence, then "How about if I come up to the island Monday afternoon and pick up Lily?"

He was confused. Kyla had never been particularly kind to him in the past about anything, so why was she offering to save him a trip back to Ann Arbor? Especially since it freed him up to be with his lover, Joe, a woman Kyla clearly didn't approve of.

"Okay," he said. "Thank you."

"We still need to talk, Louis."

He thought about the bones. "Yes, we do."

"Tell Lily to call me."

They said their good-byes and Louis hung up.

Lily came out of the bathroom. She was wearing the T-shirt. It hung past her knees and elbows. She just stood there looking around the room.

"You want to watch TV?" Louis asked.

She looked around the room and then back at Louis. There was no television in the room. Louis felt a small panic rising up in him at the thought of having to keep her entertained for the rest of the night. But Lily looked away, toward the partially opened window. It was dark, and the street outside was quiet. Her eyes drifted to Louis. She looked very tired.

"Can I lie down?" she asked.

"Of course you can."

He got up and pulled the comforter down. She climbed up on the bed, carefully holding her splinted arm. Louis tucked the comforter around her.

"I wish I had Lucy," she said.

"Lucy will be here tomorrow, I promise."

She turned away, closing her eyes. Louis went back to his bed and lay down. He wasn't really tired, and under normal circumstances he'd be searching out the nearest bar right about now. He turned off the light and lay there in the dark, staring up at the shadows on the ceiling. From the open window came a cool breeze and the clip-clop of a passing carriage.

He closed his eyes.

He had almost drifted off when he felt something warm at his side and smelled the scent of soap. He stiffened, almost afraid to move, like if he did he could roll over and crush her.

Holding his breath, he turned to his side and gently put his arm over Lily's back.

5

There was something about pancakes. Louis remembered whenever he didn't feel well his foster mother Frances would make him banana nut pancakes. Since he was so thin, she never bothered him about sugar. It was just *Eat, you'll feel better*.

Lily was staring at her stack of whipped-cream-topped blueberry pancakes. "Mama says sugar is bad for me."

"It is, but once in a while a little bit won't hurt," Louis said.

Lily picked up her fork and began to eat. Louis sipped his coffee, watching her. She had slept all night with him, waking up before he did to brush her teeth and tie up her hair. After he called down to get their bags she went into the bathroom to dress herself. She emerged wearing a pink sweatshirt and jeans, Lucy in her arms.

He had decided to do his best to make their last day on the island together memorable. The morning had started at the police station, where a big-mitted officer had gently taken Lily's fingerprints. She watched as Louis was printed and seemed thrilled when the officer gave her a copy of her print card. Next they had stopped at a souvenir shop, where Lily picked out a little ceramic horse with MACKI-NAC ISLAND stamped on the base. After that it was everything horses—a carriage ride and their pancake lunch here at the Pink Pony to be followed by a trip to the stables to see the horses get baths.

"May I join you?"

Louis had been so intent on watching Lily that he hadn't seen Chief Flowers approach. Louis gestured to the empty chair, and Flowers sat down, setting a manila folder on the table and filling the air with the scent of Old Spice.

Flowers turned his attention to Lily. "And how are you today, Miss Sunshine?"

Lily held up her right hand, which still had traces of ink on the fingertips. "I got finger-painted," she said.

Flowers smiled. "And who's this?" he asked, nodding to the stuffed rabbit on the windowsill.

"That's Lucy," Lily said.

Flowers looked to Louis, his hand resting on the manila folder. "You want to know what we found out?" he asked.

"Not really and not here," Louis said quietly.

Lily looked up. "It's okay, Louis," she said. "Did you find out who the bones belong to, Chief Flowers?"

Flowers looked to Louis for permission to answer. Louis nodded, hoping Flowers knew where to draw the line.

"The ring we found was from the Kingswood school," Flowers said. "That's the girls' school of the Cranbrook Academy. You familiar with Cranbrook, Mr. Kincaid?"

"Yeah, high-end private school outside Detroit," he said.

Flowers opened his folder and handed Louis a close-up photo of the ring next to a ruler for sizing. Louis could see it was a girl's ring, given its delicacy. The engraving KINGSWOOD and the year 1969 were clearly visible. Then Flowers set a second photo on the table, a close-up of the inside of the band. The initials J.C. were engraved in the gold.

"Did the bones belong to a girl?" Lily asked, rising slightly in her seat to see the photograph.

Flowers glanced at Louis before he looked at Lily. "We're pretty sure the ring belonged to a girl."

Lily looked at the chief. "What did she look like?"

"Well, we don't really know that yet."

Lily fell quiet, Lucy now in her lap. She didn't look upset, just curious.

"I called the school," Flowers said. "They had a student enrolled in 1969 named Julie Chapman who didn't come back after Christmas break. Her family reported her missing just after New Year's. I called the Bloomfield Hills police and found out she never turned up. They're sending their file."

"Bloomfield Hills," Louis said. "That's three hundred miles from here. And why would she be here in the middle of winter?"

Flowers nodded. "Maybe she was abducted," he said.

Louis reached for his coffee.

"John Norman Collins," Flowers said. "You remember him? He abducted girls from Michigan and Eastern and left their bodies in the woods and—"

Louis shot him a sharp look as he nodded toward Lily.

"Sorry," Flowers said.

"Collins was in prison by December of 1969," Louis said.

Flowers sat back in his chair, his eyes drifting to the window.

Louis set his coffee down. "What did you do with the remains?"

"I sent them to the state lab in Marquette," Flowers said.

The Marquette lab, located in the Upper Peninsula, was top rate. The last case Louis had worked in Michigan involved bones found on a farm. The techs in Marquette had been able to eventually establish a time and cause of death, even though the bones had been buried for eleven years.

"That was a good move," Louis said.

Flowers was quiet, his fingers tapping on the folder. "You know, I did a little research on you last night, read some articles in *Criminal Pursuits* magazine. I also called a friend of mine in Fort Myers. He said you're really good with the cold stuff."

Louis glanced at Lily. She was listening closely now but pretending not to.

"I could use a little help with this," Flowers said.

"Chief, I'm on vacation here," Louis said. "And I'm not even licensed in Michigan. I thought you called the state police in?"

"I did," Flowers said.

The tone in Flowers's voice told Louis that Flowers shared his dislike for the state police. He wondered if it went beyond the usual jurisdictional pissing matches.

Flowers's eyes suddenly looked past Louis. "Speak of the devil," he said.

Louis felt a rush of cold air and turned. A tall man in a tan trench coat had just come in the restaurant. His eyes scanned the restaurant with a laser-like proficiency, and when he spotted Flowers he came to the table.

Flowers rose and held out a hand. "Chief Flowers."

"Detective Norm Rafsky."

The name was an itch in Louis's brain, but he couldn't remember where he had heard it before.

"This is Louis Kincaid," Flowers said, nodding. "And his daughter, Lily."

"Kincaid . . . you're the one who found the bones?" Rafsky asked Louis.

"I did," Lily said.

"I'll explain later," Flowers said.

Rafsky's eyes dropped to the photographs on the table. He picked them up and gave them a glance before moving on to the folder with the crime scene photos.

"This all you have?" he asked.

"I have plenty more at the station," Flowers said.

Rafsky was trying to put the photographs back in the folder. Louis noticed that he had to brace the folder against his chest and that his right hand had a slight tremor.

"I'll need to see the lodge," he said. "Can you get me a car?"

"I can get you a golf cart," Flowers said.

Rafsky glanced at his watch. "What hotels are still open here?" he asked.

"The Potawatomi Hotel over on Astor Street stays open year-round," Flowers said.

Rafsky gave a nod and left. Louis watched him through the window. He was standing in the street as if he was trying to figure out which way to go. The man's name was still hanging on the edge of his memory.

Norm Rafsky.

Suddenly it all came back. Joe's description of the state investigator with the ice-blue eyes. It took a few more seconds for Louis to retrieve the details of the story Joe had told him about her rookie year as a police officer in northern Michigan's Leelanau Peninsula. She had pursued a monstrous serial killer and witnessed the assassinations of two fellow officers and the wounding of a state investigator.

The investigator had been Norm Rafsky.

"Louis?"

He looked over at Lily.

"Can we go look at the horses now?"

"Sure we can. You finished?"

Lily nodded and slid out of the booth. Louis looked down at Flowers.

"I'm going to stay and get a burger," Flowers said.

"We'll be here one more night if you need me," Louis said. He started to reach for the check, but Flowers grabbed it.

"Lunch is on me," he said.

Louis nodded. "Thanks."

Outside they paused on the sidewalk. Gray clouds had rolled in.

"I think it might rain soon," Louis said. "We better go find the stables."

Lily didn't answer, didn't even look up at him. She was just standing there, clutching the stuffed rabbit.

Thirty minutes ago she was eating her pancakes and singing to Lucy. Now she looked—what? He had never been able to read kids, and he sure couldn't read Lily right now.

He dropped to one knee. "What's wrong?" he asked.

"Nothing."

She was looking back at the restaurant. He tipped her face toward his.

"Tell me the truth."

"Why don't you help Chief Flowers?" she asked.

He let his hand drop and just stared at her.

"I don't think he knows how to do it," she said.

"Do what?"

"Make sure the bones get home."

"Chief Flowers will take care of the bones."

"But he sent them to a lab."

Louis couldn't think of a thing to say.

"We found her, Louis," Lily said. "It's up to us to make sure she gets home okay."

Louis sat back on his haunches. He had to force himself not to look away from her because he was remembering that day seven months ago when she had asked him why he had never tried to find his real father. He told her then that it was complicated. But for her it had been simple, just like this was now.

But it wasn't simple. In two days he was supposed to be in Echo Bay. Joe had arranged to take a week off so they could try to rebuild the bridge that had been so damaged by their separation. But he also knew that Flowers needed some help, and that without it this guy Rafsky would eat him alive.

Louis zipped up Lily's sweatshirt. He stood up and took her hand. "Come on," he said.

He led Lily back into the restaurant. Flowers was just digging into his burger when he saw them coming. He set it down and looked up at Louis.

"Okay, Chief," Louis said. "I can give you a couple of days."

6

As the Ford Explorer pulled away from the docks, Louis couldn't resist a look back.

He knew Lily was in safe hands. Chief Flowers had suggested that his dispatcher, Barbara, watch Lily while he and Louis went back to the lodge. The deal was sealed when Flowers told Lily that Barbara was taking her own daughter down to the docks to watch the first of the horses leave. Every October, as the island began to shut down for the winter, most of the horses were led in teams from their stables to the docks, where they were loaded onto ferries and taken to a farm in the Upper Peninsula. For Lily, the prospect of saying good-bye to the horses trumped any reservations she had about leaving Louis for a few hours.

After dropping Lily off at the docks with Barbara, Louis and Flowers headed out of town in the direction of the Grand Hotel. Just before the hotel's entrance road Flowers stopped the SUV.

"I was thinking about what you said about the victim being a long way from home," Flowers said. "I asked around and found out Julie Chapman's family has a cottage on the island."

"That could help explain why she ended up here," Louis said.

"Want to see the Chapman place?" he asked.

Before Louis could answer, Flowers swung the Ford left. The Grand Hotel, its awnings furled and its flagpoles bare, loomed above them until the road narrowed as they passed between two stone pillars. To the left was an unbroken panorama of water and sky. But it was the view to the right that riveted Louis's attention.

Victorian mansions, lined up like giant dollhouses, one after another. They were almost absurd in their elaborate beauty, multistoried monstrosities with great yawning porches and peaked towers topped with widow's walks. All the homes seemed to be closed up for the season, their porches shrouded in heavy plastic as if some giant had Saran-wrapped them for storage.

Flowers pulled to a stop in a cul-de-sac. "This is it."

The Chapman "cottage" was not the largest of the bunch, but to Louis's eye it was the strangest. It sprawled over its lot as if the builder had had no master plan but just kept adding rooms at whim. It also looked older—or maybe just more neglected—than its pristine neighbors. Its white paint had gone gray, and the lawn needed mowing. The only sound was the clang of halyards on the empty flagpole.

"Does the family still come here?" Louis asked Flowers.

Flowers shrugged. "I don't know anything about them, but Barbara's lived here all her life and says that after the daughter disappeared in 1969 they closed it up and no one came back for years. Barbara remembers that the father came back once or twice after his wife died but he kept to himself."

"No other kids?"

"An older brother, but he's never been back."

"It looks like no one's been here in a while," Louis said.

"Barbara heard rumors that the place might be going on the market," Flowers said. "But it's been in the family for generations, so I guess the old guy can't bring himself to sell it."

Louis looked at the house. The dark windows stared back at him, the furled awnings sitting like questioning brows above.

"We'd better get going," Flowers said.

He turned the Ford around and soon they were heading deeper into the island's wooded interior. Some bikers stared at the sight of the SUV, but most of the pedestrians just waved. There were only about five hundred permanent residents on Mackinac, Flowers explained, and everyone knew everyone else's name, face, and business.

"This is the Village, where the locals live," Flowers said as he slowed to go through a small residential area. "That's my place over there."

Louis caught a glimpse of a small green bungalow set back among the pines before they headed back into the woods again.

"So why'd you change your mind about staying?" Flowers asked.

"It was changed for me," Louis said. "Lily said it was my responsibility to help."

Flowers smiled. "I get that. Got two girls of my own."

"They stay here on the island all year long?"

Flowers smile faded. "No, they're with my ex in Kansas City."

They rode on in silence, passing a sign that read MACKI-NAC ISLAND STATE PARK.

"So where's Rafsky?" Louis asked.

"Far as I know he's checking in at the Potawatomi. I told one of my men to bring him out here in the golf cart. I don't want to deal with him any sooner than I have to."

"He's not going to like me being here."

"He'll have to adjust," Flowers said.

They turned onto a sandy road, coming up behind the lodge from the back. The chain-link fence was roped in yellow tape. A man in a blue paper jumpsuit was scouring the weedy yard with a metal detector.

Flowers led Louis to the side porch. A tech with tweezers looked up when he heard their footsteps on the planks.

"You got anything there, Henry?" Flowers asked.

The tech shrugged. "Hairs, maybe human, maybe skunks. Some brown stuff, maybe blood, maybe dirt. Maybe nothing."

"You seen the state investigator yet?" Flowers asked.

"Nope."

"Good, I want to go down in the basement and take a look before he arrives," Flowers said. "You guys done down there?"

"I think they're done," the tech said. "But the rest of this place is going to take days. You sure you want us scratching in every corner of every room for every hair?"

Flowers glanced at Louis, clearly looking for affirmation, and when he got none he gave a nod. "You never know what evidence might have survived," he said. "Just do what I asked, please."

When they were out of earshot Flowers said, "I heard of a case once where they kept a bag of stuff for thirty years that they vacuumed up from a rape scene. Turns out later they matched some hairs in the bag to someone."

"You did the right thing," Louis said. "Until you know more about this girl and why she was here you can't assume there isn't evidence in other rooms."

The boards had been removed from the front door, but the windows were still shuttered. The electricity had been turned on, and the foyer was brightly lit by a huge driftwood chandelier.

As Louis followed Flowers through the rooms he had the feeling that the place had been frozen in time. The walls were a mix of smooth logs, paneling, and peeling wallpaper. A single red chair with button cushions sat alone in one room, a three-legged piano stool in another. In the room where he had found the oil lamp there was a large deer head over a sooty stone fireplace.

"What did this place look like in 1969?" Louis asked.

"About the same," Flowers said. "It was built just after the turn of the century as a hunting and fishing camp."

"When did it close?"

"Like 1930 or something."

"You need to be sure, Chief."

Flowers glanced at him over his shoulder. "Yeah. Right. Watch that hole there. That's where your little girl fell through."

They were in the kitchen now. Louis moved gingerly

around the broken boards. It was easy to see the wood rot that rimmed the hole. A bright light coming from below gave him a view of the basement floor. He leaned over and peered down. It was a farther fall than he remembered, easily twelve feet.

Flowers opened a door leading to steep wooden slat steps. Louis went down first, surprised to see the ceiling was lower than he remembered. He was starting to wonder exactly how he had found his way back out to the sunlight carrying Lily.

At the bottom of the stairs they paused. The portable lights revealed the basement to be a large open area with stone walls and a series of small rooms. The boiler that Louis remembered seeing stood in the corner like a huge rusting robot.

But it was the place where the bones had lay that drew Louis's eyes. There was a faint whitish outline on the concrete floor, and, for a second, he took it for a chalk sketch left by the techs. But then he realized what it was. Sometimes, if the conditions were just right, the fluids from a decomposing body would soak into the surface beneath it, leaving a pale ghost image.

Louis glanced at Flowers, but he didn't even notice the stain. He was just standing there, hands on hips, surveying the scene.

"I need to confess something to you," Flowers said. "I'm not sure where to go from here. Any ideas?"

"Let's start with the basics," Louis said. "How's the identification going? You find anything else besides the ring that could link the bones to this Julie Chapman?"

Flowers shook his head. "No clothes, no purse, nothing else here so far, but we'll learn a lot more when her father gets here tomorrow."

"Her father?"

The new voice made Louis turn.

Rafsky was halfway down the stairs, and as he ventured forward his face came into the harsh light. "You called her father?" he asked.

"Why not?" Flowers asked. "We can't ID the bones without teeth. When we find the skull I figured her father could get her dental—"

"Do you have any idea what you've done?"

Flowers glanced at Louis, then back at Rafsky. "I'm just trying—"

"Do you know what parents go through when their children go missing?"

"Detective Rafsky," Louis started.

The sharp blue eyes caught the light as they swung to Louis. "You shut up," Rafsky said. He turned back to Flowers. "They live for any shred of news, so when you give them something you better be damn sure you're right."

Flowers's face had gone tight.

Louis felt a twinge of sympathy for Flowers, but Rafsky was right. Flowers should have researched other missing girls, talked to someone at Kingswood to see if the ring had ever been lost or given away. He should have waited until he had the Bloomfield Hills police report in his hands. On the basis of just the ring he had assumed the bones belonged to Julie Chapman, and now there was no way to take back whatever hope he had given her family.

Rafsky suddenly turned to Louis. "What are you doing here?"

"Chief Flowers hired me on as a consultant," Louis said.

Rafsky shook his head slowly, drew a deep breath, and opened the envelope he was carrying. "I have the preliminary lab reports from Marquette."

"I've been waiting on those all morning," Flowers said.

"You don't wait, Chief Flowers," Rafsky said. "You get off your ass and get them, even if it means driving to Marquette yourself."

Flowers started to say something, but Rafsky cut him off.

"Every bone was here," Rafsky said.

"Except the skull," Louis said.

"Which means the body was not ravaged by animals," Rafsky said. "Other bones would be missing and the skeleton would be scattered. Except for the slight disturbance from your daughter's fall, the skeleton was intact."

"So the killer decapitated her and took the head?" Flowers asked.

"The ME hasn't been able to determine yet whether the head was cut off at the time of death or detached naturally during decomposition."

"Either way, where the hell is it?" Flowers asked.

Rafsky gave him a hard stare. "It's too early to speculate."

"What else did you get from Marquette?" Louis asked.

Rafsky's eyes slid to Louis, then back to his report. "The skeleton is a Caucasian female about five-five in height, approximate age sixteen to twenty-five, with no other injuries or signs of disease."

"That describes Julie Chapman," Flowers said.

"And a hundred other girls from this state who went missing over the last twenty years," Rafsky said.

Louis took a few steps away. He was looking at the ghost stain, but he was thinking about the serial killer Joe and Rafsky had hunted in Echo Bay in 1975. That man had killed for fifteen years, and part of his signature had been to leave a bone from each victim out for animals as an offering. Also, the time period fit.

"Detective," Louis said, "I remember reading about an old case, a serial killer who operated around Echo Bay. He abducted his victims and took them up north. He hid the remains but always left a single bone exposed."

Rafsky had been looking at his report, and his eyes were slow to come up to Louis.

"Could this be related?" Louis asked.

Rafsky closed the folder. "The signature doesn't fit," he said. "The Echo Bay killer collected all the other bones in one place. And he killed only once a year, always at the same time in February. He also hung his victims in trees."

"But how do we know Julie Chapman wasn't kept for a month and killed in February?" Flowers asked. "How do we know—?"

"Because I know," Rafsky snapped. He looked at Louis and took a breath. "There were other signatures, carvings in trees. This isn't the same man."

Rafsky turned and went back up the steps.

"Asshole," Flowers said, starting after him. "I need to—"

"Let it go, Chief," Louis said.

Flowers and Louis went up the stairs, catching Rafsky on the veranda.

"I'll be in Marquette tomorrow," Rafsky said. "I have an appointment with a forensic anthropologist.

He might be able to narrow the time of death. We need to know if she's been in that basement two years or twenty."

"Detective," Louis said, "as long as the father is coming here, why don't we consider DNA testing so we can at least confirm that this is Julie Chapman?"

Rafsky hesitated, then said, "At this point it would be a fishing expedition. A very expensive one."

Louis knew bone marrow could be used for DNA and there was plenty of that, if it was not too degraded. But Rafsky was right—that it would be expensive and there was no way the state was going to foot the bill at this point. A simple dental comparison would confirm if the bones belonged to Julie Chapman, so it made sense to continue searching for the skull.

Rafsky grunted a good-bye and left.

Louis zipped up his jacket and stood at the end of the veranda looking out at the lake. They were only a couple of miles from Main Street, yet it felt like the end of the earth. And there was a strange expectant feeling in the air, as if the old lodge itself were waiting for someone to come back.

"You think it's here?"

Louis turned to Flowers. He was leaning on the railing, looking out at the tech with the metal detector in the front yard.

"The skull, I mean," Flowers said, turning to Louis.

"I don't know," Louis said. "But I do know that this place means something to the killer."

Flowers looked up at the lodge. "Nobody comes here. It's just a broken-down old dump."

Louis shook his head. "No, it's important. It's his Room 101."

"What?"

"It's from George Orwell. *1984*?"

"Never read it," Flowers said.

Flowers moved away, and Louis went back to looking at the lake. He could still recall the exact quote from the book—maybe because it reminded him of things in his foster homes he wanted to forget.

"The thing that is in Room 101 is the worst thing in the world."

7

There were thousands of them. Small, black jelly-bean creatures crawling around the big plastic bin, piggybacking one another to get to that one last shred of meat left on the bone.

The beetle larvae were hungry today.

This skull would be ready by nightfall.

He pressed his face closer to the slimy plastic. The smell was strong, and the inside of his mouth filled with the sickening sensation that comes just before the vomit.

He swallowed it away and held his breath.

He should've taken the time to remove the brain. It stunk like hell when the beetles ate the brain.

Danny Dancer made sure the lid was secure on the bin and left the room, closing the door behind him. As he walked across the cabin the floorboards gave under his weight, reminding him again that it might not be a bad idea to work on getting healthier. After all, Aunt Bitty died at sixty-four, her veins clogged with that cholesterol stuff. He missed her, but he didn't grieve. It was only because she died and left him the cabin that he was able to do what he did now. The cabin was way atop the island, too far from the other villagers for them to smell the beetles.

In the tiny kitchen, he opened a cupboard, pulled out

an industrial-size bottle of hydrogen peroxide, and filled a large metal bowl. It was his last bottle. He would have to make a trip to St. Ignace soon to restock his supplies. There were customers waiting, and he didn't want to get behind.

He let out a deep breath and set the bowl down on the counter. It wasn't easy doing everything himself. He had to feed and maintain the adult beetle colony, hunt for the perfect specimens, and package and ship the orders. He wasn't twenty anymore. His muscles were turning to blubber, and his joints were sore.

It was getting harder to do things, like building the new shelves. It had taken him a whole week to put up the three near the east window, but it had been worth it. There was now enough room to display all his favorite skulls.

He looked up at them now. He liked to sit here in the morning and watch the gold sunlight slide over the smooth skulls, turning them into pieces of art that ought to be sitting in a gallery somewhere, maybe down on Main Street for all the tourists to admire.

But he knew better than anyone that the skulls didn't belong in some shop where moms would herd their brats away, all the while sneaking peeks back.

No, only certain people could appreciate the perfection of skulls. That's why he sold only to universities, laboratories, and artists. That's why he advertised only in the classified section of *Bone Deep*, the underground magazine for collectors of the macabre.

That's where the best money was, from the decorators in Palm Beach who bought the skulls to put on pedestals in mansions. Or landscapers in Sedona who used them as garden ornaments. He had even sold a skull to a record producer in Hollywood who turned it into a bong.

Danny Dancer moved to the window by the front door and pulled aside the curtain, looking for strangers. He did this nine or ten times a day, sometimes more if he felt he was being watched. Though he had seen no one from his window today, this was one of those days when he felt like the skulls had eyes.

Maybe it was because he had heard this morning in town that the bones had been discovered in the basement of the old lodge. He turned away from the window, his eyes slipping to the large skull on the top shelf. It was so incredibly lovely. The eye sockets perfectly round, the teeth as white as pearls, the forehead as smooth as glass, except for that one small crack.

It was his favorite. *She* was his favorite. Because he had always felt it was a she.

He'd never known her name. And unlike his other skulls, he had never felt the urge to give her a name. But the police were nosing around, and maybe they'd even figure out her name. That would make her even more special.

But it would also bring trouble.

They would want her skull. The cops would want her so they could identify her. And her parents would want her so they could feel as if they had put all of her to rest. He didn't imagine the poor girl's mother wanted to live the rest of her life wondering where her daughter's head was, wondering if it was buried somewhere in the mud, lost forever under the feet of hikers who plodded through the woods looking for magic that they couldn't find in their own backyards downstate.

Well, let her mother wonder.

She wasn't going home.

Danny Dancer went to the shelf and carefully took the skull in his hands. Then, hit with an impulse he had never had before, he gave the skull a kiss on the forehead.

"No," he whispered. "You're staying right here."

8

The ferry was coming closer. There wasn't much time now. Louis looked down at Lily standing at his side.

"Bet you'll be glad to see your mom," Louis said.

Lily didn't respond, didn't even look up at him.

The ferry was docking. Louis didn't see Kyla but it was too cold to be out on the deck.

"Where's Lucy?" Louis asked, although he already knew the answer. He had helped Lily pack up all her things just an hour ago back at the Grand Hotel.

"I put her in my suitcase," Lily said.

"Good."

Kyla was the only person who got off. She spotted them and started down the dock. She was wearing a burgundy raincoat and heels, a dark blue silk scarf flowing behind her in the stiff breeze. Her eyes bypassed Louis and lasered in on Lily's splinted arm. She dropped her purse on the dock and swept Lily into her arms.

"Oh, my baby, I missed you," she said.

Lily couldn't say a thing, smothered up in Kyla's bosom. When Kyla finally let her go, Lily pulled back and smiled. Louis felt his heart give a little at the warmth of it.

Kyla touched the splint. "Does it hurt much?"

Lily shook her head. "The doctor lady gave me pain-killers."

Kyla's eyes shot up to Louis.

He pulled two vials from his pocket. "She didn't need them. Here's what they gave her."

Kyla rose slowly and took the vials. She looked tired. "Thanks," she said softly.

She touched Lily's hair. "Baby, can I have a few minutes to talk to Louis?"

"I forgot to buy a souvenir for Daddy. Can I go get him some fudge?" Lily asked, pointing to the ferry gift shop.

Kyla started to say something, then bit it back. Louis dug in his pocket and handed Lily a ten-dollar bill. She ran off to the shop.

"She seems all right," Kyla said, watching her go.

"She's a strong little girl," Louis said.

Kyla looked back at Louis. "You didn't tell me how this happened," she said.

Louis took a deep breath. "Okay, she . . . we were exploring an old house. The floorboards were rotted, and she fell."

Kyla's face tensed, but Louis didn't give her a chance to say anything. "She fell into the basement. I got down there and got her out as quick as I could."

Kyla let out the breath she had been holding.

"There's one more thing," Louis said, glancing toward the gift shop. "There were some bones in the basement. Human bones. She fell on them."

"What?"

He held up his hand. "We talked about it," he said.

"She's okay, Kyla. Believe me, if I thought there was anything really wrong with her because of this, I would tell you."

He had expected a burst of fury, anything but what he was seeing on Kyla's face now. She looked confused, then she shook her head as she looked at the gift shop.

She turned back to Louis. "*Human* bones?"

"Not a body, Kyla. Just dried-up old bones."

Kyla pushed the hair off her face, then slowly she nodded. "Okay," she said softly. "Okay."

"I'm sorry," Louis said.

"For what?" Kyla asked.

Louis didn't know how to answer.

"Louis," she said. "You can't protect them from everything. Believe me, I know. And like you said, she's a strong little girl."

Lily emerged from the gift shop, holding a bag. Louis watched her coming toward them and turned to Kyla.

"Thank you for letting me have her," he said.

Kyla hesitated. "Maybe next time, it can be longer."

Lily came up to them. "I got Daddy fudge with nuts," she said to Kyla.

The ferry horn blew, signaling its departure back to Mackinaw City.

"Louis?"

He looked down at Lily. She was holding something out to him. He knelt in front of her.

"I got you something, too."

It was a small silver-and-pink thing.

"It's a knife," she said.

He took the pocketknife, turning it over in his hand. It

was about two inches long and had a Pink Pony emblem on the side.

"It's for your keys, see?" she said, pointing at the attached ring.

Louis looked up at Kyla, who was smiling.

"Are you going to put your keys on it?" Lily asked.

Louis fished his keys from his pocket and hooked the cheap little knife onto the heavy stainless-steel ring.

"Thank you, Lily," he said, jingling the keys. "I can really use this."

The ferry horn blew again.

Lily looked at the ferry, then suddenly put her arms around Louis's neck and squeezed him. He wrapped his arms around her back and buried his face in her hair.

He was the one who had to push away. "You have to go or you'll miss your boat," he said.

The cold air rushed in where she had been. He stood up and gave Kyla a nod. He didn't trust himself to say anything.

"'Bye, Louis," Lily said.

Kyla took her hand, and Louis watched them board. Lily looked back and waved before they went inside. The ferry pulled away, and he stood there on the dock until it was just a white dot in the distance.

His bag was packed and sitting on the floor. The door of his room was open, and he could hear the drone of a vacuum cleaner. The man at the front desk had told him he was the last guest in the Grand Hotel and that he could take as long as he wanted to check out today.

Flowers had gotten him a room at the Potawatomi Hotel in town.

There was no reason to stick around. But he had one more thing to do before he left.

He picked up the phone and dialed the sheriff's office in Echo Bay. The dispatcher recognized his name but told him that Sheriff Frye was on the other line and asked him to wait. Joe picked up moments later.

"Hey, it's me."

There was a pause. "Don't tell me you're not coming," Joe said.

"No, no, I'll still be there."

"I hear a *but* in your voice, Louis."

He took a breath. "I picked up a case up here. A homicide."

"On Mackinac Island?"

He had to smile. "Yeah, I know. The chief here is in over his head. I offered to help for a couple of days."

In the long pause that followed he could almost feel her disappointment. They hadn't seen each other for eighteen months. That first summer apart, her new job as Leelanau County sheriff had prevented her from making the trips to Florida she had promised. By Christmas their phone calls had dwindled, and he drifted into depression and an affair. It took him more than six months to realize what he had lost—not just Joe but himself.

She had been the one to give voice to it: *I want you to want something for yourself.*

He knew what he wanted. He wanted his badge back. And he wanted Joe back. This trip had been for Lily, but it had also been for him and Joe. He knew that if they didn't reconnect this time they never would. But now here he was again, putting her off for work and hoping she'd understand because she was a cop.

"I've never seen Mackinac Island. How about I come up there?" she said.

"Joe, look," he said. "Everything on the island is closing down. It would be a long drive for you, and I'm only going to be here another day, I promise."

Joe was silent again. Then, in a soft voice, "I want this to work, Louis."

"So do I, Joe. More than you know."

He heard her let out a long breath. "Okay. One more day."

They said their good-byes and hung up. Louis looked around the room, his eyes lingering on the canopy bed. He picked up his suitcase and left the room. Down in the empty lobby, he waved to the man behind the desk, then stepped out onto the veranda. The rocking chairs were gone. The black carriages and red-coated livery men were gone. He hoisted up his bag and started down the long driveway.

On Cadotte Avenue, heading down toward town, he saw only one other person, a bicyclist pulling a cart filled with cords of firewood heading toward the Village.

He turned onto Main Street, walking down the middle of the empty road, passing men on ladders taking down the baskets of geraniums from the lampposts. Many of the stores had already closed, and the few that were open had signs in the windows—EVERYTHING MUST GO.

Almost overnight the island had changed. It looked like a deserted amusement park, and in that moment Louis realized his memories of this place had been distorted, refracted through his need to believe that the real world stopped at the ferry dock, that all ugliness could be forgotten and all hurts could be healed.

Everything did have to go, even illusions.

The wind coming off the lake had the feel of winter. He turned up the collar of his jacket and headed toward his hotel.

9

It was near three by the time Louis met Flowers at the docks. They took the ferry to St. Ignace. It was a good-size town, sitting in the shadow of the magnificent suspension bridge that linked the lower part of the state to the Upper Peninsula. Unlike Mackinaw City, its gaudy tourist-trap cousin on the southern end of the bridge, St. Ignace had the feel of a real town, with modest homes and a downtown of mom-and-pop restaurants and taverns where HUNTERS WELCOME signs hung in the windows. Unless you lived in St. Ignace or had a summer home there overlooking the lake, there was no real need to detour off I-75.

After Flowers picked up a loaner car from the state police post they headed out, bound for a map-speck place sixty miles north called Paradise.

They had spent most of the morning working the phones, talking to the captains of the ferries who had serviced the island twenty-one years ago. The men were easy to locate through the company records and the mariner's union. Finally, one of the captains pointed out to them that they should probably talk instead to the ticket-booth attendants.

Flowers's dispatcher, Barbara, had been able to locate addresses for only nine. None of them recalled anything special about New Year's Eve 1969 except that it had been a particularly brutal winter.

The last woman on the list was Edna Coffee. On the phone she told Louis that she vaguely remembered a young girl traveling alone one winter, but she wanted to see a photo to jog her memory. So Louis and Flowers made the ninety-minute drive through the woods of the U.P. to Paradise.

Edna Coffee was eighty-six and living with her son. She seemed delighted to see them and demanded that her son, Jeff, bring out cookies and tea. Jeff stoically retreated to the kitchen while Edna jabbered about the weather, her arthritis, and her two parakeets, Basil and Birdie. After Jeff returned with the tray, Louis and Flowers politely drank tea and ate cookies before Louis was finally able to turn the conversation to the purpose of their trip.

When he showed Edna Julie's photograph, she stared at it for a long time, then nodded.

"I remember her," she said, stabbing a finger at the photograph.

"How can you be so sure, Mrs. Coffee?" Louis asked.

"It was Christmas Eve, I remember that."

Flowers came forward. "You mean New Year's Eve?"

Louis shot him a look to be quiet.

Edna's eyes went from Louis to Flowers and back to Louis. "Yes, that's right. It was New Year's Eve. And it was really cold."

Louis pulled out his notebook. "Did you talk to her?"

Edna was nodding. "Really cold, colder than normal. I remember the captain coming into the booth and telling me the straits were freezing over and to be sure to tell anyone who was going over that they might not be able to get back."

"You have a good memory," Louis said.

Edna looked up at her son lingering by the door. "Tell him that."

The son couldn't quite hide his impatience. "Don't start, Mom, please."

Edna ignored him, looking at the photograph again.

"Did you talk to her, Mrs. Coffee?" Louis asked again.

Edna's Coke-bottle glasses came up. "Talk? No, just to give her a ticket, that's all."

"How many tickets?"

Edna stared at him. "One."

It had almost come out as a question. Louis closed his notebook.

"She was a pretty thing, with long dark hair," Edna said. "She seemed a little nervous-like, especially when I warned her there might not be a ferry coming back because of the lake icing up."

"Do you remember if she was with anyone?"

Edna's eyes clouded over, and for a moment she looked lost in a haze.

"Mrs. Coffee," Louis pressed. "Was she with a man?"

Edna blinked as she tried to focus on Louis again. "Man? No, there was no man." She held out the photograph, and Louis took it.

Flowers had been standing by the fireplace and came forward. "Do you remember if she had anything with her?"

Edna looked up at him. "Like what?"

"A suitcase, maybe?"

Edna stared at him for a moment. "No . . . don't remember seeing any suitcase . . . but I was in the booth, so I didn't see much more than her face." Edna looked upset, like she was disappointed she wasn't being more helpful. Or maybe because she realized her memory wasn't as good as she thought.

She looked at Louis. "You want to see my parakeets?"

"No, we really have to get back to St. Ignace," Louis said.

Edna's eyes dimmed behind her thick glasses. She stared hard at Louis for a moment, as if she was trying to figure something out.

Louis rose. "Thank you, Mrs. Coffee. You've been a big help."

He started to the door with Flowers.

"She had a monkey."

Louis looked back at Edna. "A what?"

"I remember she had a monkey," Edna said. "She was carrying a stuffed monkey." Edna gave him a satisfied grin. "That's not something you'd forget, is it?"

"No, ma'am, it's not," Louis said. "Thank you again."

At the front door, Edna Coffee's son stopped them.

"She has Alzheimer's," he said quietly.

Louis and Flowers exchanged glances.

"She hasn't remembered anything with clarity for years," the son said. "The parakeets died five years ago. Some days she doesn't remember who I am." He let out a sigh. "I'm sorry. I should have said something before you came all the way up here."

Flowers cleared his throat. "That's all right. We appreciate your letting us talk to her."

"She loves having visitors," the son said. "All her friends

are gone now, and no one comes. Thank you for being nice to her."

Louis and Flowers stood on the St. Ignace dock, silent and shivering as they watched the sun slide into the cloud bank behind the bridge. They had missed the ferry and now had to wait a half hour for the next one.

"Edna thinks Julie came up here alone," Flowers said.

Louis glanced at him. "Her son said—"

"My mom had Alzheimer's. Usually they can't remember what they had for breakfast, but sometimes they can remember every detail about something that happened thirty years back."

"You're dreaming, Chief."

"Maybe not."

"Okay, let's go out on a limb here and say Edna really remembers seeing one girl on one ferry twenty-one years ago," Louis said. "Then let's go even farther out on the limb and say she's right that Julie was alone. So why did a seventeen-year-old come up here on New Year's Eve all by herself? And how'd she get here? According to the missing persons report she didn't have a license, so she didn't drive."

"We haven't checked bus tickets."

Louis pulled up the collar of his jacket. "I think she was brought here by someone else, no matter what Edna thinks she remembers. I would bet my last dollar on it."

Far out on the lake, the ferry was coming into view. Flowers said nothing as he watched it.

"You found no clothes, Chief," Louis said, feeling the need to press his point. "She was nude. Nothing says abduction and rape more than that."

Flowers nodded slowly. "Okay, so let's say she was abducted. But why would the killer go more than two hundred miles downstate to grab a girl, then bring her all the way up here? And why to the lodge? You're the one who says the lodge means something."

Flowers was right that it didn't make sense for the killer to go through so much trouble to bring Julie to the island. But he was also right that the lodge meant something important. If the killer was from the island, why didn't he just murder a local girl? Why Julie Chapman? Had he known her during her last summer on the island? Had he become obsessed with her, enough to drive five hours downstate and five hours back just to bring her to the lodge to kill her?

The ferry pulled up to the dock. Louis and Flowers waited for the three passengers to disembark before slipping into the glass-enclosed interior.

"Chief," Louis said, "Edna said something about people not getting back off the island. What did she mean?"

"The straits freeze up, and the ferries can't run between the mainland and the island," Flowers said. "Usually in late January or early February."

"How do folks get off the island then?"

"If they've got money they can rent a plane. But regular folks use the ice bridge."

"There's a bridge somewhere?"

Flowers smiled. "When the lake freezes over, some fool on the island goes out on the ice with a spud bar to test the thickness. If he makes it across to St. Ignace he radios back and they mark off the ice bridge."

"Mark it off?"

"They take discarded Christmas trees out and plant them in the ice as markers to let others know where it's solid enough to cross."

"How far across is it?"

"About four miles. It's safe usually, but sometimes the currents can cause the ice to shift and break up. I've helped pull more than a few snowmobilers out, and we've had a few folks just disappear on it."

Louis looked out at the water. This ice bridge would have been a good way to get to the island unseen.

"Chief, I don't believe Edna Coffee. Maybe the killer brought Julie to the island across the ice bridge."

Flowers said nothing, and Louis knew he was seeing this grotesque scene in his head—a terrified girl dragged in the cold darkness over four miles of ice.

Edward Chapman, Julie's father, had left a message he wouldn't be on the island until tomorrow morning. Rafsky left a message that he had personal business in Marquette and would be out of contact all day. Barbara the dispatcher had left Flowers a fresh stack of former ferry employees and their phone numbers.

Louis took the list and walked back to the Potawatomi Hotel.

He called Joe's office and left a message that he was still coming tomorrow. When he hung up he looked at his room. As much as he wanted to help Flowers, he wasn't going to miss this place. The carpet was circa-1970 green shag, the bed was lumpy, and when he opened the window he got a faint odor of horseshit. He was sure that was why the place was nicknamed the Potty.

Rafsky had scored the Potty's presidential suite. When Louis asked the clerk what made the suite special he was told it came with a kitchenette.

After a hot shower, Louis took a few minutes to write out a Potawatomi Hotel postcard to Lily, then spent an hour calling ferry workers. No one remembered anything unusual about a teenage girl making her way to the island on any given New Year's Eve. Louis was crossing them off the list when his phone rang.

"Let's have dinner," Flowers said.

"Where?"

"Mustang Lounge."

"Do I need cowboy boots?"

"If you got 'em, wear 'em."

"I was kidding, Chief."

"So was I. It's a few blocks down. Can't miss it."

Ten minutes later Louis walked into the Mustang Lounge. It was a decent-size place, cut into several smaller rooms all walled in shiny pine logs. A pretty blonde in a tight T-shirt tended the small bar, chatting with Flowers while she cut limes.

Louis slid onto a stool next to Flowers and ordered a Heineken, the first beer he'd had since he picked up Lily in Ann Arbor. The blonde gave him a smile with the beer, then wandered off.

When Louis looked back at Flowers, he was bent over the bar, carefully folding a cocktail napkin. He then went about meticulously shredding and fluffing its edges.

"What are you doing?" Louis asked.

"Napkin art," Flowers said. "Look."

Flowers held up the napkin. He had created a stemmed rose, complete with petals.

"You spend way too much time in these places," Louis said.

"Not much else to do here." Flowers took a brandy snifter from the overhead rack and an olive from the garnish tray. He set the olive on the bar and placed the snifter upside down over the top of it.

"Bet you the next round you can't put the olive in the upright glass without touching the olive or letting the olive touch any other object," Flowers said.

Louis stared at the olive under the glass. He should know this. He used to play all kinds of bar games in college.

"Can't figure it out, can you?" Flowers asked.

"Let me think," Louis said.

"You'll never get it," Flowers said. He grabbed the brandy snifter and, without lifting its rim from the bar, started moving it in a tight circle. When he had it going fast enough, centrifugal force drew the olive up into the glass and Flowers flipped it upright, trapping the olive inside.

"I guess I owe you a beer," Louis said.

"I'll take a Labatt."

Louis ordered for Flowers, and for a while they sat in silence watching the baseball playoff game on the TV. Louis hadn't seen the Tigers play since he was a kid. He didn't know any of the players anymore. It made him feel like a stranger in the state he had grown up in.

"I have the Kingswood school sending us some yearbooks," Flowers said. "They're also trying to locate a teacher from back then, someone who might remember Julie Chapman."

"Chief, we still need to verify who the bones belong to," Louis said.

"Julie Chapman," Flowers said.

Louis suppressed a sigh.

"Let's eat," Flowers said. "They have really good chili-cheese fries here."

They ordered dinner and again fell into silence as they waited for their food.

"You want another?" Flowers asked, nodding toward Louis's near-empty beer bottle.

Louis shook his head. "I've been trying to cut back a little."

Flowers signaled to the bartender and ordered a shot of Jack Daniel's for himself. "Where's your little girl, Kincaid?" he asked.

"Her mother picked her up and took her back to Ann Arbor."

"Divorced, eh?"

"Not exactly," Louis said, not wanting to explain to Flowers that he never knew he even had a kid until this past spring. "What about you? You mentioned an ex in St. Louis or somewhere?"

"Kansas fucking City," Flowers said.

"Sound a little bitter," Louis said. "Rough divorce?"

"We're living down in Alpena, right? I'm a patrolman for the city police, putting in all kinds of overtime just to make ends meet so she can live in this ugly old Victorian on the lake. Everything is fine for seven years. Then out of nowhere she tells me she's not happy anymore."

Louis picked at the chili-covered fries. He didn't really

want to hear this, but Flowers, flush with booze, obviously needed to say it.

"So I let her go back to work at the bank," Flowers went on. "A year later she's made manager and putting in more hours than me, and her mother's at the house a lot with the twin girls. It wasn't a good time for us."

Flowers's eyes slid to him, then back to the empty shot glass. For a long time neither man said anything.

"Then Carol got the job offer in Kansas City," Flowers said. "She wanted me to move there, but I knew I wasn't going to be able to get on with any department there. So we split up."

Louis wondered why Flowers had taken the job here on the island. It couldn't be for child support because he doubted the chief made much here. More likely, Flowers felt he needed a title in front of his name to convince himself he was still in control of something, even if it was only a tiny island.

"Well, isn't this an impressive image of quality police work."

They both turned on their stools to see Rafsky standing behind them.

He was carrying two FedEx boxes and a manila envelope. The packages and his trench coat were spotted with rain. Louis glanced at the window. Rain rippled the glass, giving the streetlights a quivering white glow.

"How did you two make out with the ferry employees?" Rafsky asked.

"It was twenty-one years ago, Detective," Louis said. "No one remembered anything worth following up on."

"There was the Coffee woman," Flowers said.

"Excuse me?" Rafsky asked.

"One old lady said she remembered a girl buying a ticket one New Year's Eve," Flowers said.

"She has Alzheimer's," Louis said to Rafsky.

"Still doesn't mean she doesn't have the memory stored in there somewhere," Flowers said. "I told you, people with Alz—"

Rafsky stopped Flowers in midsentence by turning his back on Flowers and making a point to look at Louis, for the first time meeting his eyes with some level of respect.

"I need you to do something for me, Kincaid," he said.

"What's that?"

"When Mr. Chapman gets here tomorrow, I want you to deal with him," Rafsky said. "I want you to explain to him that the chief made a mistake by contacting him and that until we get a positive ID we cannot release the remains to the family."

Louis glanced at Flowers. In the dim light he could see the rise of color in the chief's cheeks. Louis had a sudden memory of a long-ago moment when he was facing his foster parents after getting into a fight with a bully. His foster father Phillip wanted to admonish Louis, but it was his foster mother who had the best advice.

Well, Louis, some people just need a good punch in the face.

That's what Rafsky needed, but this wasn't the time or place for Flowers to find his courage.

Rafsky set the manila envelope on the bar in front of Flowers. "This is all the missing teenage girls in the state for the years 1968 through 1972."

"Why are we wasting time on other missing girls when

we already have a solid lead on Julie Chapman?" Flowers asked.

"Because that's what an investigator does, Chief Flowers," Rafsky said. "Making the assumption that the bones belong to Julie Chapman without further investigation is amateur work. So please do as I ask. Go through this list and eliminate all the other missing girls you can."

Louis picked up the envelope and pulled out the three-page list of names. For a small department like the island PD, researching a hundred or so missing girls was going to be a tedious and time-consuming task.

Louis glanced at Rafsky, wondering why he hadn't just assigned this task to one of his underlings, but then it occurred to him that Rafsky was probably trying to keep Flowers busy while he did the real investigating.

Rafsky set one of the FedEx boxes on the bar, nearly knocking over Flowers's beer. Louis could see the return address: BLOOMFIELD HILLS POLICE DEPARTMENT. It had to be Julie Chapman's missing persons file. The box had already been opened.

"I take it you requested this?" Rafsky said.

"Yeah, anything wrong with that?" Flowers asked.

"Not at all. As I said, just don't get yourself so wrapped up in Julie Chapman that you blind yourself to other possible victims."

"Point made, Detective."

"I've already been over the file," Rafsky said. "Read it tonight and make sure you know what's in here before the father gets here tomorrow so you're prepared."

Flowers started to say something, but Rafsky roughly set the second box on top of the first. The return address on this box was the Cranbrook Academy. Like the other, this box had been opened.

"This I do have a problem with," Rafsky said. "Why did you request old yearbooks from Julie Chapman's school?"

"I thought it might help if we got a feel for her life, maybe look at her activities, maybe—"

"All the information you need right now on the Chapman girl is in that missing persons file," Rafsky said. "If and when we need more background on her we'll get it from her friends and teachers. Not from yearbooks."

Flowers looked to the mirror behind the bar.

"Homicide investigations aren't completed overnight, Chief Flowers," Rafsky added. "They're tedious and complicated and full of dead ends."

Flowers continued to stare at the mirror.

Rafsky sighed and started buttoning his trench coat. "I'll be in Marquette in the morning and back here by the afternoon," he said. "Call the Marquette post if anything comes up you can't handle."

Rafsky left the tavern. Flowers looked back at the FedEx boxes, then reached for his shot glass. Finding it empty, he set it down again.

Louis wanted to tell Flowers that Rafsky was right. Most homicide investigations took months or years, even when you had a quick ID on the victim. But he didn't have the heart to explain that right now. Flowers needed a reprieve from Rafsky's battering.

But maybe he needed a good slap on the head even more.

Louis ordered two more beers. Alcohol was a good

lubricant when you were about to get your ass handed to you.

"You know, Chief, when it comes to Rafsky, you need to grow a pair," Louis said.

Flowers's eyes shot to Louis, filled with fire. But it quickly faded, and he looked away, finding his face in the mirror behind the bar again. He didn't seem to want to look at that, either, and he turned his attention to the window.

"This is your case, Chief," Louis said. "You called the state in. You can also tell him to leave."

Flowers grabbed the fresh beer that the bartender had set before him, but he didn't take a drink.

"I need him," Flowers said. "In a couple of days, you'll be gone, and I can't do this alone."

"Then turn it over to the state," Louis said.

Flowers shook his head slowly. "I can't do that, either." He pulled in a deep breath. "I can't explain this. But this is like somebody invaded my home. I have to . . ."

His voice trailed off. It took him a moment, but he finally met Louis's eyes.

"This is my job," he said.

10

He had walked right past it the first time, mistaking the wooden carved sign for just another one of the historical markers that seemed to be fastened to every old building on the island.

The two-story white clapboard house looked more like a bed-and-breakfast than a police station. Inside, the disconnect continued as Louis stood in the tiny foyer facing a Dutch door. Its top half was open to reveal what he assumed was the heart of the Mackinac Island Police Department.

It was a narrow, long room, its walls lined with built-in desks topped with what looked to be the latest in computers, printers, and other electronics. The place smelled pleasantly of hazelnut coffee and chimney smoke, although there was no fireplace that Louis could see.

The officer sitting at the computer looked up. "Yes, sir?"

"Louis Kincaid. The chief's expecting me."

The officer went to an office at the rear of the room. Louis could see Flowers inside at his desk.

Louis looked down at the file folder he was carrying. It was the Bloomfield Hills case file. He and Flowers had stayed at the Mustang until after dark. Flowers had switched to soda water, and while he ate his dinner he read the file, scribbling notes on bar napkins.

Around eight, he'd received a radio call for a domestic fight in the village and had told Louis he needed to answer this call personally because he knew the couple. He slid the case file to Louis and asked if he wanted to take it back to the hotel and give it a look.

Louis had taken it, knowing Flowers wanted backup ready in case Edward Chapman started asking some tough questions.

It appeared the Bloomfield Hills cops had done a good job. The story that unfolded was a simple one. It was the weekend before New Year's Eve 1969. The parents were out of town; the housekeeper was visiting family in Grand Rapids; and the older brother, Ross, was at the University of Michigan. Julie had declined to go with her parents to California, telling her father she wanted to spend the holiday with her brother. Ross reported she had not told him of her intent to come to Ann Arbor and that she had never arrived.

The police had investigated her family, compiling a complete dossier. They had also talked to Julie's friends—of which there were few—and investigated Detroit-area sex offenders. They had followed hundreds of leads and had received tips of sightings as late as 1977. But in the end, despite the family's high profile, the case had gone cold.

The officer appeared back at the Dutch door. "The chief will see you now."

The officer buzzed the door open, and Louis started back to the chief's office. A black woman sitting in a chair in the corner gave him a long once-over before returning to her paperback.

Flowers's office was tiny, with none of the usual plaques and commendations hanging on the walls. Instead, there was a map of Michigan, some sepia photographs of the island, and a prominent picture of the five-man Mackinac Island Police Department on bicycles.

It was only after Flowers had closed the door that Louis noticed the old man.

He was sitting in the corner, a frail man with sparse gray hair and pale skin, almost lost in the bulk of his blue sweater. There was a tiny breathing device in his nostrils with thin tubes running back behind his ears. Louis saw the portable oxygen canister near the chair and looked to Flowers.

"Kincaid, this is Edward Chapman, Julie's father," Flowers said. "Louis Kincaid is the man I was telling you about, Mr. Chapman."

The old man extended his hand, and Louis shook it. Given his appearance, the man's grip was surprisingly strong. Louis remembered a detail from the family dossier, that Edward Chapman had been an executive vice president with Ford, in charge of overseeing the company's European operations. The Chapmans had led a high-profile life in Europe when Julie was very young. But Edward Chapman had taken an early retirement not long after his daughter disappeared. As Louis considered the fragile man before him, he thought—not for the first time in his career—about the toll murder took on those left behind.

Flowers shifted in his chair, clearly uncomfortable. "I was just telling Mr. Chapman that it was, well, premature of me to have called him because we are not sure the remains are those of his daughter," Flowers said.

"And I was telling the chief that it doesn't matter," Chapman said quickly. "If there is even the smallest chance that this is Julie, then I want to be here."

The smallest chance.

Since last night in the bar, Louis had been thinking about pushing for DNA analysis to identify the bones but had decided to wait. He wondered how much Flowers knew about the technology. His own exposure was limited to what he had read and the one case he had worked recently in Palm Beach. The remains of an illegal immigrant worker had been found and there were no records or family to identify him. They had talked about using DNA to identify him, but the police department had no interest in footing the high cost of the test. Louis suspected money would be no such barrier to a man like Edward Chapman. But he had to talk to Flowers about it first.

"You said you had Julie's ring," Chapman said.

"We think it is her ring," Flowers said. He opened a desk drawer and pulled out a small manila envelope. He took out the ring and set it on the desk.

Chapman reached beneath his sweater and pulled out a pair of glasses, slipping them on. He peered at the ring for a long time, then set it down on the desk. "I don't know if this is hers," he said softly. He looked up at Flowers. "Do you have anything else, maybe her clothes?"

Flowers glanced at Louis before he answered. "We didn't find any clothes with the remains. I'm sorry."

Chapman stared at Flowers, then his eyes closed. For a long moment the only sound in the room was the soft hiss of his oxygen. He opened his eyes. "I brought her dental records. We can use those, can't we?"

"We didn't find her skull," Flowers said. "Again, I am so very sorry about this, Mr. Chapman."

Louis realized the black woman out in the reception area was watching them intently.

"Can I see Julie?"

Louis's eyes shot back to Mr. Chapman and then to Flowers.

"Mr. Chapman, I don't think—"

"I want to see her," Chapman said. "I want to see my daughter. Even if there's only bones."

Flowers drew in a breath. "We had to send the remains to a lab in Marquette. We will have them back soon."

Chapman took off his glasses with shaking hands. He stared at the small gold ring on the desk, then looked up at Flowers with brimming eyes. "Is there anything I can do?" he asked.

Louis looked to Flowers, who gave him a silent signal that it was okay to take the lead.

"You can help by telling us about Julie," Louis said. When Chapman hesitated Louis went on. "Let's start with the day she disappeared. We have the police report, but sometimes family members can provide details that might have been missed."

Chapman wiped at his eyes. "It was the holidays, the week after Christmas," he said. "Her mother, Ellen, had been in ill health, and I thought a vacation somewhere warm would be good for her, good for the whole family, really. We decided to go to Pasadena. Michigan was playing in the Rose Bowl, and we were alums, you see, so we thought it might be good for us."

He stopped, shaking his head. "But the kids . . . well,

neither of them wanted to go. Ross was studying for finals and didn't want to be away. Julie told me she would go stay with Ross in Ann Arbor and they would watch the game on TV. So I didn't worry about her."

"Ross was nineteen at the time?" Louis asked.

Edward Chapman nodded.

"He's a state congressman now," Flowers said to Louis. "He's running for U.S. senator."

The Senate. The case had attracted only local interest so far, but that was going to change fast. "Is your son coming to the island?" Louis asked.

Chapman's eyes were slow to focus on Louis. "Yes," he said. "He's been busy with his campaign, but he told me he'd be here as soon as he could."

"That weekend you went to California," Louis said. "When did you realize your daughter was missing?"

"Not until we came home," Chapman said. "Until we called Ross we didn't know she had never even made it to Ann Arbor. Ross said Julie never called him about coming."

Louis had read this detail in the report last night, and it had struck him then that maybe Julie Chapman had lied to her parents about her plans. It didn't mean she wasn't abducted, but it raised questions.

"Mr. Chapman, do you think your daughter lied to you about going to stay with her brother?" Louis asked.

Chapman was staring at the ring again and looked up quickly.

"Perhaps she was going to go somewhere or see someone you didn't approve of?"

Chapman shook his head. "Julie never lied. Maybe she

just changed her mind about going to Ann Arbor. Maybe she wanted to surprise Ross. Maybe . . ." His voice trailed off. "Julie never lied to me."

"Mr. Chapman," Flowers said, "I have teenage daughters, too, and sometimes they get secretive."

Chapman stared hard at Flowers.

Flowers glanced at Louis and shifted in his chair. "Why don't you tell us more about Julie?" he said.

"What do you mean?"

"What was she like?"

"She was a good girl," Chapman said.

"Can you be more specific?" Flowers asked gently.

Chapman seemed confused. "She was very smart, an excellent student. She was polite, funny, and shy. She loved to ride horses and she wrote poetry."

"Poetry?" Louis asked.

Chapman was slow to focus on Louis. "Yes. She won a school prize once."

"Do you still have any of her poetry?" Louis asked.

"Why would you want that?"

"It might help us understand her," Louis said.

Chapman hesitated, then nodded. "If you think it might help," he said. "I'll have the notebooks sent up. I don't know what you think you might find in them, though. They're just poems."

Just poems, Louis thought. Julie Chapman was shy and had attended an all-girls school. When a seventeen-year-old girl lies to her parents about where she is going, it's usually about a boy. The Bloomfield Hills police had found no evidence of a boyfriend. But if one did exist Louis had a hunch he'd find him in Julie's poems.

Louis was quiet, his eyes on the photographs of Mackinac Island on the wall over Flowers's desk. And maybe he would find him here.

Twenty-one years ago, the police hadn't asked about the summer home because there was no connection to the island. But now there was—the bones in the lodge.

"Mr. Chapman, did your family spend the summer of 1969 here on the island?" Louis asked.

Chapman had been looking out the window, and it took a moment for him to turn back to Louis.

"Yes," he said. "We always came up north for the summer. We'd open the cottage on Memorial Day and close it on Labor Day." He paused. "But that last summer . . . things didn't work out like I planned."

When he fell silent Louis said, "Please go on, sir."

"I thought it was important that we all be here that summer," Chapman said. "The kids were getting older, and I had this idea that we needed that one last summer together as a family. But I was called away unexpectedly to Paris and didn't make it."

"So that summer before Julie disappeared, just your wife and the children came up here?" Louis asked.

"No, Ellen was ill. So the kids came up with Maisey."

Louis recognized the name from the police report. Maisey Barrow had been the family's housekeeper. He was about to ask if the housekeeper could be contacted, but suddenly Edward Chapman began to gasp for breath.

Flowers jumped to his feet, but before either he or Louis could make a move toward Chapman, the office door opened.

The black woman who had been sitting outside was at

Chapman's side in an instant. She checked the tubes in his nose and then adjusted the gauge on the oxygen tank.

"Try to relax, Mr. Edward," she said.

Chapman's watery eyes were riveted on her as he struggled to control his breathing. It took at least a full minute but finally the color began to return to Chapman's face.

Louis realized he had been holding his own breath and slowly let it out.

The black woman looked at Flowers. "I need to take him home," she said.

Flowers glanced at Louis and nodded. "We're finished for now," he said.

She took Chapman's elbow and helped him to his feet. He looked at Flowers and whispered something to the woman. She frowned but nodded.

"Mr. Edward wants to help you," she said. "We'll be at the cottage if you need him. But right now, he needs some rest."

"I appreciate it, Mr. Chapman," Flowers said.

The woman led Chapman out of the office. Louis watched them leave, then turned back to Flowers.

"You handled that well," he said.

Flowers rubbed his face as he sank back down into his chair. The phone rang, and Flowers looked out to the dispatcher, who mouthed the word *Rafsky*.

"Fuck," Flowers whispered. He hit the speaker button on the phone.

"Chief Flowers here."

"I'm in Marquette," Rafsky said. "I have some news."

Flowers rolled his eyes.

"The medical examiner took a second look at the

bones," Rafsky said. "He overlooked something the first time." There was a pause. "Am I on a speakerphone?"

"Yeah, Kincaid's here with me."

Another long pause.

"You going to tell us the news?" Flowers said.

"There were more than two hundred and six bones. The extras were fetal bones. I'm on my way back. I'll be there by five."

Rafsky hung up.

Louis picked up the small gold ring, turning it so he could see the initials *J.C.* He looked up at Flowers. "Looks like the perfect daughter wasn't so perfect."

11

Maisey Barrow stood on the veranda of the cottage and took in the view. She hadn't been here in five years, yet nothing had changed. The cottage—she had always thought it funny that people called a place with seven bedrooms and eight bathrooms a "cottage"—still sat in its prime position in the cul-de-sac on West Bluff Road. Beyond the sloping green lawn lay the gray-blue sweep of Lake Huron. Off to the west the little red-and-white Round Island Lighthouse still sat at the harbor like a Monopoly game hotel. And off to the east, the twin towers of the Mackinac Bridge still stood like white wicker legs under a tablecloth of gray clouds.

The cottage's paint had faded and things looked a little shabbier, but nothing had really changed much. Nothing ever changed on this island.

Why some folks thought that was a good thing she had never quite figured out.

She folded her bulky sweater tighter around her chest and went back inside, pausing in the foyer. Nothing had changed in here, either.

The same oak paneling that had always needed polishing. The same Oriental runner that always needed sweeping free of sand. The same heavy oak doors that always needed closing because things in this house were always a little off-kilter.

"Ma'am, where would you like these?"

She turned at the sound of the man's voice. The fellow she had hired at the ferry to bring up the luggage was standing just inside the archway that led to the parlor.

"Those brown ones go in the first bedroom on the right," she said, pointing. "That red one's mine." She hesitated. "Put it in the room next door to that."

The man hoisted the bags and went up the staircase. As Maisey watched him go, she ticked off the list she had written in her head. She had done this so many times in the past she could do it in her sleep. Protective plastic removed from the veranda. Dust cloths pulled off the furniture. Electricity, gas, and telephone turned on. Grocery list sent to Doud's. Cleaning girl booked. Furnace man coming tomorrow because it was too damn cold to take a chance and who knew how long they'd be here? Boy hired to rake up all those leaves. Doctor alerted at the medical center.

Doctor . . .

She allowed herself a deep sigh. She was sixty-seven now, and things weren't easy anymore. Not that they'd ever been. For more than forty summers she had been running this house, been the one who had run all the houses for the Chapmans, from that first place in Dearborn to the big house in Bloomfield Hills. She had even crossed the Atlantic on the Cunard liner to open the town house in London. She was the one who had taken care of everything.

I'm like a duck, she would joke, *it's all smooth on the top, but underneath I'm paddling like crazy.*

This was the first time she had to worry about having a doctor on call.

The man came down the stairs. Maisey handed him his money and ushered him out the door. She watched him pull up his coat collar, climb aboard the dray, and urge his horses on.

She went through the archway and into the large, cold room. She stood in the center, turning in a slow circle. Mrs. Chapman had insisted on calling it a parlor, but it was what most folks would call a family room, really, because it was the only room in the huge house where the family had always gathered. At least in those early days.

More oak paneling, a mix of wicker and lumpy slip-covered furniture, bookcases crammed with board games and Mrs. Chapman's Book-of-the-Month Club novels, a yawning stone fireplace with a mantel crowded with model sailboats, crumbling dried flowers in blue porcelain vases, driftwood, and dozens of picture frames.

Maisey went to the mantel, her eyes traveling over all the family photographs. The earliest one showing Edward and Ellen Chapman alone just after their marriage. Another of a beaming Mr. Edward, Ross just a toddler and baby Julie in Mrs. Chapman's arms. And all the later ones—Mr. Edward playing croquet on the lawn with the kids, Ross tan and lanky standing near his sailboat, Julie on a pony.

Maisey picked up one of the larger frames. It was the last photograph of Ellen Chapman taken at the cottage, two summers after her back surgery. She was sitting alone in a glider on the veranda. A book lay across her knee, and she was staring into the distance, hand to her forehead.

The sadness was there in her face, as if she knew that even as the pain pills were taking hold of her, her husband and children were slipping away.

Maisey put the frame back in its place among the others, thinking that seeing the photographs displayed like this was like watching the Chapman family age all over again, watching their small circle expand, contract, and then, with the final impact of Julie's disappearance, slowly ripple into nothingness.

One frame had fallen over. Maisey picked it up, dusted it on her sleeve, and started to put it back. She paused. It was Julie, taken when she was just seven. She was sitting alone in a wicker chair on the veranda, staring up into the camera. Her dark eyes were wide, and there was a small rare smile on her face.

Maisey felt a tightness in her chest, and it surprised her. She thought she had dealt with the hole in her heart a long time ago, thought she had managed to put Julie's memory away.

But Julie was still there, as real as anything, and Maisey could see her now, a little raven-haired thing running across the wide green lawn with the huge blue lake behind her, her arms flung wide.

"Maisey?"

The voice was a whisper, but she heard it as sure as a high-pitched whistle. She set the frame back on the mantel and went quickly up the staircase.

The door to the first bedroom was open, the Louis Vuitton cases sitting just inside. Edward Chapman was in a chair at the bay window that looked out over the lake, but his eyes were turned to the door, waiting for her.

The room was cold. She went to him, pulling a plaid wool blanket off the bed as she passed it. She laid it over his lap.

"The man promised the heat will be on by tonight," she said, tucking it around him.

"I'm fine," he said.

But she could tell he wasn't. She knelt and checked the gauge on his oxygen. The canister was full, and the flow was good. When she looked back at his face she realized he wasn't in want of a breath. He was in want of his daughter.

It had been bad enough twenty-one years ago, watching him deal with everything. Julie's disappearance, the publicity, the police, the investigation that went nowhere, the memorial service with the empty coffin. It had torn the family apart. Slowly, over the years, the hole in Mr. Edward's heart scarred, but Maisey knew it had never really healed.

But now, because someone had found bones in that old place, it had been opened again.

"Maisey?"

She looked down at Edward and took his hand. It was cold.

"Everything's going to be okay," she said.

It was just after four, and the afternoon shadows were creeping into the rooms. Edward Chapman was asleep, and Maisey was sitting in a rocker in front of the parlor's fireplace. She was tired from the long day. There was a bottle of Harveys Bristol Cream on the table—she had ordered it on impulse from Doud's—but the full glass sat untouched near her elbow.

The old Victorian house was silent around her, like a huge sleeping animal holding her in its cold embrace. Her eyes went to the bank of windows bleeding gold light and then to the game table in the dark corner where the laughter once billowed like clean white sheets in the wind.

It was so quiet, so very quiet.

She had closed her eyes and drifted off when a sharp sound drew her back.

"Hello?"

A figure standing in the archway.

"Maisey, is that you?"

A thud as the man dropped his suitcase. He came into the parlor, pausing to switch on a lamp. She squinted, and Ross Chapman came into focus.

He was forty now, she realized, and with his fine haircut and fancy clothes he had the sheen of a man working hard to impress. She hadn't seen him in more than a year, the last time he had come to the house in Bloomfield Hills, bringing his two kids and wife for a quick visit to see his father at Christmas. But she had seen him on TV a lot lately because he was having a hard time against that Burkett guy, who was giving him a run for his money in the polls.

Money . . . that was a problem for Mr. Ross right now. She had read the newspaper articles about contributions not going as well as they should and that his campaign was almost broke. She had eavesdropped on his telephone conversations with Mr. Edward, the ones where he begged for money, almost like he had when he was thirteen. She had heard, too, the anger in Mr. Ross's voice when Mr. Edward said no more.

She stared up at him. "I didn't expect you till tomorrow."

"I know. I thought I'd better get here as quick as I could."

Ross Chapman unbuttoned his raincoat, his eyes going to the bottle of sherry before locking back on Maisey.

"How's Dad?" he asked.

"Sleeping. I gave him a pill. He was very tired and pretty upset."

Ross Chapman nodded slowly. "We all are," he said.

"No," Maisey said. "It's worse than what they told you."

"What do you mean?"

"The police told Mr. Edward that she ... your sister ... the skeleton, it didn't have a head. Your father was very upset after hearing that."

She heard the creak of the wicker as he dropped into the chair next to hers. Still she couldn't bring herself to look at him.

"Do you have another glass?"

She turned. His eyes were glistening. She slid her full glass toward him. "I haven't touched it."

He hesitated, then picked it up and downed the sherry in one gulp. As she watched him, she had a memory of the day she caught him sneaking bourbon from the liquor cabinet. Ross had been just twelve, and she had given him a hard swat on the butt because Mr. Edward was gone so much he trusted her to discipline the children as she saw fit and Mrs. Chapman wasn't in any condition to care.

And she had taken that responsibility seriously. Even later when she caught him with a girl in his bedroom, even when money started disappearing from her purse.

She had always handled Ross herself, never bothering Mr. Edward.

"What else did the police tell Dad?" he asked.

"He didn't tell me very much, and I just wanted to get him back here to the house. I think the police are waiting to talk to you."

Ross Chapman let out a tired breath and pushed himself from the chair. "I guess I better get over there," he said. "Would you call and let them know I'm coming?"

"Yes, Mr. Ross."

He nodded his thanks and went to the door where he had dropped his suitcase. She followed him and closed the door behind him. She stood at the window and watched him walk down West Bluff Road toward town.

She watched until he was out of sight, then picked up his bag and took it upstairs.

12

Rafsky slammed the door to Flowers's office and slapped down three newspapers with such force it scattered the other papers on the desk.

"How the hell did this happen?" Rafsky asked, jabbing at the headline on the top newspaper.

Louis leaned forward in his chair. It was the *Lansing State Journal*. The story was at the bottom of the page, but the headline couldn't be missed.

SKELETAL REMAINS FOUND ON MACKINAC;
CHAPMAN FAMILY HOPES FOR CLOSURE

Rafsky gestured toward the outer office. "Who the fuck is talking to the press?"

Flowers rose from his chair. "Look, Rafsky, you can think what you want about me, but I have good people here. None of them would talk to a reporter."

Rafsky's eyes swung to Louis. "What about you? You got any friends at the *State Journal*?"

"I have one friend in this whole state," Louis said, "and she's not a reporter."

Louis picked up the paper. The article, bylined Sandy Hunt, was short, offering sketchy details about the discovery of bones in the Twin Pines lodge by an unnamed trespassing tourist. There was no comment from anyone official, just the line "Although a positive identification has not yet been made, sources close to the investigation say police are proceeding on the theory that they belong to Julie Anne Chapman, who disappeared from her Bloomfield Hills home twenty-one years ago." It went on to summarize the missing persons case and ended with a quote from Ross Chapman about bringing closure to the Chapman family.

Louis set the Lansing paper aside and picked up the two others. A quick read told him that both the *St. Ignace News* and the *Mackinac Island Town Crier* had picked up the *Lansing State Journal* story from the wire services—which meant the story had gone out all over the state. Four days and they had already lost control of the press.

Louis tossed the paper on the desk. "My guess is this was leaked by Ross Chapman," he said.

"Why would he do it?" Flowers asked.

"Grieving brother swoops in to bring his sister home after twenty-one years," Louis said. "Should be good for a couple of sympathy votes."

Rafsky was looking at Louis but then turned to Flowers. "It's your leak, Chief. Plug it," he said.

Flowers was about to argue, but Rafsky turned away and began reading a report. Louis noticed that Rafsky's right hand, turning the stapled papers, was trembling. Rafsky discreetly pressed it against his side to stop it.

Joe's voice was a sudden whisper in Louis's ear.

I knew from the moment I saw Rafsky that I liked him. He was different . . . he respected me, respected my idealism and my

*position as the only woman in the department. In fact, there was
a moment when I thought we might find something else, but he
was married and I was ... well, too young.*

Joe Frye was a woman with class and smarts, and
Louis couldn't help but think that to get her attention
Norm Rafsky must have been a very different man fif-
teen years ago.

"Ross Chapman's going to be here soon," Rafsky said.
"The three of us need to figure out where we're at with
this case. I want us all on the same page when we talk
to him."

Flowers nodded, waiting. Louis was finding it hard to
hide his annoyance that Rafsky had taken the lead.

"How did you make out with the missing persons list I
gave you last night at the Mustang?"

Flowers picked up a folder. "We're almost finished.
Most of the girls on the list turned up alive. Two were
murdered, but there was no evidence to tie them to our
case. We have two we couldn't find, but neither had a connection to the island here or Kingswood."

Rafsky nodded as if finally satisfied with something
Flowers had done.

"I've got more crime scene analysis and ME reports,"
Rafsky said, flipping back to the first page of the report
he had been reading. "First, they concluded that the remains were not moved after death. This is confirmed
by the residual bodily fluids they found soaked into the
concrete."

Louis remembered the ghostlike stain he had seen on
the basement floor.

"More important," Rafsky went on, "they also found

a highly degraded stream of pure blood—no decomp contamination—that ran from where the skull would have been to a drain. Which means she suffered a severe head wound that probably caused her death."

"Any indication of other injuries?" Flowers asked.

"No," Rafsky said.

"What about the missing skull?" Louis asked. "Was she decapitated?"

"All of the vertebrae were found with the remains," Rafsky said. "There were no cuts or nicks on any of the neck bones. The ME believes the head detached naturally during the decomp process."

"Okay, I know I asked this once before," Flowers said. "But isn't it about time that we started thinking about where the hell the skull is?"

"I'd guess the killer took it," Louis said.

Rafsky looked up from the report.

"Killers, especially sexual predators, often come back to relive their crimes and take trophies," Louis said. "Usually it's within days, but this guy could have waited months."

"Why wait?" Flowers asked.

"Julie Chapman disappeared in December, so the body didn't start decomposing until at least spring," Louis said. "The killer was patient. I'm guessing he waited until she was skeletonized, then came back to get the skull."

Flowers sat back in his chair. "That's really sick," he said.

"Let's move on to the pregnancy," Rafsky said, digging out another report. "The anthropologist estimates the fetal bones are sixteen to eighteen weeks."

"If this is Julie Chapman and she died around New Year's, then she got pregnant in August, when she was here on the island," Louis said.

"And that the father of the baby is our first suspect," Rafsky said.

Louis knew the stats, knew that murder was the number one cause of death for pregnant women, and the odds were better than 50 percent that the father was the killer. Violence in intimate relationships was always about power, and a pregnancy put a woman in an even more vulnerable position. For the father who had something to lose—be it a married man worried about exposure or a kid scared of being tied down for life—killing a pregnant girlfriend was all about self-preservation.

Which meant that if the bones belonged to Julie Chapman, they needed to know everything about her life. Especially the secret parts.

Flowers had picked up the file folder. He was leafing through it when he suddenly stopped.

"Oh God," he said.

He set a photograph on the desk, turning it so Louis and Rafsky could see it.

It was a picture of the fetal bones. Louis had seen fetal bones before, but they had always been neatly laid out by sections—long bones together, ribs fanned out, and the skull bones gathered like broken eggshells.

But someone in Marquette had taken the trouble to reassemble the bones so they looked like an actual fetus, and a ruler had been placed beside the bones for sizing. The skeleton—just six inches long—looked like a delicate newly hatched bird.

The three men were silent as they stared at the photograph.

A tap on the glass drew their attention to the door. An officer opened the door and looked to Flowers.

"Ross Chapman is here," he said.

Flowers turned the photograph facedown. "Send him in," he said.

13

Flowers came around the desk. As Chapman came in he gave each man a quick look before settling back on Flowers.

"Thank you for coming, Mr. Chapman," Flowers said. He quickly introduced Rafsky and Louis, then offered Chapman the only other chair in the small office.

Chapman slipped off his raincoat and folded it over his knees as he sat down. He was wearing a pale yellow cashmere sweater, dress shirt, and gray trousers. Louis had the thought that despite his polished veneer the man looked like he had been punched in the gut.

"Mr. Chapman," Flowers said, "before we go on, I'd like to apologize for contacting your family before a positive ID has been made."

Louis glanced at Rafsky, who had retreated to a corner of the small office, arms crossed. He seemed willing to let Flowers take the lead.

"No apologies are necessary, Chief Flowers," Chapman said. "If there is any chance this is my sister, I want to be here."

Chapman's voice was calm, but his hazel eyes never stopped moving—from Flowers to the officers outside the glass to the closed folders on the desk. They finally came back to Flowers's face.

"I was told my sister was found with no skull. Is this true?" he asked.

"Yes, sir, I'm afraid it is," Flowers said.

"My father also said you found her school ring, but he isn't in any state to give me any other details," Chapman said. "Could you update me on what other evidence you have that leads you to believe this is my sister?"

"Right now, the ring is all we have," Flowers said. "Except for the fact that the remains are roughly the same height and age as Julie."

"Could I see the ring, please?"

Flowers produced the ring from a drawer. Chapman turned it over, looked at the initials. "I remember the day she got this," he said.

"You were there?" Flowers asked.

Chapman nodded. "There's a ceremony at Kingswood when the juniors get their rings. It symbolizes the girls becoming women and leaders. It's a big deal, and the girls wear white dresses and the families are invited to breakfast to see it all."

He paused. The ring looked tiny in the palm of his hand. He let out a long breath and handed it back to Flowers.

"This isn't enough, is it?" he said.

"Not for a positive ID," Rafsky said.

Louis knew they would have to bring up DNA testing but decided Flowers had to handle this in his own way.

"What about her clothes?" Chapman asked. "Wouldn't they help in identifying her?"

"No clothing was found," Flowers said.

Chapman stared at him. "You mean it all rotted away?"

"No, sir. We found no clothing at all anywhere near the remains."

It took a moment for this to register, but when it did Chapman's eyes darkened. "Was Julie sexually assaulted?" he asked.

"We don't know," Flowers said. "The lack of clothing implies it is a strong possibility."

Chapman put a hand to his mouth. Louis subtly gestured for Flowers to continue.

Flowers cleared his throat. "There's one more thing, Mr. Chapman, something we didn't tell your father. Your . . . the victim was pregnant."

Chapman slowly lowered his hand. "What?"

"Your sister was pregnant."

"I thought you only found bones. How do you know?"

Flowers hesitated, turned over the photograph of the fetal bones, and slid it across the desk.

Ross stared at it for a long time. Whatever composure he had brought into the room was gone. His eyes welled up.

"May I have a glass of water, please?" he asked softly.

Flowers went to the door and hollered out to one of his men. An officer came back quickly, bearing a coffee mug of water. Chapman drank it in one long draw.

"Do they . . ." Chapman paused. "Can they tell how far along she was?"

"Four to five months," Flowers said.

Louis felt compelled to break in. "We know your family was here that summer, so we know your sister got pregnant while she was here."

"Anything you can tell us about your sister's life here at that time would be very helpful," Flowers said.

"Life?" Chapman said.

"Boyfriends," Louis interjected.

"Julie didn't have any boyfriends," Chapman said.

"You never saw your sister with anyone that summer?" Louis asked.

Chapman shook his head slowly.

"This is a small island," Louis said.

"And you and your sister ran with a small, exclusive group of kids," Flowers added.

Still Chapman said nothing. Then he let out a long breath. "Okay," he said. "I didn't think about it at the time, but something was different that summer. Julie was very moody. One minute she was sky-high, the next she would lock herself in her room and cry."

Louis noticed Flowers nodding. "I have teenage girls. What you're describing sounds pretty normal."

"Except she got pregnant," Rafsky said.

Chapman's eyes swung to Rafsky. "I don't remember Julie seeing anyone or even talking about anyone that summer."

"What about a girlfriend, someone she might have confided in?" Flowers asked.

"I . . . I don't know, really. We were at separate schools at Cranbrook," Chapman said.

Flowers reached into his drawer and pulled out the yearbook from Kingswood. "Could you take a look, please?" he asked. "Maybe you'll see someone whose face rings a bell."

Chapman hesitated, then took the yearbook. The office

was quiet as he turned the pages. After a few minutes he closed the yearbook. "I'm sorry," he said. "I don't recognize anyone. It was a long time ago."

"What about here on the island?" Louis asked.

Chapman shook his head. "I don't remember seeing her with anyone special."

"Your father mentioned a housekeeper that came up here with you every summer," Louis said. "We'll need to talk to her. Can you tell us where we can find her?"

"She's at the cottage with my father."

Louis glanced at Rafsky. He had assumed that the black woman with Edward Chapman had been a health aide.

"How long has—?" Louis paused, unable to remember the housekeeper's name.

"Maisey," Chapman said.

"How long has she worked for your family?"

"Forever," Chapman said.

"Can you be more specific?" Rafsky asked.

"Since I was two," Chapman said.

"Would Julie have confided in her?" Louis asked.

Chapman shook his head. "No, Maisey's just the housekeeper."

Louis had seen the tenderness between Edward Chapman and Maisey. This woman was not *just* a housekeeper. He made a mental note to talk to her later—alone.

Chapman set the mug on Flower's desk. His eyes were fixed on something on the wall over the desk. He seemed to be staring at an old photograph of Mackinac Island's Main Street. Finally he looked back at Flowers.

"When can I take my sister home?" he asked.

Rafsky stepped forward. "I'm sorry, but the remains cannot be released until we have a positive ID."

"So you're telling me there's nothing I can do?" Chapman said.

This was wrong, Louis thought. Wrong and unnecessary. Ross Chapman just wanted to take his sister home and bury her. Edward Chapman had waited twenty-one years and didn't have time to wait any longer.

"Actually, there is something you can do," Louis said. "Have you heard of DNA testing, Mr. Chapman?"

Louis could feel Rafsky's eyes on him, but he kept his own on Chapman.

"Yes," Chapman said. "They use blood or tissue to identify bodies."

"Bones can also be used," Louis said.

"How does it work?" Chapman asked.

"We would need some DNA that we were positive belonged to your sister for comparison, like hair from her brush," Louis said. "That's impossible in this situation."

"But you said—"

"We can test the bones for what is called mitochondrial DNA," Louis went on. "That is DNA passed on to children by their mothers. It's exactly the same for each child. We can take DNA from you, and if it matches the DNA in the bones, we know the remains belong to your sister."

Chapman stared at him. "I don't understand. Why didn't you just tell me this when I walked in?"

Rafsky took the question. "It's not as easy as Mr. Kincaid makes it out to be. The genetic material could be too degraded or contaminated. Also, testing takes a long time, and it is extremely expensive. With all due respect, Mr.

Chapman, this is not something the state is prepared to do at this time."

"You're telling me I can't bury my sister because the state is too damn cheap to do a test? You expect me to go back and tell my father that?"

"Mr. Chapman—"

Chapman cut Rafsky off with a raised hand, then looked at Flowers. "I want you to make this DNA test happen. I want to know for sure it's Julie. I will pay for it. I don't care what it costs."

Flowers made it a point not to look at Rafsky before he spoke. "Yes, sir. I will get things in motion immediately."

"What about the fetal bones?" Louis asked.

Chapman's eyes swung to Louis.

"Do you also want to pay for testing the fetal bones?"

"Why? We know it's Julie's baby," Chapman said.

"We should test for paternity," Louis said.

"I'm confused," Chapman said. "I thought you said you can only test for matches between siblings?"

"Paternity is different," Louis said. "The fetal bones contain the DNA of Julie and of the baby's father. And the father of that baby is our best suspect right now."

Chapman hesitated. "I understand," he said softly. "I know that you want to find the man who killed my sister. But you don't understand what the last twenty years have done to us. All we wanted to do was find Julie. And now all we want to do is take her home."

"Mr. Chapman—" Rafsky interrupted.

"You have to understand, Julie was my father's . . . everything, she was his princess," Chapman said. "If he found out she had gotten pregnant, it would kill him." He hesitated. "Maybe later."

Louis knew Chapman meant after his father had died.

The room was silent for a long time. Then Flowers cleared his throat.

"Mr. Chapman, we appreciate your situation," Flowers said. He picked up the *Lansing State Journal*. "The news about the bones has already gotten out. But you have my word that we will do everything we can to keep the pregnancy quiet."

Chapman considered this for a moment, then nodded. "Thank you. Now, what do I need to do for this DNA test to identify my sister?"

"You can go to the clinic here on the island and give a sample," Flowers said. "I'll have one of my officers take you over now if you like."

Chapman shook his head. "I really need to see to my father right now," he said. "I'll go tomorrow." He started for the door, then turned back. "Thank you again for your discretion."

With a quick look at Rafsky and Louis, he left.

Rafsky waited until the door had closed, then turned to Louis. "Do you have any idea what you've done?" he said. "You've hung that man's hopes of identifying his sister on a one-in-a-million chance."

Rafsky swung to Flowers. "And if you knew what the hell you were doing, you wouldn't be taking advice from this loser."

Louis straightened from his position leaning against the wall. "Wait a minute—"

"He lost his badge in this state," Rafsky said. "You want to know why? He killed his own chief."

Flowers's eyes shot to Louis.

Rafsky picked up his files and started to the door. "You want to keep him here, fine. Just don't turn your back on him."

Rafsky left, leaving the door open. Louis shoved it closed.

Damn it. He was tired of having to defend himself every time he came back to this state. He was tired of feeling like an outcast in the place where his dream of being a cop had been born. And now that son of a bitch Rafsky . . .

Flowers was staring at him, waiting.

"It was a complicated case," Louis said.

"I'm listening," Flowers said.

"We were after a cop killer. My chief was corrupt and out of control. I did what I had to do to save a boy's life."

Flowers dropped back into his chair and picked up the *Lansing State Journal.* Louis wondered if he was thinking about the shit-storm that lay ahead—or about what kind of man he had teamed up with.

"You're leaving tomorrow, right?" Flowers asked, tossing the paper aside.

"Unless you want me gone now."

Flowers leaned back in his chair. "I'll take your word you did what you had to do with your chief," he said.

Louis nodded. "I appreciate that."

"So can you give me a few more days?"

Before Louis could answer, the phone rang. Flowers picked it up, grunted a few words, and hung up. "I have to go take care of something," he said. "I'll be back in a few minutes."

Flowers left, leaving the door open.

Louis sat down in the chair Chapman had been using. From the outer office came the sounds of radio traffic and the laughter of two officers sharing a joke. He started to reach for one of the Chapman folders but pulled over the Kingswood yearbook instead.

He opened it and began to look for her. So many pretty young faces, smiling into the camera and ready to get on with their lives. And then, there she was.

The black-and-white missing persons flyer that he had shown to the ferry employees and Edna Coffee hadn't really registered in his consciousness.

But the photograph of Julie Chapman in front of him now did. The angles and symmetry that gave Ross Chapman his handsomeness were visible here but softened to beauty. Where Ross Chapman's hazel eyes telegraphed strength, his sister's darker ones conveyed vulnerability.

He hadn't noticed before, but unlike the other girls Julie wasn't looking into the camera. It was as if she was afraid the photographer was thinking she wasn't as pretty as the others.

A few more days . . .

Louis looked back up at the map of Michigan on the wall behind Flowers's desk, focusing on the little dot of Echo Bay. He had promised Joe he would be in Echo Bay tomorrow. It was only a three-hour drive. Would Joe be willing to come to him?

But what about Rafsky? He didn't want their past infecting his future with her. He'd have to tell her Rafsky was here, and he'd have to trust her.

He picked up the phone and dialed Echo Bay.

14

The front page of the *St. Ignace News* was spread out on the table before him. He closed his eyes and put his head in his hands. When he opened his eyes the newspaper was still there. So was she.

Cooper Lange stared at the black-and-white photograph that dominated the top half of the front page.

Julie.

The headline above her photograph was big and black and ugly.

BONES FOUND IN ISLAND LODGE

He had been so shocked to see her picture when he opened the paper this morning that he hadn't even read the story. He read it now, trying to go slow so his reeling mind could absorb the details.

There weren't that many. A tourist had found bones in the Twin Pines lodge. Police were calling it a possible homicide. The lodge had been abandoned and boarded up for decades. . . .

Cooper's eyes locked on one sentence: "Although a positive identification has not yet been made, sources close to the investigation say police are proceeding on the theory that they may belong to Julie Anne Chapman, who disappeared from her Bloomfield Hills home twenty-one years ago."

The photograph pulled him back. She looked exactly the same as he remembered. The same oval face framed by straight black hair and somber dark eyes. If was as if the past twenty-one years had never happened. Or as if she had been frozen in time. Frozen in his mind.

Cooper rose and went to the coffeemaker. He poured himself a fresh mug and stood at the sink, staring out the window at the flannel-gray fog.

It felt like the fog was there in his head. It had felt like this for as long as he could remember.

Like those warm nights with her in the lodge were something he had only imagined. Like that cold day on the ice bridge had never happened. Like those eleven months in Vietnam had been a nightmare and the six months in the VA hospital one big narcotic dream. Like the constant pain in his leg was something his mind made up when he needed an excuse to crawl into himself and die for just a couple of hours.

"You're up early."

He turned. His father was standing in the doorway. It was just a trick of the gloomy morning light, but for a moment he saw his father as he had that day twenty-one years ago, when they had stood in this very same spot and he had told his father—*lied to him*—that he was going ice fishing for three days up near Whitefish Bay. The next thing he remembered was his father's face above him when he woke up in the St. Ignace Hospital, half-dead from hypothermia.

"You okay? You look a little pale," his father said.

"I think I got a bug or something," Cooper lied.

His father moved into the kitchen. He glanced at the newspaper, but nothing registered. There was no reason it should. Cooper had never told him why he had been out on the ice bridge that day, never told him about the girl on the island.

For a second he thought about telling his father all of it now. Telling him, too, that maybe he needed to go to the island and talk to the police.

"The cold's coming early this year," his father said.

"Yeah."

"The storm windows—"

"I already did them."

"I better check the furnace."

"I'll do it, Pop."

His father's eyes lingered on him before he turned to the coffeemaker.

"Flu's going around," his father said. "Maybe you should stay home today. I can go open the bar."

Cooper didn't answer. He moved past his father out of the kitchen. In the bedroom he pulled on a sweater and work boots. He went to his closet, looking for his down vest because he felt the cold so easily these days. As he grabbed the vest his eyes were drawn to the old Converse shoe box on the shelf.

He pulled it down and sat on the bed.

There wasn't much in the box. But then, there had been no reason to add anything for a long time. And even less reason to look at what was there.

But he did now. He pulled out the black case and

cracked it open. He ran a finger over the Purple Heart, closed the case, and set it aside. He barely gave a glance to the faded varsity letter from LaSalle High School but took a long time staring at the Timex watch that had belonged to his grandfather. There were papers that he sifted through quickly, things that he didn't remember keeping, and the coaster from the New York Bar in Saigon made him remember a night he had tried to forget. At the bottom of the box were the photographs.

Only a few. Most faded-to-orange Polaroids of barechested smiling men with palm trees and tanks in the background. A few of the guys he had worked with on the pipeline and a blurred one of his ex-wife on the beach at San Padre Island. And then . . .

A black-and-white photograph of a girl with long dark hair and somber eyes. Its edges were curled, its image faded.

He stared at it for a long time, then turned it over.

The delicate handwriting had been lost a long time ago in the icy water. Only a few words of what she had written to him remained.

Love . . . may shatter your dream

What had happened? The newspaper told him nothing, just that there were bones in the lodge. He closed his eyes against the image in his head.

Had she frozen to death waiting for him?

Something tore deep in his chest, and it hurt so bad that for a moment he couldn't even pull in enough air to breathe.

He couldn't even move, because he knew now he wasn't going to do anything. Any thought he had of helping the police was gone. All he wanted to do now was survive.

He put the photograph back in the shoe box and stuck the box in the far corner of the closet.

Danny Dancer picked up the *Mackinac Island Town Crier*. For the tenth or eleventh time today he read the story about Julie Anne Chapman.

It told him that her bones had been found in the lodge, that she was from Bloomfield Hills and had a brother who was running for the Senate. It told him that the police weren't sure yet that it was her. But he knew it was her.

He carefully smoothed the newspaper out on the table and concentrated on the photograph. It looked like one of those school pictures, but it was in plain old black-and-white. Not nearly as pretty as the picture of her he had stored in his head.

Skin glowing gold from the bonfire. Hair black and glossy as a horse's mane. Eyes like the night sky pricked with stars, filled with love for the boy who worked at the stables.

Dancer couldn't remember the boy's name, and he didn't care. He couldn't remember the names of the fudgies or the rich West Bluff kids or even the names of the local kids who worked and played on the island.

But he remembered what they looked like. He remembered how they spent their days, what they did in the dark, because he watched them summer after summer.

They let him hang around but never too close. He never got invited up to Fort Holmes, where they went to smoke pot. Never got to share a bottle of Boone's Farm around a campfire. Never had a chance with a girl on an Indian blanket.

When he was young things like that hurt, and one day, many winters after Aunt Bitty was gone and he was all alone, he simply gave up watching them. He grew too old, grew too into himself, and stopped talking to anyone except the postal lady, the waitress at Millie's, or the grocer at Doud's.

It was just him and his skulls.

Until that day he found her, and suddenly the loneliness was gone.

When was that? He didn't know. The newspaper said she was here in 1969 and the date on the newspaper said it was now 1990, but a sense of time was something he couldn't grasp.

His life passed in seasons. Forests on fire with color. Gray skies and ice-chunked water. Melting drizzles and finally the bloom of the purple lilacs and dahlias as big as white dinner plates.

Dancer rose from the table and went to the shelves. He picked up the skull from the top.

"Hello, Julie," he said softly.

He slowly ran his fingers over the smooth curve of bone. His eyes were burning, and it felt almost like all those times when the beetles were doing their work and he got too close to the skulls. But this burning was different. It was the burn of panic.

The newspaper said police had found her in the basement of the lodge. It hadn't said anything about her skull being missing, but he knew the police would need it to figure out for sure that it was her.

They would want it back. They would come looking for it.

Had he been careful enough getting in and out of the lodge? Had the police found the hole that for so many summers had been his secret way in? Had he left fingerprints?

He had read somewhere that human beings lose eight pounds of skin cells per year. Could they sweep the floors and find him that way?

Aunt Bitty's voice was suddenly in his head. *Stop being stupid. God gave you a brain, use it.*

She was right. He was being stupid. No one could find him through his skin cells.

But he couldn't be sure the postal lady didn't know that his packages contained skulls. Couldn't be sure no one had ever seen him crawling into the lodge. Couldn't be sure someone couldn't smell the brains.

He went to the window, held back the curtain, and peered out. The wind was calm and the leaves that sometimes danced across the yard were asleep. He saw a black squirrel on a low-hanging limb. But he saw no humans.

But they would come.

He let the curtain fall and went to the kitchen. He opened the cupboard below the sink and pulled out a large shoe box. He took out the hammer and crowbar and carried them to the far corner of the cabin. Dropping to his knees, he carefully pried the nails from two planks and lifted them from the floor.

It hadn't been easy carving a hole in the concrete foundation, but he had managed. There was just enough room for him to slip in his fingers and lift the box out. He took it to the table and removed the items—a thick wad of money bound with a rubber band, the gold brooch that Aunt Bitty had always worn to church, her miniature Bible, and a silver ring with two keys on it.

He picked up the skull and started to put it in the empty box but hesitated. His eyes scanned the room, finally finding what he needed. He went to the corner, stood on his bed, and carefully took the fox pelt off the wall, bringing it back to the table.

He wrapped the pelt around the skull. After putting the wad of money, brooch, keys, and Bible back in the box, he gently set the wrapped skull inside. When the box was back in the hole, he replaced the boards, making sure every nail went back into its original hole so the police wouldn't notice they had ever been removed.

But hiding her was not enough.

He took the hammer and some nails outside to the shed. Inside he stopped to look around, at the old Tondix lawn mower, the broken rake, coils of discarded rope, and a heap of corroded beaver traps.

Aunt Bitty would be sad to see how he had let the place go, but she hadn't left him much money to keep it up. Hadn't left him anything but this three-room cabin that he was born in and her wisdom: *Don't act stupid. Don't eat rare meat. Don't kill daddy longlegs because it makes it rain.*

With a sigh he whispered a promise to Aunt Bitty to get the place in shape and went back to his work.

He dragged the shutters from the shed and started boarding up the cabin windows. He was sweating hard by the time he went back inside and put the tools under the sink.

It was past three when he put the rabbit into the boiling mixture of water, potatoes, carrots, mushrooms, and Night Train Express wine.

While his dinner was cooking he stripped and washed himself at the sink. Dressed in clean overalls, a flannel shirt, and a double pair of red-heeled socks, he sorted through the mail. There was a new skull order, but he set it aside.

Business had to wait, he decided. The next few days, maybe even the next few years, would be devoted to protecting Julie Anne Chapman.

Danny Dancer got his rifle from the closet and positioned a chair to face the front door. He sat down, covered his legs with one of Aunt Bitty's afghans, and laid the rifle across his knees. With the smell of stewing rabbit in his nose he closed his eyes and waited for the sound of footsteps in the leaves.

15

She wasn't afraid of many things. Bugs hadn't bothered her when she was a kid and busting crackheads hadn't bothered her when she was a cop in Miami. But being in a boat on open water—that had always scared the hell out of her.

When Louis called and asked her to come to the island, Joe didn't tell him she was afraid to get on a ferry.

But she did tell that she wasn't afraid to see Norm Rafsky.

Not that she hadn't been shocked when Louis told her Rafsky was on the island. It took half a bottle of wine to sort out her memories of Rafsky and the case they had worked together. She had no romantic feelings for him. But she couldn't deny she still cared about what had happened to him in the last fifteen years.

Fifteen years. . . . Did he still hate her?

The grinding engine noise stopped. She stood up, shook out her clenched hands, and picked up her bag. There was no one on the docks. Then she saw Louis at the far end, standing by the gift shop to stay out of the cold wind.

For a moment she couldn't move. Because she also hadn't told him the other thing—that after nineteen months of a long-distance relationship capped by an argument last Christmas, she was afraid it might be too late to fix things.

He spotted her and waved.

She started toward him. God, he was holding flowers. Her heart was suddenly hammering, and she had the stupid thought that she should have paid Donnie extra to put a few streaks in her hair. Or bought new underwear or painted her toenails.

Louis put his arms around her. She buried her face in his shoulder and closed her eyes. Finally she pulled back.

"I made it," she said.

"I was getting worried. You said you were coming in on the three o'clock ferry," he said.

"I know. I missed it." Because she had been too chicken-shit to get on.

Louis took her face in his hands and kissed her. His hands were like ice. His lips were warm. She realized he was wearing only jeans and a hooded sweatshirt emblazoned with MACKINAC ISLAND.

"You waited out here in the cold for the last hour?" she asked.

"I found something to do." He held out the flowers. "I wanted to get you roses, but there's no florist on the island. There are, however, a lot of really nice gardens."

She laughed and took the flowers. "I'm surprised you didn't get arrested."

"I've got juice here," he said, smiling. He picked up her bag. "Just wait until you see the hotel."

As they started down Main Street, a strange silence took hold.

"Can I ask you something?" she said.

"This sounds serious," Louis said.

"Rafsky. How is he?"

Louis hesitated. "I don't know the guy, Joe."

"You know what I told you about him."

Louis let a few moments pass before he spoke. "He seems bitter."

She wanted to ask more but decided to let it go. It didn't matter; she would see for herself soon enough. There was going to be no way to avoid seeing Rafsky, and if they were ever going to bridge the chasm between them she was going to have to be the one to reach out.

When Louis led her to the porch of the Potawatomi she gave him a wry smile. "The Grand Hotel looks a lot bigger in the photographs," she said.

"It's closed," Louis said. "This is the only place open on the island. I'm sorry."

"Don't apologize. I told you, my coming here is better than your coming to Echo Bay. At least here my officers won't bother me."

At the front desk she trailed behind holding the flowers as Louis talked to the clerk. The small lobby had fake wood paneling, a brick fireplace, and royal blue carpeting, with well-worn plaid furniture. But it was spanking clean and reminded her a little of her family's old house on Rumson Road back in Cleveland Heights.

"Here you go," Louis said, coming over to her.

She hesitated, then took the key he was holding. From the moment she saw him standing on the dock she had felt the stir of longing. She was sure he felt the same, but she was glad he had made no assumptions.

Upstairs Joe unlocked the door to room seven and turned to take her bag from Louis.

"Where is your room?" she asked.

"Right across the hall." He glanced over her shoulder. "You have a kitchenette."

"You don't?"

"I have a Mr. Coffee, but it doesn't work."

She smiled. "You can come over to my place for breakfast."

He returned the smile. She had forgotten how much she liked seeing him smile. His smiles had come easily when she first met him two years ago, when they were both still in Florida. But then she took the sheriff's job in Michigan, and things started to change. It wasn't just the strain of their long-distance relationship. Something inside of him began to change, like a strange moroseness had taken hold of him. He wouldn't talk about it when she asked. When he called her from Palm Beach last Christmas there was a bitterness in his voice. She knew it was because he hated working as a PI, but it was more than that. He was adrift. And worse, he didn't seem to care. She told him they needed a break from each other.

Six weeks ago he called. He said he was coming to Michigan to visit Lily and wanted to know if he could come up to Echo Bay. No pressure, he said. I just want to see you again.

The awkward silence was there again, filling the small space between them in the narrow hallway.

"It's going on five. You want to get something to eat?" Louis asked.

She nodded. "And a glass of wine."

"Okay, let me just change my shirt."

She tossed her bag on the bed, set the flowers down, and took off her leather jacket. At the mirror she blew out a breath. Her lipstick was gone, and her hair was a wild mess. She thought about fishing her brush out of her bag but with a dismissive wave at her reflection she turned away.

Louis's door was open. She went across the hall and stood in his doorway, arms crossed, watching him. It had been four months since she had been with a man. Stephen was a doctor in Petoskey, and the sex had been good and the companionship just what she needed. The affair with Stephen had lasted three months, and there had been no one since.

Louis was standing at the sink, his back to her. His shirt was off, and his back rippled as he reached for the towel.

"You've been working out," she said.

He turned. Again, there was that smile.

"For me?" she asked.

"For Lance Mobley."

She stared at him.

"I've put in for a job with Lee County."

She came further into the room. "You're going back in uniform?"

Louis nodded. "Mobley's in trouble with the EEOC. I just have to go through certification, and I'm in."

"Detective?" she asked.

"Probably not."

"You're okay starting at the bottom again?"

He nodded. "You're the one who told me I had to want something for myself. I want my badge back."

From the moment she saw him on the dock she had sensed that something had come alive in him again. Part of it was probably Lily. Some of it was undoubtedly this case here on the island. But she felt certain most of it was because he was going to be a cop again.

She went to him and wrapped her arms around his waist. He pulled her closer. All the awkwardness vanished, and the silence filled with sweet expectancy. She reached back and closed the door.

16

Flowers's call woke them up early. He wanted Louis to meet him at the lodge.

"What's up?" Louis asked.

"We found out how he was getting inside," Flowers said.

"I'm on my way."

When Joe, curled by his side, asked to go along he didn't hesitate. They had worked two cases together, and though he sometimes felt a tug of competitiveness he wanted her with him. He had planned to go to the Chapman home this morning to interview the housekeeper, Maisey, but that could wait for now.

It was cool, but the sun was climbing in a blue sky as they headed to the lodge in the police golf cart Flowers had sent for them. The officer positioned on the back road to keep out the curious waved as Louis drove past.

Louis could see a CSI tech with a metal detector working the brush at the edge of the property. The side yard was roped off in a grid pattern and stabbed with small red flags.

Joe took his hand as they trudged through the weeds, her eyes taking in the lodge. Flowers was standing on the side porch, and as they approached, his eyes locked for a moment on their intertwined hands and lingered on Joe's face.

"Hey, Chief," Louis said. He looked to Joe. "This is my friend Joe Frye from Echo Bay. She's—"

"Good to meet you, Chief," Joe interrupted, sticking out her hand.

She had stopped him from introducing her as a sheriff, which surprised Louis. Last night, Joe had pumped him about the case, but he realized now that she was going to keep a low profile for his sake. With her hair loose and dressed in a gray sweater coat, white blouse, and jeans, she looked like anything but a sheriff.

Louis nodded toward the tech in the yard. "Looks like you're being pretty thorough," he said.

"You bet I am," Flowers said. "I'm tired of that prick Rafsky chewing on my ass."

At the mention of Rafsky's name, Joe gave Louis a look and slipped her camera off her shoulder, wandering away to take some photos.

"Hey, Pike," Flowers said.

A second tech had emerged from the front door carrying a brown bag sealed with evidence tape. His face was smeared with dirt.

"Louis, this is Pike, my lead tech guy," Flowers said.

Louis gave him a nod.

Pike looked up to the second floor. "This is one big place to process, Chief."

"You find anything?"

"Zip-o so far. No clothes, jewelry, or skull anywhere in this place. Nothing but a couple of Faygo cans and hundreds of prints and hairs."

"You finish with the luminol?"

"Almost. But other than the blood in the basement, we haven't found a trace anywhere else."

"So how did he get in here?" Louis asked.

"He's got a little rat hole. Follow me," Pike said.

Joe held up a hand, indicating she would stay on the veranda. Pike led Louis and Flowers around to the far side of the lodge. An orange flag hung from the porch railing, and a section of the latticework had been removed to allow a clear view of the crawl space.

Pike pointed. "There's a hole in the foundation. Take a look."

"I've already seen it," Flowers said, handing Louis his flashlight.

Louis dropped to his knees and crawled under the veranda. The flashlight beam picked up the gray stone of the foundation. Then he saw it—a ragged three-foot hole. It looked as if the concrete had deteriorated and instead of repairing it, someone had framed out the hole with studs and nailed boards over it. The intruder had simply removed the boards to get inside.

Louis shined the flashlight on the nail holes in the studs and ran his fingers over them. They were worn smooth. He picked up one of the boards, and its nails easily went into the holes. It was obvious the boards had been removed and put back repeatedly. The hole opened into the basement. It was maybe a four-foot drop to the floor.

He backed out from under the veranda and gave the flashlight to Flowers. "The boards and nail holes are worn," Louis said. "I think he came and went many times."

"That supports your theory that he returned to watch the body decompose," Flowers said.

As they started back toward the front of the house, Louis spotted Joe on the front veranda. Below her, down on the perimeter road behind the iron gates, two women were straddling their bikes, taking pictures of the lodge.

"Have you had any trouble with reporters trying to get up here?" Louis asked Flowers.

"Yeah, we caught some photographer from the *Lansing State Journal* scaling the fence yesterday. We threw him off the island."

"That reminds me, Chief," Pike said. "Could you post an extra officer to watch the interior paths?"

"Why?"

"Some guy's been lurking back there in the trees. I think he's local, because he just walks in from the woods."

"Has he tried to get under the tape?" Flowers asked.

"No. Just stands there and watches us."

"What's he look like?"

"Stocky fellow, unshaven, and walks with a shuffle," Pike said. "He wears overalls and one of those old red-and-black-checkered hunting hats."

"That's just Danny," Flowers said.

"Danny who?" Louis asked.

"Danny Dancer," Flowers said. "He's a hermit who lives up around the bend in one of the old cabins left on state land."

"Why would he be so interested in what the techs are doing here?"

Flowers shrugged. "Hell, Kincaid, everyone on this is- land is interested in this case."

"Is he dangerous?"

"Danny? Shit, no."

"How old is he?" Louis asked.

Flowers had to think. "I don't know, forty, maybe?"

"Then he was here the winter of 1969. He might know something. He might be the—"

Flowers quickly raised a hand. "Look, I know Danny. He's harmless. He was raised by his aunt Bitty, a sweet old lady from what I hear. He comes into town once a week for groceries and eats a tomato-and-lettuce sandwich on the fifteenth of every month—the day his aunt passed—at her favorite restaurant."

"I don't care what he does now," Louis said. "In 1969 he would've been around the same age as Julie, and he lives near this lodge."

"I'm telling you Danny Dancer is no killer," Flowers said. "Look, you said at one point you thought the killer might have abducted Julie from downstate. Danny doesn't even own a car. I don't think he's been off the island in his entire life."

"The pregnancy changes our theory, Chief," Louis said. "Maybe she wasn't abducted. Maybe she came back will- ingly to meet the father of her baby. And maybe that boy didn't want to be a father. And maybe Dancer was that boy."

Flowers laughed. "If you only knew how crazy that was."

"Why?"

"Danny's a likable guy, but he's homely, real shy, and a little dim," Flowers said. "A guy like him would've been invisible to a girl like Julie Chapman."

"Sometimes girls play cruel games with dumb boys."

Flowers shook his head. "From what we know about Julie Chapman that doesn't make sense."

"We need to talk to him," Louis said.

"Good grief, Kincaid."

"Humor me, Chief."

"Okay," Flowers said. "But you'll see what I mean when you meet him. Come on, we can walk to his place from here."

Joe was sitting on the railing on the veranda. Louis went up to her. "I have to go with the chief to talk to someone," he said.

"I heard." Joe glanced over his shoulder at Flowers. "I can't believe he doesn't see this Dancer guy as a suspect," she said softly.

"Now you see what I've gotten myself into?"

"You never could resist a cold case or a lost cause."

"The chief's not a lost cause, just a little lost."

"Well, go help him," Joe said with a smile. "Give me the golf cart keys. I want to go take some pictures of that old cemetery we passed coming in."

He was fishing the keys from his pocket when Flowers came up to them.

"I just had a thought," he said. "It might be a real help if Joe came along with us."

"What for?" Louis asked.

"Danny tends to clam up around men," Flowers said. "He's been that way since his aunt died." He looked at Joe. "I think he'd be intimidated by two cops. Having a lady there would make him feel better."

Joe looked questioningly at Louis.

"You mind?" he asked her.

"Not at all. I'm happy to help out, Chief," Joe said.

It was a small log cabin sitting in a copse of peeling white birch trees. A rock chimney rose up on the right, a small porch jutted out from a rough-hewn wood door. The two front windows were shuttered, and the shed set back in the tall grass had a padlock on the door. A wrought iron table sat in the yard, its two chairs tipped over into the carpet of leaves.

"The place looks deserted," Joe said.

"He's in there," Flowers said, starting toward the cabin.

Still scanning the yard, Louis and Joe fell into step behind him.

Suddenly, the front door of the cabin swung open.

A man stood in the doorway.

"Danny!" Flowers called out as he walked toward the door.

The man took one step forward. Something in his hands glinted in the sun.

Louis froze and threw out a hand to stop Joe.

"Gun! Get down!" he yelled.

The crack of the rifle split the silence.

Louis dropped to his belly, searching for cover, but he was caught between trees, each six feet away.

More rifle fire. Three, four, five shots.

"Joe, you hit?"

Her voice came from behind him. "I'm okay."

"Chief?"

No answer.

Louis raised his head. The cabin door was still open, but Dancer had retreated into the dark interior.

Oh God.

Flowers lay in the leaves about ten feet to Louis's right.

Suddenly more gunshots, zinging through leaves and snapping bark off trees. Louis waited a few seconds, then crawled forward. When he reached Flowers, he tugged on his uniform jacket and it fell open.

Blood . . . his white shirt was soaked at the collar. He had been hit in the neck.

Flowers moaned and coughed up blood.

Louis put a hand to Flowers's chest, trying to keep him from moving.

"Joe! Flowers is hit!"

A crack of a bullet smothered her answer.

Louis grabbed the radio from Flowers's belt and keyed it.

"Dispatch, Dispatch, this is Louis Kincaid. We're at the cabin of Danny Dancer, and Chief Flowers is down with a GSW. Need medical assistance now! Right now!"

Another volley of bullets zipped overhead.

"Dispatch, approach with extreme caution. We're still under fire!"

The dispatcher spat out a shocked expletive but then acknowledged. Louis stuck the radio in his jacket and pulled the gun from Flowers's holster.

He looked down into Flowers's face. His eyes were wide and liquid.

"Chief, I've got you. It's okay," Louis said. "You're going to be okay."

He looked back at Joe. She had found cover behind a

woodpile and was sitting up, her breathing fast and her face flushed.

Louis took a quick look at the door. "Dancer! Stop shooting! We're not here to arrest you!"

Two more rifle shots ripped into a nearby tree. It sounded like Dancer was shooting a .22 rifle, what hunters called a varmint gun. Dancer could keep them pinned down and just reload. Which meant he could outlast them—and Flowers.

He had to do something. And to do it, he had to leave Flowers. He crawled on his belly back to Joe.

"How bad is the chief hurt?" Joe asked.

"Bad. Hit in the neck."

"What do you want to do?" Joe asked.

"I need to get up there."

"And do what?"

"The windows are shuttered, so he can't see me if I go for the porch. If I can get close enough, I can grab the rifle and take him down."

He held out Flowers's .45. "You need to distract him."

"You're going to go up there unarmed? Are you nuts?" Joe said.

Maybe he was, but they had no choice. Joe's Glock was locked in a safe back at the hotel, so they had only the chief's gun. If Dancer managed to turn the rifle on Louis it would be up to Joe to drop the bastard.

Louis pressed the .45 into her hand. "Shoot at the door to keep him inside until I make the porch. If we're lucky he'll think you're reloading and stick his head out."

Joe gave him a nod and took aim at the cabin.

Louis began crawling toward higher brush at the side of the cabin. Joe started firing.

Immediately Dancer ripped the air with bullets in the direction of the woodpile. Louis used the distraction to scurry to the side of the cabin. He pressed back against the logs.

Everything suddenly seemed sharper and louder. The rustle of the leaves sounded like someone chewing potato chips into a microphone, his breathing like wind whistling through a canyon. How could Dancer not hear him?

Move. Keep moving.

At the corner of the house Louis slid along the front of the cabin toward the door.

Joe's bullets continued to splinter wood on the far side of the cabin, forcing Dancer to stay hidden.

Louis stopped inches from the open door and held up a hand to signal Joe to stop firing.

Suddenly, it was quiet.

One, two, three seconds.

The barrel of the rifle popped into view. Louis had only inches of steel to grab, but he went for it. The barrel was hot, but he held on and yanked it outward.

Dancer stumbled out, stunned, but didn't let go of the rifle. Louis flung him to the porch. He hit hard but still wouldn't let go.

"Give me the damn gun!" Louis yelled.

The rifle went off, the recoil and shock of the concussion almost making Louis lose his grip on the barrel. Furious, he ripped the rifle from Dancer's hands and slammed the stock down against his head.

Dancer's hands flew to his face and he rolled to his side, moaning.

Louis put a foot on his shoulder to keep him there. He jerked the radio from his jacket and radioed the station.

"Clear! We're clear! Get that ambulance in here now!"

His heart was finally slowing, but he still had to blink to clear things in his head. Joe was kneeling by Flowers, and from somewhere down the dirt road sirens wailed.

He heard a kitten-like whimper and looked down at Dancer.

The bastard was crying. Curled up like a baby and crying.

17

How could he have been so stupid? He knew that anyone who showed an abnormal interest in a crime scene was someone to be treated with suspicion.

Yet he had allowed Flowers, who was blind to the idea that anyone on his island could be a cold-blooded murderer, walk into a crazy man's line of fire.

Louis rubbed his face and looked toward the double doors of the trauma room. No one had come out or gone in for fifteen minutes. All Louis knew was that Flowers was clinging to life.

His thoughts turned to Joe.

She had been in the ladies' room a long time. She said she wanted to get Flowers's blood off her face and hands. But he sensed there was something else she was trying to wash away.

Maybe it was the memories of her own close calls on the job. The knife attack on the case they had worked together in Florida. The countless times she had confronted crackheads and gang thugs in Miami. And the brutal ambush during her rookie year in Echo Bay that had left Rafsky wounded. He knew she had held the bleeding Rafsky in her arms that day, just as she had held Flowers today.

The squeak of the elevator doors at the end of the hall broke his thoughts, and he looked up.

Three of Flowers's officers stepped off the elevator, whispering to one another and shaking their heads. The tallest one, a man wearing sergeant's stripes on his jacket, motioned for the others to stay near the elevator before he started toward Louis.

He pulled off his cap as he walked. When he stopped in front of Louis, the fluorescent light played hard against his ashen face and red-rimmed brown eyes. Louis had heard his name around the station but right now couldn't remember it and had to look to the man's nametag—DON CLARK.

"Mr. Kincaid," Clark said. "How's the chief doing?"

"No word yet. All I know is that he's lost a lot of blood."

Clark's eyes moved to the trauma center doors.

"You get ahold of Detective Rafsky yet?" Louis asked.

It took Clark a moment to refocus on Louis. "Yes, sir," he said. "We caught him in his car going to Marquette. He's on his way back. Should be here in an hour or so."

"Did he have any instructions for you?"

Clark shook his head. "I didn't talk to him, Barbara did. I understand about all he said was to make sure Dancer was secure and left alone."

"Where are you holding Dancer?"

"I was going to put him in a cell, but he's talking to himself. So I thought we should tape him. He's under guard in a secure room with a video camera."

Louis nodded. "Detective Rafsky's right about no interviews, but if Dancer asks for a lawyer, then you find him one. Watch him for suicide and keep the officers away from him."

"Sir?"

"There's a lot of emotion in the air right now," Louis said. "The last thing your department needs is someone losing it and beating the shit out of Dancer. Do you understand what I'm telling you?"

Clark nodded. "Oh, yes, sir. But he doesn't have a mark on him, except the bump on the head you gave him with the rifle."

"Good. Keep it that way."

Clark wiped his mouth, and again his eyes moved to the trauma center doors.

"You okay, Sergeant?" Louis asked.

Clark nodded. "Yeah, but can I ask you something, Mr. Kincaid?"

Louis nodded.

"I'm the only officer of rank here, so I guess I'm in charge until Detective Rafsky gets back. I was wondering if you might give me a second pair of eyes right now so I don't miss anything important in these first few hours."

The last thing Louis wanted was to step into a case that would fall uncontested into Rafsky's jurisdiction—the shooting of a small-town police chief whose department had no means to investigate the crime. But the last thing Clark needed was Rafsky crawling up his ass over a missed step in procedure amid the chaos.

"Okay, what have you done so far?" Louis asked.

"Well, as I said, we're videotaping him."

"Did you post something that said the room's under surveillance?"

"Already a sign there. It's the room where prisoners are held before their hearings."

Louis nodded.

Clark pulled in a deep breath. "I got two officers securing the cabin, but I told them not to touch anything," he said. "Pike, the crime scene fellow, showed up here at the hospital, but I asked him to get his team out there and start processing the cabin."

"Good. What else?"

"I've roped off about a hundred feet in all directions from the cabin because I figure that even if this shooting doesn't have anything to do with Julie Chapman, Dancer was protecting something, and we need to find what that is."

This guy was sharp.

"Go on."

"I wanted to keep the reporters away from the woods, so I created a corral for them outside the station," Clark said. "I told them that no one would talk to them unless it was from the station steps, so they might as well wait there."

"How many reporters are on the island?" Louis asked.

"We've had two hanging around for days, hoping to get a statement from the chief or from Congressman Chapman. But I already got word from a friend at the ferry in Mackinac City that two more are waiting to board."

"Tell your officers not to talk to any of them."

"Yes, sir."

Louis heard the trauma center doors open and spun around. A nurse in pink scrubs was walking toward them. She carried three or four plastic bags of different sizes.

"How is Chief Flowers?" Louis asked.

She hesitated, her eyes moving from Louis to Clark. "I'm not supposed to say—"

"Come on, Candy, it's us," Clark said. "Screw your rules. How is he?"

Tears filled her eyes. "It's not good," she said. "They can't stop the bleeding, and they don't want to move him until he's more stable, so right now it's a rush just to keep his heart going. We'll know more in an hour or so."

Clark turned and started back to the other officers. The nurse caught his arm.

"You want to take these, Don?" she asked, holding out the bags.

Clark stared at the plastic bags. Inside were Flowers's boots, jacket, navy blue pants, utility belt, and, in a separate bag by itself, his uniform shirt. The bloody white fabric was compressed, leaving a red smear on the inside of the plastic.

Clark took the bags but he seemed rooted to the spot, as if he had Flowers himself in his arms.

Louis touched his shoulder. "Separate everything into its own bag, reseal it, and log each piece into evidence," he said. "Protect the chain of custody and send everything to the Marquette lab."

Clark nodded slowly.

"I have one more bag," the nurse asked.

The last bag held Flowers's badge, keys, loose change, and wallet. Clark looked at it, blinking fast to hold back the tears.

"Someone has to call Carol," he said softly. "Is there a number in his wallet?"

Louis took the plastic bag and pulled out the worn calf-skin wallet. Inside was a driver's license, ID card, credit card, forty-three dollars, and two pictures in yellowed photo sleeves. One was of the Flowers family when it was intact: Jack, his wife, and his daughters sitting on the sand at the Sleeping Bear Dunes. The other photo was of the twins when they were little, posed in front of a Christmas backdrop offered in mall photography studios.

No phone numbers.

Clark shifted the plastic bags, reached for his radio, and walked away. Louis waited, thinking Clark was going to have the dispatcher make the phone call to Kansas City, but Clark came back a few seconds later with a telephone number written on a piece of paper.

"I'll do it if you want, Mr. Kincaid," he said, "but I don't think I could get through it without breaking down. Plus I really need to keep my head together right now. Would you call her?"

Louis accepted the slip of paper. "Sure."

"Thank you," Clark said. "And if you get some news, especially if it's bad news, would you call me first? I want to be the one to tell the guys. I don't want them hearing it on the street."

"I understand."

Clark walked back to his officers. It took him a minute or so, but he finally convinced them to get on the elevator with him and leave. The door had just closed when Louis heard footsteps behind him.

He turned and watched Joe come down the hall toward him. Her face was scrubbed pink and her hair was damp around the edges. There were smears of blood on her jeans and white shirt as if she had tried to clean the stains with paper towels.

"Where's your sweater?" Louis asked.

"In the bathroom," she said. "I threw it away. I couldn't stand to look at it . . ."

Her voice trailed off, and she looked around the hallway, then she closed her eyes in exhaustion. There was no place to sit down, so Louis pulled her into his arms to steady her. She gently eased away from him.

"I have to go back to the hotel," she said. "I have to change. I feel so . . . so . . ."

"Okay, okay," Louis said. "You go ahead. I'll call you if I hear anything."

She nodded and moved away. He watched her until the elevator doors opened, wondering if he should go with her. Then he looked down at the phone number in his hand and knew, like Clark, that there were things to do. Joe was tough. She'd be okay in a few hours.

Louis went down the hall to the nurse's station. A nurse looked up as he approached.

"Any word on the chief?" she asked.

"No. May I use the phone to call his family?" Louis asked.

The nurse set the phone on the counter. "Of course. Dial nine for an outside line."

Louis dialed the number and turned his back for some privacy. It rang six times before a woman picked up. Van Halen's "Jump" pounded in the background, and the woman sounded breathless, like she'd been exercising.

"Hello?"

Louis realized he didn't know her last name. "May I please speak to Carol?"

"This is Carol," she said. "And who is this calling me on this fine autumn day?"

"My name is Louis Kincaid," he said. "I'm calling on behalf of Mackinac Island Police—"

"Stop. Stop. Wait."

The music was suddenly gone, and when she came back on the phone she was still out of breath.

"What's happened to Jack?" she asked.

Louis wanted to begin with "I'm sorry" or something like that, but she already sensed something was wrong. He just said it.

"Jack's been shot," Louis said. "He's alive, but things don't look good. They need to move—"

Carol interrupted him. "I'll be there as soon as I can," she said. "When I get in, if it's too late for a ferry, then you make sure I have a way over to that damn island, you understand me?"

Somehow it didn't surprise Louis that she sounded tough-as-nails. Most cop wives were.

"Yes, ma'am. Is there anything else I can do for you? Do you need to know where—"

"No. No. I know the island. I'll be . . ."

Carol suddenly fell quiet, and he thought for a moment she had hung up, but then he heard her draw a deep breath. He waited, listening as muffled gasps began to fill the line.

"Are you okay?" Louis asked.

"Yes, yes," she whispered.

"Is there anything I can do for you?" Louis asked.

"No . . . yes, there is," she said. "If Jack's awake enough to understand, would you make sure he knows I'm coming? Could you do that for me?"

"Yes, ma'am," he said. "If not me, I'll make sure someone tells him."

Again the other end of the phone was quiet except for the hard breathing of a woman trying to hold herself together. Louis waited, not wanting to cut the call short if there was something else she needed to ask him but not sure what else to say. After a long time, her voice came back, clearer and a little stronger.

"I'm sorry, what was your name?" she asked.

"Louis Kincaid."

"Yes, yes," she said. "I'm sorry, I need to go get my girls now. Thank you for calling, Mr. Kincaid. Thank you."

The phone clicked softly as she hung up. He set the receiver down and stood there at the nurse's station, taking a moment to compose himself before starting back to the trauma center doors.

He was passing the elevators when they opened. He turned, hoping it was Joe, but it was Sergeant Clark. Clark saw him and hurried toward him.

"What's wrong?" Louis asked.

"You need to go to the cabin and take the lead there for me."

"Why? What's happened?" Louis asked.

"They found some skulls," Clark said.

18

There were hundreds of them. Skulls, covering almost every inch of every surface. Some as small as golf balls, others as huge and horrific as horned gargoyles.

Louis stood in the middle of Danny Dancer's cabin, trying to wrap his mind around what he was seeing. What had gone on in this place? What in the hell had Dancer been doing shut up here all alone?

And what in God's name was that smell?

Louis hadn't wanted to leave Flowers, but Clark had thrust a police radio into Louis's hand and promised he would call if there was any news. Clark said he needed to stay in town to direct the evidence logging, oversee Dancer's custody, and deal with the media. But Louis understood that the young sergeant also didn't want to be far from his boss.

They decided that there was to be no mention of the skulls at Dancer's cabin on the police radios, not even to the other officers. With reporters monitoring the frequencies they had to keep this quiet as long as they could.

By the time Louis arrived at the cabin the place had already been cordoned off with yellow tape, two officers guarding the perimeter. Except for removing the shutters they had obeyed Clark's orders and done nothing. They told Louis they hadn't even picked up the casings on the porch from Dancer's rifle.

Inside, Louis found Pike's assistant taking photographs. But Pike was nowhere to be seen. Louis stood just inside the door, careful not to touch anything. They were working two crime scenes here at the cabin. One was a cop shooting. And the other?

Louis stared at a deer skull on a shelf. The question pressed forward again. Was Julie Chapman's skull in here somewhere?

The radio in Louis's jeans pocket crackled with traffic. One officer stating that a TV reporter and cameraman had just gotten off the ferry. Another officer asking for help on erecting barricades. Barbara the dispatcher telling Clark that the mayor wanted to see him immediately, and Clark telling her he was too busy.

Suddenly a new voice cut in.

"Sergeant Clark, this is Rafsky. I just hit the island. Meet me at the hospital."

"No need, no news yet," Clark answered.

"Then I'll come to the station."

Louis quickly keyed the radio. "Kincaid to Rafsky. I could use you at Dancer's cabin."

"Negative, I'm heading to the station."

"Detective, I repeat. You need to meet me here at the cabin."

There was a long pause from Rafsky, and Louis knew he had figured out Louis didn't want to go public. Then, "I'll be there in ten minutes, Kincaid."

Louis stuck the radio back in his pocket. An interior door opened, releasing more of the putrid smell. Pike came out of the room and pulled off a mask. He looked pale and disoriented.

"Did you find anything?" Louis asked.

"Oh yeah," Pike said softly.

"A human skull?"

Pike wiped a hand over his sweating brow. "No, but I think you'd better come see this."

Louis followed him into the room. The smell grew stronger. It wasn't quite the sweet-sour smell of decomposition he was used to. It was something stronger and more vile—dense and wet like vomit—an odor that seemed to wrap itself around him. He stopped just inside the door. He felt his stomach heave and had to go back out into the main room. He retched, but he hadn't eaten all day, so nothing came up. Finally he drew in a deep breath, covered his nose and mouth with his hand, and went back in.

Pike was standing at a table that held four large plastic bins, like the kind sold at Wal-Mart to store winter clothes. But as Louis drew closer to the nearest bin he saw that something inside it was moving.

Pike removed one of the plastic tops and Louis peered inside.

Oh God.

He pulled back, repulsed. Then he forced himself to look again into the bin. Inside was a huge animal head—but he couldn't tell what kind of animal because most of its skin was gone. It was covered in thousands of squirming black wormlike things.

"What the fuck is that?" Louis said.

"I'm guessing that's a deer skull under there." Pike gestured to three other plastic bins. "There are others. Nothing human."

The smell was making Louis sick. He motioned to Pike to follow him out into the main room of the cabin. They shut the door. The smell was still bad, so Louis went onto the porch and pulled in several deep breaths of clean, cold air. Pike came up to his side and did the same.

"What the hell is going on in there?" Louis asked.

Pike shook his head slowly. "I think your man Dancer is using bug larvae to clean skulls."

"What?"

"If you want to clean bones you can boil them, but the fat can make the bones turn yellow," Pike said. "And you can't use bleach because it weakens the bones. So you get bugs to eat the flesh away. You'd need to ask an entomologist, but I'm guessing those are dermestid beetle larvae. There's an aquarium full of adult beetles. It looks like Dancer is raising them. He's got Tupperware bowls filled with raw meat to feed them and a heating pad under the aquarium to keep them nice and warm."

Louis shook his head slowly. "But why?"

Pike reached into his pocket and pulled out a pair of latex gloves, holding them out to Louis. "That's your department."

Pike put his mask back on and returned to the room. Louis waited a moment before he ventured back into the cabin. The smell was everywhere, like a swirling mist. He tried to concentrate on the task at hand.

It was too big a coincidence that Dancer collected skulls and Julie Chapman's was missing. He had to search not only for her skull but also for any evidence that she might have been here.

His eyes traveled over the kitchenette, the black potbellied stove, the rough-hewn pine table and chair, the old sofa covered with a plaid blanket, and the small bed tucked in the corner. Despite the grotesque displays of skulls and the smell, the cabin was clean and neat.

Louis pulled on the latex gloves and went to a desk by the window. There was a shelf of books above it, but a quick scan of the titles told him there was nothing odd. A second shelf held what looked to be a collection of sketchbooks. Louis pulled one down and flipped through it.

Drawings . . . it was filled with drawings of horses, carriages, figures, and places around the island. The style was childish and cheerful. He put the sketchbook back and opened another. More drawings, mostly portraits, but the style was assured and carefully detailed. There were many drawings of an old woman with wild hair and a weathered face. Others looked to be workers and shopkeepers on the island, a man wearing a ferry boat captain's hat, a lady in a waitress uniform, a cop on a bike.

Louis slipped the sketchbook back among the others on the shelf. There had to be at least forty sketchbooks here. Had Dancer done them? Where had he learned to do this?

He turned his attention to the desk. It held a coffee can of pencils and pens, a box of manila envelopes, and a neat stack of papers. There was a file cabinet tucked next to the desk. Louis opened the top drawer. It was crammed with more sketchbooks.

He closed the drawer and turned to the pile of papers on the desk. Bills mostly, all carefully marked PAID. He focused on a catalog. It was from a company in Wyoming called Skullduggery: "The World's Leading Supplier of Osteological Specimens."

Louis flipped through it. It featured every kind of animal skull imaginable for sale—dogs, cats, birds, cattle. There were also human skulls for sale with the disclaimer "Due to stringent regulations, these specimens are only available to medical or educational academic institutions."

Stuck inside the catalog was an invoice from a company in Alaska called Wild Things. It was for one COLONY STARTER KIT. For forty-five dollars and ten dollars handling, Danny Dancer had bought "an assortment of two hundred live adult beetles, larvae, and pupae."

There was a second invoice. It was hand-printed on lined school paper. At the top was Dancer's address. It was made out to a Los Angeles company called Architectural Accents. It was for one DEER SKULL (ANTLERED, LARGE) at a price of three hundred and forty dollars.

"Kincaid."

Louis turned. Rafsky was standing at the open front door. His eyes swept slowly over the skulls and finally came back to Louis.

"Jesus," Rafsky said.

Louis held out the invoice. "Dancer is running some kind of business selling skulls."

Rafsky came forward and gave the invoice a glance before his eyes went back to scanning the room.

"What the fuck is that smell?" Rafsky asked.

"Rotting animal heads. He's got a skull-cleaning setup in the other room. They haven't found any human skulls yet."

Rafsky let out a long breath. "Now I see why you didn't say anything on the radio."

Louis pulled off the latex gloves. "I need some air."

They went out onto the porch. For a long time the only sound was the rush of wind through the pines and the soft babble from the police radio in Louis's back pocket.

"Any word on Flowers?" Rafsky asked finally.

"None. Clark said he'd call if there was any change."

Rafsky fell quiet again. His trench coat was wrinkled, and his face had a dark growth of stubble. The guy looked spent, and Louis suspected it wasn't just from the fast drive back from Marquette. He wondered if Rafsky was remembering the last scene in Flowers's office and how he had insulted both of them.

Pike appeared at the door. His mask was hanging around his neck, and he was wiping his eyes. "I need better equipment," he muttered.

"What did you find?" Rafsky asked.

"Okay, this is only preliminary, but I didn't find any human skulls or bones anywhere in the cabin," Pike said.

"What about an attic?" Rafsky asked.

"No attic."

"Crawl space?"

Pike nodded to the other tech, now out in the yard taking photographs. "Sam checked it out. Solid concrete foundation."

Rafsky looked out over the woods. "Then he buried it out here in his yard somewhere."

"It's not his yard, Detective," Pike said. "It's all state land. You going to dig up the whole damn island?"

"I am in charge here now. We'll dig wherever I say we'll dig."

Pike shook his head. "I hope you have a lot of troopers and a lot of fucking shovels."

"Look, I suggest you get your ass back in that cabin and find something to connect this bastard to Julie Chapman," Rafsky said.

Pike looked like he wanted to punch Rafsky, and Louis started to step between them but held off. Everyone was on edge. Finally, with a glance at Louis, Pike headed back to the porch. Louis waited until Pike was inside before he turned to Rafsky.

"You know, you're a real prick," Louis said.

Rafsky faced him. "And you have no reason to be here anymore."

"At least I was here," Louis said.

Rafsky's eyes locked on him. "What the hell does that mean?"

Louis started to walk away, but Rafsky grabbed his arm. Louis spun out of his grip.

"What the hell are you saying?" Rafsky demanded.

"I'm saying that you want to be in charge but you never seem to be around for any of the real work." Louis paused. "Where the fuck do you disappear to? Why aren't you here when it counts?"

Rafsky glared at him, then his eyes moved over Louis's shoulder. Louis realized the two officers at the tape perimeter had heard them. But he didn't care.

"Are you saying this is somehow my fault?" Rafsky said.

"I don't know. Is it?"

Rafsky started to say something, then stopped. His expression shifted, as if he had suddenly gone somewhere else. It lasted only a second or two and then he was back. But the ice in his eyes was gone.

"I have work to do," Rafsky said quietly. He walked away, ducking under the yellow tape and ignoring the stares of the officers.

19

Quiet. There were always these strange hours of quiet after a shooting. Maybe it was a natural reaction to the first moments of terror and the following lost time of chaos. Or maybe it was just that the fire of adrenaline finally burned out for everyone.

Louis rubbed his face and looked up. It was nearly seven, and the tiny office of the Mackinac Island Police Department was almost empty. Clark was outside dealing with the press. His second in command was busy logging evidence. The other officers were helping the techs process at the cabin and lodge. Even the radio was silent for the moment. Barbara, the dispatcher, pulling her second shift of the day, was staring vacantly at the wall, her hands cradling a cold cup of tea.

No one was talking. The tension was too thick. Word had come from the hospital fifteen minutes ago that Flowers's condition had stabilized, but he was still unconscious. If he made it through the next twelve hours, the doctor said, his chances were good.

Louis turned his attention back to the form in front of him. He had been here an hour now and still had not finished writing out his statement or drawn the diagram of what had happened at the cabin.

It wasn't the process. He had written countless statements far worse than this. But there was something gut-wrenching about this one. It was like it should never have happened in a place like this.

He thought back to the scene at the cabin with Rafsky. As angry as he was at the man he shouldn't have said what he did. It had come out of frustration and anger at himself for walking into Dancer's trap.

He glanced at the phone. He had called Joe twenty minutes ago. She said she was fine and would be there soon so they could go get something to eat.

Eat . . . he couldn't remember the last thing he had eaten. And right now, a big hamburger, two cold beers, and a warm bed with Joe at his side were the only things he wanted.

Clark came back in. He looked beleaguered as he walked up to Louis.

"How'd it go out there?" Louis asked.

"One of them asked where Ross Chapman is."

The Chapmans. *Shit.*

"You better call him and fill him in," Louis said. "We're not going to be able to keep Dancer's skulls quiet long. I don't want Chapman hearing about it from a damn reporter."

"I'll go out to their house myself tonight."

"Make sure he understands that right now we have no solid connection between Dancer and his sister."

Clark nodded.

"Where's Rafsky?"

"I think he's still upstairs with Dancer."

"Did Dancer ask for a lawyer?"

Clark shook his head. "The only thing he asked for was a pencil and some paper."

"Why?"

"He wouldn't say. I thought maybe he wanted to write out a statement or something, so I gave him a notebook."

"You didn't give him a pencil, did you?"

"No. Barbara had some of her daughter's crayons in her desk. I gave him those."

Louis nodded. "Good."

Clark looked down at the statement form. "Are you going to be leaving the island soon?" he asked.

"I don't know yet," Louis said. "I want to make sure the chief is going to be okay first." He leaned back in the chair. "Have you heard from his ex-wife yet?"

"She called me from the airport in Kansas City. She has a flight to Detroit tonight, but there are no connections until morning. She'll be here tomorrow. I assigned a man to go pick her up and accompany her here."

A sound drew Louis's eyes to the foyer. Rafsky had come down the stairs from the courthouse. He gave Louis a quick look, then started back toward Flowers's office. Suddenly he stopped and came back to the desk where Louis sat.

"I can't get anything out of the bastard," he said. "He said he wanted to talk to the black guy and the lady. What lady?"

The sound of the front door opening and a rush of cold air drew Louis's eyes to the open Dutch door. He was sitting at an angle that gave him a clear view of the front entrance.

Joe.

She came into the office and every head turned in her direction. Just hours ago back at the hospital she had been shaking and smeared in blood. Now, in black jeans, black leather jacket and boots, her hair back in a neat ponytail, she was all business again.

Rafsky's back was to the door, and he couldn't see her. There was no way to stop it, no way to make this easy. Louis rose, his eyes on Joe.

Rafsky turned to follow Louis's gaze.

A look of surprise moved across Joe's face—not at seeing Rafsky, Louis knew, but at how he had changed.

Rafsky's eyes flicked to Louis and then went back to Joe as he tried to figure out what was going on. When Joe came up to Louis's side and put a hand on his arm—a small but obviously intimate gesture—Rafsky watched her carefully. Slowly, gradually, a look of comprehension settled into Rafsky's face, followed by something else. At first Louis couldn't read it, but then it registered—barely concealed contempt directed at Joe.

"Sheriff Frye," Rafsky said.

"Detective Rafsky," she said.

Again Rafsky's eyes went from Joe to Louis and back to Joe. Louis wondered if Rafsky was going to ask about him and Joe, but Rafsky said nothing. The ringing of a phone finally split the awkward quiet.

Rafsky turned to Louis. "Dancer's upstairs. Follow me," he said. He glanced at Joe. "You, too, Sheriff Frye."

20

The three of them stood at the window, watching Danny Dancer in the room beyond. There was a table and two folding chairs in the room, but Dancer sat on the floor in the corner. His head was bent over a notebook, his knotty-knuckled hand furiously working a crayon across the paper.

"Whose idea was it to give him the crayons and paper?" Rafsky asked.

"Sergeant Clark," Louis said. "Dancer asked for it."

"I wouldn't have given the bastard shit," Rafsky said. "But it seems to be keeping him calm."

Rafsky unlocked the door, and they went inside. Dancer looked up only long enough for the fluorescent light to wash once over his face. He had the healthy weathered look of an outdoorsman, but his eyes were strange, two circles of iridescent silver, like tiny round mirrors.

"Here they are, Dancer," Rafsky said. "The black guy and the lady, just like you asked for. Start talking."

Dancer pushed up the wall to his feet and clutched the notebook to his chest. He looked at Louis and Joe but said nothing.

"Talk to them, Dancer," Rafsky said.

"I'm sorry," he said softly.

"Sorry?" Louis asked.

Dancer looked at the floor. "I shouldn't have done what I did. I'm really sorry, sir. And ma'am."

"You shot at three people," Louis said. "And all you can say is you're sorry? You think that fixes anything?"

Dancer cringed at the edge in Louis's voice. "Is Chief Flowers okay?" he asked.

Louis's first instinct was to grab Dancer and yell at him that the chief wasn't okay, that he would never be the same again because he had a hole in his neck that this bastard had put there. But then Dancer looked up again, clearly straining to keep eye contact. His expression was contrite. And something about it was very genuine.

"No, he's not okay," Louis said. "He's hurt badly."

"Can I tell him myself that I'm sorry?" Dancer asked.

"No," Rafsky said. "Sit down."

When Dancer didn't move, Rafsky grabbed Dancer's sleeve, dragged him to the table, and forced him into the chair. Dancer went down hard, then lowered his head and started to rock.

Rafsky sat down across from him. "Okay, asshole," he said. "It's time to talk to me."

Rafsky had basically dismissed them, but Louis was reluctant to go. A few days ago all he could think about was Lily and Joe, but this afternoon had changed all that. A man Flowers had described as harmless had picked up a rifle and fired at a cop he knew and respected. The key to a cold case homicide—a young woman's skull—was missing, and now they had uncovered a collector of skulls. And then there were the Chapmans. A father and son who had waited two decades to find out what happened to Julie.

Louis had made a promise to the chief, but with Flowers out of commission Louis now had no authority to even be in the room. And neither did Joe. He gave her a motion that they should leave and reached for the door.

"No, no, no," Dancer said. "Don't leave. Don't leave."

Rafsky leaned across the table. "Look, you son of a bitch, you don't dictate the rules here. I do."

Dancer's eyes filled with fear.

"Dancer, talk to the detective," Louis said. "You'll be okay."

Dancer's head dropped and he started whispering something that sounded like a children's song.

Rafsky slammed his palm on the table. "Don't play the village idiot with me! Start talking!"

Dancer jumped from the chair, clutching his notebook. "I'll talk to them!" he shouted. "Not you! Them!"

Rafsky glared at Dancer and pushed away from the table so hard he nearly tipped it. He reached for the door, then changed his mind and just stood there, staring out at the empty hallway. It wasn't hard to guess what he was thinking—that he was being pushed around by a dim-witted cop shooter and there wasn't a damn thing he could do about it.

"Kincaid," Rafsky said finally, "you know what we're looking for out at that cabin. I don't care how you do it, but you make him tell us where it is."

Dancer was still in the corner, holding his notebook, staring at his shoes. Louis stepped toward him.

"You want to come back and sit down?" Louis asked.

Danny shook his head.

Louis reached for his sleeve, intending to guide him

back to the chair, but Dancer jerked away and pressed deeper into the corner.

"Don't touch me."

Louis backed off. "Fine. But if you want to talk to me you need to sit down."

Dancer hesitated, then slid into the chair. Louis took the chair across from him.

"Why did you shoot at us?" Louis asked.

"I was scared," Dancer said.

"Scared of what?"

"I was scared you were going to take away my skulls."

"Why would we do that?" Louis asked.

"It's not legal to sell skulls. I was scared you were going to stop my business."

"Bullshit," Rafsky said. "You know it's not illegal."

Dancer shrank lower in his chair.

Louis was thinking how organized Dancer's record keeping was and about Skullduggery's catalog. Rafsky was right that Dancer knew damn well his business was legal. Maybe he wasn't as dim as they assumed.

"Where do you get your skulls?" Louis asked.

"Everywhere."

"You can't hunt on the island," Louis said. "Where do you get them?"

"I find them in the U.P."

"You don't have a car," Louis said. "How do you get around in the U.P.?"

"I *do* have a car."

"No you don't," Rafsky said. "We checked."

"Yes, I do," Dancer said. "It's Aunt Bitty's 1966 Ford pickup. License plate RFS456. I keep it in a garage in

St. Ignace for ten dollars a month. I drive it to find the animals."

"Do you hunt the animals?"

"No, I never kill," Dancer said, "I pick them up off the road, and I make them clean."

Louis could actually see this guy scraping up roadkill. But he also remembered seeing some large skulls in the cabin.

"Where do you get the big skulls?" Louis asked.

"Max trades me sometimes. Big skulls for skins and eyeballs and claws."

"Max?"

"Max the taxidermist in Escanaba," Dancer said. "He hunts places he's not supposed to and gets me big skulls. We trade lots of things. That's how I got Callisto."

"Who's Callisto?" Louis asked.

"My bear skull."

Rafsky sighed loudly.

Louis knew now where he wanted to go with his questions. He also decided to get more personal and use Dancer's first name.

"Danny," he said. "Do you name all your skulls?"

Dancer started to fidget, as if he knew naming skulls made him look childish. "Some of them."

"Can you tell me the names?"

Dancer shrugged. "Callisto, Penelope, Lycus, and—"

"Do you have a skull named Julie?"

Dancer bolted from the chair, but Louis caught the back of his overalls and yanked him back. Dancer fell, tipping over the chair. His notebook skidded across the floor.

Joe picked it up. Dancer's eyes were riveted on her. Louis tapped the table to get Dancer's attention.

"Danny," Louis said. "You didn't answer me. Do you have a skull named Julie?"

Dancer wrapped his arms around himself and lowered his head. He began to rock gently.

"Louis?"

He looked back at Joe. She had the notebook open.

"May I speak with both of you?" she asked Louis and Rafsky.

Dancer didn't look up as they left, closing the door behind them.

"I think Dancer's autistic," Joe said.

"Autistic?" Louis asked.

"He has many of the symptoms," Joe said. "The rocking motion, the recoiling from touch. And he has trouble looking people in the eye."

"The man runs a business," Rafsky said. "Autistic people aren't that high-functioning."

"You're wrong. There's a wide spectrum to autism and often they're highly intelligent," Joe said. "Those names he mentioned, they're Greek. The name he has for his bear skull, Callisto, is from Greek myth about a girl who was changed into a bear."

Rafsky let out an annoyed breath.

Joe held out the notebook. "Look at this."

Louis looked at the notebook page. It was a sketch in brown crayon of Joe. It was a perfect likeness right down to the tiny mole near her left eye. Louis knew Dancer had seen Joe only once before she walked in this room—for those seconds outside his cabin as he fired his rifle and maybe as he sat in the back of the SUV before the police took him away. How had he so accurately captured her likeness?

Joe flipped the page. "And look at this one."

Another crayon drawing, and this time Louis felt as if he were looking at himself in a mirror. Again every feature was perfectly rendered.

Louis looked up at Joe. "How the hell—?"

"Autistics sometimes have remarkable talents," she said. She turned to the next page.

Julie Chapman stared back at them.

It wasn't the somber senior class portrait that had been printed in the newspapers. It was a different Julie. A dazzling smile, windblown hair, long-lashed eyes dotted with carefully drawn little stars.

"May I question him?" Joe asked Rafsky.

Rafsky's eyes went from the drawing up to the window. Dancer was still rocking, head down.

"Go ahead," he said.

They went back into the room. When Joe sat down across from Dancer, he looked up. He held out his hand for the notebook but Joe shook her head.

"Who is this?" Joe asked, showing him Julie's picture.

Dancer's mirror eyes clouded.

"Who is this, Danny?"

"It's Julie Chapman," he whispered. "But I didn't know it was her until I knew it was her."

"You mean you didn't know her name?"

"Not until the newspaper told me it was her."

"Why did you draw her?" Joe asked.

"I don't know."

"Yes, you do."

"I saw her in the newspaper."

Joe leaned over the table. "But she didn't look like this in the newspaper," she said. "You drew her very happy with a big smile. Where is she in this picture, Danny?"

"Bonfire. Bonfire on the beach."

"When?"

"Summer."

"Which summer?"

"Just summer."

"Were you friends with her?"

"No, she never talked to me."

"How old were you the summer Julie went to the bonfire?"

"I don't know."

"Was your aunt Bitty alive that summer?" Louis asked, hoping Dancer could give them some point of reference.

Dancer didn't look up at him. "I don't know," he said.

"Do you have other drawings of Julie?" Joe asked.

"Lots of them. At home."

"Do you have photographs of her?" Joe asked.

"I don't understand."

"Photographs," Joe repeated. "Your picture of her is very accurate. Did you take pictures of her to look at later so you could draw?"

"Yes, photographs here," Dancer said, pointing to his temple.

"What do you mean?"

"My camera is up here," Danny said, tapping his head again. "My brain-camera takes the picture and later if I want to draw it I just go get it."

Joe stared at him for a moment, then flipped back a couple of pages in the notebook. "When did your brain take this picture of me?"

Dancer slumped. "When you were scared. I'm sorry I scared you."

Joe held up the sketch of Louis. "When did your brain take this picture?"

Danny wiped his nose with his sleeve. "When he was trying to help Chief Flowers."

Joe started to flip back to Julie's sketch, but Rafsky stepped in. He took the notebook from Joe, and she sat back in the chair.

"You're a liar, Dancer," he said. "You can draw Julie Chapman at seventeen because you knew Julie Chapman when she was seventeen. You watched her. She was pretty, you liked her, and one day you decided you wanted to fuck her."

"Don't curse," Dancer said softly. "Aunt Bitty said don't curse."

"When she left the island you decided to go get her back," Rafsky said. "You drove downstate and brought her back up here to that lodge."

"No," Dancer said.

"Then you murdered her," Rafsky said.

Dancer pressed deeper into the corner, murmuring incoherently.

"And you waited," Rafsky said. "You waited and watched her as she rotted away. And when she was nothing but bones you took what you wanted."

Dancer wrapped his arms up over his head and began to rock.

"Look at me, Dancer."

Dancer was crying softly.

Rafsky straightened and gave the notebook back to Joe. "He's done," he said. He looked at Louis. "You two can stay if you want. I'm out of here."

He left the interview room.

Joe watched Rafsky, then with a glance at Dancer, she rose. Louis followed her out into the hallway. When Louis looked back at Dancer through the wiandow, he was curled up on the floor, arm under his head.

"Maybe I can try later," Joe said.

Louis shook his head. "We're all tired. I say we call it a night."

Joe was looking at something in the notebook. Louis saw it was a drawing of Rafsky.

"I think Rafsky's burned-out, Joe," Louis said. "I'm worried about what he might do."

She closed the notebook. "I'm worried, too."

21

It was only nine thirty, but it felt much later. It was, she knew, the stress of the long day. A day that had started with the warmth of the sun on her face as she looked out over Lake Huron and ended with the cold of the water on her hands as she washed away Chief Flowers's blood.

Joe finished rubbing lotion into her hands and came out of the bathroom. Louis was hunched over the desk, and except for his reading glasses had nothing on except a towel around his waist. When they had arrived back at the hotel neither had said a word as Louis moved his things into her room. There had been no need for words, either, when they made love or afterward as they lay in each other's arms listening to the rain. Words didn't seem to have a place at the end of this day.

"The bathroom's all yours," she said.

He was busy writing something and gave a grunt but didn't look up.

"What are you doing?" she asked.

"Postcards."

"What?"

He turned and held up one. "It's for Lily. I'm writing out a week's worth tonight so I can mail one every day."

"That's cheating."

"I know, but I might not have time later." He held her gaze for a moment. "You okay?"

She nodded as she fished a hairbrush from her travel bag.

"You feel like going downstairs to get a glass of wine?"

She came over to him and ran a hand over his neck. "I don't think so," she said. His hand came up to grasp hers, and he kissed her fingers. Then he let go and went back to his postcard.

Her eyes drifted down to his back, to the small scars just below his shoulder blades. She had seen them before, of course, the first time they had made love. But she had been hesitant to ask him about them because she knew he had been a foster child and she had a feeling the scars were something he wanted to forget. Finally, when she did ask, he told her he had fallen off a bike. She had let it go. There were doors she knew he would never open, not even for her.

Dancer's notebook was sitting on the desk by Louis's elbow. She picked it up and went to the window seat. She sat down and opened the notebook to the crayon drawing Dancer had made of Louis.

She realized now that Dancer had captured Louis in those first moments as he was kneeling over Flowers after the shooting. It was all there on Louis's face—anger, anxiety, and the fierce need to right the wrong. There was something else there, too. It was in the eyes, a soft swirl of pain. But whose pain?

She turned the page. Dancer's drawing of her. Her eyes wide and liquid, her mouth agape as if caught in midquestion.

She shut her eyes. But it didn't help because the images were all there in her memory. Fifteen years and it was still there, every detail of the ambush that had killed two of her fellow officers and left her for dead in the snow.

And Rafsky . . .

She opened her eyes and turned to the next page in the notebook.

The man in the sketch had Rafsky's features—the long straight nose, concave cheeks, thin lips, and pale eyes. But there was something disturbingly empty about the likeness, as if there were nothing behind the skin, nothing alive in the eyes. Dancer hadn't drawn a man. He had drawn a ghost.

Joe shut the notebook and drew up her knees. She looked over to the desk, but Louis was gone. She heard the groan of the plumbing and then the rush of the shower in the bathroom.

She drew back the curtain and looked down. The rain had stopped, and the street was dark and quiet. She saw someone step out of the shadows and then a flick of a lighter as it caught the tip of a cigarette. A face was revealed just long enough for her to see it was Rafsky.

He turned in a slow half circle, as if trying to figure out where he wanted to go. But then he just stood there in the middle of the street.

He was Section-Eighted to Siberia.

That's what her friend at the state police had told her when she made a discreet inquiry about what Rafsky had been doing for the last fifteen years. She had felt guilty about checking up on Rafsky after Louis told her he was on the island, but she gave in to her curiosity.

Section Eight was the official name of the district of the Upper Peninsula covered by the state police. But it was also military-discharge jargon for mental cases. Norm Rafsky, once one of the state's most respected investigators, had been exiled to a remote post in the U.P. Her friend at the state police didn't know all the details, just what he had heard. That after the ambush at Echo Bay fifteen years ago, Rafsky's injury had sidelined him to a desk job for two years. And when he returned to active duty he was never the same. Something had been lost, iced over.

Joe looked toward the bathroom. She knew Louis would stay in the shower until the water went cold. She went to the desk, scribbled a note that she was taking a walk, grabbed her leather jacket, and left the room.

Rafsky was still standing in the street when she emerged from the hotel. His back was to her, but he heard her and turned. In the light spilling out from the hotel windows, she saw his face tighten.

As she came closer he looked up at the night sky, as if trying to avoid meeting her eyes.

"It's a blue moon tonight," he said.

The cloud cover was so dense there was no moonlight at all. The air was so cold it almost smelled of snow.

"Do you know what a blue moon is?" he asked. When she didn't answer he went on. "Two full moons in one month, a rarity. Once in a blue moon."

He finally looked at her. "I've done everything I could not to run into you in the last fifteen years, and now you show up here."

"I didn't plan on it," she said.

Rafsky took a final drag on the cigarette, tossed it to the street, and crushed it out with his heel. "How do you know Kincaid?" he asked.

"We met two years ago when I was with Miami homicide. I helped him with a case."

"Two years," Rafsky said. "That's a relationship."

Joe didn't say anything. The silence lengthened.

"How have you been, Norm?" she asked.

Maybe it was because she used his first name when they had always called each other by their surnames. Rafsky-Frye, it had always been Rafsky-Frye. Maybe he took it as a signal that their old relationship of mentor-rookie was long gone. Maybe he thought she was patronizing him. Whatever the reason, he took a half-step away from her.

"I'm okay," he said. "You know how it goes."

She touched his sleeve. "How's your arm?"

He flexed his forearm beneath the trench coat. Then, suddenly, she felt him relax.

"It's not worth a damn anymore, Joe," he said.

Her hand moved up to his shoulder, and she gave him a squeeze. He met her eyes for a moment, then looked away.

"I had to learn how to shoot all over again lefty," he said.

"You don't need a gun to do your job," she said.

He gave her a withering look.

"Okay, forget that," she said. She struggled to find something neutral to talk about.

"How's Gina?" she asked.

"We split up twelve years ago."

"Oh. I'm sorry."

"Yeah." He reached into his coat and pulled out his cigarettes again. He lit one and drew deep on it.

"When did you start smoking?" she asked.

"Twelve years ago."

"How's your son, Robert?" Joe asked.

"Ryan," Rafsky said.

"Sorry. He must be, what, in his twenties now?"

"Twenty-five. Married. Associate professor of biology at Northern. He's got a daughter, five years old."

Joe stayed quiet, waiting for Rafsky to go on. He took a step away, then looked back at her.

"I need to walk. You want to come?" he asked.

She nodded, and they started down the street. They turned onto Main Street, where the old globed lamps left pearly puddles on the wet street.

"Your son and granddaughter," Joe began, "do you get to see them much?"

It was a long time before Rafsky answered. "After Gina left we lost touch." He paused. "It was my fault. I let them both go without a fight."

He took another drag on the cigarette, and it was a few more steps before he spoke again. "When Ryan got the job at Northern last year I called him. I wanted to reconnect."

Joe had a sudden memory from the case fifteen years ago. Over dinner, Rafsky had given her advice on not letting the job take over her life. She could still remember his exact words.

You have to be careful. You have to have another life. A lot of cops let their work become their life. And my God, that will kill you.

She remembered that after enough wine he had pulled out his wallet and proudly showed her a picture of Ryan. She could remember, too, how the boy had looked—a small replica of his father, right down to the spiky sandy hair.

"So are things going well with Ryan now?" she asked.

Again he was slow to answer. "He's having a hard time forgiving me for not being there. And he's having a hard time believing me when I tell him I want to be there now for Chloe."

They stopped under a streetlamp, and she could see his face clearly now. She could see now that what Danny Dancer had captured wasn't emptiness. It was something as hard and ungiving as stone. Norm Rafsky, she realized in that moment, wanted to be forgiven, yet he didn't know how to do it himself.

That was the source of the contempt in his eyes when he had first seen her today. Fifteen years and he still hadn't been able to forgive her for what happened in Echo Bay.

It had taken her a long time to get over what she had done during her rookie year, conspiring with her fellow officers to leave a killer in the woods to die instead of taking him in to stand trial. Rafsky had been there, and she could still hear his words. *You'll be murderers, all of you.*

He hadn't turned them in, and when she asked him why his voice had gone cold.

I made a choice about what I could more easily live with— letting you get away with what you did or sending three decent young cops to jail.

But she knew now that he had never forgiven her. Not

just for what she had done but also for what keeping silent about it had done to him.

"Forgiveness is easy to ask for," she said. "But it's hard to give."

He just stared at her.

"Good night, Rafsky," she said. She turned and started back to the hotel.

22

It was still drizzling by the time Louis got to the station the next morning, and a heavy fog had turned Main Street into a smudged charcoal drawing. Head turtled into his collar, he didn't even see the crowd until he was almost upon it. It was the press scrum. Like a lab experiment gone bad, it had doubled in size since yesterday.

He did a quick count: six reporters, three photographers, and two TV camera guys were huddled under umbrellas at the side of the station's steps in the area Clark had cordoned off that was normally used for the police bikes. No one looked at him as he went up the steps.

There was no room to move in the small foyer; two huge state troopers in black rain slickers had taken up the space. Louis nudged past and went to the Dutch door. Two more state guys were inside, crowding a harried-looking Barbara at her radio console. Louis caught her eye, and she pressed the buzzer to let him in. Heat was blowing down from a ceiling vent. The small office was hot and stuffy with the smell of wet wool. Rafsky was back in Flowers's office on the phone.

Clark saw Louis and came over.

"What's with the heat?" Louis asked.

"The janitor turned on the furnace last night and no

one seems to know how to turn it off," Clark said. "I'm working on it."

"Any word on the chief?" Louis asked.

"He was transferred to St. Ignace Hospital this morning."

"So he's better?"

Clark nodded. "Still not conscious, but they said he was stable enough to be moved. He should be in surgery by now. I just sent one of my guys down to Pellston to pick up his ex-wife. Her plane gets in in a half hour, and we're taking her right over there."

"Good," Louis said. He pulled a manila envelope from his jacket. "I wanted to make sure you got Sheriff Frye's statement," he said.

Clark took it reluctantly. "So this means you're out of here?"

"It's Rafsky's show now."

An officer came up to Clark. "Sergeant, somebody better get out there and feed the animals."

Clark's eyes went to Rafsky. "Like you said, it's his show now, right?"

Clark went to Flowers's office and said something to Rafsky. Louis heard Rafsky spit out a string of obscenities. A moment later he came out. He gave Louis a glance as he passed, stuffing his arms into his sports jacket. Louis decided he had to see this and followed him outside.

The moment Rafsky took his place on the station steps the TV camera lights went on. They created an eerie glow in the mist. The reporters tried to shout out questions, but Rafsky quieted them with a raised hand.

"I have a statement about the events of yesterday," he

said. "We have a suspect in custody in the shooting of Chief Jack Flowers. His name is Daniel Albert Dancer, and he is a resident here on the island."

"Why were you at Dancer's cabin?" someone yelled out.

"We just wanted to ask him some questions," Rafsky said.

"Was it because you found skulls at Dancer's cabin?"

There was a rumble in the crowd. Louis's eyes shot to the scrum, but he couldn't figure out who had asked the question. It was a female voice, and there were two women in the crowd. He focused on a blonde in a red raincoat.

"Detective, did you find skulls at Dancer's house?"

Rafsky was staring at the blonde as if his eyes could turn her to a pillar of salt.

"No comment," he said.

"Is Dancer a suspect in the Julie Chapman case?" the blonde called out.

"I said no comment. That is all for now. There will be no questions."

Rafsky turned and went back inside. He stopped in the middle of the crowded office. Everyone was staring at him. For a second Louis thought Rafsky was going to start screaming about someone leaking the information about the skulls to the press. Then Rafsky caught Louis's eye.

"Kincaid, I need to see you," he said.

Louis followed him back to Flowers's office and closed the door. Rafsky ripped off his sports coat and threw it on a chair. He turned his back to the outer office.

"Who the fuck is talking to the press?" he said.

"It's a small island, Detective, it could be anyone," Louis

said. "Guys talk to their wives. Things get loose at the bar. And Dancer mailed skulls to customers. The people at the post office could have known."

Rafsky drew in two deep breaths and went back around the desk to sit down. He sat there for a long time just staring out at the people beyond the glass.

"You've got good people out there, Detective," Louis said. "No one here is trying to undermine you. Especially where it concerns the chief."

Rafsky wiped the sweat from his brow and began to roll up his shirtsleeves. "Clark told me you and Sheriff Frye are leaving today," he said.

"Yeah, Joe's back at the hotel packing up. I'll be staying with her in Echo Bay, and I left my contact info with Clark if you need me for anything."

Rafsky started to say something, but the phone rang. He picked it up, listened for a moment, then said, "Tell him I need dogs. If I don't find that skull in the cabin I'm going to dig up the whole damn island."

Rafsky gave some more instructions, hung up, and looked at Louis. "Look, Kincaid," he said. "I need to say something to you."

"Make it quick," Louis said.

"I don't have much use for PIs," Rafsky said.

The phone rang again. Rafsky pounced on it. "What?" Immediately, his face softened.

"Yes, I know," he said quietly. "Look, Ryan, I have a wounded officer here and—"

Rafsky fell silent, listening for a long time. "I know I promised her," he said. "Okay . . . yes, I will call her tonight. You have my word."

Rafsky hung up. He leaned forward and laced his hands together. "Look, Kincaid," he said. "I owe you an apology."

Louis waited.

"That day we talked to Ross Chapman, I was out of line with what I said. I'm sorry."

"Maybe you'll get a chance to apologize to the chief, too," Louis said.

Rafsky rubbed his eyes. "Yeah," he said softly.

Louis waited, but when Rafsky said nothing, he turned to leave.

"Wait," Rafsky said.

Louis turned back.

"I looked deeper into what happened to you here in Michigan," Rafsky said. "I didn't have all the information, but now I do." He paused. "You did the right thing."

Louis hid his surprise. "Thanks."

Rafsky sat back in his chair. "I want to ask you something," he said. "You've got a good grasp of this case and experience with cold cases in general. I'm asking if you'd considering staying on to help."

Before he could answer, Clark rapped on the glass door. He didn't wait to be asked in. "Detective," he said, "I think you'd better get back outside."

"Why?"

"Ross Chapman is making a statement."

Rafsky shot to his feet. "Goddamn it," he said. He didn't even bother to grab his jacket as he bolted for the door. Louis followed.

They stopped in the open doorway just behind Ross

Chapman, who had commandeered the porch of the station as if it were a podium.

Chapman was in midsentence, so there was no way for Rafsky to stop him without looking heavy-handed.

"This has been a terrible time for my family," Chapman said. "And I just wanted to say that my wife, Karen, and I appreciate all the kind words of support we have received." He paused. "This has been particularly hard for my father, who, as you know, has not been in good health in recent years. Twenty-one years ago my sister, Julie, disappeared, and we did what we could to mourn her and move on with our lives."

"Congressman," someone yelled out. "The man in custody collects skulls. Does he have Julie's?"

Ross stared down at the man. He opened his mouth to speak but couldn't.

"Have you seen it, Congressman?"

"I . . . don't—"

"Fuck," Rafsky whispered to Louis. "He's done."

Rafsky stepped in front of Chapman and lifted a hand. "No more questions for today."

Rafsky put a firm hand on Chapman's sleeve and pulled him back into the foyer. Louis shut the door.

"I could have handled that," Chapman said.

"No, you couldn't," Rafsky said.

"Look, Detective, I can—"

"I'm going to tell you this once and only once. Stay away from the press. And don't make any assumptions about your sister's case."

"But I—"

"Go home," Rafsky said.

Chapman was silent. When he started to open the door Rafsky pushed it closed. Looking around, he spotted Clark and waved him over.

"Sergeant, would you please escort the congressman home? And use the back door."

Clark nodded. "Yes, sir."

Chapman yanked up his raincoat collar and followed Clark.

"You're not going to keep him quiet," Louis said. "He's her brother."

"And a fucking politician," Rafsky said.

Rafsky pulled out his cigarettes and started to light up. He hesitated, then went outside. Louis followed him out onto the porch.

Rafsky lit his cigarette and turned to Louis.

"You didn't answer my question," he said. "Will you stay?"

The reporters were moving away, probably headed to the Mustang. A ferry horn sounded, even though there were probably no passengers to summon.

Louis saw a spot of black emerging from the fog. It was Joe. She was pulling her small rolling suitcase and had his duffel slung over her shoulder.

Rafsky saw her coming. "I know you have plans," he said. "I could use Sheriff Frye's help, too."

When Louis didn't say anything, Rafsky tossed his cigarette to the street and went back inside.

Joe stopped at the foot of the steps and dropped the duffel. "We missed the ferry," she said.

"I know."

Joe's eyes went to the closed station door and back to Louis's face.

"You want to stay, don't you?"

He came down the steps. "Yes."

"Why?" she asked.

He had been asking himself that question all day, and the answer had come from Lily and what she had said that morning in the restaurant. *It's sad that the bones were down there in the dark for so long and no one knew it.*

"I promised Lily I would make sure the bones get home," he said.

Joe smiled, shook her head, and started dragging her suitcase back toward the Potty. Louis picked up his duffel and followed.

23

The fog grew thinner as they climbed higher. The only sounds were the steady thuds of Sergeant Clark's footsteps behind him and the soft jingle of his keys.

Ross glanced back, but Clark didn't meet his eyes. Last night he had come to the cottage and efficiently briefed Ross on the chief's shooting and Dancer's arrest.

But now he was clearly uncomfortable, and Ross knew why. Clark wasn't like Rafsky or Kincaid. Clark was a local who knew how to treat people.

They made the turn onto West Bluff Road.

People who lived up here.

Ross thought back to the press conference. It had been his campaign manager's idea, to use the spotlight of the chief's shooting to get some camera time. But he hadn't been prepared when the reporter blurted out, "Have you seen it?"

Julie's skull. He felt a rise of bile in his throat and swallowed hard. This was so ugly, and it was only going to get worse. He had to stay in control somehow.

Ross stopped and turned to Clark. "Sergeant," he said. "This man Dancer. Tell me more about him."

"Well, sir, I'm not at liberty to discuss the case."

"I just want to know what kind of man he is."

Ross saw Clark's eyes flick over to the big shuttered houses. "He's lived here his whole life, sort of a hermit. Some folks say he's retarded. They also know he's been sneaking in and out of the old lodge."

"What about these skulls of his? Did you see them?"

Clark hesitated and ran a hand under his nose as he gave a small nod. "Yeah, I saw them. His cabin is filled with them and all these bugs that eat the skin away. None of the skulls are human, though, sir."

"Does Detective Rafsky think this man killed my sister?"

"I don't know, sir, but he's got a lot of people digging up Dancer's yard."

Ross nodded slowly. He looked down the road to the last house. "Thank you, Sergeant. I can make it from here."

Clark turned and started back down the road. Ross headed to the cottage.

Inside, the house was chilly, the drapes drawn. Ross knew Maisey closed them to keep the house warm, but it didn't help. Nothing helped. Like the house down in Bloomfield Hills, the island cottage was old and drafty. Sometimes he felt as if he'd been raised in a chill, which was one reason that when he married he built a big modern house in Rochester, with three fireplaces and two furnaces.

Ross took off his raincoat and hung it on a coatrack in the foyer. He heard the creak of footsteps above and looked up the staircase. The lights were on in the front bedroom. He needed to go up and see his father, but he needed a drink first.

He went to the parlor and switched on a lamp. He

poured a half glass of Hennessy and sat down in the chair by the phone.

Maisey had left a small pile of messages. He took a quick drink and sifted through them.

Six calls from four different reporters, including a name he didn't recognize from the *Washington Post*. Two messages from the Reptile—as he called his campaign manager—asking when he was coming back to Lansing. And two messages from Karen, one reminding him that the boys' Cranbrook tuition was due and the other warning him that she wasn't going to the Michigan Leadership Conference dinner alone.

Karen . . .

Image was everything to her, and she was so good at burnishing it. Everything from what pictures of the family were released to the press to the color of his ties. It was a talent she had gotten from her mother, a distant relative of the Piedmont family, who had made a fortune building tract homes in the suburbs during the fifties. Karen's parents didn't have money but nonetheless Karen had been raised to believe privilege was her right. That mind-set led her to a college junior named Ross Chapman, a Ford executive's son with a bright future.

And when Ross chose politics over business it had been a pregnant Karen who told him that she wasn't going to spend the rest of her life living in Lansing married to a state representative. If Ross wanted politics, then he better want it all, because she wanted to live in Georgetown, host cocktail parties for diplomats, and get invitations to inaugural balls.

Ross took another swallow of brandy and closed his eyes.

But the images wouldn't go away.

Retard.

Bugs eating skin off skulls.

A skeleton like a baby bird.

This was beyond ugly. It was grotesque. Not even Karen would be able to paint over it.

Everything would come out, and Ross knew exactly what would happen when it did. He understood the "disgust factor," understood that a man like Dancer was irresistible to the public and media. The story would play out in endless loops on Court TV and in the *National Enquirer*.

It wouldn't stop with Dancer. If it went to trial, Dancer's defense attorneys would go after Julie, paint her as a troubled runaway with no close friends, a girl with an absent father and a drugged-out mother. A girl who teased the retarded kid, ended up pregnant, and got what was coming to her.

Ross looked toward the stairs.

Dad . . .

He hadn't told him about the pregnancy. Or any of the other things Clark had told him. In his darkest moment he had hoped this would all somehow stay quiet until after his father died. But he couldn't chance that any longer.

He downed the last of the brandy and pushed himself from the chair.

The door to his father's room was open. His father was reading in a chair facing the window. Maisey was folding towels at the bed, and she glanced at Ross but said nothing as he came in.

"Hello, Dad."

His father looked up, tucked his book between his thigh

and the chair, and removed his glasses. "Ross. Where have you been?"

"At the police station." Ross leaned down and touched his father's hand. "How are you feeling, Dad?"

"Pretty good, considering," Edward said.

"We should talk, then," Ross said. "I have some things to tell you."

"I have something to ask you first," Edward said. "Maisey tells me you held a press conference this morning. Is that true?"

Ross glanced at the housekeeper. "Word travels fast," he said.

"It's a small island, Mr. Ross," Maisey said, without looking up.

"Why did you do that?" his father asked.

"Dad, I just thought—"

"You thought you could use the press to your advantage," Edward said. "This is your sister, for God's sake!"

"They wanted to know how the family was doing," Ross said evenly. "I couldn't just walk away from them."

Edward shook his head and looked out the window. It put his face in the hard granite light. Ross had noticed how quickly his father seemed to be aging, especially the last few months. His heart, the doctor had told him last month, had become as thin as paper.

"Tell me about this man they arrested," Edward said. "Did he kill my Julie?"

My Julie. Not just Julie. Not even our Julie. My Julie.

Ross eased in front of his father and sat on the window seat. Choosing his words carefully, he told his father what Clark had said about Dancer. Even though he was careful to tell his father that the police had no proof Dancer had killed Julie, he could see that his father was putting things together in his head—and he was horrified.

"Do you need some water, Dad?" Ross asked.

Before his father could answer, Maisey was there with a glass and a pill. She waited while Edward took the medication before going back to her folding.

Ross glanced after her, knowing she was taking her good old time to eavesdrop. He thought about dismissing her before he told his father about Julie's pregnancy, but it didn't matter. Dad would tell her later. He had been telling her everything for years.

"Dad, there's something I haven't told you yet," Ross said.

"What can be worse than what I know?" Edward asked softly.

"Julie was pregnant when she was killed."

Edward dropped his glass of water in his lap. Ross looked to Maisey. She was frozen, dumbfounded.

"Maisey, bring a towel," he said.

She grabbed one and hurried over. She took the wet blanket and book and brought Edward a fresh coverlet.

As she turned to leave, Ross caught a look from her that at first he wasn't sure how to read. Then he remembered. It was the same look she had always given him when he was a boy and he had done something to disappoint his father.

Edward's mumblings brought his attention back to his father. "I just can't believe it," his father whispered. "My little Julie. My baby, my baby."

Ross said nothing.

"How do they know?" Edward asked.

"What?"

"How do they know she was pregnant?"

"The police found fetal bones."

Edward shut his eyes, and for a long time the two of them just sat there.

"How far along was she?" Edward said.

Ross was stunned his father had even asked. Before, whenever something bad had touched the family, his father would tell everyone that no one should speak of it. Like when Uncle Rawlins was arrested for embezzling. Or when Ross's mother started walking around like a zombie from taking the pain pills.

"What does it matter?" Ross asked.

"It matters to me," Edward said.

Ross sighed. "Four to five months."

"Then she got pregnant that summer," Edward said slowly. He looked back out at the gray windows. "This man they have arrested, this Dancer, do they really believe he . . . do they think he raped her?"

"They don't know yet," Ross said. "Apparently Dancer is mentally ill, so it's possible."

"If Julie was raped that summer by this . . . this man, she would've . . ." His voice trailed off, and he was quiet for a long time. "She would have told me," he said softly. "If something like that had happened to her, she would have told me."

A drawer closed loudly behind Ross. He looked over his shoulder to see Maisey watching him.

"Maisey, leave us alone, please," Ross said.

The housekeeper took her time folding one last

towel before she left the bedroom, closing the door behind her.

Edward's gaze drifted back to the window. The rain started up again, spotting the glass and turning the lake and trees into a blur of gray and green.

"Did you know your sister wrote poetry?" Edward asked.

"I'm sorry," Ross said, needing a second to come back to the moment. "What did you say?"

"Poems, she wrote poems," Edward said. "Do you remember those red leather journals I gave her every Christmas? She wrote poems in them. I found the journals after she disappeared, years later when we were packing up her things. But I was too consumed by my grief to understand how important they were."

"What do you mean?" Ross asked.

"I don't think I would have even thought about them even now if the police hadn't asked to see them."

"The police? Why would they want to see them?"

"They think they could reveal something about what happened up here that summer."

Ross rose slowly and took a few steps away, trying to think. Julie wrote poems? Why didn't he know about this?

"I was just reading a few of them this morning," Edward said softly. "The ones she wrote that last summer here."

Ross turned back. His father's profile was silhouetted against the gray window.

"I was reading them, and I realized Julie had left a piece of herself for me to hang on to, a piece of her heart to help fill the hole in mine," Edward said.

Ross looked at his shoes, biting back his words, words he had wanted to say for a long time. Was now the moment? Did it matter anymore?

"Dad," Ross said softly, "don't you realize . . . have you ever realized that you never really knew either of us? Julie and I were just pictures in your wallet, something you could pull out when the other men talked about their families."

When Edward turned to him Ross was surprised to see no anger in his father's eyes, just a sort of sad resignation. Edward looked away toward the windows. For a long time it was quiet, just the splatter of rain against the glass and the soft hiss of the oxygen. Ross felt suddenly very tired, and right at this moment all he wanted to do was get away. Away from this house, away from his father, away from this damn island.

"I think she fell in love that summer."

Ross's eyes shot back to his father.

"It was there in her poems," Edward said. "It had happened here that summer. She found someone to love."

Ross came back to stand in front of his father.

"I want to know who the father of her baby is," Edward said.

"What?"

"I don't think this man Dancer is the father of Julie's baby. I think she fell in love with someone and maybe his name is in her poems somewhere. I want to find out who he was. I want to talk to him."

Ross almost said it: *You can't accept rape, so you believe in love.*

Edward was looking around the room. "Maisey?"

"She left, Dad."

Edward tried to get up from his chair. "I need something . . ."

Ross put a hand on Edward's shoulder and eased him back into the chair. "What do you need? I'll get it."

"My address book. It's over on the desk."

"Why do you want—?"

"Just do what I ask, Ross!"

Stunned by the anger in his father's voice, Ross got the book from the desk. He handed it to his father, who put on his glasses with shaking hands.

"What are you looking for, Dad?" Ross asked.

"John Manning's phone number."

"Dr. Manning? What do you need him for?"

"He can tell me about testing the bones."

"What bones?"

"The baby's bones. Maybe they can be tested to find out who the father is."

"Dad, listen to me," Ross said.

Edward ignored him as he flipped through the address book.

"Dad, please, will you just listen to me for a minute?"

Edward looked up.

"Did Julie say in the poems who the boy was?"

Edward looked confused for a moment. "I don't remember."

Ross knelt down in front of Edward. "Dad, I know you think this will bring you some sort of comfort, but the fetal bones can't be tested."

"How do you know that?"

"The police told me there probably isn't enough genetic material to determine paternity."

"Of course there's enough," Edward said. "They use marrow. Don't baby bones have marrow?"

"I'm just telling you what—"

Edward went back to flipping through the address book. "Dr. Manning can tell us for sure. We went to school together. I know he would help me with this. He can get the university to—"

Ross pressed his hand down over his father's.

"Dad, stop it. Even if it could be done, it would be very expensive."

Edward slowly pulled his hand away. "Money? Is that what you're worried about?"

Ross sat back in the window seat, forcing himself not to look away from his father's glare.

"All the money," Edward said. "All the money I've given you for your campaign and you're talking to me about what something costs?"

Ross stood up slowly and moved behind the chair so his father couldn't see him. There was nothing more to say, nothing more to do. He started toward the door. Then he stopped and turned back.

"Dad, where are Julie's journals?" he asked.

His father didn't turn. "Why do you ask?"

"I'd like to read her poems." He paused. "I miss her, too, Dad."

"Not now, Ross," Edward whispered. "Please leave me be."

Ross left the bedroom and went down the stairs. Maisey came out of the parlor and with barely a glance went up the stairs.

He went back into the parlor. He poured himself another brandy and took a chair near the phone. He stared at his messages for a moment, then pulled the phone into his lap. He dialed his office in Lansing, not his secretary's line but his private number, the one he had given out to only two people.

Only one new message. The Reptile.

Ross, where the hell are you? The last poll is bad, buddy. You've dropped two and Burkett's right on your ass now. I need you back here now. You've got to be visible, Ross. You don't win an election hiding out on an island. Your sister will still be dead after November sixth.

The message ended. Ross hung up the phone and sat back in the chair, the phone in his lap.

The hell with him. The hell with them all.

Ross reached for the brandy, took a drink, then set it aside. He picked up the receiver and dialed the number he had memorized. There was no answer. Ross shut his eyes but didn't hang up. On the twelfth ring, someone picked up.

"Hello?"

"I need to see you," Ross said. "Right now."

24

Louis zipped up his jacket and pulled up the hood of the sweatshirt he wore underneath. The rain had stopped, but it was so cold he had been forced to stop in Doud's to buy some gloves. The grocery didn't sell winter gloves, the bemused woman behind the counter had told him, but her husband did have some cotton work gloves she was willing to lend him.

He pulled out the bright orange gloves from his pocket, tucked the manila envelope under his arm, put on the gloves, and continued down West Bluff Road. The Chapman cottage was the only house with lights on, sitting like a lonely outpost at the end of the street.

It was time to talk to Maisey Barrow.

He had called ahead, and she was expecting him, holding the door open as he mounted the steps. She gave him a stiff nod and pulled her heavy sweater tighter around her as he came in.

"Leave your coat there," she said, pointing to the rack. "I have some fresh coffee brewing."

Taking the envelope with him, he followed Maisey toward the back of the house. The kitchen, compared to the rest of the dim and dank house, was ablaze with light and warmth. There was something cooking that made Louis's mouth water. He had been working with Rafsky all morning and had a hunger headache from eating only doughnuts at the station. Maisey saw him staring at the stove.

"It's beef stew for dinner," she said. "But it's probably ready now if you want some."

"If you can spare it."

"Mr. Ross had to go back to Lansing. It's just me and Mr. Edward tonight, so we have plenty."

She ladled out a bowl of stew and set it before Louis with an old silver spoon and a linen napkin. He tried to eat slowly, but it was several minutes before he even looked up. Maisey was bending over the oven and came up a moment later with a cookie sheet of biscuits. Without asking, she set two on a plate before him and went back to the stove.

"How is Mr. Chapman today?" Louis asked as he buttered one of the biscuits.

"He had a really bad night," she said. "He's been resting all day."

"I'm sorry to hear that," Louis said.

She came over with the coffeepot, and Louis nodded. She refilled his cup and sat down across from him at the table. She looked very tired, her soft brown eyes heavy with emotion.

"What did you want to see me about, Mr. Kincaid?" she asked.

"Louis. Call me Louis, please."

She gave him a look that told him that was never going to happen.

"I understand you've been with the Chapman family for a long time," Louis said.

"Almost forty years," she said. "I came to work for them soon after Mr. Ross was born. I raised those children. They were like my own."

Louis remembered a detail from the Bloomfield Hills police dossiers. Except for one brother, Maisey Barrow had no family.

"You stayed on after the children were grown?"

She nodded. "Mrs. Chapman was in poor health. Mr. Chapman needed me."

Louis suspected Maisey's job description had expanded and contracted over the decades as the Chapman family dynamic changed. She had gone from nursemaid to surrogate mother and now was Edward's caretaker.

"I need to ask you some questions about Julie," Louis began. "Mr. Chapman told us that Julie was very shy and well behaved."

Maisey nodded.

"But that weekend before she disappeared, she lied to her father about where she was going," Louis said.

Maisey was quiet. "I know," she said finally. "I don't know why she did it."

Everything the family had told him so far was consistent with what he had read in the original police report from twenty-one years ago. As with Ross, the only thing new he could learn from Maisey was what had happened here that summer.

"I'd like to ask you some questions about that last summer you were here with Julie," he said.

"I don't know what help I can be."

"Do you know that Julie got pregnant while she was here?"

Maisey nodded slowly. "Mr. Ross told us yesterday."

"We have a man in custody named Danny Dancer. We don't know if he is connected to Julie's death yet. Did you ever hear Julie mention him?"

She shook her head.

"You're sure? It's an unusual name."

Again she shook her head, now avoiding his eyes.

Maisey was obviously distressed about the pregnancy. Louis decided to change direction. "Ross told us that Julie was acting strange that summer," he said.

"Strange?"

"Mood swings." Louis paused. "I need you to think back, Maisey. Did you notice anything about Julie's behavior that might indicate she had been attacked? Did she say anything to you, anything at all?"

Maisey's eyes welled. "No," she whispered.

Louis sat back in his chair. "Okay. There's something else we have to consider," he said. "Did Julie have a boyfriend?"

Maisey had been looking away and when her eyes refocused on Louis they were confused. "Boyfriend?"

"Someone she met that last summer here."

Maisey thought for a moment, then slowly shook her head. "No," she said. "I would have known."

"Well, how did she spend her time here?" Louis said. "Did she go anywhere, do anything special?"

"She went riding and went for walks," Maisey said. "Mr. Edward was always worried about her being too shy, so he told Mr. Ross to take her to the dances down at the yacht club." She paused. "I don't think she enjoyed it much, truth be told."

"Were you and Julie close?" Louis asked.

Again her eyes welled. She picked up the empty bowl and took it to the sink. "I should go check on Mr. Edward," she said, her back still to him.

"There's one more thing," Louis said. "I'd like you to look at some drawings."

Maisey turned. "Drawings?"

Louis took a sketchbook from the envelope. They had found a hundred and forty-two sketchbooks during the processing of Danny Dancer's cabin. Joe had suggested the drawings might help them find persons of interest or witnesses. She had gone through every sketchbook, finally giving one to Louis that contained drawings of teenagers in sixties-era dress and in settings like the beach at British Landing or Fort Holmes, places Sergeant Clark told Louis were popular for the local kids to hang out at.

Louis opened the page that Joe had marked with a Post-it. It was a picture of Julie. She looked beautiful, her long hair wind-whipped around her face, her mouth tipped in a smile, and her eyes focused on someone unseen off to her right.

Maisey came to the table and stared at the drawing for a long time. Finally she sat down and looked up at Louis.

"Where'd you get this?" she asked softly.

"Danny Dancer drew it," Louis said. "He drew almost everybody on this island for more than twenty years. We think he might have done this that last summer here."

Maisey nodded slowly. "Yes, I recognize that blouse."

"She looks very happy," Louis said.

A small smile came to Maisey's face. "This is how I remember Julie that summer." She ran a finger lightly over the drawing. "A boyfriend," she said softly. "How could I have not seen it?"

"Maybe you did," Louis said.

He flipped the sketchbook back to the first page. "He could have been the boy who delivered groceries or someone she met in town, maybe someone she was afraid to bring home," Louis said. "Please look, see if you recognize anyone."

Maisey began to turn the pages. The kitchen was quiet as she studied each drawing. She was on the last few pages when she suddenly stopped. She turned the sketchbook around toward Louis.

It was a drawing of a girl. Round-faced, large-eyed, a gap-toothed smile, a cascade of curly light hair held down by a braided headband across her forehead.

"You recognize her?" Louis asked.

Maisey nodded. "She came to the house a couple of times. She and Julie used to sit out on the porch. I remember her because . . . I heard her making jokes about Julie having a mammy."

She gave Louis a wry smile, which he returned with one of his own.

"Do you remember her name?" he asked.

Maisey frowned. "It started with an *R*. It was . . . Roberta." She paused. "No, wait. Rhoda. That was it. Rhoda."

"Can you remember her last name?"

"No, but I think she worked here on the island because she always came here after five or so." She looked up suddenly at Louis. "She smelled like chocolate."

Louis took the sketchbook back, slipping it into the envelope. He was disappointed Maisey hadn't been able to recognize Julie's boyfriend, but this Rhoda could be a lead.

"If there's nothing else you need, Mr. Kincaid, I really should go see to Mr. Edward," Maisey said.

"Actually, there's one more thing," Louis said. "Can I see Julie's room?"

"Her room? Why?"

"It helps me get a sense of a person. Sometimes if I see where they spent their time, what things they had, it helps me figure out what might have happened to them."

"The room's not the same as it was then," she said.

"I'd still like to see it."

She gave him a nod. Louis followed her up the staircase. At the first open door, she paused, listening for a moment. Louis got a glimpse of the interior—burnished antiques, the edge of a plush bed, and light streaming in from the bay windows.

Maisey moved on down the hallway. All the other doors were closed. At the end of the hallway Maisey stopped and opened the heavy oak door.

The air inside was stale, the drapes drawn. Maisey touched a wall switch and an overhead light went on.

Louis had been expecting something different, maybe like the room back at the Grand Hotel with the canopy beds. This was just a small plain room with two twin beds, one oak bureau, a small bookcase, and a braided rug on the wood floor. Except for the white chenille bedspreads the only thing that looked remotely feminine was the wallpaper dotted with pink rosebuds.

"It's not what I thought it would look like," he said.

"What were you expecting?" Maisey asked.

"I don't know. Something that tells me a teenaged girl used to be here." He turned to Maisey, who was still standing by the door. "Stuffed animals. A monkey, to be exact."

"A monkey?" Maisey pulled her sweater tighter around her. "Julie wasn't much for that kind of thing."

Louis went to a closet and opened the door. It was empty. "There's nothing left of her things?" he asked.

"After Julie disappeared Mr. Ross ordered that everything be taken away. He said it upset Mr. Edward too much to see the room like it was."

Louis heard a sound, like someone calling out. Maisey stepped out into the hallway and looked toward the far end.

"That's Mr. Edward," she said quickly. "Do you mind seeing yourself out?"

"Not at all. Thanks for your help, Maisey," Louis said.

She gave him a brisk nod, then went down to the first bedroom at the top of the stairs.

Louis watched Edward Chapman's bedroom door close and stepped back into Julie's room. He went to the drapes and pulled them open. The room looked out over the backyard. He let the drapes fall and turned to consider the room again.

There were seven bedrooms in this place. Why had Edward Chapman's "princess" been given this small one in the back?

He went to the bookcase and scanned the titles of the books, but they all appeared to be novels. He started for the door but something tucked in the shelf of the bookcase caught his eye. It was a small ceramic horse, similar to one he had bought Lily, right down to MACKINAC ISLAND painted on the base. Just a cheap souvenir, and it seemed out of place in such a grand house, even in this plain little room.

He put it back on the bookcase and left the room, quietly making his way down the stairs.

Outside he paused to look back at the house. He saw Maisey standing at the upstairs bay window. He felt her eyes follow him as he walked back down West Bluff Road.

25

Louis stared out the window of the police station. This morning when he had walked up to the cottage to see Maisey, the watery horizon had been bloated with steel-gray clouds. Now it was snowing.

"Louis?" Clark came up next to him. "Dancer's attorney wants to talk to you."

"Attorney?" Louis asked.

"Don't ask me what got into him all of sudden, but Dancer asked for one late last night. Mackinac County sent a public defender a few hours ago. Name is Lee Troyer."

It was inevitable that Dancer would get a lawyer for the shooting charges, but the problem was that a good attorney would steer Dancer away from answering questions about Julie Chapman.

"Do you know where Rafsky is?" Louis asked.

"He's over in St. Ignace, visiting the chief," Clark said.

"How's the chief doing?"

"I went and saw him this morning," Clark said. "He's mad as hell that he can't eat or talk. But I know one thing. He's real glad Carol is there, even though he'll never say it out loud."

"I understand."

Clark smiled. "I guess when it comes to women we're all too stubborn sometimes."

Louis was quiet. Stubborn. Was that what it was? Last night, in the cool darkness of their hotel room, wrapped in each other's arms, listening to the clinking of the old radiator and the faraway crash of water against the giant boulders, he had almost said it.

I love you.

Until that moment he had not realized that when Joe wasn't with him there was a strange emptiness that nothing else—no one else—could fill.

He had been about to say it, but then Joe rolled away from him and reached for her wineglass. The moment—and his courage—was gone.

"Almost forgot," Clark said. "Rafsky said to tell you that Dancer is being transferred to the county jail in St. Ignace first thing tomorrow."

"Okay, thanks," Louis said.

He headed upstairs, taking Dancer's sketchbook with him. At the top of the stairs he was met with the pungent smell of gardenias. Lee Troyer was seated in a folding chair, head down. Everything about her seemed cut on severe angles. Even her hair looked sharp, a blond page-boy style that reminded Louis of the kid in the Dutch Boy paint commercials.

"Miss Troyer? Louis Kincaid."

She looked up from her legal pad. "You're the person who so roughly subdued my client on the steps of his cabin."

"After your client shot at me and two other officers."

Louis glanced at Dancer. He was in one of two cells, drawing.

"And you, a Miss Frye, and a Detective Rafsky questioned my client that same evening?"

"Yes. And it's Sheriff Frye."

"You questioned him without giving him a Miranda warning?"

"He was read his rights in the cruiser, Miss Troyer."

"For the shooting of Chief Flowers, yes," she said. "But you then proceeded to question him about the homicide of Julie Chapman."

"Now wait a—"

"So," Troyer went on, "not only was he *not* advised of his rights pending any charges in the Chapman case but he was also questioned by two people who have no jurisdiction on this island."

Louis studied the woman. Was she good enough to somehow tangle up the Chapman investigation with motions and accusations, or was she grasping at legal clichés?

"Dancer was not given his rights for the Chapman homicide because at the time of questioning he was not in custody for that crime," he said. "By voluntarily drawing a picture of the victim *he* brought the subject of her murder into the discussion."

Lee Troyer squared her shoulders. "I could argue that you set my client up by giving him a sketch pad, knowing he draws obsessively."

"That's ridiculous."

"Detective Rafsky thinks Dancer killed Julie Chapman," she said. "Even as we speak he has officers searching my client's property for her skull. That act makes Danny a suspect in the Chapman murder, and for you to deny he isn't is the ridiculous part."

She was right, but he'd be damned if he would admit it.

"Look," Louis said. "The fact is, your client has not yet been charged with Julie Chapman's murder and won't be on the basis of a single drawing."

Troyer was quiet, trying to keep her gaze level.

"Off the record," he said, "I don't happen to think he killed Julie Chapman, and I don't think Detective Rafsky is going to find proof out there that Dancer killed anyone."

Troyer looked down at her legal pad. He could see she had jotted down bullet points of her argument and was now out of bullets. She couldn't be more than twenty-five, and he knew she had been sidetracked by Julie Chapman's case. With the simple act of drawing a picture Dancer had elevated a small-town cop shooting to a high-profile cold case homicide, complete with a locally connected politician running for national office.

"Look, Miss Troyer," Louis said. "You're probably right about Mirandizing Dancer before we asked him about Julie Chapman, but that aside, if you want my advice you need to focus on the crime he is charged with—the attempted murders of three people, two of them police officers."

"Well, I do know that, of course," Troyer said.

"I know I have no real say here, but if you want to help Dancer you need to find him a say-what-the-defense-pays-you-to-say psychiatrist," Louis said. "That's the only way you'll keep him out of prison for the rest of his life."

"He can't afford that, and my office can't—"

"Then you petition the court to provide equal resources," Louis said.

"Excuse me?"

"You argue that Dancer can't compete with the state's criminal psychiatrists on the public defender's budget. If you make a good argument you can get the court to order that the state pick up the tab for your experts."

Troyer raised a thin brow. "I never heard that kind of advice from the law enforcement side of the table before."

"I have an ulterior motive to keep things friendly with Dancer," Louis said.

"Which is?"

Louis opened the sketchbook. "Dancer has thousands of drawings of people whose names he doesn't remember." He pointed to Rhoda. "This girl was a friend of Julie Chapman's. I need to talk to Dancer about her."

Troyer stared at the drawing for a moment, then looked at Dancer.

"I won't ask him any questions about Julie's murder," Louis said. "I just need to know who this girl is."

"What if he blurts out something incriminating?"

"I can't control that and neither can you," Louis said.

There was something about this woman that reminded Louis of himself when he was a rookie investigator in rural Mississippi. Way in over his head, floundering for clues, afraid to make the wrong decision, but determined to go it alone.

"I won't screw your client," Louis said. "I promise."

Troyer gave Louis a nervous smile, then looked back at Dancer. "You feel like talking today, Danny?"

"Yeah, okay."

"Come to the bars, please," Troyer said.

Danny didn't get up. All his attention was on finishing his drawing. He was also mumbling.

"What are you saying, Danny?" Louis asked. "We can't hear you."

"Fifty-three, fifty-four, fifty-five."

"I think he's counting the wrinkles," Louis said to Troyer. He looked back to Dancer. "Is that Aunt Bitty?"

"Yeah."

"How many wrinkles do you have to draw?"

"A hundred and twenty-two."

"Danny, can you stop for a moment and please come to the bars?" Troyer asked. "I've brought you some chocolate fudge."

Like a robot reacting to a command, Danny set his pad aside and came to the bars. Troyer gave him a square of fudge. He ate it in two bites, licked his fingers, then wadded up the paper and gave it back to her through the bars.

Troyer leaned close to Louis. "When I met with him last night I had a box of fudge in my purse to take home," she whispered. "When he didn't respond to me I'm ashamed to say I used it to get him to talk."

Louis held up the open sketchbook to Dancer. "Danny, can you tell me the name of this girl?" he asked.

Danny was still licking his fingers, eyeing Troyer. Finally, he looked at the drawing.

"Summer," he said.

"Yes, I know. Can you tell me her name?"

Danny shook his head.

"Danny, listen to me," Louis said. "Can you tell me if you ever saw this girl with Julie?"

Danny reached through the bars and touched the drawing, tracing Rhoda's jawline with the tip of his finger. Louis sensed he was remembering and he stayed quiet.

"Cold," Dancer said.

"What do you mean 'cold'? You said it was summer."

Danny formed a V with his fingers and put them on the eyes of Rhoda's drawing. Still he said nothing.

Louis watched him, remembering how Dancer had captured emotions in the drawings he had done of Joe and Rafsky and himself. He looked at the sketch of Rhoda, and he suddenly saw what Dancer had seen.

"You mean she was cold on the inside," Louis said.

"Eyes like ice," Danny said. "Heart like ice."

Louis leaned closer to the bars. Danny quickly took a step back, but he didn't walk away, interested in Rhoda in a way Louis had not seen from him before. There was some sort of connection.

"Danny, someone told us this girl's name might be Rhoda," Louis said. "Do you remember anyone named Rhoda from when you were a teenager?"

Danny's eyes were glazing over. Louis started flipping through the notebook to keep Dancer's attention.

"Danny, look at this guy's picture," Louis said, showing him another face. "Do you know this person's name?"

Danny shook his head.

"What about this one?" Louis asked, trying another unknown.

As if his batteries had died, Danny returned to his bunk and picked up his pad. He started mumbling again.

"Ninety-six, ninety-seven . . ."

Louis watched him for a moment, then closed the sketchbook. He had worked complicated cases before, but this one was driving him crazy. A skeleton with no skull. A cop shot for no good reason. Hundreds of possible witnesses in the sketchbooks but only one name.

"You okay, Mr. Kincaid?" Troyer asked.

"Frustrated."

"I understand," Troyer said. "But I can't allow any more interviews with Danny until we get a psychiatric evaluation. I also need to speak with the prosecutor about a possible plea on the attempted murder charges. I'm sorry."

Now the lady grows a pair, Louis thought. Not that it mattered. For the first time in his career he was okay with a cop shooter taking a plea that might land him in a hospital rather than a maximum-security prison.

And Julie Chapman's case?

The DNA test on her bones could take months. Anyone who might recognize Rhoda's face was already gone from the island. Rafsky's team had finished searching the cabin, even opening some walls. The cadaver dogs had alerted on nothing inside the cabin or the yard, and the teams were now working their way deeper into the woods. No one was willing to say it to Rafsky's face, but it was becoming clear that Dancer didn't have Julie Chapman's skull.

Louis looked at the barred window, where the snow was starting to pile in the corners. Things were fast going cold.

And the truths they needed to know about Julie Chapman's murder were very possibly trapped inside Danny Dancer's enigmatic brain.

26

It was past midnight when Ross put the key into the front door of the cottage and slipped inside. The parlor was dark except for the glow of a dying fire in the hearth.

Ross hung up his coat and pulled off his scarf. He stood for a moment, eyes closed, holding the scarf to his nose. Her smell was still there in the cashmere, and so was his memory of the scarf draped between her bare breasts. It had been only a few hours since he had made love to her, but his desire stirred again. It was as powerful as it had been that first time five years ago when they began their love affair.

He hung up the scarf and went to the liquor cabinet in the parlor to pour himself a drink.

Love affair? No, that's not what it was. There wasn't a shred of love between them. It was all sex. Sex and professional favors. She needed an interview or some gossip at the state capital, and in exchange he needed . . .

Sandy Hunt. Sophisticated, intelligent, and gorgeous—one of the most familiar faces in the Michigan media. Her public reputation was as a street-smart woman playing hardball in a man's world. But privately Ross knew what people thought of her. He had heard what the other reporters said, the jokes they made and the names they called her in Stober's bar as they watched her on TV. Sandy the slut . . . that was the kindest one.

Ross drank the Hennessy, letting it burn its way down his throat.

A few hours ago he had been in her Lansing apartment, listening to Sinatra croon from the other room. It was a drizzly day, the kind of day that lulled a man toward sleep, and her bedroom had been a grotto of silver-blue shadows.

He had lain there, wondering why the fuck he kept coming back to a woman he couldn't trust, wondering how he was going to get his attack ads on the air when he didn't have the money to pay for them, wondering about—

The memory of Sinatra's voice momentarily interrupted his thoughts.

"Today the world is old. . . . You flew away and time grew cold."

He shut his eyes. Sandy had sensed something was wrong, because she started to stroke his chest, a tender gesture that she seldom offered. Her voice had the smoothness and burn of brandy.

Too bad your father doesn't just fly away one night in his sleep, then you would have everything you need to be the man you were meant to be.

I love my father, Sandy.

Uh-huh. Right.

She rolled away from him, smoked a cigarette, and fell asleep. Soon after, not wanting to be near her anymore, he slipped from her apartment and chartered a flight back to the island. On the way, he made a decision. He would tell his father that he wasn't going to sit out the campaign waiting around the island for news about Julie. And he was going to demand that his father unlock an untouched trust left to Julie by their grandfather and give him the money he needed to win this election.

She was dead, damn it. His father had never been willing to admit it. Five years ago, Ross had finally petitioned the court to declare Julie legally dead. After his father saw her death announcement in the newspaper, the last of his father's affection for him seemed to disappear.

Ross rose and went upstairs. As he passed Maisey's room, he paused to make sure she was snoring, then moved on to his father's room, stopping at the open door.

His father was sleeping, frail-looking in the enormous four-poster bed.

Ross went to the bed and stared down at his father. For several months now he had known Dad wouldn't make it much past the New Year. While Maisey was already grieving in her own way, he had felt so little he often wondered what was wrong with him.

I love my father, Sandy.

But he had known since he was about twelve that it wasn't the kind of love a son should have. It was obligatory, forced, sometimes offered desperately in the hopes of getting a splinter of the affection his father saved for Julie.

As Ross grew older he gave up on love, becoming instead the consummate actor playing the role of a loving son, because that's what people expected of the Chapmans. And even as his father grew sicker and more distant, even as Ross had his own children and made a name for himself in Lansing, he continued to play the same role.

Decades of pretending.

And now, as he stood there and looked at the old man who had once been the indomitable Edward W. Chapman, he was stunned to feel an ache in his chest. It was the ache of needing love from someone who didn't love you back, and it was real. He knew because he'd felt it once before.

Ross looked down at the oxygen tank, at the gauge that monitored the flow rate. A tiny red needle quivered over the number two. The voice of Dad's doctor in Bloomfield Hills drifted to Ross, like a cold breeze from a crack in the window.

It's important the oxygen flow stay consistent. Too much or too little could be fatal in a matter of minutes.

Ross shut his eyes, trying to erase what he was thinking. *Wouldn't it be nice if your father just flew away?*

It would get him the money he needed to finish his campaign. It would buy the bigger house Karen wanted. It would allow him to set Sandy up in an apartment in D.C. And he could get rid of Maisey.

Slowly Ross reached down and turned the dial on the oxygen tank up to four.

His instinct was to watch his father's face, but he forced himself not to look, afraid that his father's eyes would open and he would see his son standing over him.

Ross listened for some indication that death had come, but the seconds passed so slowly he began to count them in his head. Still, he heard nothing but the hiss of the oxygen growing louder and louder and louder.

Shame suddenly engulfed him.

Ross tightened every muscle and closed his eyes.

Fifteen, sixteen . . .

Then, as soft as if it had come from another room, he heard a cough.

Or had he?

Ross forced himself to look down at his father. Nothing about the old man had changed. There was no sudden gray hue to the skin, no flop of his head toward the side, nothing to confirm the horror of what he had just done.

Ross put a finger to his father's neck, then to his wrist, holding it there for nearly a minute even though there was no pulse.

Ross turned the oxygen dial back to number two. Then he stepped away from the bed, feeling as he had with Sandy that afternoon—suddenly sickened by the thought of being there a moment longer.

He moved to the window.

It was pitch-black but the pale light behind him haloed his reflection in the glass. The image was almost transparent, defined only by patches of frost and slivers of light.

I have killed my father.

How had he become this man? A man who cheats on his wife, who drinks with criminals for donations, who lies to old women for votes.

"You flew away and time grew cold."

The tears came. He stayed at the window, letting them fall.

His only thoughts were, as always, for himself.

How did I become this monster?

27

The phone jarred him from a deep sleep. Louis knocked the receiver to the floor and lunged for it.

"Yeah?"

"Mr. Kincaid?"

He rubbed his eyes. The room was dark and cold. "Who is this?"

"It's Maisey Barrow." A long pause. "Mr. Kincaid, I . . . Mr. Edward is dead."

Her words dissolved into sobs. Louis swung his legs over the bed and fumbled for the light, switching it on.

"Maisey, calm down," Louis said. "Are you sure?"

Joe touched his arm. "Louis, what is it?"

He held up a hand to silence her.

"He's cold, Mr. Kincaid," Maisey said. "I went into his room a few minutes ago, and I found him. I touched him. He's cold as ice."

"Okay, okay, listen carefully, Maisey." Louis rubbed his face. "Is Ross there?"

"I . . . yes, he came back last night. I think he's asleep."

"Go wake him up, but it's important that neither of you touch anything."

She was sniffling.

"Maisey? Did you hear what I said?"

"Yes, sir."

"I'll be there with the police as soon as I can."

He depressed the receiver and dialed the police station. He directed the dispatcher to call Sergeant Clark and tell him that Edward Chapman was dead. Then he asked the dispatcher to send a car immediately to the Potawatomi Hotel. He hung up and turned to face Joe, who lay propped on one elbow staring at him.

"Edward Chapman is dead," he said.

"Good Lord," Joe said softly.

Louis reached for his jeans. "Get dressed. I'll go wake Rafsky."

Ten minutes later, Clark was behind the wheel of the police SUV waiting for Louis outside the hotel. Louis climbed in the front, Joe and Rafsky in the back. Clark was wearing a police parka, but Louis saw the striped collar of his pajamas beneath. No one said much as Clark drove through the dark deserted streets.

A pale smudge of pink was coloring the horizon over the lake as they pulled up to the Chapman cottage. The first floor was ablaze with lights, but the second floor was dark. The grass, hardened with frost, cracked under their shoes as they went up the lawn. Louis was surprised when Ross, not Maisey, met them at the door.

"I can't get her to leave his room," Ross said, gesturing toward the stairs as they went in.

Ross was wearing sweatpants and a rumpled black sweater. His hair, always so carefully styled, was a wild mess. His eyes were red, and his face was puffy. It was obvious he had been crying, but the faint odor of liquor was also on his breath.

"She won't leave him," Ross said. "Please, you have to talk to her."

Louis glanced at Rafsky and Joe. "Give me a minute with Maisey, okay?"

Rafsky nodded. "We'll wait down here for the doctor."

There was no way to get a coroner here quickly from the mainland without chartering an expensive plane, so Clark had called the island doctor who had been caring for Edward Chapman during his stay at the cottage.

Louis went upstairs. The door to the first bedroom was open, and the room was dark except for an orange glow. It took Louis a moment to realize what it was—a space heater positioned near the bed. As he ventured closer, Louis saw Edward Chapman lying in the bed, a small bump amid the snowy white mountains of blankets.

Louis heard a mewing sound and turned. It was Maisey, sitting in the shadows. The chair creaked as she got up and came to him. They stood side by side, staring down at Edward Chapman.

"I couldn't leave him cold like that," Maisey whispered. "I put the blankets over him and brought the heater in."

Her eyes glistened in the orange glow, and her face was streaked with tear tracks. Louis stepped between her and the bed and put his hands on her shoulders.

"You need to go downstairs now, Maisey," he said. "The doctor's coming. We'll take care of Mr. Edward now."

"I can't leave him alone," she whispered.

"It's all right," Louis said. "I'll stay here with him. The best thing you can do for Mr. Edward now is to go downstairs and wait for the doctor. Bring him up when he gets here, okay?"

Maisey was straining to look beyond Louis to the bed, but he tightened his grip on her shoulders. "Maisey, please. You have to do what I say, okay?"

Her body seemed to give suddenly, as if she were exhaling every bit of air from her lungs. Eyes glistening, she turned slowly and left the room. Louis went back to the bed. Except for his mouth hanging slightly open, Edward Chapman looked as if he were asleep. His eyes were closed, and his arms were at his sides under the blankets Maisey had put over him. The plastic tubing was still in his nostrils, and Louis could hear the faint hiss of the oxygen.

A sudden stab of a buried memory came to him—his own mother, Lila, lying motionless in her bed, her body wasted from alcohol poisoning, her skin yellowed with hepatitis, her face frozen in a death grimace. There had been nothing peaceful about her leaving, nothing much peaceful about her life, in fact. At least Edward Chapman looked like he hadn't suffered, in death or life.

Louis heard a sound and turned to see a short, round man coming into the room. He carried a black doctor's satchel.

"I'm Dr. Mitchell from the island health center," he said, nodding to Louis. His glasses caught the glow of the space heater as he looked down at Edward Chapman.

Louis took a step back and watched as the doctor examined Edward Chapman's eyes, prodded his limbs, and then checked the oxygen tank and every pill vial on the nightstand. With a glance at Louis, the doctor looked up something in a black notebook and then picked up the phone and dialed Chapman's personal physician in Bloomfield Hills. The conversation was short, and it seemed Mitchell was not alarmed by Chapman's death.

As Dr. Mitchell hung up, Ross appeared in the doorway.

"It looks like your father died from natural causes," Dr. Mitchell said to Ross. He glanced at Louis. "Mr. Chapman had an atrioventricular septal defect." When he saw Louis's blank expression he added, "It's a large hole in the middle of the heart. He was born with it."

"He had surgery when he was just seven," Ross said. "And open-heart surgery five years ago."

Dr. Mitchell reached down and turned off the oxygen. "I'm surprised he lasted this long."

"I'd like to take him home as soon as possible," Ross said.

Dr. Mitchell nodded. "You can make arrangements. I'll have a death certificate for you in a couple of days."

"Thank you," Ross said quietly.

Dr. Mitchell pulled a card out of his pocket and held it out to Ross. "This is a funeral home in St. Ignace. They can take care of everything for you."

Ross took the card and pulled the doctor aside to talk privately. Louis used the moment to head back downstairs. Rafsky and Joe were waiting in the parlor. The room was full of bright light, the slanting morning sun falling full and warm through the big windows.

"What's it look like?" Rafsky asked.

Louis shook his head. "Natural death. He had a hole in his heart."

Rafsky got up from his chair and picked up his coat. "Then we're finished here. Where's Clark?"

"He went outside," Joe said.

Rafsky left, presumably to find Clark and get a ride back to town. Joe stayed in her chair, looking at Louis.

"I need to get going, too," she said. "Not just from here but back to Echo Bay."

Louis was quiet. It had been pulling at him for days now, this feeling that things were coming to an end. The season here on the island, the search for Julie's killer, his chances to fix things with Joe. If he wasn't careful, his moment would be lost.

He looked around the room. "Where's Maisey?" he asked.

"I don't know," Joe said.

Louis was wondering if she had gone back upstairs when he saw a blur of green move past the window. Maisey was out on the porch. He excused himself from Joe and went outside.

Maisey was standing on the far end of the porch, staring out at the lake. It glistened in the bright morning sun like a broad, flat mirror. Not a wave in sight, not a cloud on the horizon.

Louis moved to her. She didn't seem to see him. She was wearing a green plaid overcoat but hadn't even bothered to button it. She had just wrapped herself in it as if she were trying to retreat into a cocoon. He touched her arm.

"I know you cared for him," Louis said. "I'm sorry."

Maisey didn't look at him. "I loved him," she said. "We loved each other."

Louis looked out at the lake. He wondered what would happen to her now, if Ross would keep her on. Where did a sixty-something caretaker find a new home? Where did you fit in when your family had broken apart?

"Mr. Kincaid, I'd like you to do something for me," Maisey said.

"Anything."

"When they get Mr. Edward back to Bloomfield Hills, I want you to ask his doctor there to make sure he died naturally."

"What?"

"I need to know."

"Know what, Maisey?"

She faced him. "I need to know Mr. Ross didn't do something to him."

Louis was stunned into silence.

"Before Mr. Ross went back to Lansing, they had words," she said.

"What do you mean?" Louis asked.

"Mr. Ross and Mr. Edward. They had words about Julie."

"What did they say exactly?"

"I don't know for certain because Mr. Ross sent me out of the room, but I know it upset Mr. Edward."

Her eyes suddenly darted past Louis. He turned to see Ross standing just outside the door.

"Maisey," Ross said, "I need your help, please."

With a glance at Louis she went inside. Louis stayed on the porch, thinking about what Maisey had said. Edward Chapman had been near death, so why would Ross take the chance of killing him amid the media glare of Julie's investigation and his own campaign?

But Maisey, by her own admission, loved Edward. Maybe she just needed someone to blame.

Something caught Louis's eye and he turned to the window. Ross Chapman was standing inside looking out at him, his figure a rippled blur behind the old glass.

28

The interior of the Mustang Lounge was as dark as a tomb and deserted except for one man sitting at the bar. It took Louis a moment to realize it was Rafsky. He hesitated, thinking he'd go back to the hotel and wait for Joe. But she told him she had at least an hour of phone calls to catch up on and that he should go on without her.

The smell of frying meat drifted over to Louis. Finally hunger overcame any trepidation he had about having to make lunchtime small talk with Rafsky and he went to the bar.

"What's good today?" Louis said, sliding onto the stool.

"Try the Mustang Burger," Rafsky said.

The bartender placed a plate of fries and a towering burger in front of Rafsky.

"I'll have the same, no pickles," Louis said. "With a Heineken, please."

The bartender left, and Louis watched Rafsky as he took the top bun off his burger. He dismantled the stack of tomato, bacon, onion slices, pickles, and lettuce and then carefully put the hamburger back together again.

"You always do that?" Louis asked.

"Do what?"

"Restack your burger?"

Rafsky turned to stare at him. "Yes. Does it bother you?"

"No."

"The tomato should always be on top," Rafsky said.

Louis nodded as though he understood. The bartender brought his beer, and he took a long draw.

"I need to fill you in on something," Louis said. "After you left the Chapman house this morning Maisey took me aside and told me she thought Ross might have done something to the old man."

Rafsky stopped in midchew. "Done something? She say what he did exactly?"

"No. She says they argued before Ross went to Lansing."

"About what?"

"Something about Julie. I think she believes Ross killed his father."

"Why would Ross Chapman do that?"

"She didn't have a chance to tell me more."

Rafsky was quiet, eating.

"Maisey's just really upset." Louis paused. "I think she and the old guy were lovers."

"That doesn't surprise me. I noticed it between them the first day I saw them together."

"Yeah. She seemed very protective of him."

Rafsky nodded. "Every time he looked to her through the glass I got the feeling he wanted her in the room with him, holding his hand while he talked about his daughter."

Louis was quiet. Had Edward asked for Maisey to be in the room they would have let her come in. But he knew a man like Chapman would never ask such a thing. He thought of his own parents in that moment, something he rarely allowed himself to do. His black mother, his white father, coming together in the deep shadows of the South just long enough to give him life. Things might have been easier for Maisey and Edward twenty years ago but he doubted it. And he was sure their relationship had been carried on in secret in what he was beginning to believe was a house full of secrets.

"If it's all the same to you, I'd still like to alert Chapman's doctor in Bloomfield Hills and ask him to take a look before they bury the old man," Louis said.

"Be my guest," Rafsky said. "But I can tell you what he'll say. I had an uncle who was in bad shape, oxygen tank, heart pills, the whole HMO bonanza. He died in his sleep a day before he was going to take his life savings out of the bank and start a cruise around the world."

"That sounds suspicious," Louis said.

"One cousin accused the other, and they ended up spending half his money getting expert opinions. It was always the same. There was no way to tell if someone gave him one too many pills or pinched the oxygen tube closed."

"I'm still going to make the call."

"Go ahead," Rafsky said as he slathered his fries with ketchup. "It's the right thing to do."

The server set Louis's burger down in front of him. He ordered another beer.

"How's Frye like being a sheriff?" Rafsky asked without looking at him.

Louis was surprised at the question—or rather the fact Rafsky had brought up Joe. The tension he had noticed the first few days between Joe and Rafsky had seemed to fade some, but things were still awkward between them.

"She loves it," Louis said.

"I've heard her name mentioned over the years," Rafsky said. "She's got a kick-ass reputation."

"I believe that."

"You know, I knew her when she was a rookie," Rafsky said.

Louis took a swallow of beer and set the bottle down. "I know," he said. "She told me."

"Did she tell you about the case we worked?"

"Yeah."

Rafsky was quiet. He set his burger down and just sat there, staring at himself in the mirror on the other side of the bar.

"Did she tell you she saved my life that day?" Rafsky asked.

"She told me everything," Louis said.

Rafsky was still looking at himself in the mirror, but Louis saw nothing in his eyes. It was as if the man weren't seeing his own reflection but something—or someone—else.

"She saved my life, too," Louis said.

It took Rafsky a moment to turn to him. "I'm sorry, what?"

"I said she saved my life, too," Louis said. "Put six bullets in a man holding a knife over me."

Rafsky raised a brow, then picked out a french fry, swirling it in the ketchup.

"How do you two manage a relationship twelve hundred miles apart?" he asked finally.

Louis was chewing, and it gave him time to consider his answer. The question didn't bother him, but he wasn't sure how honest he wanted to be with this man. But then, they had both been saved by the same woman. Maybe they had a cosmic connection.

"It's not easy," Louis said.

Rafsky was wiping his fingers, probably wanting to hear more but too polite to ask.

"You like PI work?" Rafsky asked.

"It pays the bills," Louis said. "But I've been accepted to the Florida Department of Law Enforcement police academy. I start in mid-February."

Rafsky continued to pick at his fries. They ate in silence listening to Stevie Wonder's "Part-Time Lover" on the jukebox.

"Mark Steele and I graduated the academy together back in the seventies," Rafsky said.

Steele was the state investigator who had worked the case that had cost Louis his badge. When Steele was promoted later he red-flagged Louis's file, making certain Louis could never again work as a cop in Michigan.

"What's your point?" Louis asked.

Rafsky turned on his stool, beer in hand. His eyes glistened with the buzz of alcohol. "I can talk to him about you if you want."

"No, thanks, I'm no good at groveling," Louis said. "I got a shot at the FDLE academy, and I'm taking it. I'm thirty this year. I might never get another chance."

Rafsky eyed him for a second, then his gaze moved over Louis's shoulder toward the front door.

Louis turned to see Joe walking toward them. Tight jeans, leather jacket, a strange fur hat on her head. Her face held a glimmer of puzzlement at seeing him with Rafsky.

Joe gave Louis a kiss on the cheek, filling his nose with the scent of her Jean Naté cologne.

"How is everything? Any news?" she asked.

"Nope," Rafsky said. "In fact, we have a problem."

"What's that?"

"We're at a dead end," Rafsky said. "My men spent yesterday taking the sketch of Rhoda to every house on this island. No one remembered her. And the owners of the fudge and ice-cream shops, where this girl probably worked, are all in Florida or Arizona."

"What about the search for Julie's skull?" Joe asked.

Rafsky shrugged. "My boss says it's time to pack it in," he said. "Hell, maybe it's just not there. Even the cadaver dogs are getting bored."

"When do you expect to get the DNA results?" Louis said.

"They won't be back until at least after Christmas," Rafsky said.

"What about Dancer?" Joe asked. "I'm sure with some more prodding I could get him to open up to me."

"His lawyer put him off-limits to us until the shooting charges are resolved," Louis said. He looked back at Rafsky. "Any indication he'll take a plea?"

Rafsky shook his head. "His lawyer has it in her head that not only can she get the state to pay for her experts but also that she can get Dancer a long stay in a psych ward instead of prison."

There was an edge of disgust in Rafsky's voice.

"And you think he deserves to be in a maximum-security prison?" Louis said.

"He shot a cop, Kincaid."

"But is prison justice for a man like him?" Louis pressed.

Rafsky set his bottle down and turned it slowly in the watery circle beneath it. "A long time ago I could've answered that without having to think about it," he said. "But I don't know anymore what real justice is."

Rafsky's eyes moved to Joe's face. "Nor am I sure anymore who should issue it," he said.

Louis felt Joe's hand tighten on his shoulder, and for a long time the three of them were quiet. Plates clattered in the kitchen, and Madonna's voice came from the jukebox.

Rafsky finally reached for his wallet. "I think our little party on this island is over," he said. "I've got some things to finish, but for the most part the investigation's on hold until our potential witnesses come back to the island, we get our positive ID with the DNA, and we're allowed to interrogate Dancer."

"So you don't need us anymore?" Louis asked.

"No," Rafsky said. "But I appreciate your help. Leave me your address in Florida. I'll get a check in the mail for you."

"Send it to the sheriff's office in Echo Bay," Joe said. "We're going to my home for a while." She glanced at Louis. "If it's all right with you, I'd like to leave first thing in the morning."

Rafsky was laying money on the bar, and Louis noticed a split-second pause in his motion. Then Rafsky looked up—at both of them. For the first time the cool blue eyes had something warm behind them. Louis thought for a moment it was just the beer, but then he recognized it for what it was.

Envy.

Not the ugly green kind but more of a melancholy re-alization that what Louis and Joe had, Rafsky had lost. And for a second Louis had the feeling *he* was looking in the mirror. Fifty years old, living alone in a beach shack, married to his badge, and at odds with his only child be-cause somewhere along the line he had stopped sending her postcards.

Rafsky pushed off his barstool and extended a hand to Louis.

"Good-bye, Kincaid," he said. He looked to Joe and held out his hand. "Good-bye, Frye."

She hesitated, then took his hand in both of hers. "Good-bye, Rafsky," she said. "Be well."

29

The waves were crashing against the pilings, and the dock was groaning under the onslaught of wind and water. Louis stepped outside the shelter of the ferry office and peered into the rain, but there was nothing to see but grayness. He went back inside.

Joe was huddled on a bench in the corner, clutching a Styrofoam cup. She held it out to him, and he took it, taking a drink of the hot coffee even though it had no sugar in it.

"I can't wait to get off this island," Joe said.

"I'm sorry this wasn't the great getaway I had planned," Louis said, sitting down next to her.

She burrowed closer to him. "We'll make up for it when we get to Echo Bay. Did you think about what we talked about?"

Last night Joe had suggested he stay with her through Christmas. Her mother, Florence, was coming up for Thanksgiving, and it was time for Louis to meet her, she said. At first Louis had been reluctant, but he really had no reason to go back to Florida right now. He had cleared all his PI cases in anticipation of going into the academy, and he sure as hell wasn't looking forward to spending another Christmas alone.

"Yeah, I thought about it," he said. "I'd like to come stay with you for a while."

She smiled broadly and wove her arm through his. They were silent as Louis finished the coffee.

"Where's Rafsky?" he asked finally.

"He left on the first ferry this morning," Joe said. "He was pretty anxious to get home to Marquette. It's his granddaughter's birthday today."

Louis looked to the open doorway. A seagull took flight off a piling, straining against the wind, but finally gave up and turned back to land.

Through the rain, Louis spotted a smudge of red coming down the dock from Main Street. It was an umbrella, the person beneath bent low against the wind. Suddenly, a gust caught the umbrella, turning it inside out.

It was Maisey.

She struggled to right the umbrella but was clearly losing. Louis ran out to her. He grabbed the shredded umbrella and tossed it aside. Locking an arm around her shoulders, he steered her into the ferry office.

"Oh Lord," she gasped, stopping just inside the open door. "Thank you, Mr. Kincaid."

"Louis," he said.

Her green plaid overcoat was sodden, and her plastic rain bonnet had blown down around her neck. She pulled the bonnet off and wiped her face.

"I went to the police station," she said. "They told me you had gone home. But I took the chance you might be here."

Her eyes slipped past him to the open door. Louis turned and saw the ferry far out on the lake, coming toward the island.

Maisey touched his sleeve. "I have to talk to you."

"Is it about Rhoda? Did you remember something?"

"Rhoda?" Maisey shook her head. "No, no, it's about Julie."

With a glance toward Joe, Maisey turned so her back was to her and faced Louis. She closed her eyes for a long time and when she opened them Louis was surprised to see tears threatening.

"Maisey, what is it?"

"I wanted to tell you this yesterday when you came to the house, but I couldn't talk of it. I just couldn't."

Louis waited while Maisey took a deep breath.

"I couldn't tell anyone before now because it would have killed Mr. Edward to know." She paused. "But he's gone now, and I can't keep it inside anymore."

The tears flowed down her face.

"Mr. Ross . . . he did things to Julie," she said.

Her words came out as a low hiss. And Louis understood immediately what Maisey was saying.

"He molested her?" Louis asked.

Maisey stared at him, and Louis had the sense the word *molested* wasn't strong enough for what Maisey was trying to tell him and for the anger she was feeling.

"He never let her be, Mr. Kincaid," she said. "It started when she was about twelve, and it went on right up till that last summer here."

Louis let out a hard sigh and looked over Maisey's head to Joe. She had questions in her eyes, but Louis gave her a look that told her not to come over. It was clear Maisey was angry and embarrassed, but he suspected she was also deeply ashamed.

"Do you know this for certain, Maisey?" he asked.

She hesitated, then shook her head slowly. "I never caught him. And Julie never told me. But I know. I just know."

Louis knew enough about incest to know that it usually began in childhood and often went on for years. He knew, too, that the victims often blamed themselves and rarely told anyone. Knowing what he knew now about the odd dynamics of the Chapman family, he suspected it would have been impossible for Julie to find a safe place within its cold comforts.

A horn blew. The ferry was at the dock.

Maisey saw it and her eyes shot back to Louis.

"Mr. Ross did it," she said.

"Did what?"

Maisey wiped her face roughly with her sleeve. "One day Julie came home and she was all muddy and her blouse was torn. She told me she went hiking down the trail that leads from the cottage down to the lake and fell. But I know he did it."

"Did what, Maisey?"

"He raped her, Mr. Kincaid," Maisey said. "He raped her and got her pregnant."

"I wish you had told me this when we first talked," Louis said.

"If I told you, Mr. Edward would have found out," she said. "I just couldn't do it to him. I couldn't break his heart."

Joe stood up and was coming toward him, pointing at her watch and then the ferry. He waved her back.

"You've got to do something," Maisey said.

"Maisey, I—"

"I didn't protect her," she said. "That's something I have to find a way to live with. But it's not right that Mr. Ross doesn't have to pay for what he did to her."

The ferry horn blew again.

"Maisey," he said, turning back to her. "I have to go. I can't do anything right now."

"But you will?"

He didn't know what to say. "I'll think about it and call you. When are you going home?"

Her eyes clouded. "I won't be going back to Bloomfield Hills. Mr. Ross let me go."

"What?"

"He told me he didn't need my services after this week."

He remembered she had no family of her own. "Where will you go?" he asked.

She gave a small shrug. "My brother's widow lives down in Grand Rapids, and she might take me in until I figure things out. Mr. Ross gave me six months' salary."

Louis fished in his jeans pocket and came out with a business card and a pen. He wrote Joe's phone number on the back. "You call me when you get wherever you're going, okay?" he said.

She took the card and put it in her coat pocket. "I have to get back now," she said. "Mr. Ross wants to leave today, and I've got to close down the house."

Her eyes held his for a moment, then she retied the plastic rain bonnet over her hair. She touched his arm.

"Please don't forget about Julie," she said.

She set off back down the dock. Louis watched her until he lost sight of her green plaid overcoat.

Joe came up to him. "What was that all about?"

"I'll tell you on the ferry."

He picked up his duffel, and they went out into the rain.

At the gangplank, he stopped suddenly. "I have to make a call," he said.

"Louis—"

"I have to call someone. Go ask the captain if he can wait five minutes."

Louis went quickly back inside the office. The old guy manning the desk looked up from his newspaper.

"Can I use your phone?" Louis asked.

"Be my guest." The guy swung the old black rotary phone toward Louis and went back to his paper.

Louis pulled out his notepad and flipped through the pages. He found the number of the lab in Marquette and dialed. He was trying to remember the name of Rafsky's friend at the lab when a woman answered.

"Dr. Bloodworth's office."

"Is the doctor in? This is—"

"No, I'm afraid he's out of the office today. I'm his assistant. Is there something I can help you with?"

"I'm calling about the Chapman case. Julie Chapman. You're doing a DNA test."

"Yes, the bones found on Mackinac Island."

Once he told this woman who he was there was no way she would do what he wanted.

"This is Norm Rafsky," he said.

"Oh, yes, Detective. What can I do for you?"

"I need another test done. I need you to test the fetal bones for paternity. I want them compared with the sample we took from Ross Chapman."

"We'll need you to fax the lab order."

"No problem. One more thing. I'd really appreciate your giving this test priority, even if you have to move it ahead of the familial test."

"We can do that, Detective."

He thanked the woman and hung up. He was skating on thin ice here, and he knew it. Not only was Rafsky going to be pissed when he found out but Louis also wasn't certain ordering the second DNA test was even legal. Ross had given a sample of his own DNA only to identify his sister and had never given his permission to do a paternity test. Even if the paternity test was legal, it would never hold up in court if it came to that.

The ferry horn blasted twice.

Louis started to dial Rafsky but set the receiver down. It could wait for now; he didn't want to interrupt Rafsky's granddaughter's birthday party.

When he went back outside Joe was waving him frantically from the ferry.

He hustled on board. The engines kicked to life, and the ferry began its retreat from the dock. He stayed out on the deck, watching the island slowly dissolve into the mist. He thought of Lily and how this place had looked when they first saw it, a riot of color and life. Now it looked empty and cold.

He'd have to deal with Rafsky soon, but his part of this was over. He'd spend the holidays with Joe and then he had to go back to Florida and learn how to be a cop again. Whatever happened now was up to Rafsky alone.

PART II

Tread lightly, she is near
Under the snow,
Speak gently, she can hear
The daisies grow.
                    —Oscar Wilde, "Requiescat"

30

It was snowing again. The tracks that he had left this morning on his walk down to the mailbox were already gone. Louis turned away from the window and went back to the kitchen to refill his coffee mug and add four sugars.

He sat down at the small table, staring contently off into space as he stirred his coffee. The sound of the shower running started up from the next room, and he knew Joe was finally awake and getting ready to go in to the station. In the eight weeks he had been staying at her cabin he had learned a lot about her—that she could sleep through any noise, including the two alarm clocks she used. And that she could—in defiance of everything he had ever learned about women—get dressed in ten minutes.

He knew she wasn't going to have time for breakfast, so he poured coffee into her travel mug and grabbed a chocolate doughnut from the Entenmann's box on the table. Finally, for something to do while he waited for her, he pulled the copy of the *Echo Bay Banner* closer and scanned the front page.

The annual Polar Bear Dip had had its biggest turnout in ten years. A leaky pipe had caused $17,000 worth of damage to the county government building. Seventh grader Dina Bidwell had won the Leelanau County spelling bee by correctly spelling *cockatoo*. But the big story was the inauguration of the new Echo Bay mayor this morning at the high school auditorium.

Louis sipped his coffee, staring down at the photograph of the Polar Bear men standing around the hole that had been cut in the ice of Lake Michigan. In all this time here, he had never seen news that got any spicier than old guys in Speedos.

Not that he minded. He had come to like it, in fact, this weird feeling of ease. It was cold as hell outside, but here inside Joe's cabin he felt as if he were floating in a warm and buoyant sea. So much of it was just being cocooned here in this place. But it was more than that.

All his life he had been moving. From one foster home to another, from one job to the next, from Michigan to Mississippi to Florida and back here again. He had been moving, too, away from people—from partners who had died, from women whose faces were just blurs in his memory. Even from his foster parents Phillip and Frances. When he called them at Christmas, Frances said that they were thinking of making a trip down to Florida to look at condos. He knew damn well Phil didn't want to move to Florida, but he also knew they were getting older and wanted to be nearer to him.

He reached across the table to the pile of mail he had brought in earlier and found the red envelope. He had already read the Christmas card inside, but he slipped it out and read it again. Glitter sprinkled to the table.

Dear Louis,

I am sending you a Christmas card that I made my-self with glitter. I hope you like it. Thank you for the pretty sweater. I wore it to school today. Momma said you were still up north working on getting the bones home to their family. I told my friends at school that I helped find some bones, but no one believed me. Boys are stupid anyway. I sent away for some pictures of Tahquamenon Falls, so we can go there next summer when you come back to Michigan for my birthday. Do you think that on the next trip I could meet your girlfriend?

XOXOXOX
Lily

Girlfriend . . .

The sweater had been Joe's idea. When they had gone shopping in the little stores in downtown Echo Bay to look for a Christmas present for Lily, Louis had headed straight for the bookstore and picked out a kid's science book on the origin of horses. Joe had steered him next door to a yarn boutique where she found a nubby pink girl's sweater with white lilies knitted down the front. And she had given him a warning.

Don't even think about getting me a DustBuster.

He didn't. The next day, while Joe was at work, he found a women's boutique where he picked out a silver bracelet set with a Petoskey stone. Two months ago he hadn't even known what a Petoskey stone was. But during one of their walks on the wintry beach Joe had told him she had been scouring the shoreline for one of the prehistoric fossils for months but had never been lucky enough to find one.

She had surprised the hell out of him by crying when he gave her the bracelet. She had worn it to the New Year's Eve party hosted by Augie Toussaint, the *Echo Bay Banner* editor. But he had the feeling that he—not the bracelet—was the thing she was most proud to wear on her arm that night.

Girlfriend . . .

When Joe had first introduced him to people at the party she had hesitated. Finally she had just said, "This is my friend Louis Kincaid."

It made him feel strange, to be half of a couple. Once during the party, standing there with Joe's arm entwined in his, he had felt that old urge to pull away. But he hadn't. Because for the first time in his life he didn't want to move away from people. For the first time in his life he wanted to move toward them.

"So how do I look?"

Louis turned.

Joe was standing in the doorway. She was wearing her dress uniform—double-breasted dark brown jacket and pants with a crisp white shirt. Gold buttons, gold braid on the left epaulette, gold bars on the jacket cuffs, and a gold six-pointed star on her left breast pocket.

Louis stared, dumbstruck. He had seen her in her usual uniform—plain shirt, slacks, and usually a Leelanau County Sheriff's Department ball cap over her ponytailed hair. But he had never seen her looking like this.

"Well?" she pressed.

"You look—" He shook his head. "Impressive," he said finally.

"I feel like George Patton in drag," she said, heading toward the coffeepot.

Her hair was done in a neat braid. She carried white gloves and the stiff gold-braided garrison hat that he had seen wrapped in plastic at the top of her closet.

"How long will the mayor's swearing-in take?" he asked.

"I don't know. His wife is holding a lunch afterward. I can't get out of it."

He held up a hand.

"What are you going to do today?" she asked.

"I was thinking about doing the laundry."

She sighed. "I'm sorry about leaving you alone so much."

"Joe, don't be ridiculous. You have a job to do."

"I know, it's just—"

The phone rang. Joe grabbed the receiver off the wall.

She listened for a moment. "Yes, he's here," she said, looking at Louis. She put a hand over the receiver. "It's Rafsky."

She handed him the receiver, then ducked beneath the coiled cord to put the cap on her coffee and wrap her doughnut.

Louis drew a breath, readying his words. A couple of days after he had arrived in Echo Bay, he had called Rafsky's office, intending to tell him that he had ordered the second test—the paternity test—to compare Ross's DNA to that of the fetal bones. But Rafsky had been on family leave, and Louis had no home phone number for him, which made it all too easy to forget about it.

"Hey, Rafsky," he said.

"'Hey'? That's all you have to say to me—hey?"

Louis blew out a breath. "Look, I called your office, but you weren't there and—"

"And you couldn't be bothered to track me down?" Rafsky said.

Louis looked up at Joe. She was watching him quizzically.

"Ordering a test without telling me is bad enough. But telling them you were *me*? That's low, Kincaid, even for a fucking PI."

"Cheap shot, Rafsky. Look, I know it wasn't a smart thing to do—"

"Actually it was," Rafsky said. "That's why I'm letting you off the hook." He paused. "The first test I ordered, the familial test, is still pending, thanks to you pushing it lower down the list. But I just got the results this morning on the paternity. Ross Chapman is the father."

Louis leaned back in the chair.

Maisey had been right. Ross Chapman sexually assaulted and impregnated his own sister.

"Bastard," Louis said softly.

"Listen," Rafsky said. "This isn't information we need out there right now. Not until we know if it had anything to do with her murder."

"I understand."

"So how quick can you get back to the island?" Rafsky asked.

Louis glanced at Joe. She was standing nearby, holding

her travel mug and hat, obviously anxious to hear what Rafsky wanted.

He covered the receiver. "There's been an unexpected development," he said to her. "Rafsky wants me back on the island to help him finish the case."

For a moment she said nothing, and he wondered what was behind the play of emotions on her face. Maybe a little jealousy that she wasn't going to be part of it. Clearly disappointment that he was going to leave. But there was something else there, too, and he knew what it was because he was feeling it as well—uncertainty about where they as a couple were going to be after this case was over.

Joe stepped forward and gave him a quick kiss on the cheek.

"Go," she said. "You have a job to do, too."

31

When Louis got off the ferry the blast of wind hit him like a hard slap in the face. He set down his duffel and zipped up his down parka. The coat had been a Christmas gift from Joe, and he was damn glad to have it now. He spotted the Mackinac Island police SUV sitting on Main Street, its exhaust pluming in the icy air.

He was surprised to see Rafsky behind the wheel as he got in, tossing his duffel in the back.

"Where's the chief?" he asked.

"He's home," Rafsky said. "He's not a hundred percent yet. His ex-wife is still here taking care of him."

Rafsky put the SUV in gear, and they started away from the docks. Main Street was snowed over and crisscrossed with snowmobile tracks. The lamplights blinked on, a concession to the gloom of the early January afternoon. Louis had forgotten how early darkness came in winter this far north.

They were headed away from town. "Where are we going?" Louis asked.

"The airport."

"Why?"

"To intercept Ross Chapman," Rafsky said. "His plane lands in thirty minutes."

"How'd you get him to come up here?"

"I told him we found Julie's skull and made a positive ID from the dental records. I told him he had to come up here and sign the papers to claim the remains."

"You lied," Louis said.

"I had to. I need to question him about Julie, and if he knew he was a suspect he'd never come."

"You can't get him on incest. The statute of limitations has run out. You're going for murder?"

Rafsky nodded. "Why not? We've got Maisey, who said he was fucking his sister for years. She gets pregnant. Abortion is illegal. By December she starts showing. He's a nineteen-year-old prince and now all he can see is his life going down the toilet. He does the only thing he can do."

Louis didn't say anything because this was exactly what he had been thinking about all night. It was why he hadn't slept.

In the orange glow of the dash lights Rafsky's profile was etched with deep lines. It was obvious Rafsky hadn't slept, either.

"Does Flowers know about this?" Louis asked.

Rafsky was silent for a moment. "No," he said finally. "I haven't told him anything. I haven't even told him about the DNA paternity test yet."

"Why not?"

Again it took Rafsky a second to answer. "I don't think the chief should be around when we question Chapman."

"It's still his case."

"He's a fuckup, Kincaid," Rafsky said. "I like the man, but he's a fuckup. We're going to get only one shot to question Chapman, and we've got to do this right."

It started to snow. Louis watched the wipers slap the flakes away. Rafsky was right. Not so much about Flowers but about Chapman. Once he knew he was a murder suspect he would wrap himself in lawyers and public-relations hacks. And he was coming back here now only because he thought he was finally going to be able to bury Julie forever.

When they got to the airstrip Rafsky parked in the small lot facing the runway. Everything was gray and still as they watched for a speck in the sky. There was a strange tension in the car.

"What's going on with Dancer?" Louis asked.

"His lawyer's still trying to prove he's nuts."

Rafsky went silent again.

"What about Edward Chapman's doctor in Bloomfield Hills? Did he find anything suspicious?"

"No."

Louis suppressed a sigh. "Anything from the lab in Marquette on the lodge processing?"

"No."

The SUV was silent again. Rafsky was staring up at the darkening sky. Louis thought about asking him to turn up the heat but just burrowed down into his parka and closed his eyes.

"He's here," Rafsky said.

The Learjet touched down in a spray of snow. When the airplane door opened and the steps unfolded, Rafsky pushed from the SUV. Louis was going to stay inside, but there was something about Rafsky's quick—no, angry—walk that made Louis follow. Ross was alone, no aide, no entourage. He didn't even have an overnight bag with him.

Louis watched Rafsky carefully. Nothing but politeness for Chapman, a smile, a handshake. After a few seconds Ross ducked his head against the wind and walked with Rafsky toward the SUV.

Louis opened the door to the front passenger seat and got in. No way was this prick riding in front.

Ross gave Louis a look as he slid into the backseat. He filled the SUV with the smell of lemon cologne.

Fresh snow speckled the windshield as they drove from the airstrip. Louis peered up at the sky. The clouds to the west, where the storms came in off Lake Michigan, rolled toward them like a swell of blue-gray smoke.

"Thanks for picking me up," Ross said. "I was wondering if I was going to have to rent a damn horse or something."

Rafsky said nothing as he turned the SUV back onto Garrison Road, his eyes darting between the windshield and the rearview mirror. Louis glanced in the backseat. Ross had a small black book in his hand and was checking his watch and making notes. Not one iota of curiosity about his sister's skull or why he was being allowed to finally bury her.

"Excuse me, Detective Rafsky," Ross said, leaning forward. "Do you know how long all of this will take?"

"Why?" Louis asked. "You got somewhere you need to be?"

"No, not tonight," Ross said. "But I have an interview in Detroit with the *Free Press* at eight in the morning and a phone interview with the *Washington Post* at noon."

"Freshmen senators must be busy guys," Rafsky said.

Ross gave an awkward laugh. "It's been hectic, yes," he

said. "My wife and I have been in Washington all week trying to find a decent place to live. We found a nice town house in Georgetown, but it's a little small and things are a lot more expensive than in—"

Rafsky slammed on the brakes. The SUV skidded a few feet, then spun a hundred and eighty degrees, coming to a stop right in front of the iron gates of St. Anne's cemetery.

"Jesus Christ," Ross said, his hand gripping Louis's headrest. "What happened?"

Rafsky sat there, both hands on the wheel, staring straight ahead.

"Do you know where you are, Mr. Chapman?" Rafsky asked.

"Who cares? Why are we stopped?"

Rafsky turned in his seat and looked back at Ross. "You're in a place people around here call Dead Center. Right in the middle of the island, triangulated by three cemeteries."

Ross looked to Louis, then back to Rafsky. Before he could say anything Rafsky got out of the SUV and opened the back door.

"Get out," he said.

"What? Why?" Ross asked.

Rafsky stared at him. "Get out or I'll pull you out by your balls."

Ross looked at Louis and, seeing no help there, slid uneasily from the backseat. He stood, looking around while Rafsky leaned his head into the open door of the SUV.

"You might want to come, too, Kincaid."

"What for?"

"To keep me from killing the motherfucker."

Rafsky closed the door and gave Ross a shove toward the iron gates.

"What's going on?" Ross asked. "Why aren't we going to sign the papers for Julie?"

Rafsky stopped and turned to face Ross. "There are no papers and there is no skull. I lied to you."

Ross looked to Louis and back at Rafsky. It was dark now, but in the glare of the headlights Louis could see Ross's face clearly. He was getting scared.

"I want to go back to my plane," Ross said. "Now."

"No, we have some business to take care of first," Rafsky said.

Ross looked around, at the old tombstones just visible in the snowdrifts and the thick ring of trees that surrounded them. He seemed to know how far away he was from anyone who could hear him.

When he didn't move Rafsky gave him another shove toward the gates. Ross trudged forward, his shoes sinking into the snow, his eyes darting back over his shoulder at Rafsky.

Rafsky pulled on his black leather gloves as he talked. "This is one of the oldest cemeteries in the country," he said. "Mr. Chapman, do you know who was the first person known to be buried here?"

Ross turned. "I don't give a fuck who's buried—"

Rafsky smacked him on the side of the head with an open hand. "Wrong answer, Senator."

Ross glared at Rafsky, his hand to his temple.

"The first person buried here was a little girl," Rafsky said. "Her name was Mary Biddle. She fell into the lake while trying to cross the ice bridge. They rescued her, but she later died from pneumonia. Do you know how old she was?"

"I don't care how—"

Rafsky smacked Ross again, harder this time. Ross lost his balance and almost fell. He spun to Louis.

"You better stop this crazy bastard."

Louis didn't know how far this was going to go, but he was willing to give Rafsky some rope. "I have no authority here," he said with a shrug.

Ross started back toward the SUV. "I don't have to take this shit from people like—"

Rafsky punched Ross, blindsiding him. Ross tumbled to his hands and knees. Blood spotted the snow under his head.

"You're not going anywhere," Rafsky said. "I'm not finished telling my story."

Ross drew to his feet slowly, wiping his mouth. The snow was falling harder now, swirling in the headlights and salting his hair and overcoat.

"Mary was eight years old," Rafsky said, "just four years younger than your sister, Julie, was the first time you fucked her."

Ross's panicked breaths clouded the air. "That's perverted," he said. "I would never—"

Rafsky grabbed the lapels of Ross's overcoat and slammed him against the gate.

"You're the father of Julie's baby and the DNA you gave proves it."

Ross's hands flew up to Rafsky's wrists but he didn't fight. And Louis knew he wouldn't.

"No," Ross said. "No, it's wrong. The test is—"

Rafsky jammed his fists up under Ross's chin, slammed his head against the bars, and kneed him in the groin. Ross grabbed his crotch and slumped down, but Rafsky jerked him back up.

"DNA doesn't lie," Rafsky said. "You're a freak. A twisted, perverted freak who got off on his own little sister!"

"No! No!"

Rafsky punched him again. Ross dropped to his knees, eyes closed, gasping for air.

"Admit it or I'll start kicking. Your choice, sicko."

"All right!" Ross shouted, throwing out an arm. "All right. I did it! We did it. But it was consensual. Every damn time. I swear."

"So that made it okay?" Rafsky said. "You're a loser who went after his baby sister because he couldn't get laid by real girls."

"Shut up," Ross said.

"And that last summer up here," Rafsky said. "You raped her that year, didn't you?"

"No! I told you—"

Rafsky leaned over him, his mouth at Ross's ear. "You took her to that lodge—"

"Lodge? What lodge?"

"You took her there and you raped her," Rafsky said.

"I never raped her!" Ross screamed. "I loved her!"

Rafsky grabbed Ross by the hair. "*Loved her?*" he shouted. "You ruined her!"

Ross shoved Rafsky's hand away and sat back on his haunches, his lip dripping blood. Rafsky started toward

Ross again, but Louis stepped forward, clamping a hand on Rafsky's sleeve.

"Enough," Louis said.

Rafsky's eyes shot to Louis. With a slow draw of breath, he turned away. Louis watched him walk a tight circle. Rafsky knew he had gone too far.

Ross used the iron bars of the gate to pull himself up.

"What difference does it make now anyway?" he mumbled.

"What did you say?" Louis asked.

"I said what difference does it make?" Ross looked up at him. "The statute of limitations on incest is expired. Even I know that. And you can't prove I raped her. Your victim is dead."

The word *victim* came out of Ross's mouth dripped in acid.

Louis leaned into him. Ross flattened himself against the gate.

"Show some fucking respect," Louis said. "Her name was Julie."

Louis turned away. Rafsky was standing by the SUV, rubbing his bad right arm. Louis grabbed Ross's sleeve. "Let's go."

Ross shuffled forward, wiping at his bleeding lip. His steps were slow and unsteady.

"I'm going to sue that son of bitch for everything he has," Ross said, eyeing Rafsky.

"No, you won't," Louis said. "You'd have to take the stand and testify. And you don't have the guts to tell a jury the shit you told us out here."

"I know people. I'll have his badge in a week."

Louis grabbed Ross's coat and spun him to a stop. "If you tell anyone what happened here, I will make sure that paternity report is faxed to every newspaper in the state."

Ross stared at him.

"We clear, Senator?"

Ross blew out a long breath and headed to the SUV. Louis followed, and they got back in the car.

Rafsky took a moment to light a cigarette before he started the engine.

"Take me back to my plane," Ross said.

"We're going to the police station," Rafsky said.

32

"**S**it down."

Ross Chapman's eyes moved slowly over Chief Flowers's office. Louis wondered if he was remembering the first time they had questioned him here more than two months ago. The confident man who had sat here then was gone. The man standing here now was bloodied, physically and mentally.

Ross had taken off his camel overcoat before coming into the station, folding it so the blood did not show. But Barbara, the dispatcher, couldn't have missed Chapman's bloody lip as he walked in.

Ross was staring at something on the desk.

Rafsky had placed three photographs out for Ross to see—the reassembled fetal bones, the skeleton in the lodge basement, and the school portrait of Julie.

Rafsky was holding a file folder, and he used it to gesture toward the chair. "Sit down," he said again.

"Am I under arrest?" Ross asked.

"No," Rafsky said. "Just being detained for questioning."

"I think we covered all the nasty little details of my life already, don't you?"

Rafsky stared at him long enough to make Ross visibly uneasy, then slapped the file folder down on the desk.

"I think you murdered your sister," he said.

It took Ross a few seconds to understand. "You're crazy," he said. "I'm calling my lawyer."

He reached for the phone but Rafsky hit his hand with the folder. Ross drew back and looked at Louis.

"Take a good look out that window there," Louis said.

Ross's eyes swung to the window. Barbara was sitting at her console. A couple of locals wrapped in parkas stood at the door with an officer holding a clipboard. They were all looking their way but trying to act like they weren't.

"You think those people don't know who you are, Senator?" Louis asked.

"So what?" Ross said.

"Right now all they think is that you're a grieving brother who selflessly came all the way here to make arrangements for his dead sister before flying off to Washington to take his oath of office."

Ross was silent, looking again at the people in the outer office.

"If you have a lawyer fly in here tonight, what do you suppose folks will think then?" Louis asked. "And what about the reporters who still come around from time to time? What will they sniff out? Maybe even that pretty blonde from the *Lansing State Journal* would come back up here for this."

Ross sank into a chair and yanked at his tie.

Louis knew Ross was stuck. A United States senator as a murder suspect. Once that was the headline it would never matter if he had done it or not.

Rafsky slid a small tape recorder toward Ross and punched a button. Ross stared hard at it.

"Let's start at the beginning," Rafsky said. "When your sister disappeared, did you know she was pregnant?"

Ross shook his head.

"I think you did," Rafsky said. "I think she told your parents the truth about going to Ann Arbor that weekend. I think she was alone and scared and came to see you for help."

Ross shook his head again.

"And your idea of help was to take her to Canada for an abortion."

Louis had been looking at the floor. His eyes came up quickly but Ross was a blur. Instead, Kyla was there and so were his words to her eleven years ago—*get rid of it*.

Rafsky smacked the desk with the folder.

"But Julie was a good girl, wasn't she?" Rafsky said. "She wasn't going to let you just get rid of it. I think she threatened to tell your father."

"She never came to see me!" Ross said. "I spent all weekend partying at the Phi Psi house."

"Who saw you?" Rafsky asked.

"Hell, I don't know," Ross said. "It was New Year's. There was an open party all weekend. Everyone was coming and going. We were drowning our sorrows because Michigan lost to USC."

Rafsky pushed a notepad across the desk. "Give me some names. Start with your frat friends," Rafsky said.

Ross leaned over the desk. "Listen to me," he said. "These guys are professionals now, lawyers, doctors, CEOs. You're not going to go traipsing into their offices asking about my college days."

Rafsky looked at Louis. "Traipsing? Do I traipse?"

"I did not kill Julie!" Ross said. He ran a shaky hand over his face. "You don't understand," he said softly. "I wanted . . . all I ever wanted . . ."

Ross put his head in his hands.

Rafsky took a step forward, but Louis put up a hand. Ross Chapman had just opened a vein. He was vulnerable. They had to exploit the moment carefully.

Louis pulled a chair close to Ross and sat down.

"What did you want?" he asked.

Ross didn't move.

"Senator, what did you want?"

When Ross looked up his eyes were glistening. "All we had was each other," he said softly. "We were always together. We were best friends. Nothing about it felt wrong."

Louis glanced up at Rafsky.

"But when we got older, things changed," Ross said. "When I went off to college I missed her so much. But then that last summer . . ."

Ross looked at the tape recorder. Louis reached over and turned it off.

"What about that summer?" Louis asked.

Ross pulled in a deep breath. "I thought it would be our last chance. I knew that if we didn't reconnect this time we never would. That's why I came up here."

Louis glanced at Rafsky. Arms crossed, he was listening intently.

"But she ended it," Ross said. "She ended everything."

"You're breaking my heart," Rafsky said.

Louis shot him a look, but Ross hadn't seemed to hear him. He was staring at the three photographs on the desk.

"I went crazy after that," Ross said. "For a month I

fucked everything that moved. But finally I couldn't stand being here—being around her—and I went home."

"When was that?" Louis asked.

Ross shook his head slowly. "It was right around my birthday, on August 20," he said. "I remember because I went back to Ann Arbor and drank myself sick."

Ross was quiet for a long time. He was staring at the bulletin board behind the desk. Or maybe the old sepia-toned photographs of Main Street. Louis couldn't tell.

"I thought maybe things would change when Julie came home," Ross said softly. "I thought I could talk to her, convince her that we needed each other." He paused. "I had this crazy idea that we could run away to another country where we could be together."

"Where were you going to go?" Louis said.

"Sweden," Ross said. "They let siblings get married there."

Rafsky jerked open the door. "I'll be right back," he said. "I'm going to go puke."

Rafsky slammed the door behind him. Ross didn't seem to notice. For a long time the room was quiet, then a furnace thumped on and heat poured from an overhead vent. Ross was looking at the sketch of Julie. He reached out and ran a finger over it.

"I'm not a monster," he said.

He looked up Louis.

"Julie was only my half sister," he said.

It was the last thing Louis had been expecting to hear. But now that the words were out there it didn't seem so incredible. Because everything about this fucked-up family had seemed unreal.

"Explain," Louis said.

"My father and Maisey," Ross said slowly. "They had been having a relationship for years, since I was boy."

Louis's mind flashed to Maisey's face the last time he had seen her on the dock eight weeks ago. He picked up the photograph of Julie.

The dark hair, the solemn dark eyes. Was it there? One drop, they had always said, that was all it took. He was sure he should have been able to see it, but he couldn't. Maybe back in the fifties and sixties no one else could, either.

"Julie was born in London," Ross said. "We lived there for two years."

It made sense. Living abroad, it had probably been easier for Edward and Maisey to keep their secret. Whatever strange arrangements Mrs. Chapman had signed off on, Louis would never understand.

Louis set the photograph down. "How do you know this? Did your father tell you?"

Ross shook his head. "I just knew it."

"Did Julie know?" Louis asked.

Ross looked him straight in the eye. "No," he said.

Another black woman's face flashed into Louis's head. His sister Yolanda, sitting next to him on the porch, teasing him again about his hair, telling him that he wasn't really one of them because his daddy was white. The memory was gone as quick as it had come because he had been only four. But he had somehow understood even then that he didn't fit.

"I didn't kill her," Ross said. "Why don't you believe me?"

"You're the best suspect," Louis said. "You had means,

motive, and opportunity. And unless someone can place you in Ann Arbor all weekend twenty-one years ago, a jury will make the leap that you were on this island killing your sister in that lodge."

Ross put his head in his hands.

The door jerked open, and Rafsky came back in the room. He looked more agitated than when he had left, rubbing the bruised knuckles of his right hand.

"You can go," Rafsky said.

Ross looked up. "What?"

"I'm sick of looking at you."

Ross stood up slowly, his eyes going from Louis and then back to Rafsky. "What happens now?" he asked.

"We tear your life apart," Rafsky said. "I'll be sending investigators downstate. We'll be talking to your college friends, your Cranbrook buddies, old girlfriends, your wife."

Ross's face reddened with anger, but beneath it Louis could see his fear. "You said that if I talked you wouldn't make me a public suspect," Ross said.

"I never said anything like that," Rafsky said. He opened the door. "Get out of here."

Ross picked up his overcoat and started to put it on, then draped it over his arm. He was halfway out the door when he looked back at Rafsky.

"I want a copy of that DNA report."

"Why?" Rafsky asked.

"I need to know I'm really the father," Ross said.

Rafsky thought about it for a moment, then sifted through some papers in the folder and produced the lab report.

Ross took the report, stuffed it into his pants pocket, and pushed out the door. As he started across the outer office, two officers stopped to shake his hand and congratulate him on his election. Ross managed a few handshakes and abruptly broke away.

Rafsky gathered up the three photographs. When he looked up he seemed surprised Louis was watching him.

"You upset about what happened at the cemetery?" Rafsky asked.

Louis shook his head. "No, we're good. But we need to talk about something Ross told me."

The phone rang, and Rafsky held up a hand to Louis before picking it up. He said something, then covered the receiver, looking at Louis.

"I'm going to be a while with this," he said. "Let's meet at the Mustang in an hour."

Rafsky went back to his call, and Louis left the office. He started away but then looked back. Rafsky was sitting down at Flowers's desk, taking notes. He rose suddenly and, still talking on the phone, tacked the three photographs on the bulletin board behind Flowers's desk—Julie, the skeleton, and the fetal bones.

Rafsky had started a murder board.

33

He decided he needed fresh air more than a drink. Instead of waiting for Rafsky at the bar he took a walk through town. The wind had died, and the air was icy and still. Main Street was deserted, and he kept to the middle of the street where the snowmobile tracks gave him sure footing. Louis didn't know where he was going, but it felt good to be out, away from the weird masculine energy that seemed to dominate this island now.

Where the hell were all the women, anyway? Even the blond bartender at the Mustang had vanished, replaced by a fat guy with a beard. Louis had a flash of memory—Joe sitting by the fire reading a book. He had been sprawled on the sofa, half-asleep from sex, wine, and lasagna.

What are you reading?

Mansfield Park by Jane Austen.

What's happening in it?

Henry and Maria are just about to cross the ha-ha.

The what?

The ha-ha. It's a big trench in an English garden that keeps the cows from wandering. But Henry and Maria are having a secret affair and the ha-ha stands for the moral line they are going to cross.

Louis trudged up the hill through the snow. He was

thinking of Rafsky. It was clear he had reached the edge of his own trench. What wasn't clear yet was if he was going to try to jump it.

He didn't realize he had walked all the way up the road to the Grand Hotel. It stood in the gloom like a big gray ship, moored and silent. The streetlamps on the road below the hotel glowed like beacons in the mist. He followed them all the way to the last house on West Bluff Road.

He drew up short. There were lights on inside.

It couldn't be Ross. He had left a half hour ago in his chartered plane.

Louis trudged through the drifts and up onto the porch. He tried the front door. It was open. He went in, stopping in the foyer. One lamp was on in the parlor, another deeper in the house, probably in the kitchen. He could also see lights at the top of the dark staircase.

"Hey! Anyone here?" he shouted.

There was a loud bump from above and then the creak of the floorboards over his head. A moment later, Maisey's face appeared over the banister above.

"Who's there?"

"It's me, Maisey. Louis."

She was clutching something against her chest, maybe a load of books? Louis switched on the hall light. Maisey hesitated, then came down.

"What are you doing here, Mr. Kincaid?" she asked.

"I saw the lights—"

"I mean on the island." She searched his face. "You found out something, right?"

How much should he tell her? He couldn't tell

her that Ross was now a suspect in Julie's murder. But didn't she have a right to know her suspicions about the incest had been correct? And what about the rest? Didn't he have a right to know if Maisey was really Julie's mother?

"You were right about Ross and Julie," Louis said. "He confessed everything to us."

Maisey's face sagged, and she carefully put the books on the table, then went into the parlor. Louis followed her. She seemed to be searching for something. Finally she went to the bookcase and picked a picture frame from a group on the top shelf. It was a family portrait of all the Chapmans, taken on the front lawn of the cottage when the kids were very young.

Maisey stared at it for a moment, then put it back on the shelf. "I don't know what to take," she said, as if to herself. "The lawyer said it was all mine now, but I don't know what to take."

"Yours?" Louis asked.

She looked at him. "Mr. Edward left me this house." Her eyes wandered around the room. "I don't want any of this. The real estate lady said I could leave it all and she'd sell it."

So Edward had taken care of her after all. The cottage would probably bring Maisey about a million dollars. No matter how much Ross protested that the island meant nothing to him, it had to have stung to find out the house that had been in his mother's family for three generations was now owned by "just a housekeeper."

Maisey picked up another frame. It held a small photograph of Julie sitting in a wicker chair holding a rag doll.

Maisey used her sleeve to wipe the glass, then folded it to her chest.

"Maisey," Louis said. "I have to ask you something."

She looked up expectantly.

"I don't know how—" he began. Then he let out a long sigh. "Is Julie your daughter?"

Her mouth dropped open. It took a few seconds, but then the shock faded and something else replaced it.

"How could you ask me such a thing?" she said.

It wasn't anger he was seeing in her face. It was indignation that he knew instinctively came not from guilt but from deeply bred modesty. It was one thing for a woman like Maisey to admit that back in the fifties she had loved a man like Edward. It was something else entirely for her to hear a near stranger give words to what had to be a painful secret.

"I'm sorry," Louis said. "I have to know."

"Why?" she demanded.

How did he explain this? How did he explain to her that family dynamics—and race—could factor into a murder motive?

"The family is important in a murder investigation," he said.

"Family," Maisey said quietly, turning away. She set the frame back on the mantel and started away.

"Maisey—"

She spun around. "Mr. Kincaid, you need to leave."

"Maisey, you don't understand."

"No, you don't understand," she said, pointing a finger at him. "You think you do because you're black. But you're too young, and you don't know."

She went out into the foyer, and he followed.

"Maisey," he said. "Please. I need an answer."

She was halfway up the stairs but turned and came down a few steps. Her eyes glistened, but Louis knew she wouldn't cry until she was alone.

"I'm not Julie's mother," she said.

He almost said it, almost said that a simple test would prove it. But this woman had trusted him with her family's darkest secrets. He couldn't push this. He would have to take her word for it.

"I'm sorry, Maisey," Louis said. "I am just trying to help you take Julie home."

Her hand went to her chest and she wiped at her eyes. She came down the steps, reached into the box, and pulled out a small red book.

"This is Julie's journal, the one from that summer, with her poems," she said, holding it out to Louis. "Take it. Maybe it will help you."

34

The ferry was moving slowly, carefully maneuvering through the channel the coast guard ice cutter had forged in the straits. The day was bright with a stinging sun, but it was too cold to be outside, so Louis stayed inside.

When the boat docked in St. Ignace Louis picked up the small bag and hurried off the ferry. It was six blocks to the Mackinaw County substation and jail. His shoes were soaked from the snow by the time he got there, and he made a mental note to buy some boots, since it was apparent he was going to be here awhile longer. Rafsky had asked him to stay on indefinitely and had even issued him a temporary state police ID.

The investigation was progressing in fits and starts, but at least they were moving forward. Rafsky was shepherding the investigators he had sent to Ann Arbor and Bloomfield Hills to dig into Ross Chapman's life. He was hell-bent on proving Ross Chapman guilty of murdering his sister. But Louis wasn't convinced. And it was something small that triggered his doubt, something Ross had said at the cemetery.

Lodge? What lodge?

Louis had felt from the beginning that the lodge was important to the killer. But the place didn't seem to register on Ross's radar.

That's why Louis had spent last night reading the poems in the journal Maisey had given him. He was hoping to find some reference to the lodge or to the boy he was convinced Julie had been seeing that last summer on the island.

Julie Chapman's poems were strange and often beautiful but all were painful to read. She wrote about her mother's spiral into addiction. She wrote about her father's long absences in words that careened from anger to aching loneliness. She wrote about feeling smothered in what she called Kingswood's "velvet coffin."

There was an undercurrent of repressed rage. One chilling poem called "Slammed and Damned" detailed Julie's ostracism by a clique of girls using "slam books." Louis had heard of slam books. They were a fad in the sixties where kids wrote anonymous biting comments about one another in spiral notebooks. Julie's poem ended with the subject thinking about killing her tormenters but committing suicide instead.

In a poem called "Lost in the Mist" the narrator was a color-blind girl who lamented that she was "not black, not white, but just shades of gray."

And then there were the poems about Ross. None of them mentioned him by name and none used the word *incest*. Still they were almost unbearable to read. One called "Tick Tock" was about a clock that ran backward "to the time when I was new, back to the time before there was you." Another called "Night Creature" was about a sharp-clawed beast slipping into her bed and tearing her open with "claws like razors, a tongue like a blade." The hardest one to read was "Twelve." Louis had memorized the last lines.

Your fingers are ice on my body
Your heart is ice on my soul
I let you take
What should have been mine to give

Louis had almost stopped reading after that. But then he got to the poems that dated to Julie's final month on the island. They seemed as if they were written by a different girl.

The tone was brighter, almost hopeful. One poem called "Phoenix" was a long tale about a girl whose home burned down, but she hatched out of a golden egg and flew away to make a new life on a tropical island. But there was nothing in any of the summer poems that spoke about being in love and nothing about a special boy.

Except for maybe one poem. It was called "Centaur" and it was about a creature, half man and half horse, that was "wise and gentle" and carried the girl away from earthly tormenters.

Was "Centaur" Julie's island love?

It was a long shot, but the poem was why Louis was now on his way to see Danny Dancer. His plan was to show Dancer the poem and hope it triggered him to remember an image from his own sketchbooks.

At the county building, a sign on the front door directed Louis to the jail around the side. The desk sergeant behind the Plexiglas spoke without looking up from his paperwork.

"Visiting days are Saturdays and Wednesdays."

"I have an appointment with Danny Dancer. Special

visit, granted by your sheriff as a favor to state investigator
Norm Rafsky."

The sergeant flipped through some papers on a clipboard. "You Louis Kincaid?"

"Yeah."

"ID and sign the book."

Louis slid his license and state police ID through and
signed in. The cop pushed Louis's license back through but
fingered the state ID as if it were a counterfeit twenty before he finally gave it back.

"Dancer's lawyer here yet?" Louis asked.

"Nope."

When Louis called Lee Troyer this morning it had
taken all his charm to convince her that all he needed was
information on kids Dancer knew when he was young.
She had finally agreed and told him she'd meet him at
eleven. It was eleven fifteen.

"The roads are bad north of here," the sergeant said. "It
might be hours before anyone gets through. You better go
in. You wait too long the inmates will be at lunch."

"If Troyer shows up, tell her I'm here."

The sergeant hit a buzzer, and a steel door to Louis's left
slid open, leading to a second waiting area. The guard in a
wire cage handed Louis a plastic tray through a slot.

"Empty your pockets and leave the bag here."

"I have books in here I need to take in," Louis said,
hoisting up the bag.

The cop used his pencil to point to a sign that said no
contraband was allowed inside.

"I have permission from your sheriff to take the books
in," Louis said.

The cop eyed him, then picked up the phone and asked for a Captain someone. Louis waited, listening to the sounds of the jail—buzzers, shouting, clanging. This place was a stark contrast to the island station with its coffee-scented office, boxes of doughnuts, and framed pictures of the island.

Louis looked back at the cop on the phone. The officers here were different, too, a tough bunch with weathered skin and military tattoos. Louis knew he was in a place where cops were *us* and inmates were *them* and there was nothing in between.

The guard hung up the phone. "Captain says you can take the books in but you'll have a guard with you the whole time."

"Not a problem."

With another buzz the second door slid open. Louis followed a guard to the end of the hall. Inside an eight-by-eight-foot cell Dancer sat cross-legged on the floor, staring at the drain. He was wearing an orange jumpsuit, had a small yellow-black bruise on his cheek, and his dirty hair hung uncombed in his eyes.

"I'm not wasting time down here babysitting your cop-shooting retard, so make this quick," the guard said, unlocking the cell.

Louis went inside. The clang of the door closing reverberated off the walls, but Dancer didn't look up.

"Hello, Danny," Louis said.

Dancer didn't answer, his attention still focused on the floor. Louis realized he was counting the red speckles in the tile.

"How many are there?" Louis asked.

"I'm not done yet."

Louis pulled some books from the bag. "I have something to show you. Can you take a break?"

Dancer looked up at him, his eyes lighting up when he saw the sketchbooks. He held out his hand.

"I'll give them to you in a minute," Louis said. "Can we sit on the bunk?"

When Dancer came to the bunk and sat down a week's worth of sweat wafted off him. Louis made a mental note to tell Lee Troyer to demand her client get special hygiene attention. And protection.

"Are my beetles okay?" Dancer asked.

"Your beetles?"

"My beetles," Dancer said. "Is someone feeding my beetles?"

Louis hadn't been to the cabin since that day with Rafsky months ago, but he could only assume the bins were now full of dead bugs.

"I don't know about your beetles, Danny," Louis said.

"I need to go home."

"They're not going to let you go home," Louis said. "You shot Chief Flowers, remember? That's why you're here."

Dancer looked down.

"Do you understand what I'm telling you?" Louis asked.

Dancer said nothing. Was he counting speckles in the floor again?

"Danny, do you understand what you did?" Louis asked.

Dancer's eyes shot up. "I understand! I'm not stupid. I understand. I understand everything!"

To Louis's surprise, there were tears in Dancer's eyes. He had thought that autistics were devoid of deep emotion, but that stereotype was now gone.

"When you get out—" God, he hated lying like this. "When you get out, you can get some new beetles."

"What about Callisto, Penelope, Lycus and—"

The damn animal skulls.

"I'm sure they're still there in your cabin. No one would take them."

"My skulls aren't safe there," Dancer whispered.

"I'll go your cabin. And I'll pack up Callista—"

"Callisto. Cal-lis-*toe*."

"I'm sorry. I'll pack them and store them. Okay?"

Dancer looked away again. His fingers were wrapped tightly around the edge of the bunk as if he were afraid he would fall off.

"Did you hear me? I said I'd get them," Louis said.

"You repeat yourself a lot," Dancer said.

"I'm sorry. But I'll get them."

"You got to get them all."

"I will."

"All of them."

"Yes, all of them."

Dancer was quiet again, his attention back on the floor. Louis set the sketchbooks on the bunk, keeping Julie's journal in his hand.

"Do you know what poetry is, Danny?"

No answer.

"Do I have to repeat myself again?" Louis asked.

Dancer shook his head. "'The woods are lovely, dark, and deep. But I have promises to keep. And miles to go before I sleep. And miles to go before I sleep.' Robert Frost."

Greek mythology and American poetry. Aunt Bitty must have been a remarkable woman.

"Yes, that's good," Louis said. "Now, do you remember talking to us about Julie Chapman?"

"Bones now. Julie Chapman is just bones."

"Yes," Louis said. "But you and Julie had something in common. You and she were sort of the same. Do you want to know how?"

Dancer's head came around slowly. Louis had wondered if Dancer understood that he wasn't the same as everyone else, and now he had his answer. Dancer's eyes were wide with curiosity as to how he and someone like Julie Chapman could be anything alike.

"Julie was a lonely girl who got her feelings out by writing poems," Louis said. "That's how she coped with her life and her sadness. She put her heart into her poetry."

Dancer just stared at him.

"You cope by drawing pictures," Louis said. "Your pictures are your . . . friends, sort of, people you could have around you but who you didn't have to talk to."

For a split second there was a hint of a smile but then Dancer turned away. "I can't draw here," he said.

"I know," Louis said. "Maybe we can fix that. But today I want to do something else with you, something that will help us find out who killed Julie. Are you okay with that?"

The guard's voice boomed from across the hall. "Hey, how about hurrying up this little shrink-rap session. I got other work to do."

Dancer suddenly slid off the bunk to the floor, hugging himself like a sulking child.

Louis glanced at the guard. "Thanks a lot."

The guard looked at his watch.

Louis leaned down to Dancer's ear. "I want you to listen to me," he said. "I'm going to read one of Julie Chapman's poems to you, because I think you will understand her words better than I can."

Danny put his forehead on his knees.

Louis opened Julie's book to the poem "Centaur." Then he leaned back down to Dancer, keeping his voice low.

"'You came to me in the golden rays of the sun, half a horse and half a man . . .'" Louis began.

"Like a centaur," Dancer said.

Louis looked up. "Yes, that's right."

"Finish the poem," Dancer said.

"'Your brown velvet flanks so strong and smooth,'" Louis went on. "'Your gentle eyes of sea-foam hues. You carry the wilderness in your soul, you carry me away and melt the black ice of my heart.'"

"Give me a fucking break," the guard said.

Louis rose quickly and went to the bars. "You've got no idea what I'm doing or why I'm doing it. Now shut the fuck up or go find something to do."

"All right, smart-ass," the guard said, reaching for his keys. "You're done here."

Louis glared at the guard. Damn it, he shouldn't have mouthed off to him. He couldn't risk getting thrown out now. The closer Dancer got to trial, the harder it was going to be to get permission for another visit.

The guard unlocked the door. "Let's go."

Pissed, Louis turned back to gather up the books. But Dancer was flipping pages in one of his sketchbooks. Louis held a hand up toward the guard.

"Give me ten seconds, man. Please."

Dancer finally stopped turning pages and stood up, drawing back into the shadows. Louis looked down at the open book on the bunk.

It was a head-and-shoulders portrait drawn in pencil. The boy had light wavy hair, a hint of a smile, and was wearing a madras shirt. Dancer had concentrated most on the boy's eyes, carefully shading them and pressing the pencil tip deep enough to literally carve the eyelashes in the paper. There was something very feminine, very romantic in the pose, and Louis thought he knew what Dancer had captured—the moment this boy fell in love with Julie.

"Cooper the Yooper," Dancer said. "Cooper the Yooper."

"What?" Louis said. "Is Cooper his name?"

"Cooper the Yooper, Cooper the Yooper . . ."

The guard stepped in the cell. "Let's go, mister. Now."

"Danny, is Cooper the boy's last name?" Louis pressed.

"I said let's go!"

The guard clamped a big hand on Louis's shoulder. Louis resisted the urge to shrug it off and picked up the books and followed the guard out of the cell. The hard clang of the door brought Dancer forward.

"Those are mine," Dancer said, pointing through the bars at the sketchbooks.

"I know but you can't have them in here," Louis said.

"Will you take care of them for me?" Dancer asked.

"Yes."

"And my skulls? You'll find them all and take care of them, too?"

"Yes. I promise."

Dancer retreated back into the shadows of his cell. As Louis walked away, he glanced back and saw that Dancer was back sitting on the floor again, staring at the tiles.

At the door, the guard paused before he hit the buzzer and looked back at Louis.

"You working for Dancer's lawyer?" the guard asked.

"No, I'm working with state investigator Norm Rafsky," Louis said. "I'm on your side here, man."

"Sure didn't sound like it," the guard said.

"I'm just trying to find out who killed a girl."

"The one whose bones they found on the island? You working that case?"

Louis nodded.

The guard's eyes narrowed as he stared at Louis. Then he hit the buzzer again and the door slid open. Louis stopped at the cage to gather his pocket items and wallet. He felt eyes on him and looked back to see the guard leaning against the wall, arms folded across his chest.

"Did that retard know the girl?" the guard asked.

"Yes. And maybe the man who killed her."

The guard pushed off the wall, nodding toward the sketchbook. "Can I see the picture?"

Louis opened Dancer's sketchbook, and the guard stared at the drawing of the boy for a long time.

The guard looked to be around forty, the same age Julie's boyfriend would be now. "You recognize him?" Louis asked.

The guard shook his head. "Nah, but I heard that name before."

"Cooper?"

"Yeah, Cooper the Yooper." The guard pursed his lips. "When I was playing football for Newberry I remember there was a kid they called that. He played for LaSalle. Helluva wide receiver if I'm remembering right."

"Is Cooper his last name?"

"His name is Cooper Lange," the guard said. "Him and his old man run a bar over on High Street called the Ice House."

Louis gave the guard a nod. "Thanks."

"I got a sixteen-year-old daughter," the guard said. "I hope you find the fucker that killed that girl."

35

The bar was almost deserted, just Bald Billie and his wife, Tammie, holding down their usual spots by the waitress station and a couple of snowmobilers at the high-top in the window. Business had been slow all month after a summer that had been the worst in years.

Not the first time Cooper Lange wondered if he shouldn't talk to his dad about getting one of those big projection TVs like the place down on Main Street had. Serving the best whitefish sandwiches in the U.P. just didn't cut it anymore.

"Hey, Coop, where's the game, man?"

Cooper looked toward the pool table where his friend Nick was reracking the balls and grabbed the remote off the cash register. He was about to turn the channel when he saw the crawl below the newscaster.

COP SHOOTER TRIAL SET FOR MARCH

And then there he was. Older, fatter, and wearing orange jail clothes. But it was definitely Danny Dancer.

Danny had been charged only with shooting the island police chief and shooting at two other cops—a black guy and a woman. But Cooper had heard the talk around the bar that Danny was connected to the bones found in the lodge. Wild rumors about his cabin in the woods, with human scalps hanging from the rafters and the stink of decomposing body parts.

Cooper stared at the TV screen. But he was seeing Danny Dancer as he had been twenty-one years ago. The quiet blob of a boy who hung around the edges of their clique, who never spoke, never did anything but sit there drawing his pictures while the other kids drank, laughed, made out, and made fun of him.

Retard! Retard!

Leave him alone, damn it. He's not hurting anyone.

Cooper had always tried to defend him, telling the other kids Danny was harmless. But maybe he had been wrong. He had been wrong about a lot of things that happened twenty-one years ago.

Cooper quickly changed the channel and upped the volume. The quiet was split by the *thwamp-squeak-squeak-thwamp* of the Pistons-Bulls game.

Cooper started to wipe down the bar. He didn't realize he was cleaning the same spot over and over until a bright band of sunlight cut across the wood laminate.

He looked up, squinting. A man was standing in the open doorway silhouetted against the white backdrop. He was tall and wearing a heavy parka, but it wasn't until the door closed and Cooper could see his face that he realized he was black.

He had seen this guy before, seen his face in the newspapers. It was one of the other cops Dancer had shot at.

A second later, light flooded the bar again as another man pushed open the door. The light glinted off a badge hanging around his neck. He said something to the black man and looked to the bar.

Cooper froze.

How had they found him? How did they find out?

The voice in his head screamed before his brain could react.

Run!

Cooper slammed open the door at the waitress station and ran toward the back hallway. He heard one man yell to the other but he kept going.

At the men's room door he looked back in time to see Nick thrust out a pool cue, and the black man went sprawling to the floor. The other guy had disappeared, but the front door was wide open.

The alley was the only escape.

He vaulted over some liquor boxes and shoved out the heavy back door into blinding sunlight. He flailed his arms to keep his balance as he ran down the icy alley, dodging crates and boxes. But his legs didn't work so good anymore and he was stumbling, his mind racing with fear.

"Stop! Police!"

Cooper heard the pounding of footsteps behind him, but he didn't look back. He caught the edge of a Dumpster, trying to hold on as he turned a corner, but lost his grip on the icy metal. He went sliding into a snowbank like a speed skater skidding out.

Someone was on top of him, crushing him, pushing his face into the snow and wrenching his arms behind his back. Cooper struggled and kicked.

"Stop fighting, man!"

He felt the hard pinch of the cuffs on his wrists. Cooper stopped fighting. The black cop grabbed his arm and yanked him to his feet.

Cooper gulped in air, icy water dripping in his eyes. A circle of faces and ball caps came into focus. The other cop—the older white guy—thrust out an arm.

"Stay back! Police!"

The crowd was from the bar, his friends, his father's friends. People he'd known all his life, watching him get arrested. He rubbed his face on his shoulder to dry the snow.

"You Cooper Lange?"

"Yeah," Cooper said.

"Come on," the older cop said, taking ahold of Cooper's shirt. "You're under arrest. Eluding a police officer and re-sisting."

"Coop! Coop!"

It was Nick's voice.

"Coop, you want us to call your dad?"

"Yeah," Cooper said. "Yeah, do that, Nick. Tell him they're taking me to the island."

The *fwump-fwump-fwump* of the helicopter was heavy in his ears. He had forgotten how awful the sound was, like you were buried deep in the earth and your head was filled with dirt. The sound was triggering a cascade of images— the vivid green of the jungle below, the drab green of his uniform as he stared at his knees, the heaviness of the rifle on his shoulder, the stink of fear-sweat coming from the soldier sitting next to him.

Cooper closed his eyes, stuffing Vietnam back in the duffel.

When he opened them he saw white. The helicopter was out over Lake Huron now.

A ragged line of tiny black dots in the white. Christmas trees marking the ice bridge.

Connect the dots . . . connect the dots.

How had they found him? What did they know? Why in God's name had he been so stupid to run?

But he knew why. Because he was guilty. He could pretend all he wanted, hide away all these years, but he couldn't escape the fact that Julie was dead and he was to blame.

The black man was shouting something to the older cop, but the helicopter noise made it impossible to hear what they were saying. Cooper shifted in the seat, trying to ease the tension on the cuffs behind his back.

The island was coming into view now. It looked weird from way up here, all white and bare of its cover of leaves. He could see the white hulk of the Grand Hotel up on the bluff and the curling wisps of chimney smoke from the small houses in the Village. Then the helicopter took a dip and there through the black lacy trees he saw it.

The lodge.

He hadn't seen it in twenty-one years. It looked different, a cold and empty place now, nothing like it had been then.

The memories had always been there, as if they were asleep. But now they were awake and they were shouting in his ears. He shut his eyes.

"So, did you fuck her?"

Cooper looked up at the tall detective.

They had kept him in this small room for an hour now, his right wrist cuffed to the metal loop bolted on the table. He was sweating from the heat pouring out of the ceiling vent and his mouth felt like it was stuffed with cotton. He hadn't told them anything, and now the cop whose name was Rafsky was getting pissed.

Cooper's eyes slid to the black man—Kincaid, Rafsky had called him. He thought he saw a look of sympathy in Kincaid's eyes, but he had to be wrong. These men were convinced he had killed Julie. And because he had run he was under arrest. He was trapped.

Rafsky leaned on the table, his face close to Cooper's. "I asked you if you fucked Julie."

Suddenly he couldn't stand it anymore. "Don't say it like that," he said.

Rafsky pulled back, moving out of view. "How should I say it?" he said. "How about . . . did you bang your little girlfriend? Did you take her to that lodge and pop her little cherry?"

"Shut up!" Cooper shouted.

Rafsky was suddenly back in front of him, hands on the table. "Then talk to us, Lange."

Cooper hung his head. He heard the scrape of a chair and looked up to see Kincaid sitting across from him.

"You loved her, didn't you?" Kincaid said.

Cooper hesitated, his eyes sliding up to Rafsky.

Kincaid caught the look. "Detective, I think Mr. Lange would like something to drink." He glanced at Cooper, who nodded.

Rafsky left and the room was quiet. Kincaid was just sitting there watching him. Despite the heat, the guy didn't seem to be breaking a sweat. Cooper used his free arm to wipe his brow.

He didn't know what was going on here. He didn't know how they had found him or what they knew about him and Julie. The only thing he knew was that he felt a sudden overwhelming weariness. It had been more than twenty years, and he was so tired of carrying this around, so tired of having no one to talk to about it.

As he looked into Kincaid's calm gray eyes, he saw something that told him it was finally safe, safe to risk a walk across the ice.

"Tell me about that summer," Kincaid said.

"I met her at the stables," Cooper said.

Kincaid moved the tape recorder closer and sat back in his chair.

"She was alone and was sort of quiet and shy," Cooper went on. "She said she wanted to go riding, and I asked her if she knew about horses. She laughed a little and said she used to have one."

Cooper took a deep breath.

"She was so pretty but so . . ." Cooper couldn't find the right word because he had never found out what it was that caused that swirl of sadness in her eyes.

"So you hooked up for the summer?" Kincaid asked.

Cooper nodded. "I knew she was a West Bluff girl, and I thought I didn't have a chance with her. But she kept coming back to the stables. Then one day I took her up to Fort Holmes. I kissed her there." He paused. "I got the feeling it was the first time for her."

Kincaid was staring at him oddly now. "When did it become sexual?" he asked.

Cooper wiped his sweating face. "In August," he said quietly.

"You took her to the lodge?"

Cooper nodded, the images flooding back in a torrent now. "She didn't want her family to know. I couldn't take her back to my room in the employee dorm. It was the only place we could be alone."

"How'd you get in?" Louis asked.

"There was a broken window in one of the front rooms. The shutter half off the hinges, so we snuck in. I had a transistor radio. Julie brought blankets and candles."

He was surprised to feel a small smile coming to his lips. "It's a weird old place, but Julie made it beautiful. She called it Pelion. I never knew what she meant."

"It was the home of Chiron," Kincaid said.

"Who?"

"He was a mythical creature, a centaur."

The door opened, and Rafsky came in. He was holding a folder and set a can of Vernors on the table. Cooper popped the tab with his free hand and guzzled half the can.

"He was telling me about Julie," Kincaid said.

Rafsky said nothing, just took his spot against the wall again. Cooper waited until Kincaid's eyes came back to him.

"Did she ever talk about her family?"

"No, never," Cooper said. "I asked her about them once, and she just shut down. I didn't ask again. I figured she was worried I would ask to meet them or something."

"What happened at the end of summer?" Kincaid asked. "Did you just split up?"

Cooper shook his head. "She left suddenly. I heard

it was because her mother was sick and she had to go home. I stayed here until the stables closed in October. We promised to write, but Julie didn't want her parents to know, so we sent the letters to each other through a girlfriend."

Kincaid sat forward. "Rhoda?"

How did they know about her?

"Rhonda," he said slowly. "Her name was Rhonda Grasso."

Kincaid wrote the name in a notebook. "Do you know where we can find her?"

"She was from Cedarville and worked here during the summers like me," Cooper said. "She was part of the summer crowd we hung with. She and Julie were friends, and she volunteered to help us."

"I need her address," Louis said.

"I lost track of her a long time ago."

"What about Julie's letters," Louis asked. "Do you still have them?"

Cooper shook his head. "I didn't keep them."

Rafsky came forward. "When was the last time you heard from Julie?"

Cooper picked up the Vernors and drained it. His hand shook as he set the can down. How much should he tell them? Would it make any difference now? Julie was dead. He himself might as well be.

"I called her on December 1, 1969," he said.

"Why are you so sure about the date?" Rafsky asked.

"It was the night of the draft lottery," Cooper said. "I drew the lowest number."

Cooper could tell Rafsky knew what this meant and

that Kincaid had no idea. "I had to talk to her, so I broke my promise to never call her house. I told her I was going to Vietnam. She cried. I couldn't get her to stop. Maybe that's why I said it." Cooper let out a long breath. "I don't know now why I did, but it came out."

"What did you say?" Kincaid asked.

"I asked her to run away with me to Canada."

Kincaid and Rafsky exchanged looks.

"I didn't have any money, but I had a friend up there who I knew would help us out," Cooper said. "I told Julie she had to find a way to get to St. Ignace, and she said she would take the bus. But then she said she wanted me to meet her on the island at the lodge."

"Why?" Kincaid asked.

"She said she had hidden something there and she had to get it. She said it was a surprise for me."

"What was it?"

"I never found out. I never made it to the lodge."

Cooper shut his eyes.

A loud crack, like a rifle shot.

Suddenly the world dropped.

Blackness. Water. Cold.

"Mr. Lange?"

Cooper opened his eyes. Kincaid was staring at him.

"I had to cross the ice bridge to get here," he said. "I fell through. I was lucky. An ice fisherman saw me go in and pulled me out."

The room was still hot but Cooper felt a shiver go through him. It was quiet for a long time as he waited for one of them to say something, to tell him he was free to go. Now they understood why he ran.

"So when you fell in," Rafsky said, "were you coming or going from the island?"

Cooper blinked. "I told you—"

"Prove you weren't leaving the island."

"The hospital, there's a record I was there—"

Rafsky leaned close. "Prove to me you didn't meet her at the lodge. Prove to me you didn't kill her."

"I loved her!" Cooper's eyes shot to Kincaid, then back to Rafsky. "Why would I kill her?"

"Because when you got to the lodge she gave you your little surprise," Rafsky said. "She told you she was pregnant."

Cooper was stunned into silence. "Pregnant? That's not possible," he said finally. "I was always careful. I always used a condom."

Rafsky set a photograph on the table.

"This is Julie," he said.

He slapped down a second photograph. "This is her baby."

Cooper stared at the photograph of the tiny bones. He felt a tear in his chest and choked back a sob. He reached out toward the photograph but couldn't pick it up.

"You're right, Lange," Rafsky said. "You were careful. The baby wasn't yours."

Cooper looked up at him. "I don't understand."

"Yes, you do," Rafsky said. "She told you she was pregnant. You didn't want to give up your whole life for a baby that wasn't yours. So you lost it and you hit her."

"No . . ."

"You took her down to that basement—"

"No, no!"

"You killed her. You took her clothes to make it look like a stranger did it and then you left her there to rot."

"Shut up! Shut the fuck up!" Cooper jumped up, pulled against the cuff, trying to get to Rafsky. His chair clattered to the floor.

"Got a bit of a temper there, Lange?" Rafsky said.

Hands clamped down on his shoulders and Kincaid righted the chair, shoving him into it.

Cooper wiped his face. "I want a lawyer," he said.

Rafsky picked up the photographs and put them back in the folder. "You're going to need one," he said.

36

Louis followed Rafsky downstairs and into Flowers's office. Rafsky closed the door and went to the murder board. He tacked the sketch of Cooper Lange on the board and reached for the phone.

The bulletin board wasn't very big, so Rafsky had added two large drugstore poster-boards to the wall to extend it. But everything was there. The photographs of Julie, the skeleton, and the fetal bones. Danny Dancer's mug shot and a blowup of Ross Chapman's license photograph. A close-up of the school ring and shots of the basement from all angles. On one of the poster-boards Rafsky had written out in black marker a time line for all the dates and events. There was also a map of the island that showed the distance between the lodge, Dancer's cabin, and the Chapman cottage. Another map marked the usual route downstate to Bloomfield Hills, noting the miles and driving time.

"I don't have a fucking clue if we can get phone records from 1969," Rafsky snapped into the phone. "Have you ever heard the term 'Give it a shot'?"

Rafsky listened for a moment before he launched into a tirade about getting ahold of the Mackinac County DA Greg Thom and securing a quick search warrant for Cooper Lange's home in St. Ignace. Louis knew Rafsky was hoping to find anything to put Lange in a bad light. Maybe Lange had lied and had kept Julie's letters. Maybe he had lied about not knowing she was pregnant.

Rafsky hung up and dropped into the chair. "Good job with Lange," he said.

"Thanks," Louis said.

The phone rang, but Rafsky let it go. He picked up the pile of pink message slips and spent the next minute sorting through them. Finally he tossed them aside and tipped his chair back. The man looked exhausted.

"Do you think he killed her?" Rafsky asked.

"I don't know," Louis said.

Rafsky swung his chair around to the murder board. He stared up at it for a long time.

"I blew it," he said.

Louis understood. If Rafsky hadn't been so aggressive, Lange might have kept talking. He could have told them more about Rhonda Grasso and other kids who had been involved with Julie. Lange clearly needed to unload something, and if they had kept him talking through the night he might have even confessed to killing Julie.

"Look," Louis said, "something will break. We could find something of Julie's at Lange's place. Your investigators in Ann Arbor might uncover something about Ross. Hell, the skull still might turn up at Dancer's cabin."

Rafsky pushed from the chair and reached up to straighten the photograph of the fetal bones.

"I have to get this right," he said. He turned to face

Louis. "I don't want my last case tainted ten years down the road with an overturned conviction when it comes to light we arrested the wrong man."

"Your last case?"

Rafsky picked up a set of stapled papers. "These are my retirement papers. I filled them out weeks ago. I just haven't turned them in yet."

"You having second thoughts?" Louis asked.

"Maybe," Rafsky said. "I don't know. It's just hard to pick up the pen and make it final. Once a decision like this is made you can't go back."

There was a knock on the door, then it opened.

"Hey, guys, am I interrupting anything?"

Flowers. The last time Louis saw him was in the medical center more than two months ago. Flowers had been unconscious then, and there had been no time for Louis to say a proper good-bye before he left for Echo Bay.

Flowers's voice was soft and raspy, but Louis was surprised how good the guy looked. There was a healthy glow to his face and a fresh trim to his mondo-grass hair. He was wearing jeans and a turtleneck instead of his uniform, and Louis remembered what Clark had said last month when Louis called to check on the chief's health. Flowers's release from the St. Ignace hospital had been complicated by a respiratory infection and his recuperation at home had been long and hard.

"Come in, Chief," Rafsky said. "It's still your office."

Flowers shut the door behind him. He gave Louis a big smile and stuck out a hand. "Hey, man, what are you doing back?"

Before either Louis or Rafsky answered, Flowers

noticed the murder board. He moved around the desk toward it. It took almost a full minute before he turned back to Rafsky.

"What's all this?" Flowers asked.

"Things are heating back up, Chief," Rafsky said.

When Flowers glanced back at the board, Louis saw something flit across his face, like the chief knew he had never been a big part of the investigation and the shooting and his long recovery had shoved him even further into the margins.

Flowers pointed to the drawing of Cooper Lange. "Who's that?"

"Our latest best suspect," Rafsky said.

"His name is Cooper Lange," Louis said. "He was Julie's boyfriend her last summer here."

"How the hell did you find him?" Flowers asked.

Louis gave him a rundown of the visit to Dancer and how Lange had run when they confronted him in the bar.

"Who's this?" Flowers asked, pointing at the drawing of Rhonda Grasso.

"A local girl who worked on the island. She was Julie and Cooper's go-between to keep their relationship secret."

Flowers nodded. "Makes sense. A girl like Julie would have to keep it a secret. She wasn't a pop-and-drop."

Rafsky looked up. "A what?"

"It's what the Bluff boys call it when they take up with a local girl." Flowers shook his head. "But for a Bluff girl like Julie to be with a local kid like Cooper? It just doesn't happen, even now."

The office was silent as Flowers went back to looking at the murder board. Louis wondered if Flowers thought it was odd that Ross's picture was up there, but the chief probably thought Rafsky was just keeping track of the case's cast of characters. Louis and Rafsky had agreed not to tell Flowers about the incest.

"I heard they set Danny's trial date," Flowers said.

"Yeah, but his lawyer is still fighting for psychiatric commitment," Rafsky said. "And if that happens, he'll be right back here in a year."

Flowers was staring at Dancer's mug shot now. "I know in my heart Danny didn't want to hurt anyone," he said. "And I know he's different than us and doesn't understand things like we do."

He pulled down the collar of his turtleneck, revealing a jagged red scar. "But every time I look at this thing in the mirror I don't know if I can forgive him."

No one said anything. The awkward silence lengthened.

"I need a drink," Rafsky said suddenly.

"I need some food," Louis said.

"Chief?" Rafsky asked.

Flowers looked surprised Rafsky had invited him.

"My treat," Rafsky added.

Flowers cleared his throat, wincing. "Okay, but don't you guys laugh at me when I cut my burger up into little tiny pieces. I lost some of my swallowing room when they patched me up."

The table was a mess. Three empty burger baskets, seven empty shot glasses, five empty beer bottles, crumpled wet napkins, cigarette butts that had tumbled from Rafsky's ashtray, and a scattering of pretzel crumbs.

Except for a big bearded guy in a flannel shirt at the bar, they were the last three customers in the Mustang.

Louis picked up his Heineken and looked around the table. Flowers was wasted. He had announced when they got here that this would be his first drop of alcohol since the shooting, and it hadn't taken him long to make up for lost time.

Rafsky was drunk, too, but he was holding it well. Just sitting there hunched over the table, turning his bottle as he talked shit about his bosses, his days as a trooper, and his first car—a 1949 Kurtis in which he had "deflowered" his future wife during the summer of 1964. *It wasn't easy, either. It was a fuckin' two-seater.*

His side of the conversation finally deteriorated to passing around pictures of his granddaughter, whose name Louis couldn't remember at the moment.

That prompted Flowers to pull out a picture from his wallet of his twin girls. Rafsky peered at it, grunted out a compliment, and handed it back to Flowers. Flowers turned to look at Louis.

"Show him yours," he said.

"My what?"

"A picture of your daughter."

Rafsky's head swiveled to Louis. "You got a daughter?"

Louis hesitated, then fumbled for his wallet. He felt an odd swell of pride as he pulled out the picture from behind his license. Rafsky took it, stared hard at it, then even harder at Louis before he gave it back.

"Pretty girl," he said.

Louis nodded. The three men were quiet, each taking

a moment to look at their own pictures before stashing them back in their wallets.

"So your ex-wife . . . Cathy, is she's still—" Rafsky said finally.

"Carol," Flowers corrected him. "And yeah, she's still here. Took a leave of absence from her job."

"She gonna stay?"

Flowers shook his head. "No, she has a really good job in KC," he said. "But she wants to reconcite, recon . . . she asked me to come back with her."

"You gonna go?" Louis asked.

"I don't know," Flowers said. "I don't know how to do anything but this and electrical work, and I sure as hell don't want to go back to that. With my luck I'd probably electrocute myself."

"Apply to the Kansas City department," Rafsky said.

Flowers gave a small shake of his head and took a long drink of his Labatt. Rafsky glanced at Louis, then back to Flowers.

"You don't have a degree," Rafsky said.

"No," Flowers said. "And all the big departments—the ones that pay—want one now. I don't want to go KC and have my wife supporting me."

"Not the worst thing in the world," Rafsky said. "Being a househusband. I bet your girls would love that."

"Didn't you see *Mr. Mom*?" Flowers asked. "The guy was a moron, sitting around in his robe watching soap operas all day. I ain't that guy. I'm a cop. I'm a fuckin' cop. I'm not a fucking Mr. Mom."

Rafsky sat back in his chair, nearly falling out of it.

Once he regained his balance, he pulled out his wallet again and opened it. He stared down into it for a moment, then carefully pulled out a business card. He slid it across the table to Flowers.

"Call this guy," Rafsky said.

"Who is he?"

"Friend of mine," Rafsky said. "Specializes in getting cops grants to advance their education so they can keep their jobs."

"In Kansas City?" Flowers asked.

"Hell, I don't know," Rafsky said. "Just call him and use my name. He'll do right by you."

"Thanks, Rafsky."

Flowers reached for his own wallet but couldn't seem to figure out what pocket he had put it in, so he slipped the card into his shirt pocket.

"That'll keep you with Cathy," Rafsky said. "That's the most important thing. Cathy. Remember that."

"Carol," Flowers said.

"Who?" Rafsky asked.

"Never mind," Flowers said.

"And *you*," Rafsky said, looking across at Louis. The blue eyes were a little duller, muted by the alcohol and who knew what else.

"What about me?" Louis asked.

Rafsky pointed a finger at him. "You are the stupidest one of us all. Going back to Florida. What the fuck you got in Florida?"

"A badge, man," Louis said.

"What else?" Rafsky asked.

"What do you mean, 'What else?'" Louis asked. "Right now, there is nothing else for me."

Rafsky shook his head. "Like I said, you're the stupidest one of us all. Where does your lady live?"

Louis stared at him.

"Come on," Rafsky said, "tell me and Flowers here where your lady lives."

"I already know where she lives," Flowers mumbled.

"Shut up," Rafsky said, waving a hand. "I'm making a point here. Tell him where she lives."

"Here in Michigan," Louis said.

"Where's your little girl live?" Rafsky asked.

"Here in Michigan."

"You got parents alive?"

"Foster parents."

That made Rafsky pause for a second, then he went on. "Where do they live?"

"Here."

Rafsky threw up both hands. "Could it be any more fucking obvious, Kincaid?"

Louis glanced around the bar. The bearded man was looking at Rafsky like he was crazy. But he wouldn't say anything. Everyone in town knew they were cops.

Louis leaned toward Rafsky. "I want my badge back. After I get that I'll figure everything else out. Now get off my back."

"Don't fight, guys, come on," Flowers said. "I don't want to see anyone fight."

"No one's fighting, Chief," Rafsky said. He picked up his wallet, fished out two twenties, and tossed them on the table. He hesitated, then added one more. It took him three tries to get his wallet back in his pocket. "I'm done for the night."

"Not me," Flowers said. "I don't have anything to do tomorrow. I'm going to close the bar."

"I thought you were back on this case with us," Rafsky said.

Flowers blinked. "Well, I'd like to be, but I wasn't sure . . . I don't know what I can do."

"You can go to Cedarville."

"What's in Cedarville?" Flowers asked.

"Rhonda Grasso, hopefully," Rafsky said.

Rafsky finished off his beer and stood up. As he tried to put his overcoat on he stumbled and knocked over a nearby chair. Louis jumped to catch his arm, but Rafsky caught himself on a post.

Louis watched him struggle to get his bad arm in the sleeve but resisted the urge to help.

"You going to be okay to get home?" Louis asked Flowers. "It's snowing pretty heavy out there."

"I'll call one of my guys," Flowers said. "You go ahead and tuck Rafsky in. The last thing we need is to find him frozen stiff in a drift tomorrow morning."

"I don't need an escort," Rafsky mumbled.

"I'm going your way anyway," Louis said, standing. His head started to spin, and he put a hand to the table. He realized he wasn't much more sober than Rafsky.

Rafsky wandered toward the door, trying to button his coat.

Louis looked to Flowers. "Where's Cedarville?" he asked.

"About a half hour from St. Ignace. I'll run a check in the morning for her address."

"If you find her, I'd like to go," Louis said.

"Sure, company is good."

"I'll see you in the morning."

Louis threw some money on the table, grabbed his parka, and hurried to catch up with Rafsky. He stepped out into a blast of snowy wind coming off Lake Huron.

It took him a moment to spot Rafsky. He was sitting in a snowbank, staring at his shoes.

"Watch that step," Rafsky said. "It's a little slippery."

Louis went to him and held out a hand. "Come on, you old drunk," he said. "Let's go home."

Louis pulled Rafsky to his feet, and the two of them started down Main Street toward the Potty. Rafsky trudged through the snow like an exhausted husky pulling a sled.

"Did I show you the picture of Chloe?"

"Yeah. Keep walking."

"Did I tell you about my papers?"

"Yeah. Keep walking."

"I've spent my whole life doing this fuckin' job," Rafsky said. "My whole life, and sometimes I feel like I haven't learned a fuckin' thing."

"Here's the hotel," Louis said. "Watch your step."

Rafsky grabbed the railing and shuffled in ahead of Louis. Louis stopped in the lobby to stomp the snow off his shoes, but Rafsky just walked toward the stairs, trailing puddles. He stumbled again halfway up, and Louis had to catch him.

"Thanks. I'm sorry."

"No problem."

"I can't find my key . . . where's my key?"

"Look in your pocket."

Rafsky patted every pocket and finally came up with his

key. Louis took it from him and unlocked the door. When he pushed it open Rafsky nearly fell inside. Somehow he found his way to the bed and plopped down, face-first, coat on and wet shoes hanging off the end of the mattress.

Louis tossed the key to the dresser, turned off the light, and started to close the door.

"Kincaid."

"Go to sleep."

"Kincaid."

Louis sighed and stepped closer to the bed. Rafsky's face was buried in the pillow.

"What?" Louis asked.

"Tell Frye . . ."

Louis waited.

"Tell Frye I forgive her."

Louis stood by the bed, waiting, wondering if Rafsky was going to say anything else. When he heard Rafsky snoring, he turned and left the room, closing the door behind him.

37

They followed a snowplow into Cedarville. What should have been a half-hour drive from St. Ignace had taken more than an hour because of the snowstorm that had dumped six fresh inches overnight. The other side of the two-lane highway was still covered in high drifts, so Louis had no choice but to stay in the plow's wake.

Flowers was snoring in the passenger seat. He had dozed off soon after they left St. Ignace, giving in to his hangover. Louis had let him sleep because it had given him time to think.

About Joe. About Lily. And what Rafsky had said last night: *Could it be any more fucking obvious, Kincaid?*

What was obvious? That hearing Lily's voice when he called her on Christmas Eve made his heart ache to see her again? That it had felt so right being with Joe those eight weeks in Echo Bay, even during Thanksgiving when her mother, Flo, was around? That he had never felt so comfortable living with another person before? That he loved her? That he felt like a coward because he still hadn't told her?

All of that was obvious. But it was also obvious that, as he had told Rafsky, he wanted his badge back. What wasn't obvious was how he was going to reconcile the two things in life he now needed most.

There was a single blinking traffic light ahead. They were coming into the scattering of stores that was Cedarville's small core. Louis gave Flowers a sharp poke.

"Chief, we're here. Where do I turn?"

Flowers came to life and rubbed his face, looking around. "Turn right after the bookstore," he said.

"Bookstore?"

"Yeah . . . there it is. Turn here!"

Louis skidded to a stop in front of a gray bungalow bearing the sign SAFE HARBOR BOOKS. He had to slow to a crawl on the unplowed side street as Flowers peered at the house numbers.

"That's it," Flowers said, pointing to a faded two-story clapboard house. Louis pulled to a stop.

The yard was heaped with high drifts, with no car, footprints, or any sign of life. The house was fronted with a glassed-in porch, but the panes had been covered with heavy plastic sheeting, sections of it flapping in the wind.

"It looks abandoned," Louis said.

"Not for the U.P," Flowers said. He zipped his parka and got out. Louis followed, trudging behind him through the snow.

Flowers had run a quick record search for Rhonda Grasso this morning, but there had been no current address for her in Cedarville. Or anywhere in Michigan for that matter.

The only things that turned up were an expired Michigan license issued in 1967 when Rhonda was sixteen and her employment record. It included two summers working in Ryba's Fudge Shops on the island and a short stint at the post office in Cedarville.

But Flowers had found a Chester Grasso in Cedarville. Repeated calls to Grasso's number had gone unanswered, but they decided to make the trip anyway. Flowers said that, like Cooper Lange, Rhonda could have come home as so many Yooper kids did when they got older and eaten up by the bigger world. She was probably married and living two doors down from her childhood home.

Louis kept back while Flowers knocked on the porch storm door. If Chester Grasso was inside he was more likely to open the door to a guy in a Mackinac Island police parka than a strange black man.

They heard a dog barking inside. It grew more frenzied the harder Flowers banged on the storm door. The interior door jerked open, and a man poked his head out. A second later, a huge red chow chow bounded out and launched itself at the porch door.

The man came out onto the porch and grabbed the dog's collar. "Pearl! Knock it off!"

The dog retreated behind the man's legs. The man's watery blue eyes narrowed as he stared at the police patch on Flowers's parka. He opened the door a crack.

"Mackinac? Whatcha doing up here?"

"Mr. Grasso? Chester Grasso?" Flowers asked.

The man nodded, now staring at Louis. Louis was staring at the chow chow, but it was sitting calmly behind the man.

"We're looking for Rhonda Grasso," Flowers said. "We need to talk—"

"Rhonda? Rhonda doesn't live here anymore."

"Is she your daughter?"

Chester Grasso hesitated, then gave another nod.

"Do you know where we can find her, sir?"

"I haven't seen Rhonda in years," Grasso said. "She left home a long time ago."

Louis stepped forward. "So you haven't had any contact with your daughter, sir?"

The man shook his head. He was rubbing the dog's ears, and it leaned against his legs, its black tongue hanging from its mouth.

"Your daughter used to work on Mackinac Island, right?" Louis asked.

Chester Grasso's eyes came alive a little. "Yeah, yeah, she did. Not a lot for a kid to do in a town like this, so she used to go live over there during the summers." He paused. "Rhonda was a hard worker, and she made enough to buy herself a used Impala when she was just seventeen. After that, she wasn't home a lot."

"Did you know a girl named Julie Chapman, Mr. Grasso? Did your daughter ever mention her?" Louis asked.

"No, don't remember her talking about a Julie anybody."

"What about Cooper Lange?"

Grasso shook his head. "What's this all about, anyways? Is Rhonda in some kind of trouble?"

"No, sir," Flowers said. "We're investigating the disappearance of this girl, Julie Chapman, and we just need to talk to Rhonda."

"Well, I can't help you," Grasso said. "Like I said, Rhonda moved away a long time ago."

"Do you remember the date?"

Chester scratched his jaw. "It was after she graduated, I remember that much."

"Where did she go?"

Chester shrugged. "She just left one day. She talked a lot about going up to live with her brother in Sault Ste. Marie."

Louis had his notebook out. "What's his name?"

"Fred," Grasso said. "His name is Fred. He used to work at Algoma Steel up there."

"We need his address," Louis said.

Chester looked down at his dog. "Don't got it. I haven't talked to Fred in years."

Flowers let out a breath, glanced at Louis, then back at Grasso. "Well, thank you—"

"Wait, Chief," Louis said. "Mr. Grasso, is this the same house Rhonda lived in?"

Grasso nodded. "Yup."

"Could we see Rhonda's room?"

"Her room?" Chester Grasso ran a hand over his whiskered jaw. "There's nothing in her old room."

"Your daughter left nothing here?" Louis asked.

"My wife . . ." He cleared his throat. "Rhonda was, well, she had a wild streak to her. I always said she was just a little high-strung, but Dot said she was boy crazy and Dot was always after her. They were always going after each other. You know how mothers and daughters can be."

Louis saw Flowers nodding.

"When Rhonda ran off for good, Dot sort of went nuts," Grasso said. "She packed up all of Rhonda's things and cleaned out her room. It was like she was so mad at her she just didn't want to look at anything to do with her, you know? There's nothing left of Rhonda here, except some old boxes."

"Can we look through them?" Louis asked.

Grasso closed the storm door a little. "I don't think—"

"Mr. Grasso," Louis said. "Wouldn't you like to see your daughter again?"

Chester Grasso's face went slack.

"When we find her we can ask her to contact you," Louis said.

The chow chow whimpered, pushing its head under Grasso's hand. He ignored it, his eyes on Louis.

"The boxes are in the garage out back," he said, nodding toward the left. "I can't help you because my hip's gone, but you're free to go look. The man-door's open."

"Thank you, sir," Louis said.

Grasso stayed at the door, watching them as Louis and Flowers trudged through the drifts, going around the side of the house.

"When we get back we need to run a search on the brother. Maybe we can get an address through his old company," Louis said.

"Algoma Steel," Flowers said. "That's in Canada."

There were two Sault Ste. Maries, one in Michigan and the other across the river in Canada, Flowers had to remind him. Maybe that was why they hadn't found anything on Rhonda yet.

"Remember when Lange said he and Julie were going to run away to Canada?" Louis said. "He said he had a friend there. Maybe it was Rhonda's brother."

Louis found a small door on the side of the garage and pushed it open. The interior was dark. Louis couldn't see a light switch, but as his eyes adjusted he could make out the shapes of a tool bench, a snowmobile half covered by a stiff tarp, broken furniture, fishing poles, and a battered metal canoe suspended by straps from the rafters. A dirty Chevy Fleetside pickup took up the center. The place was stacked with so much junk it was hard to move.

"You see anything?" Flowers asked.

Louis headed toward some cardboard boxes stacked against the far wall near a small window. "Yeah, over here."

Flowers came over to him. "Shit," he said, looking up at the stack.

Louis had already started working his way through the boxes. The first two were filled with old linens and clothes. A third held dishes, mismatched glasses, and bowling trophies. The fourth was flattened from the weight of the others. A faded ink scrawl on the top read RHONDA.

Louis pulled it out. The yellowed, cracked tape gave easily. There were clothes on top, and Louis set them aside. He pulled out a small red box with a plastic handle, but it was filled only with old records. Louis glanced at the top one—Jefferson Airplane's "White Rabbit" single—and handed the box off to Flowers. A battered loose-leaf binder came out next, its blue surface scarred with faded peace signs and other doodles, the inside papers just routine schoolwork.

Louis's hopes rose when he pulled out a macramé purse, but there was nothing in it but a bottle of Oh! De London perfume that filled the garage with a powdery scent.

Louis tossed the purse back in the box. "That's it," he said.

Flowers was about five feet away, tugging on another box buried under two tires. "I found two more with RHONDA on them."

Louis went to help him drag the top box into the thin light under the window. When he opened the flaps, he let out a long breath. It was filled with papers.

"Maybe we should just take this one with us," Flowers said.

Louis pointed at the bottom of the box. It was sodden from sitting in a puddle. The second, smaller box, also with RHONDA scrawled on it, was also wet.

"I'll go ask the old guy for some garbage bags," Flowers said.

Flowers left. Louis blew on his cold hands and began sorting through the papers in the first box. More schoolwork, tattered copies of *Teen, Tiger Beat*, and *16 Magazine*, pages pasted with photographs of fashion models, a Sears catalog, an application for a beauty school in Ishpeming, a crumpled report card from Cedarville High School. Louis held it up to the light, squinting to read it without his glasses. Rhonda Grasso had flunked algebra and science and had skated by English, home economics, and gym with C's. She had fourteen absences for the six-week marking period. Louis tossed it back in the box and dug deeper, finally unearthing a pack of old envelopes bound with a faded blue ribbon. There were about thirty, all addressed to Rhonda at the Cedarville house, all with a return address on Clayton Street, San Francisco. He opened the top envelope.

It was a single piece of unlined paper, the writing too small and faded for Louis to read—except for the LOVE, DIRK at the end. Louis stuck the letter in his parka. It was the longest of long shots, but maybe Rhonda, like so many other troubled kids, had decamped to Haight-Ashbury in 1967.

Louis dug back into the box, looking for something, *anything*, that might connect Rhonda to Julie.

Photographs.

He pulled out a handful. They were old snapshots, most faded to orange. He sifted through them quickly, discarding the ones that looked like family pictures or shots from school events. Then, suddenly, there she was.

Not Julie but Rhonda. He didn't need his glasses to tell it was her. It was a close-up, as if the photographer had surprised her. Her head was thrown back, exposing her neck. She was smiling broadly, blond curls wind-whipped around her face, eyes like blue pilot flames.

Louis stared at the photo, stunned by how accurate Danny Dancer had been in capturing Rhonda's likeness.

He heard a rustling, and a second later Flowers appeared with a black garbage bag.

"Look," Louis said, handing him the photo of Rhonda.

Flowers took it and let out a low whistle.

Louis went back to plowing through the box, pulling out more snapshots. There were plenty of other teenagers, many of young men or Rhonda with a young man. None had names on the back.

He dug out another handful. Street scenes, blue water, and horses. The photos were of Mackinac Island. He tossed the landscapes in the box and sorted through the rest. He stopped.

It was a group shot, six teenagers standing in front of a grassy knoll. Louis couldn't make out their faces. He held it up to Flowers.

"Is that Rhonda?" he asked.

Flowers took the photo. "Yeah," he said. "This was taken up at Fort Holmes." He pointed to tiny lettering on the photograph's edge. "'July 1968.'"

Louis stood up. "The summer before Cooper met Julie. Is that Cooper Lange next to her?"

"Looks like him." Flowers was sniffling from the cold. "Come on, let's pack this up and get out of here."

Louis slipped the group shot and the close-up of Rhonda into his parka pocket. Flowers held the garage bag open while Louis dumped in the contents of both wet boxes.

A small metal box missed the bag and fell to the floor. It was an old Band-Aid tin. Flowers was about to throw it in the bag, but Louis stopped him.

"Open it."

Flowers shook it. "It's empty."

"Open it anyway."

Flowers popped the top and shook the tin over his palm. Six tiny pieces of fabric fell out.

"What the hell?" Louis said.

Flowers fingered them and chuckled. "Fruit loops," he said.

"What?"

"Man, I haven't seen these since I was a kid."

"What are they?" Louis asked.

Flowers paused. "Where's that group picture?"

Louis fished it from his pocket and held it out. Flowers pointed to one of the boys. "See the shirt this kid is wearing? There were little loops on the back. Girls would cut them off and collect them."

"What for?"

"Conquests. Guys notched their belts. Girls collected fruit loops."

Louis was thinking about Danny's sketch of Cooper. He was almost positive Lange had been wearing a madras shirt. He retrieved his glasses from his parka pocket and held the group photograph up to the window.

Cooper Lange at age eighteen—blond and slender, wearing chinos, a T-shirt, and a confident smile. He looked like the whole world was spread out before him. He looked nothing like the faded man who had sat hunched in the interrogation room.

And Rhonda . . .

She was dressed in tight white shorts and a pink blouse tied below her breasts. One of her long tan legs was bent like a model's, and her arm was draped over Cooper Lange's shoulders.

Her father had described her as "boy crazy," but it was more than that. Even at sixteen, Rhonda Grasso was a girl at ease with her sexuality.

"Chief," Louis said, holding out the photograph, "I think we might have a triangle—Rhonda, Cooper, and Julie."

Flowers looked up, letting the garbage bag fall. He came over and took the photograph, looking at it for a long time.

"If it was, it was a pretty ugly triangle," he said softly.

"Aren't they all?"

"Yeah, but you've got to understand what it's like up here," Flowers said. "The locals are stuck here all winter and then summer comes and the fudgies take over. They make a big mess, then leave everything for us to clean up.

If a townie girl like Rhonda thought a Bluff girl like Julie wanted her guy, she wouldn't give him up easily."

Flowers handed Louis the photograph and went back to bagging up the papers.

Louis started to put the photograph away, then stopped. He stared at Rhonda Grasso, thinking about Danny Dancer's description of her—*eyes like ice, heart like ice*—and he had the feeling he was looking at a killer.

38

The first thing Louis did when they got back on the island was drop Flowers off at his home. It was clear the trip had taken all the starch out of him. Louis caught a glimpse of Carol waiting for him at the front door as he trudged up the walk. She waved to Louis, wrapped an arm around her ex-husband, and ushered him into the house.

Louis turned the police SUV around and started back to town, eager to tell Rafsky about Rhonda Grasso. But then he stopped at an intersection, remembering his promise to Danny Dancer.

I'll take care of your skulls.

Dancer's cabin was just up the road from Flowers's house. What the hell he was going to do with the damn skulls, he had no idea.

A few strands of yellow crime scene tape hung limply from the trees. Apparently it had been enough to keep trespassers out, as Louis saw no fresh footprints close to the cabin and no sign anyone had poked around. The evidence tape that sealed up an active crime was gone from the front door, so Louis knew the police and DA were finished. He could enter without disturbing anything.

The door was locked. The shutters had been taken down, so Louis tried the front window. It took him a while to get the frozen window open, but finally he was inside.

He hadn't been back since the shooting. Parts of that day were a little fuzzy, blurred by the memories of bullets whizzing over his head and Flowers bleeding in his arms. Yet the place seemed less gruesome. Then he knew what it was—the stench was gone. All the beetles were dead.

Louis looked around. The cops had cleared the shelves of Dancer's sketchbooks. But his other books remained and Louis took a moment to scan the titles: *Greek Mythology for Children*, *The Road Less Traveled*, and a third book, *The Empty Fortress: Infantile Autism and the Birth of the Self*.

So Joe's hunch had been right.

He opened it to the copyright page. It had been published in 1967 and checked out of the St. Ignace library that same year, when Dancer would have been about sixteen. He thought of Aunt Bitty and how hard it must have been for her to raise a child she had probably not understood very well.

Louis turned to the task of gathering the skulls. The only containers he could find were the plastic bins with the dead beetles in them. He took two of them outside and rinsed them out with half-frozen water from the spigot.

Back inside he lined each bin with sheets off Dancer's bed and started putting the animal skulls in them, starting with the large ones. When both bins were full, he began gathering up the smaller skulls. It was freezing in the cabin, and he hadn't had anything to eat since breakfast. He thought about leaving the smallest skulls, then realized he couldn't.

You got to get them all.

He went through the kitchen cabinets, finally spotting a large shoe box under the sink. He dumped out the hammer and small crowbar and started back to the skulls. Halfway across the room, he stopped and looked back at the tools.

He was remembering what Pike said that day at the lodge.

Want to see his little rat hole?

The hole in the foundation that was Dancer's secret entryway. The hole where, each time he left, he would carefully re-place the boards' nails into the same well-worn holes.

Louis turned a slow circle. The interior wood walls already had holes cut in them from where Rafsky's men had searched inside.

Louis looked up. Nothing but a peaked roof and rafters.

He looked down at the floorboards.

Pike had said the foundation under the cabin was concrete. Louis had a sudden memory of the movie *Escape from Alcatraz* and Clint Eastwood chipping away at the old concrete in his cell with a spoon.

Louis grabbed the crowbar and scanned the floorboards again, looking for uneven slats or protruding nails. He saw nothing, so he started moving the furniture.

He dropped to his hands and knees. Starting in the farthest corner from the door, he crawled along the wall, sliding his palm over the worn boards and tapping to find a hollow spot.

In a corner by the bed he found what he was looking for. A hollow sound beneath three boards, which all had holes wider than those of the abutting boards.

It was easy to use the crowbar to pull up the boards. Beneath, set down in a hole in the concrete, was a wooden box about the size of a twelve-pack of beer. He wedged his fingers down each side, lifted the box out, and opened the lid.

Fur. Brown and red fur.

An animal pelt wrapped around something else. He peeled away the top flap of fur.

Julie Chapman's skull lay on the leathery underside of the pelt.

Rafsky had been right. Dancer had Julie's skull all along. And it had been well cared for. It was clean and smooth and Dancer had even used fine wire to attach the jaws, giving the skull the look of a perfect laboratory specimen.

Louis gave the pelt a shake. A wad of money, a brooch, a tiny Bible, and a set of keys tumbled to the floor. He was sure the keys were for the Ford Dancer kept garaged in St. Ignace. He stuffed them and the other things in his parka pocket, pushed, to his feet, and took the skull to the window so he could get a better look at it.

There it was—a small crack in the right temple area. Now they had a cause of death.

He turned the skull around to the front.

There was something about seeing a human skull that conveyed a reality that a photograph could not. As he stared at Julie Chapman's skull he could imagine the white bone with long black hair and brown eyes. But as his eyes moved over the curves and ridges, an uneasy feeling started to settle inside him.

It was the teeth.

There was a bottom molar missing and the two front teeth . . .

There was a gap between them.

Jesus.

Louis set the skull on the counter and reached into his parka, pulling out the photographs he had taken from Chester Grasso's garage. He held the close-up of the smiling Rhonda Grasso next to the skull.

He let out a long breath. He was no expert, but to his eye there was no doubt that this was not Julie Chapman. It was Rhonda Grasso.

39

It took Rafsky a good five minutes to open his hotel room door. He was wearing a wrinkled T-shirt, sweatpants, and his face was lathered with shaving cream. His eyes looked like a road map, blue shot through with red, and his hand holding the razor trembled slightly.

"Kincaid, where have you been?" he asked.

"Cedarville," Louis said.

Rafsky frowned, then nodded. "Oh yeah. Rhonda Grasso. You find her?"

"I think so."

Rafsky stepped aside, and Louis came into the room. The drawn drapes glowed gold with the afternoon sun. The room smelled stale, and there was a pile of clothes on the floor and a scattering of case folders on the unmade bed.

Louis set the wood box on the desk near the window along with the folder holding Julie Chapman's dental records. He had swung by the station and picked them up before coming to the hotel because he knew Rafsky would want to see hard proof.

Rafsky came out of the bathroom, wiping his face with a towel. "Look, I know I made an ass out of myself last night," he began.

"Forget it," Louis said. "You need to see this."

Louis opened the box and carefully took out the skull. Rafsky's mouth dropped open, and he came forward. He switched on the desk lamp and stared at it.

"Where'd you find it?" he asked.

"Dancer had a hole carved in the cabin foundation. I found the loose boards."

Rafsky took the skull and turned it around. "There it is," he said, pointing to the fracture. "That's what killed her."

Louis pulled the dental X-ray from the folder and held them out to Rafsky.

"What's that?"

"Julie Chapman's dental records."

Rafsky took the X-ray, holding it against the lamp. It took him a few moments, but when he looked back at Louis his face was gray and it wasn't from the hangover.

"Jesus Christ," Rafsky said softly. "It's not her."

Louis pulled the snapshot of Rhonda from his pocket and held it out to Rafsky. "I found this in Chester Grasso's garage in a bunch of Rhonda's stuff."

Rafsky stared at the picture for a long time. Then he set the X-ray aside and, still holding the skull, went to the bed and sank down on the edge.

Louis had known that Rafsky would take this hard. Not just because they had spent three months, countless man-hours, and a lot of money racing down the wrong road. But also because when this got out, Rafsky would be crucified as an incompetent burnout who had tried to rebuild his reputation on the bones of a young girl.

"I should have known better," Rafsky said.

Louis said nothing.

"I should have waited for the DNA identification on the bones," Rafsky said.

Louis took off his parka and sat down in the chair across from the bed. Rafsky was still staring at the skull in his hands. Finally he rose slowly and set the skull down on the desk. He went to the window and moved the drape aside, looking out at the fast-gathering darkness.

"Norm," Louis said. "What do you want to do?"

"We start over," Rafsky said, his back still to Louis. "And this time we don't make any fucking assumptions."

"When's the DNA identity test coming back?"

"I called the lab yesterday. Our test got pushed back in line by a triple homicide. They said it will be at least three more weeks."

"Without DNA, we can't even assume this skull is part of the skeleton found in the lodge," Louis said. "We can't even assume whoever died in that lodge died twenty-one years ago." He paused. "We need to get in to see Dancer again. We need him to admit he took the skull from the lodge."

Rafsky was quiet, just staring out the window.

"Ross is still the father of the baby," Louis said. "We at least know that's a fact. Which puts him back as our number one suspect."

Rafsky finally turned around. "That certainly explains his behavior when we picked him up at the airport. He waited twenty-one years to take his sister home, and all he could think about was his new house in Georgetown. He knew the bones weren't Julie's."

"When do we bring Chapman back here?" Louis asked.

Rafsky picked up the skull. "Not until we know beyond

a shadow of a fucking doubt that this skull is part of the skeleton and that the skeleton is Rhonda Grasso."

"I'll go back to Cedarville tomorrow and track down Rhonda's dental records," Louis said. "I'll also stop by the jail and get Dancer to confirm he took the skull from the lodge."

"We need to know more about Rhonda. Maybe she told someone she was pregnant. Maybe she told someone she was meeting Ross. Did you talk to her family?" Rafsky asked.

Louis quickly summarized what Chester Grasso had said about Rhonda having a wild streak, working summers on the island, and leaving home sometime after graduating from high school in 1969. When Louis mentioned that Rhonda had a brother living in Sault Ste. Marie, Canada, Rafsky said he'd contact an inspector he knew in Ontario.

"We still need to link Rhonda with Ross after that summer," Rafsky said.

"Flowers said it's common for the Bluff guys to pop and drop the local girls," Louis said. "Ross said that after Julie rejected him, he screwed around a lot. So maybe when he got Rhonda pregnant she figured she had caught a big fish. When she demanded Ross marry her, he freaked and killed her."

"Assumptions," Rafsky said quietly.

"The time line fits," Louis said. "Ross said he left the island around August 20, and we know that Rhonda was about four months pregnant when she was killed. Our time of death is still late December."

Rafsky set the skull down on the desk. His eyes drifted to the mess of case folders on his bed. He gathered up the folders, slipped the photograph of Julie back into the Bloomfield Hills missing persons file, and set it aside.

The clanking and hissing of the radiator filled the silence.

"What are you going to tell your boss?" Louis asked.

Rafsky shook his head slowly. "I don't know," he said. He glanced at his watch, then picked up the phone. But before he dialed he gently put the receiver back in the cradle.

"We don't tell anyone anything yet," he said. "Not my boss, not the press. Not even Flowers."

"We hauled two garbage bags of Rhonda's stuff back, and he took it back to the station to sort through."

"Let him. It'll keep him busy. But don't tell him anything we've talked about."

And don't tell Joe, Louis thought. Because he knew what Rafsky was asking him to do. He was asking him to go off the grid and try to clean this up before anyone found out how badly they had screwed up.

"I'll understand if you want out," Rafsky said.

Louis realized in that moment that while his head had been telling him he needed to go back to Florida, his heart was pulling for him to stay with Joe. But if he went all in with Rafsky now and this backfired, he didn't have a prayer of working in Michigan again, not even as a security guard.

A light came on. Rafsky was standing next to the bedside table, his face drawn in the harsh upward glare of the bulb.

And Rafsky? Louis knew he wouldn't survive.

Louis rose and went to the desk. He set the skull back in its fur-lined box and closed the lid.

"All right," he said. "I'm in."

40

The sun was hovering above the lake, and the wind was cutting across the water like knives. Louis hustled from the police SUV to the porch of the lodge.

He fumbled with the key in the frozen lock, yanked open the door, and stepped inside. It took him a second to catch his breath. It was just as cold inside as out.

The lodge windows were still shuttered, and the entrance hall was dark. He hit the light switch. Nothing. The power had been turned off again.

He opened the front door to let some light in and glanced at his watch. It was only four but it felt later.

First the long drive to Cedarville on icy roads to get Rhonda Grasso's dental records. On his way back through St. Ignace he stopped at the jail and got Dancer to confirm that the skull he had hidden in his cabin had come from the lodge.

Rafsky had been working the phones since last night, trying to squeeze any results from the Marquette lab on the processing of the lodge months ago. An hour ago, Rafsky had relayed a message through Barbara the dispatcher asking Louis to meet him at the lodge.

Louis was glad Rafsky was late. It would give him time to walk through the lodge alone. And it had nothing to do with looking for evidence.

He went to the kitchen. It was the only room not shuttered, and for the first time he got a good look at it. It was large and lined with old wooden cupboards marked with smudges of black fingerprint dust. A stone fireplace dominated one corner.

What was he looking for here? He didn't know. He never knew. He just knew he had to stand here and feel things.

It was why he had asked Maisey to see Julie's room. Why he had asked Chester to see Rhonda's room. Why he always asked to see the places where people had lived and maybe died.

Most times the places were silent, like it had been in Julie's bedroom. But sometimes, like in the trash-strewn rooms of an abandoned asylum or in a crumbling root cellar on a farm south of Hell, Michigan, there was something left in the air. Something visceral and usually unsettling, but something that always took him closer to the truth.

And now that they had a new victim, he needed to find out what this old lodge could tell him about Rhonda Grasso.

Louis unzipped his parka and went to the parlor. There was nothing in the room except empty bookcases, a tattered red chair, and a stone fireplace with a deer head over the mantel.

Going down the hallway, he peered into all of the rooms, each with the same log walls, scuffed floors, shuttered windows, and silence.

Back in the entrance hall he paused. He was tempted to go down to the basement but decided to wait for Rafsky. Instead, he started up the staircase to the second floor, careful to test his footing for rotten wood.

It was colder upstairs. The rooms were like those downstairs, shuttered and dim, holding nothing but cobwebs. He was about to give up and chalk the lodge up to one of the places determined to keep its secrets when he found a room that made him pause at the doorway.

It took him a moment to understand what had stopped him here. It was the light.

There were three windows, but only two were shuttered. Louis went to the open window and looked out.

It couldn't have been prettier if it had been a painting from one of the galleries on Main Street. A sloping bluff of snowcapped pines was silhouetted against an exploding sunset of lavender and pink. And the lake lay below, as smooth as antique milk glass.

He turned and went to the spot on the floor where he imagined someone would put a bed. There was no bed now, but he knew they hadn't needed one.

That last summer this spot had been covered with blankets and pillows stolen from the linen closets of the Chapman cottage. There had been candles purchased from the Wick Shoppe in town. And music playing from a transistor radio—the Righteous Brothers or the Temptations, maybe.

Something on the log wall in the corner caught his eye. He went to it and knelt down. Someone had carved something in the log wall—JC+CL.

It was so small and faint it was easy to understand why the techs might have missed it during their search. But would it have made any difference if they had had this clue months ago? All it proved was that Julie and Cooper had been in this room.

Assumptions, Kincaid.

But it felt right.

His eyes drifted back to the windows, and his breath billowed in the icy air. It took him a moment to figure out where his melancholy was coming from.

There was a time when he would not have understood two kids creating a hideaway in such an ugly old place. Or understood the kind of love that would drive Cooper Lange to cross an ice bridge. But he did now.

He heard the door downstairs bang shut. When he went back to the parlor, he found Rafsky sorting a stack of file folders. Dancer's wooden box sat on the red chair.

Rafsky glanced over his shoulder. "We have lights?"

"Nope."

"Be right back."

Rafsky left and returned with two Maglites. He tossed Louis one and stuck the other in the pocket of his coat.

"You get the final report from Marquette?" Louis asked.

Rafsky nodded, picking up two folders. "This is it, everything they found during the processing of this place."

"I found some initials, JC plus CL, carved in the wall upstairs," Louis said.

Rafsky arched an eyebrow. "I'd bet that's in here somewhere. They noted all marks and graffiti. What'd you find out in Cedarville?"

"I found Rhonda's dentist in De Tour Village," Louis said. "The guy pressed me about a warrant or permission from her family."

"How'd you get around that?"

"I told him we didn't want to give the father any cause for concern until we were sure," Louis said. "I'm not sure he believed me, but he finally handed the X-rays over, telling me he expected a warrant faxed to him as soon as possible."

"He's got a long wait," Rafsky said. "Let me see them."

Louis handed Rafsky an envelope. Rafsky took the skull from the box and set it on the fireplace mantel. He shined his flashlight first on the X-rays, then on the skull, then repeated the motion.

"Three fillings, one missing tooth, and a quarter-inch gap between the front teeth," Rafsky said. "We have an ID for our victim now."

Rafsky slipped the X-rays back in their envelope and tucked his flashlight back in his coat. "Did you get in to see Dancer?"

"Yeah," Louis said. "It took a while, but he finally admitted he took the skull from the basement and left the other bones."

"You're sure he was clear?"

"I got him to write out a statement. It says 'Bones, lots of bones. I was afraid to take the skull, so I just visited it sometimes. Then I took it. It was so clean I didn't need my beetles.'"

"I don't suppose our man of all seasons could give us a year?" Rafsky asked.

"No, just that it was cold."

"Okay," Rafsky said. "We got a positive ID. We know that the skull belongs to the skeleton."

"What about prints?"

Rafsky opened the top folder. "There are matches here for Cooper Lange, Danny Dancer, and Rhonda Grasso."

"Did Rhonda have an arrest record?" Louis asked.

"No, she was fingerprinted when she worked for the post office. Guess who doesn't show up anywhere?"

"Ross," Louis said.

Rafsky set the folder on the mantel and blew out a sigh. "I need a smoke." He headed back out to the entrance hall. Louis picked up the folder and followed him.

Rafsky was staring out the door at the setting sun. Louis put on his glasses and started flipping through the fingerprint report. It was at least twenty pages long, detailing the hundreds of prints found in the sixty-year-old lodge. Every print was assigned a number, and most were listed as unidentified. Every time a print was lifted, its number and location was noted. Louis saw his and Lily's names on the list as IDENTIFIED PRINT #1 and IDENTIFIED PRINT #2, with locations around the milk chute, kitchen, parlor, and basement. Dancer's IDENTIFIED PRINT #3 showed up around his rat hole and in the basement. Cooper Lange, IDENTIFIED PRINT #4, had left a trail throughout the lodge, heaviest in the southwest upstairs bedroom with no prints in the basement.

Rhonda Grasso's prints were listed as IDENTIFIED PRINT #7, with dozens of locations throughout the lodge.

Hundreds of prints. And not one from Ross Chapman.

Louis was about to close the folder when he noticed it. UNIDENTIFIED PRINT #15. Unlike the other unidentifieds, this one appeared at dozens of locations—including the basement. Louis flipped back to the page with Rhonda's prints and back to the page with #15. Many of the locations were parallel, as if someone had been following in Rhonda's shadow.

"Rafsky," Louis said, ripping out Rhonda's page. He held it next to the page for #15. "Look at this," he said.

Rafsky took the two pages. It took him only a second to see the pattern. He handed Louis the page for #15, keeping the page for Rhonda.

"Let's walk through this," he said.

He went to the parlor, stopping at a shuttered window. When he turned on his flashlight it picked up black smudges of fingerprint dust. "They found Lange's prints here."

"This must be the broken window he said they used to sneak in."

"Rhonda's prints show up on the windowsill here," Rafsky said. "And all over the room."

"I've got prints in the room for number fifteen but none on the sill."

Rafsky went to the entrance hall. "You have prints here?"

Louis nodded. "Just on the banister."

"No banister prints for Rhonda," Rafsky said. "Let's move on."

There was nothing in the long hallway leading to the back of the lodge or in the back rooms of the first floor, so they headed to the kitchen.

"Lots of good prints for Rhonda here," Rafsky said, surveying the smooth countertops and wood cupboards.

"Same for number fifteen," Louis said. He went to the fireplace. "I have a lot of good hits here."

"I have none on the fireplace," Rafsky said. "My next print is at the door leading to the basement."

"I have one there, but it's tagged no value," Louis said. "It's too smeared."

They paused at the top of the steps as Louis shined his flashlight down into the darkness.

"Rhonda left several good prints on the wall going down," Rafsky said, "including one full handprint."

"I have nothing along the steps," Louis said. "Let's go down."

At the bottom they stopped. The Maglite beams pierced the darkness. Louis swung the beam slowly over the basement, picking up the rough walls, the concrete floor, and the old boiler.

"I've got two good prints for number fifteen on one of the steps," Louis said. He went behind the steps and found the black fingerprint dust on the back of the fourth step.

"Maybe number fifteen was hiding back there, waiting for Rhonda," Rafsky said.

Louis came out and shined his flashlight onto a spot about three feet from the steps. "I have multiple no values for number fifteen here," he said.

"Same for Rhonda," Rafsky said.

"I'm guessing there was a struggle," Louis said. "That's why the prints here are all smeared."

"But Rhonda died over there," Rafsky said, shining his light at the drain four feet closer to the furnace.

Rafsky blew out a long sigh. "Fuck, no prints for Ross anywhere, and none for Cooper in the basement."

"It was winter," Louis said. "They could have worn gloves."

"Maybe. But who the hell is number fifteen?"

They were quiet for a long time. Louis swung his flashlight beam up the steps, pausing it on the step where the two prints had been lifted. He turned the beam onto the report for UNIDENTIFIED #15. Again he scanned the locations throughout the lodge, focusing finally on SW UP-STAIRS BEDROOM.

The same bedroom where he had seen the initials carved in the log wall—JC+CL. The same initials—JC—engraved inside the Kingswood ring.

"It was Julie," he said. "Julie is number fifteen."

Rafsky's beam swung to him.

"I found a picture of Rhonda and Cooper in Chester Grasso's garage," Louis said. "I thought Rhonda might have killed Julie out of jealousy."

"But then Rhonda became our victim," Rafsky said.

They both swung their flashlights to the spot in the floor where all the smeared prints had been found.

"There was a struggle," Louis said. "And Julie won."

"So where is she?" Rafsky asked.

Louis took a few steps forward, moving his flashlight beam over the ghost stain on the floor.

"I don't know where she is, but I know she's alive," Louis said.

"Assumptions, Kincaid," he said softly. "Bring me some proof."

41

Louis stood down the slope from the Chapman cottage, watching the two women on the porch. One of them was Maisey, who he knew was still readying the place for sale. He didn't know the other woman, but from the way she was gesturing toward the house he suspected she was a real estate agent. He was waiting for her to leave so he could talk to Maisey alone.

Bring me some proof.

Rafsky's words had brought him back here, to the woman who was figuratively—if not literally—Julie's mother.

The agent and Maisey shook hands, and as the agent came down the walk and passed Louis, Maisey's eyes found his.

He knew she was still angry that he had asked her to take a DNA test, so he just stood there hoping she would relent. Finally, with a small shake of her head, she motioned him toward the house.

The foyer was stacked with cardboard boxes. Maisey stood in front of him, arms crossed, waiting for him to speak.

"I'm sorry, Maisey," Louis said. "My questions about you and Julie last time I was here were intrusive and rude."

Maisey's lips drew into a straight line.

"But it's my job to speak for the victim," he said. "Sometimes that takes me places that are uncomfortable for everyone."

Maisey uncrossed her arms. "I'm still not going to take that test," she said.

"I'm not going to ask you to again."

She gave a small nod. "Okay, then. Would you like a cup of coffee, Mr. Kincaid?"

"Love one."

"I've closed the heat vents in most of the rooms already. But the parlor's warm. Go have a seat," she said. "I'll bring you a cup."

Louis wound his way through the boxes to the parlor. Maisey had mentioned before that she wasn't sure what to take from the house but apparently had found enough keepsakes to fill at least two horse carts with boxes.

He took a seat next to a table with a carafe on it, rubbing his hands to warm them. Maisey appeared a moment later with a cup and poured him some coffee. She had left some picture frames on her chair, and she picked them up before sitting down. She kept them on her lap.

"What do you need this time, Mr. Kincaid?" Maisey asked.

"First, I need to ask that you not share what we talk about today with anyone," Louis said.

She hesitated, then nodded. "You were fair with me about Mr. Ross, so you have my word."

Louis decided to just start laying things out and watch her for a reaction.

"The remains we found in the lodge do not belong to Julie," he said.

Maisey kept her eyes on his, but there was no shock in her expression. Finally she looked away, focusing on the picture frames in her lap. She was frozen, not a muscle moving. He wasn't even sure she was breathing.

"Maisey, are you okay?"

"I don't know what to say," she said. "How could . . . how could you, how could the police let everyone think . . . let Mr. Edwards die believing you had found his little girl?"

Louis set his cup down. It was a deft recovery, Maisey turning her inability to find an appropriate response back onto the police in the form of blame. It was also interesting that she didn't name herself as a wounded party in the police's screwup.

"On behalf of the police all I can do is apologize," he said.

Maisey's fingers tightened on the frames. She had just been told that her family's twenty-one-year search for closure ended with a case of mistaken identity, yet her face was a mask.

"Do you want to know whose remains they are?" Louis asked.

Maisey's voice was soft and far away. "If it's not Julie, why would it matter to me?"

"Because it was Julie's friend," Louis said. "The girl you picked out of the sketchbook. Her name was Rhonda Grasso."

Maisey shook her head. "God Bless her soul, but I barely remember her. I didn't even get her name right."

Louis was quiet, and so was Maisey. If she knew nothing of Julie's whereabouts, why wasn't she asking questions? Why wasn't she asking why Julie's ring had been found in the lodge? Why wasn't she asking about Ross being the father of Rhonda's baby?

Maisey started to get up from her chair, but Louis put a gentle hand on her forearm. She sat back down.

"Julie had a boyfriend named Cooper Lange," Louis said. "She was going to run off to Canada with him so he could avoid the draft. Did you know that?"

"No. I told you, I didn't know anything."

"Back then you didn't know anything," Louis said. "What about now?"

"What do you mean?"

He had gone too far to turn back. He had to put the question out there and see what it got him.

"I believe Julie is alive," Louis said.

He could feel Maisey's arm trembling under his hand. He could see something in her face, the same thing that had been in Cooper's face that day in the interrogation room when he talked about Julie. It was the need to not be alone any longer with a secret.

"Maisey," Louis said gently, "do you know where she is?"

Maisey opened her mouth to say something but then clamped it shut. She started to pull away, but Louis tightened his hand on her arm as a subtle pressure, hoping that if he waited long enough the weight of what she knew would become unbearable.

But Maisey drew her arm away and rose. She was gathering herself together, and he knew he had lost the moment of her vulnerability.

"I can be of no help to you, Mr. Kincaid," she said.

"I know you want to protect Julie but—"

Maisey interrupted him. "I have things to do upstairs. Please see yourself out."

He stood up quickly, pissed at himself for not being more aggressive with her.

"Maisey."

She was almost to the stairs and she stopped. There was one open cardboard box, stuffed with newspapers. She set the frames she was carrying on top of the newspapers, reached into the pocket of her sweater, and pulled something out. Louis saw it was the little ceramic horse he had seen up in Julie's room.

She set the horse on top of the picture frames and looked up at him. Her eyes were brimming.

"I've given you all I can, Mr. Kincaid," she said. "In the only way I can."

She turned and went up the stairs.

There was no reason to call to her because he knew she would just ignore him. And he wasn't going to drag her down to the station and rip the truth from her by tag-teaming her with Rafsky as if she were a common criminal. There had to be another way.

I've given you all I can. In the only way I can.

What had she given him besides Julie's journal?

Louis moved to the open cardboard box and picked up the ceramic horse. Underneath was the framed photograph of Julie sitting in a white wicker chair holding a rag doll, the same picture he had seen before. Except . . .

Louis pulled out his glasses. It wasn't a rag doll, he could see that now. It was a sock monkey.

Edna Coffee had seen a teenage girl carry a monkey onto the ferry that winter day twenty-one years ago. If Julie treasured the stuffed animal that much, surely Maisey would have noticed it was missing after Julie disappeared. But that day up in Julie's room, when he had asked Maisey if Julie had a stuffed monkey, she had said no.

He knew now Maisey hadn't lied to protect Julie. She had lied to protect herself. She knew Julie had not been abducted. She knew Julie had left voluntarily.

Why had she kept the secret from Edward? Maybe because she knew Julie was running away from something and didn't want to be found?

He looked up the staircase. Maisey had wanted him to find the photograph. She wanted him to find Julie now.

But one photograph was not enough proof. He looked back at the open cardboard box. The only other things sitting atop the newspapers were some books. They were so thin he was able to grab all four with one hand.

They seemed to be a set of some kind, the dust jackets all featuring landscapes—snowcapped mountains, a deserted beach, a shadowed forest, jagged ocean rocks, a log cabin on a lake. The author's name, Emma Charicol, meant nothing to him. The titles held no clues—*The Path to Acheron, Elysian Echoes, From Pelion, Island of the Sun.*

His heart gave a kick.

Pelion.

The place in Julie's poem where the centaur Chiron lived. The name she gave to the lodge.

The drawing on the jacket of *From Pelion* was of a log cabin high on a bluff overlooking a lake. He turned the book over. There was no author photo, just a brief biography.

> Emma Charicol is the author of four books of poems. She is an adjunct professor of creative writing at Berkeley City College, where she is a founder of the Lyrics and Odes Reading Series.

Louis flipped through the poems, scanning them for something that would resonate with Julie's journal. Finally, he found it. The last poem in the book, titled "Seventeen."

> From a chrysalis of ice
> Into the August sun I glide
> A flight too brief
> On wings of grief
> Now my heart beats a dirge
> For the girl who died

There had been a poem in Julie's journal called "Twelve." It had clearly been about the incest. Was this one—also titled with what could be an age—about the death of Rhonda Grasso?

Louis closed the book, looking again at the author bio on the back. There was a small rush of adrenaline moving inside him, but there was also something else. Something more sobering—the knowledge that if Emma Charicol was Julie Chapman, then his next step would be exposing a woman who had spent her entire adult life trying to escape her childhood.

But she was also a murder suspect.

He gathered up the four poetry books, the ceramic horse, and the photograph of Julie and started toward the door.

Masiey's voice came soft and weary from the quiet shadows of the second floor.

"Good-bye, Mr. Kincaid."

He paused, his hand on the doorknob. "Good-bye, Maisey," he said. "Thank you."

42

Louis drove slowly up the narrow winding road, leaning forward to see the house numbers through the light fog. Then, around another bend, there it was—290 Rose Street.

He pulled to a stop, looking up at the big shake-shingled house. It had come down to this one moment, all the months of investigation, all the hours of work he and Rafsky had put into this case. It had all come down to this moment and his instinct—that Julie Chapman was dead but had come alive again as Emma Charicol.

Rafsky had decided not to make the trip to California. There would be no way to explain it to his boss without revealing how far things had gone off the rails. Except for finding her address in Berkeley, they had also decided not to alert any authorities in California or run any computer checks on Emma Charicol. First Louis had to see her himself.

During the long flight from Chicago to San Francisco, Louis had read all the *From Pelion* poems. They had none of the desperate despair that infused Julie's childhood verses. Emma's poems were about gardens that bloomed in winter, deaf children who sang, and mythical worlds where three moons burned so white that "the night was benign and belighted."

Louis picked up the *From Pelion* book from the passenger seat and turned to "Seventeen." It was the only one of Emma Charicol's poems that had a hint of darkness and perhaps a hint to what happened in the lodge in 1969.

My heart beats a dirge for the girl who died.

Louis took out the two Xeroxes he had used as a bookmark. He had stopped at the library in San Francisco to find whatever he could on Emma Charicol. The first copy was from a reference book published by the Academy of American Poets that listed the same bio as her book jacket with one new piece of information, that Emma Charicol was thirty-eight, the same age Julie would be now.

Louis put on his glasses and unfolded the second Xerox. It was a short article from the *San Francisco Chronicle*, coverage of a benefit for the Lyrics and Odes Reading Series. But it was the black-and-white photo that had given him the confidence to come to this house in the Berkeley hills. The photograph showed four people holding wineglasses, the lone unsmiling woman identified as Emma Charicol. He had stared long and hard at the picture, looking for the somber girl in the Kingswood yearbook.

It was there, he was sure of it. It was there in the way Emma couldn't bring herself to look into the camera, the way Julie couldn't bring herself to trust anyone, even a yearbook photographer, to see what was inside her.

He slipped the copies back in the book and put his glasses away. Holding the *From Pelion* book, he got out of the car. At the top of the stone steps he paused. Four mailboxes, number three marked E. CHARICOL.

The front door was unlocked, so he went in. The old house had been divided into apartments, bikes crowding the narrow hallway. He went up the stairs and stopped at number three.

Music was playing faintly inside the apartment. He knocked.

The door jerked open. A woman stared at him. "Yes?" she said sharply.

He almost said it, almost said, "Julie?"

"Emma Charicol?" he asked.

Her eyes dropped to the book tucked in his arm. "I'm sorry, but I don't sign my books," she said.

"I'm not here to get a book signed," Louis said.

Something shifted in her expression, and she took a step back from the door. "What do you want?" she asked.

He wanted to know *why*. Standing here, looking at this woman, he wanted to know why the girl had done what she had done.

"My name is Louis Kincaid," he said. He pulled out his state police ID and held it out to her. She pushed her glasses up her nose and peered at the card.

"Michigan," she said softly, her eyes going up to his face.

"It's been a long trip," Louis said. "Can I come in?"

The music was still playing in the background. Through the soft murmur of Bach came the piercing whistle of a kettle.

She glanced over her shoulder, then back at Louis. "All right," she said and opened the door wider.

She went quickly into the kitchen, and the whistling stopped. Louis took the moment to look around the room. She had the front apartment of the house and had filled it with homey old furniture and modern paintings. Bookshelves took up every wall but one, which was given over to a picture window. There was a large oak desk in front of it, heaped with papers. But he didn't see one personal photograph anywhere.

She came back into the room holding a tray with a pot and two cups. "I was just going to have some tea, Officer. Would you like some?" she asked. She started to use her elbow to shove aside a stack of papers on the desk, and Louis quickly moved them so she could set the tray down.

"Thank you," she said. She hesitated, then picked up the pot. "How do you take it?"

"Just plain," Louis said. He unzipped his jacket and sat down in a chair near the desk. As she poured the tea he took stock of her.

She was slender, though her loose blue-flowered dress hid her body. Her long hair, pulled back in a ponytail, was still black but with a faint streak of gray at one temple. There were two pencils stuck in the elastic band holding her hair. She was barefoot. Her toenails were painted light purple.

She set a china cup in front of Louis and sat down behind the desk, taking off her glasses. She folded them carefully and set them down, not looking up at Louis.

"What do I call you?" Louis asked.

"Emma," she said. "Please."

"You've been Julie to me for months now," Louis said.

There was a flash of panic in her eyes before she looked away to the window. As the light caught her face full-force, he tried to see Maisey in her, but there was nothing of the housekeeper in her features. He saw, instead, Edward and his melancholy, the kind that grew in people when they realized their lives had not been as well lived as they migh have been.

She rose abruptly and walked away, pausing in the cen ter of the room with her back to him. Louis thought bacl to his last talk with Maisey, how she had gone to the edg but he had let her slip back. He had come too far to let th same thing happen now with Julie.

"I've brought you something," he said.

He reached into his pocket and pulled out the cerami horse. He set it on the table, but it took her a few moment to turn.

When she saw the horse, her eyes widened. She cam forward slowly, her eyes never leaving the horse. Sh reached out to pick it up but then drew her hand back.

She looked up at Louis. "How did you find me?" sh asked softly.

Louis set the *From Pelion* book on the desk, then reache inside his jacket and pulled out the red journal, the on from the last summer on the island. He held it out to hei

She drew a deep breath and took it, running her finger lightly over the scuffed leather surface.

"There's a poem in the journal called 'Twelve,'" Lou said. "There's another poem called 'Seventeen' in you book *From Pelion*. I think the same person wrote both them."

She opened the journal, slowly turning the page "Where did you get this?" she asked.

"I found it in the island cottage."

"You just *found* it," she said softly.

"Maisey gave it to me," Louis said.

She sat down at the desk, her eyes brimming. Sh

wiped a hand across her face. "After it happened I wasn't going to contact anyone," she said.

"What changed your mind?" Louis asked when she didn't go on.

"I read my death announcement in the paper," she said. She hesitated, then began to search for something among the stacks of papers on her desk. Finally she pulled out a newspaper and set it in front of Louis. It was the *Birmingham-Bloomfield Eccentric.*

"I subscribed to it after I moved here to Berkeley," she said. "I don't know why. Maybe I needed a connection."

"So you know about the bones being found?"

She nodded. "When I read about it, it was almost a relief. Julie has been a ghost in my house and after that it was like I could finally bury her."

He almost said what he was thinking—what about Rhonda's ghost? Where was the sympathy for her?

"Do you know about your father?" he asked.

She nodded, looking away and blinking back tears. For a long time the only sound was the Bach playing in the background.

"She's not in any danger, is she?" she said. "I mean because of me."

It took Louis a moment to realize she was asking about Maisey. Depending on what Maisey knew, she could face charges for aiding a fugitive or even as an accessory to murder after the fact.

"I can't tell you anything about that," Louis said.

"Maisey didn't know anything," she said. "She didn't know anything about what happened and she doesn't know where I am."

"But she knows you're alive," Louis said.

She nodded. "After I read the death announcement I knew I had to make contact with her somehow. My first book had just come out, so I sent it to her hoping she would know it was me. After I sent her the second book I got a letter. It was addressed to my publisher, and they forwarded it to me. It was from Maisey. All it said was—"

"I think we should stop talking about this now," Louis said. "I am not a police officer, but I'm acting as an agent for the state police and anything you say to me I can testify to."

She stared at him for a moment, then nodded. She picked up her teacup and took a sip. When she set the cup back down in the saucer her hand was trembling.

"How is she?" she asked. "Can you at least tell me that?"

"Maisey is fine," Louis said. "Your father left her the cottage."

She allowed herself the smallest of smiles, but her eyes had a faraway look.

Louis picked up the journal and put it back inside his jacket. "I'd like you to come back to Michigan with me," he said.

Her eyes shot up to his. She was frozen in the chair, her hands gripping the edge of the desk. "I can't . . ." she said.

Louis wasn't certain what he felt for her. Sorrow for the little girl who had been dragged into the dark, sympathy for the teenager who had tried to find her way back to the light. But what about the person who had allowed her family to mourn a ghost? What about the person who had taken another girl's life and coldly disappeared? Someone had to answer for that.

"It will be better for everyone if you just tell the truth," Louis said.

"There's no one left," she said.

"It will be better for you," Louis said.

"I'm gone," she said. "Julie's gone."

She rose and walked away, going to the stereo and turning off the music.

"Cooper Lange is in custody," he said.

She turned. "What?"

"Cooper Lange has been arrested, and the police believe he killed Rhonda Grasso."

"He didn't do it," she said.

"Miss Chapman—"

"Charicol. Emma Charicol," she said.

Louis rose. "You're the only one who knows what really happened in that lodge twenty-one years ago. That means you're the only one who can help him."

It was a bluff, but he had to play it. He had no authority to arrest her, but she didn't know that. She also didn't know that Cooper Lange would never be charged in Rhonda's murder. But right now Cooper wasn't the one who needed her to come back to the island. Rafsky was.

"Whoever comes here the next time will come with handcuffs," Louis said.

She covered her face with her hands. He thought she was going to cry, but she didn't. She let her hands fall and her body seemed to cave in on itself.

"When do we have to go?" she asked softly.

"Tonight. There's a flight back at ten thirty."

She didn't move. "Can I? . . . I need to pack a bag."

Louis nodded.

Still she didn't move. She looked around the apartment, then back at Louis. "What do I bring? I don't even have a pair of boots. I don't . . ."

Her voice trailed off. She turned slowly and went into the bedroom. Louis went to the window. The fog had lifted. Just over the tops of the trees he could make out the sliver of silver that was the San Francisco skyline.

Several minutes later she emerged, dressed in a sweater, slacks, and raincoat. She was carrying a small suitcase and a brown bundle. She set the suitcase on the floor and opened it.

Louis watched as she carefully set the tattered sock monkey in the suitcase. She started to zip the case, then hesitated and went to the desk. She picked up the ceramic horse.

"Cooper gave me this," she said. "I lost it a long time ago. Where did you find it?"

"Your bedroom."

When she frowned, he added, "The little room at the end of the hall."

"Oh," she said. "That wasn't really my bedroom. I only slept there. It was the only room with a lock on it."

She looked at him. "Can I keep this?"

He nodded.

She knelt and put the horse in her suitcase. When she stood up and looked at Louis her gaze was steady.

"I'm not a monster," she said softly.

"I know," Louis said.

43

Louis didn't understand why she had brought it with her. But now, as he watched Julie Chapman holding the sock monkey, he knew.

Twenty-one years ago, Julie had taken the stuffed animal with her because she knew she was never going back to Michigan. And she had brought it with her now because she believed she would never return to her life in California.

On the red-eye flight from the West Coast she had asked a few questions about Maisey, her father, and Cooper, but Louis told her the answers had to wait. The first thing Rafsky had said after Louis called him from the San Francisco airport was that he was not to tell her anything. The second thing was that they had to keep this as quiet as possible.

The name on her Delta ticket was Emma Charicol. The woman who boarded the ferry was just another faceless visitor.

Once they reached the island, the plan was to question her. But after that it was up to the district attorney. Depending on what she said happened in the basement of the lodge in conjunction with the evidence they had, the DA could charge her with anything from murder to flight from prosecution.

Louis glanced over at her. She was sitting at the window of the ferry, staring out at the lake with its crags of ice. She had managed to sleep some on the long flight, but she looked exhausted, the dull afternoon sun bringing every line of her face into high relief.

The ferry was moving slowly, staying in the narrow channel carved by the coast guard icebreaker. When it made its final turn around the lighthouse, she sat up straighter.

The island came into view, a white and dark green mass pinpricked with a few faint yellow lights, the outlines of the fort and Grand Hotel visible on the bluffs.

She was motionless, her hands pressed against the window. He wondered if she could see the single light there below the dark hotel.

They were the only people who got off the ferry. She stood on the dock shivering in her raincoat, looking as if she expected someone.

"I'm sorry, but I couldn't tell anyone we were coming. We'll have to walk," Louis said.

"How far is the police station?" she asked.

"We're not going there," he said. "We're going to the cottage."

"The cottage? Why?"

"We have to take your statement and we thought it was best if no one saw you yet."

If she thought this was strange she said nothing. She just turned up her coat collar and let Louis pick up her bag. They walked through the deserted snowy streets, heading uphill away from town. She was silent, her head hunched into her coat, her hands thrust into her pockts. After a few minutes Louis stopped her and gave her his gloves.

They didn't stop until they reached the twin stone pillars that marked the entrance to West Bluff Road.

At the end of the street a lone yellow light beckoned. She stopped again when they reached the cottage. She stood staring up at it for a long time.

There was another reason, beyond secrecy, to bring her to the cottage for questioning. Rafsky wanted to surround her with reminders of her life here and what she had done, hoping it would help shatter her defenses.

Louis wondered if it was the right thing to do, to submerge this fragile woman into a sea of painful memories to force a confession. But he had to remind himself that there was still a victim here—Rhonda Grasso. And sadly, she was the kind of victim, unlike Julie Chapman, who could be easily dismissed.

The only hitch in their plan had been Maisey. Rafsky had been forced to tell her that Julie was coming back. Her joy was tempered when Rafsky asked to use the cottage but told her she couldn't be present during Julie's questioning. Maisey agreed to stay away as long as she got to see Julie before she was taken into custody.

As they neared the veranda Rafsky came out the door.

"Who is that?" she asked.

"Detective Norm Rafsky. He's in charge of the case."

She looked to him. "You're staying, aren't you?"

"Yes."

Rafsky held the door open and followed them in. In the foyer, Louis set their bags on the floor. Rafsky was staring at Julie as if he didn't believe she was real.

"Miss Chapman," he said, extending a hand.

She took his hand. "Please, call me Emma."

Rafsky glanced at Louis, then back at her, his eyes dipping to the sock monkey in Julie's arm. "I've set things up in the kitchen," he said.

She was looking toward the parlor and it took a second for her to turn back to Rafsky. "May I have a moment?" she asked softly.

Rafsky hesitated. "Go ahead."

Julie set the sock monkey on top of her suitcase and wandered away, her footsteps a soft echo through the empty house. She paused in the middle of the parlor, her gaze moving over the sheet-covered furniture, the rolled carpets, and bare wood floors. She moved to the empty bookshelves, running her finger over the edges.

"There's nothing left," she said.

"We need to get started, Miss Chapman," Rafsky said.

In the kitchen, she paused to look around. A coffeemaker was spitting out a fresh pot. A half-filled bottle of Harveys Bristol Cream sat on the counter next to a plate of cookies covered with Saran wrap.

Louis saw Julie's eyes move to the cookies. The look reminded him of how Lily had stared at the fudge slabs in the shops in town. He remembered Julie hadn't eaten on the plane.

"You want one?" Louis asked.

Julie glanced at him and shook her head. "I don't think they're for me," she said.

Louis suspected the cookies had been made especially for her, but he let it go.

"Can I take your coat?" Rafsky asked.

"I'm cold," she said. "I'd like to keep it on if that's okay."

Rafsky nodded. "Sit down, please," he said.

Julie slid into a chair. There was a tape recorder and a legal pad on the table, but Julie didn't seem bothered by them.

Rafsky turned on the tape recorder and stated the date, the time, and the people present. Julie just sat there, slightly hunched. It struck Louis how different this was from most interrogations. No handcuffs, shackles, or hard metal chairs.

"You have the right to remain silent," Rafsky said.

"Am I under arrest?" Julie asked.

"Not yet," Rafsky said. "These rights are for your protection. You are a suspect in a homicide."

"I understand."

Rafsky finished the Miranda warning. "Would you like an attorney?" he asked.

"No," she said.

"Okay, then let's start with New Year's Eve 1969," Rafsky said. "Where were you and what were your plans?"

She pulled in a breath. "I was at home in Bloomfield Hills," she said. "I was planning on coming up here to Mackinac Island to meet Cooper. We were going to run away to Canada."

"Why had you decided to run away?"

"Cooper was going to be drafted. We thought it was our only way to be together. We were going to stay with a friend of his, Fred Grasso."

"How did you plan to get up here?" Rafsky asked.

"I was going to take the bus," Julie said. "But when I told Rhonda what Cooper and I were going to do, she offered to come down and get me."

"Rhonda who?" Rafsky asked.

Julie looked at Rafsky, confused. Of course they knew who Rhonda was, but they needed Julie's statement to be complete, with nothing that could later be interpreted as being suggested by the police.

"Please answer the question, Miss Chapman," Rafsky said.

"Rhonda Grasso," Julie said. "I met her that last summer and we became friends. Cooper didn't want anyone to know we were going to Canada, especially his father, but I was so excited I called Rhonda."

"So she drove down to Bloomfield Hills and brought you back up here?"

Julie nodded. "She was going to just drop me off at the ferry, but at the last minute she decided to come with me to the island. She told me it was too dangerous for me to be alone at the lodge."

Louis was thinking about what Edna Coffee had told them, that the girl she saw with the stuffed monkey wasn't with a man. They hadn't thought to ask her about two girls traveling together.

"You were going to Canada," Rafsky said. "Why didn't you just cross the bridge to St. Ignace and go from there?"

"That was what Cooper wanted me to do," Julie said. "But I told him I needed to go to the island first."

"Why?"

Julie drew a deep breath that flushed her cheeks. "I had been stealing money from my father's wallet and hiding it at the lodge," she said. "I knew Cooper didn't have much money, and I wanted to surprise him with it."

"How much had you taken?"

"About a thousand dollars," Julie said.

Louis had been standing near the door and came forward. "You stole a thousand dollars in one summer?"

Julie looked up at him. "I had been stealing on and off since I was about twelve. I guess I always thought about running away. But after I met Cooper I started taking more because I think I knew in my heart we would need it someday."

"What happened after you got to the island?" Rafsky asked.

"The ticket lady at the ferry told us there was a snowstorm coming. Rhonda said I shouldn't stay at the lodge alone and offered to come with me," Julie said. "I was worried Cooper would be upset that I brought someone, but I thought he'd be okay if it was Rhonda. She had been helping us exchange letters."

"Cooper was supposed to meet you at the lodge?"

"Yes. Rhonda and I got to the lodge about two. Cooper was supposed to get there by three. When he didn't come, I didn't get too worried because in winter the ferry is often delayed."

"What did you do while you waited?"

"By four it was really cold and getting dark because of the storm. We only had one flashlight, so Rhonda and I huddled in one of the front rooms and just talked."

"What did you talk about?"

Julie looked down at her hands clasped in her lap.

"Miss Chapman, please."

"We talked about our parents, school, and horoscopes. Rhonda told me I probably had a lot of trines in my chart because my life was so charmed."

She paused.

"She asked me a lot of questions, about going to a private school, about living in Bloomfield Hills. She really liked my Kingswood ring, so I let her try it on. She said she'd be rich one day, too, designing her own jewelry in San Francisco."

When Julie paused again, Louis thought he saw a flicker of impatience in Rafsky's eyes and hoped he didn't start pushing her as he had Dancer and Cooper. He glanced at the coffeepot, then back to Julie.

"Would you like a cup of coffee, Miss Chapman?" Louis asked.

"No, thank you."

"Then let's go on," Louis said. "You're doing fine."

Julie wet her lips and nodded. "I knew Rhonda had a brother in Canada, and I asked her what it was like up there, what it would be like for Cooper and me. Rhonda got quiet and she changed the subject. She started asking me what my surprise for Cooper was. I didn't want to tell her because I was afraid to trust her. But Cooper said he had known her for a long time and she was a good friend to us."

"So you told her about the money?" Rafsky asked.

Julie nodded. "She said she wanted to see it. So I decided to go get it from my hiding place."

"Where was that?" Rafsky asked.

"In the kitchen," Julie said, "behind a loose stone in the fireplace. It was dark, so I asked Rhonda to come with me to hold the flashlight."

Julie shook her head slowly. "I trusted her," she whispered.

"What happened?" Louis pressed.

"I showed her the money. She told me she had never seen a thousand dollars before and she asked if she could hold it. I let her. Then she shined the flashlight right in my face and I knew something was wrong. I couldn't see her but I could *feel* something change."

Julie pulled in a deep shuddering breath.

"I couldn't see her but I could hear her, and I could hear her voice change. She said . . . she said, 'You know Cooper doesn't love you.' She said, 'You're just his little West Bluff whore. He brags to all his friends about screwing you.'"

She was gulping for air, her body bending with each inhalation.

"Miss Chapman, take a breath," Louis said gently.

She didn't seem to hear him. "She said that Cooper really loved *her,* that they had loved each other for a long time and that she could prove it. She said she was pregnant with Cooper's baby and that they were going to run away to Canada."

Her eyes came up to Louis.

"Then she told me I needed to disappear," she said.

Tears fell slowly down her face.

Louis looked around for a Kleenex but saw only a roll of paper towels. He ripped off two and held them out to her, but she didn't take them.

"What happened next?" Rafsky said.

Julie was just sitting motionless.

"Miss Chapman," Rafsky said. "What happened next?"

Her eyes swung to Rafsky. "She picked up the stone from the fireplace and came at me," she said. "She hit me on the shoulder but I got away. It was so dark, but I saw a door. I pushed through it and suddenly I was falling down some steps. I hit my head and thought I was going to black out."

When Julie didn't go on, Louis prompted, "Could you tell where you were?"

"Not at first," Julie said. "It was completely dark. But then I saw a light. It was coming toward me, and I knew it was the flashlight and that Rhonda was coming down the stairs. I knew then I was in a basement. I crawled away and hid under the steps."

Her face had gone ashen, her eyes dark.

"I could hear her boots on the stairs, and I could see the light's beam. Then I saw her legs through the steps."

She held her hands out. "I grabbed her and pulled hard. She fell and the light . . ."

Louis put a hand on Julie's shoulder to calm her, but she didn't seem to feel it.

". . . the flashlight. She dropped the flashlight, and it was laying there on the floor. I tried to get up the steps, but she grabbed me and pulled me back down. She was strong and she was on top of me, hitting me, choking me. I couldn't see her, I couldn't see anything. But I felt something. My hand touched something hard, and I knew it was the stone from the fireplace. I grabbed it and I . . . God, oh God."

She covered her face with her hands, sobbing. Louis looked up at Rafsky. He was sitting ramrod straight in his chair, the pen poised above the pad.

Louis touched Julie's shoulder and held the paper towels under her bowed head. She took them, pressing them to her face. She took two deep breaths and looked up. Her face was streaked with mascara.

"Suddenly she was gone," she said. "I gulped for air and couldn't see anything for a few seconds. I was afraid she would come back after me, so I got on my hands and knees and tried to crawl away."

Julie shut her eyes. "I saw the light first, from the flashlight on the floor. Then I saw her. She was lying over by the boiler. She wasn't moving."

"Did you go to her?" Louis asked.

Julie shook her head slowly.

"What did you do?"

"I went back upstairs to wait for Cooper." She opened her eyes. "But he never came."

"How long did you wait?" Louis asked.

"All night," she whispered.

The tape clicked off. Rafsky opened the recorder, turned over the tape, and hit the RECORD button.

"Rhonda was right," Julie said.

"About what?" Louis asked.

"Cooper. She was right. He didn't love me."

Louis glanced at Rafsky, who gave him a subtle shake of the head.

"What did you do in the morning?" Louis asked.

She had drifted away and it took her a moment to come back to him.

"I knew I couldn't go home," she said. "I had killed someone, and all I could think about was what Rhonda had said."

"What was that?" Rafsky asked when she didn't go on.

"That I needed to disappear."

Her eyes had gone blank.

"But to do that, you couldn't just leave Rhonda in the basement as she was," Rafsky said.

She looked at him.

"You need to tell us what you did, Miss Chapman."

When she reached up to push her hair back her hand was shaking. "I remembered my father talking about this man who had killed some students in Ann Arbor. He was worried about me going to school there. I had this idea that I could make it look like someone like him had killed her. So I took her clothes and the stone from the fireplace."

"But you left your school ring," Rafsky said.

"I didn't mean to," Julie said. "I had forgotten I gave it to Rhonda to wear."

"What did you do after you left the lodge?" Rafsky asked.

"I threw the stone out in the weeds outside. I got Rhonda's clothes and her purse and I took the ferry back to Mackinaw City. I got in Rhonda's car and drove away. I drove for two straight days."

"Why did you go to California?"

"Rhonda had told me about a friend she had there named Dirk. He worked in the free clinic in Haight-Ashbury. He took me in and helped me get a fake ID."

She let out a long tired breath. "It was easy to disappear in those days."

Rafsky sat back in his chair and glanced up at Louis. Louis knew it was a signal. Julie Chapman had told them what they needed to know. Now they could tell her what she needed to know.

Louis looked at her. She had wrapped her arms around

herself, and her head was bowed. Her hair had come loose from its ponytail and hid her face. She was rocking slightly.

"Miss Chapman," Louis said.

Nothing.

"Julie."

She looked up at him, her eyes wet and expectant.

"Rhonda Grasso was pregnant, but Cooper wasn't the father," Louis said. "Your brother, Ross, was."

Her face lost all its color, and she tipped forward as if her bones had dissolved.

"There's something else you need to know," Louis said. "Cooper was coming to the island to meet you. He fell through the ice bridge and nearly drowned. He spent a week in the hospital."

Julie crumbled to the side and let out a cry. Louis started to reach for her, but Rafsky was there first, on one knee to catch her as she collapsed into his arms. She buried her face in his shoulder, clutching him.

44

Louis heard a faint rapping sound. It was coming from the front of the house, someone at the door. He looked back at Rafsky. He still had his arm around Julie, but she had stopped crying.

He left the kitchen and went to the foyer. When he opened the door he was surprised to see Maisey—and coming up the steps behind her was Flowers.

Maisey's eyes went beyond Louis, and she tried to push by him. "Is she here?" she asked.

Louis took her by the shoulders, holding her back. "Maisey, wait. You can't go in."

"Where is she?" Maisey demanded.

"I can't let—"

Maisey's eyes dipped to the two suitcases, and she saw the sock monkey. She picked it up, her eyes welling.

"I made this for her. Please let me by," she said. "I have to see her."

Louis let her go, and she ran toward the kitchen. He turned back to Flowers. He was staring hard at Louis, his mouth pulled in a thin line.

"Why didn't you tell me about this?" he asked.

"Chief—"

"You knew Julie Chapman was alive, and I had to hear

it from the housekeeper? If I hadn't seen her leaving the coffee shop and offered to drive her back here I might never have found out."

Damn it. Maisey had told him. It wasn't her fault; she assumed that because he was the chief he had to have known.

"Look, Chief, Rafsky and I didn't even—"

"Rafsky's here?" Flowers shoved past him, heading for the kitchen. Louis followed.

Julie and Maisey were in a tight embrace, crying. Rafsky was standing near the stove, watching them, and looked up at Flowers as he came into the kitchen, Louis a step behind.

Flowers stopped abruptly. He stared at the two women for a moment before his eyes went to Rafsky.

"Chief, please," Louis said quietly. "Don't do this now."

Flowers was rooted to the spot. Rafsky put a hand on Maisey's shoulder as he stepped around them and came toward the door.

"You son of a bitch," Flowers said.

Rafsky positioned himself between Flowers and the women. "Let's take this somewhere else," he said.

Flowers spun and headed back to the foyer. Rafsky let out a sigh as he and Louis followed. Flowers was standing, arms crossed, in front of the door.

"What the hell is going on?" he demanded.

"How much did Maisey tell you?" Louis asked.

"Just that Julie was alive and you were talking to her at the cottage." His eyes shot back to Rafsky. "I want to know what the fuck is going on. I want to know everything!"

Rafsky blew out a breath. "The bones in the lodge belong to Rhonda Grasso. Julie killed her."

"What?"

"We couldn't bring you in on this because—"

"How did you find her? How did—"

Rafsky held up a hand. "Let me explain."

Flowers listened, arms still folded over his chest, as Rafsky laid everything out. When Rafsky was finished, Flowers shook his head.

"Who made the decision to cut me out?" he asked.

"I did," Rafsky said.

Flowers looked to Louis. "And you agreed?"

"Things were moving fast," Louis said.

Flowers stabbed a finger at Louis's chest. "This is my island," he said. "This was my case." His eyes swung to Rafsky. "Right from the start you didn't think I could handle this, and when you fucked it up, all you could think about was covering your ass."

Rafsky was quiet.

Flowers looked toward the kitchen, and when he spoke again his voice was lower but no less angry.

"You people," he said, shaking his head. "You come up here and take over everything. You make your messes and then you leave."

It was the same thing Flowers had said back in Chester Grasso's garage about Rhonda and Julie, but now Flowers was looking at Louis and it stung.

"Excuse me."

They all turned. Julie and Maisey were standing in the hallway. Julie was still wearing her raincoat and looked as if the only thing holding her up was Maisey's arms.

"Julie is really tired," Maisey said, looking to Louis. "I

made up a room for her. Would it be all right if I took her up so she can rest?"

Louis nodded.

Julie gently disentangled herself from Maisey and came to Louis.

"No matter what happens, thank you for bringing me home," she said.

She picked up the small suitcase and the sock monkey and slipped her arm through Maisey's. About halfway up the stairs, Maisey stopped and looked down.

"Are you leaving?" she asked, looking at Louis.

Louis glanced at Rafsky but his face was a blank.

"I'd like to talk with you, Mr. Kincaid," Maisey said. "Can you stay for a while?"

When Louis nodded Maisey gave him a small smile and led Julie up the stairs.

With a final glare at Louis, Flowers jerked open the door and went outside, jamming his hat on his head. Rafsky blew out a tired breath and headed back to the kitchen.

Louis watched Flowers trudge down the walk and went after him.

"Chief, wait!"

Flowers kept going toward the SUV.

"Jack, wait!"

Louis caught up as Flowers got to the driver's door and grabbed the sleeve of his parka.

Flowers slapped Louis's hand away. "I trusted you!" he said.

Louis held up his hands. "I know."

Flowers moved away, turning in a small, tight circle, his head down.

"I'm sorry," Louis said.

Flowers wouldn't look at him. He pulled out his gloves and jerked them on. He looked up at the house. "What's going to happen to her?"

"I don't know. We haven't even told the DA yet. Right now, other than me and Rafsky, the only people who know Julie Chapman is alive are Maisey and you."

"You think you're going to keep something like this quiet?"

"We have to, at least for a while. It could still blow up on us."

Flowers looked at him over the hood of the SUV. "You mean it could blow up for him."

"Yes."

Flowers shook his head slowly, then he got in the SUV and started the engine. Louis stood shivering as Flowers pulled away. After Flowers turned around in the cul-de-sac, he stopped the SUV in front of Louis. The window whirred down.

"There's a bad storm coming tomorrow," he said. "You'd better stock up on supplies while you can."

The window went back up. Louis watched the red tail-lights disappear down the road and then went back in the house.

He stopped long enough to stamp the snow off his shoes before he headed to the kitchen. Rafsky was standing near the refrigerator, connected to the kitchen wall phone by a long coiled cord.

"Yes, Greg Thom," Rafsky said. "No, I need him now."

Louis looked to the coffeemaker, then to the bottle of Harveys Bristol Cream on the counter. He started quietly opening cupboards but found nothing but a second bottle of Harveys.

Louis reached for two glasses, listening as Rafsky began updating the Mackinac County DA on the events of the last week. Louis knew the DA was up on the case, but like Flowers he couldn't possibly expect what Rafsky was about to tell him.

When Rafsky finished explaining that Julie was now on the island, Louis could hear the squawk of Thom's voice from the receiver but couldn't understand what he was saying. On Rafsky's end it was mostly "Yes, sir" and "I understand."

After he hung up, Rafsky rubbed his brow and looked at Louis, his eyes dipping to the glass in Louis's hand.

"What is that?" he asked.

Louis handed Rafsky a glass and filled it. "Harveys Bristol Cream."

Rafsky took a drink and grimaced.

"What did the district attorney say?"

Rafsky sank into a chair at the kitchen table. He downed the sherry like a shot of whiskey and held his glass out for a refill. "He was pissed until I told him we had our suspect right here on the island," he said. "He wanted me to arrest her now, but I talked him out of it until he reviews her statement. He wanted me to bring the tape over today."

He looked to the Harveys in his hand and finished it. "Fuck it. I'll go tomorrow."

"Did Thom indicate what direction he was going to take this?"

Rafsky tapped the rim of his glass and Louis refilled it again. "He asked me if I believed her story of self-defense."

"What did you say?"

"I told him I did. But then he said that if it was self-defense, why did she run?"

"She was seventeen and scared," Louis said.

"That's no defense."

"She thought she couldn't go home."

"Still no defense."

"She was afraid of Ross."

Rafsky gave him a raised eyebrow. "Do you really think an incest defense will mitigate murder charges?"

Louis picked up his glass but set it back down. He was so exhausted from the trip to California he could barely think.

"You've done all you can," Rafsky said.

Louis heard a sound and turned toward the door. Maisey was standing there, holding Julie's raincoat.

"Did I hear you mention Mr. Ross?" she asked.

Louis and Rafsky exchanged glances. Rafsky reached for the bottle of Harveys to refill his glass as a pretense to not answer.

"Yes," Louis said.

Maisey came forward. "If that boy shows up here I'll kill him," she said.

45

Louis believed her. He believed that if Ross showed up at the house, Maisey would in fact kill him. Her guilt over not protecting Julie as a child had new life. Before today Maisey might have been able to go to her grave bearing its weight. But not now, not since Julie had been given back to her.

As for Julie, she didn't ask one question about her brother.

She did ask about Cooper. Last night, as Louis and Rafsky were getting ready to leave the cottage, Julie had come downstairs. She had pulled Louis aside and asked if there was any chance she could see him.

I'm going to prison. I know that. I just want to see him once.

Later, back at their hotel, Louis had brought it up to Rafsky. It took Rafsky a long time to answer, and it was not what Louis was expecting.

I think I can make that happen.

What was behind Rafsky's decision? It wasn't sentimentality; that wasn't in Rafsky's bones. Louis suspected it was something deeper, something that came from that part of Rafsky that had whispered, *Tell Frye I forgive her.*

Whatever it was, it had brought Louis here, to the Ice House bar in St. Ignace.

It was lunchtime, but the place was almost deserted,

just two men hunched over beers at the bar. Rafsky had told Louis that Cooper's father had put the bar up as collateral for his son's bail. Louis suspected the publicity had not been good for business.

There was a man behind the bar cleaning glasses. He was tall and thin like Cooper but older, and as Louis stepped up to the bar he gave Louis a hard stare.

"You're that cop," the old man said.

Louis didn't bother to correct him. "I'm looking for Cooper Lange. Is he here?"

"No, he's not. Now why don't you get out of here?"

Over the man's shoulder, Louis saw someone come out from the back carrying a beer keg. Cooper's eyes were on Louis as he set the keg down.

"It's okay, Pop," he said. "I'll handle this."

The old man moved away to the end of the bar but didn't take his eyes off Louis.

"What do you want?" Cooper asked Louis.

"I need to talk to you."

"I don't have to talk to you. I got a lawyer. Talk to him."

"It's not about the charges against you," Louis said. "It's something else."

Cooper shook his head and started to turn away.

"Look, it's personal," Louis said.

Louis looked down the bar. Cooper's father was still watching them, and Louis knew he could hear every word.

"Come outside with me," Louis said.

"Forget it."

"Cooper, you've got to trust me on this. It's personal and it's important."

In the glare of the neon sign behind the bar, Louis could

see something change in Cooper's face. With a glance at his father he followed Louis outside.

An icy wind was blowing hard from the lake. Cooper, standing there in his flannel shirt, didn't seem to feel it. Louis pulled up the hood of his parka.

"I need you to come to the island with me," Louis said.

"What? What the fuck for? You guys want to play hockey with my balls again?"

"Cooper—"

"Fuck this, man."

Cooper started to go back in the door. Louis grabbed his sleeve. Cooper slapped his hand away but then stepped back, realizing he couldn't risk even looking cross-eyed at a cop at this point.

"Goddamn it," he said softly. "It's bad enough I had to tell my dad everything. I had to tell him about Julie, I had to tell him I was running away to Canada, man! And here you are again. What the fuck more do you want from me?"

"I want you to come to the island with me," Louis said.

Cooper shook his head. "Why?"

"I can't tell you. Not here. You have to trust me," Louis said.

Cooper hung his head.

It was time to play the ace.

"If you come," Louis said, "I can make sure the resisting arrest charges against you are dropped."

Cooper looked up at him. "Don't fuck with me," he said softly.

"I'm not," Louis said. "Let's go."

* * *

When they got off the ferry, the kid handling the ropes told them the last ferry back to St. Ignace left at four. Louis assured Cooper he would make it, and they started up Main Street.

"Where are we going?" Cooper asked.

"The Chapman house."

Cooper stopped. "What for?"

"You'll find out when you get there."

Cooper glanced back toward the docks, but the ferry had already left. He said nothing until they were almost to the end of West Bluff Road, where he stopped and stared up at the house.

"I've never been inside," he said. He looked to his left to a small break in the trees. "Julie always met me over there, on the path down to the lake."

Louis put a hand on Cooper's shoulder. "Let's go in," he said.

In the foyer Cooper took off his gloves and pushed off his red wool hat. His eyes were everywhere, taking in the oak paneling, the curving staircase, and the parlor with its sheet-draped furniture and cardboard boxes.

He took a step closer to Louis. "Why am I here?" he asked softly.

The creak of the wood floors made them both look to the hallway. Julie was coming in from the kitchen.

A night's sleep and Maisey's tender care had transformed her. She was wearing jeans and a dark red sweater. Her hair was loose around her shoulders.

"Hello, Cooper."

He just stared at her.

She took a step forward. "It's me, Cooper," she said softly.

"My God," he whispered.

Julie's eyes brimmed. "I know. I know."

Cooper didn't move. Couldn't move, Louis thought as he watched the man. Julie went to Cooper and gently, tentatively, held out her arms. He stepped into them, awkwardly at first, then he clasped her to him and closed his eyes. Julie buried her face in his shoulder.

Louis heard a sound and saw Maisey coming from the kitchen. She came over to stand next to him, her hand to her mouth. For a long time the only sound was the wind ticking against the windows. Then Cooper let out a hard breath and took a step back, out of Julie's arms.

He wiped a hand roughly over his face.

"How?"

His question was for Louis, but his eyes never left Julie's face.

"Later," Louis said.

Cooper gave Louis the barest glance before looking back at Julie.

Maisey put a hand on Julie's shoulder. "Why don't you take Cooper in the kitchen, honey. I'll make some fresh coffee."

Julie smiled and nodded. She took Cooper's hand, and they walked down the hall.

Louis saw Julie sit down at the kitchen table across from Cooper. Even from this distance he could see it in her face, see that as happy as she was to see Cooper again, she knew their moment had passed.

Maisey was watching them, too, her eyes bright with tears.

"What's going to happen to her?" she asked.

Louis glanced at his watch. Rafsky was meeting with the DA Greg Thom right now. It was the kind of meeting that would take hours. The final decision about what to do with Julie Chapman was in the hands of a small-town district attorney who, depending on his decision, could end up either crucified or canonized by the media.

"We'll know by tomorrow," Louis said.

Maisey nodded and started toward the kitchen. But she stopped and came back to Louis.

"Thank you, Mr. Kincaid," she said.

She held out her hand but then instead drew him into a tight hug.

46

It was midmorning but the house was as dark as if it were dusk. The Canadian front that had been threatening for two days was making its way onto the island, bringing an ice storm that had brought down electrical wires and left a hard glaze on the trees that sent them groaning and cracking with each shift of the wind.

Maisey pulled her bathrobe tighter and headed to the fireplace. All the logs from last night were burned down to ashes, and there was no more wood in the basket. Julie and Cooper had used it up last night, sitting down here wrapped in quilts and talking to God knows what hour.

Maisey had slipped away around nine to give them some privacy. For a long time, though, she had lain upstairs with her door ajar, knowing it was wrong to eavesdrop but wanting to make sure Cooper said or did nothing to upset Julie. But all she heard was murmuring voices and eventually she had fallen asleep. This morning she had found his pillow and blankets folded neatly on the sofa in the parlor.

"Still no power, Miss Maisey?"

Maisey turned to see Cooper standing in the foyer. It was so cold in the house he was wearing his parka. Julie was still sleeping, she knew. There hadn't been a sound from her room.

"No, the ice storm took the lines down," she said. "Th
phone's still working. I called the electrical people th
morning, and they said they're working on getting th
power back."

Cooper nodded. "Maybe I better go get some mo
wood, then," he said.

"Yes, that would be good," Maisey said.

Cooper disappeared, and a moment later Maisey hea
the back door bang closed. She looked back to the pile
blankets and quilts on the sofa, wondering what it mu
feel like to be them—to be Julie and Cooper—and see ea
other again after all these years, after all the lies and a
sumptions.

With that thought came a rush of regret that she h
never told Mr. Edward that she suspected that Julie w
alive. Maybe she should have, but she had no real proc
And even if she had found out for sure, and no matter hc
much she loved Mr. Edward, her first loyalty had alwa
been to Julie. And if that was wrong, then let God be h
judge.

"Here you go, Miss Maisey."

Cooper came in, carrying a bulging canvas tote in ea
hand. He set them by the fireplace. "It's getting pretty ug
out there now," he said. "I should probably get going dov
to town and see if the ferry—"

"Nonsense," Maisey said. "There isn't going to be
ferry today or probably tomorrow. You'll just have to st
here until they start running again."

Cooper gave her an awkward smile. "Thank you,"
said. "I'd like that."

Maisey nodded. "But if you want to help you can r

own to Doud's and get us some food," she said. "I wasn't
lanning on company, and the cupboards are pretty bare.
ou'd better get some more candles and batteries, too, just
n case."

"Not a problem," Cooper said. He pulled his gloves and
ed wool cap from his pocket and started toward the door.
Anything else you need?"

"Try to find a bottle of Harveys Bristol Cream. Some-
ne drank all mine yesterday."

"Yes, ma'am."

Cooper left in a swirl of snow, and when the door
losed the house was quiet again. Maisey heaped some logs
n the grate, lit a fire, and started to the kitchen.

As she passed through the foyer, she heard the clump
f footsteps on the porch. A shadow appeared behind the
eveled glass. Cooper probably forgot his wallet and had
ome back to get money, she thought. She should've of-
ered some.

She reached for the door but it burst open, almost
nocking her over. Ross stood in the doorway. Snow caked
is hair and the shoulders of his dark overcoat, and he was
ooking around the foyer like a rabid animal. His eyes
opped on Maisey.

"Where is she?"

Maisey stepped toward him. "Get out of my house."

"*Your house*," Ross said. "A house you whored your way
ato. Where's my sister?"

Maisey wanted to smack him. "Who told you she was
ere?"

"I'm a fucking senator, and I am her brother," Ross said.
The DA's office called me. Now, where the hell is she?"

"She doesn't want to see you!"

Ross shoved Maisey aside and walked quickly to th parlor. Seeing no one, he spun back and headed to th kitchen. Maisey hurried after him.

"Get out!" she shouted. "Get out or I'll call the police.

Ross stopped, his eyes pinballing around the kitcher He started back toward the foyer.

God, no. He was going upstairs!

Maisey grabbed a knife off the counter and ran afte him. "Get out of here or I'll kill you!" she screamed.

Ross spun, saw the knife, and smacked it from he hand. It skittered into a corner by the door.

Ross headed toward the stairs. Maisey launched herse at his back. He slipped on the wet floor but then caught h balance on the stair post and knocked her away.

She saw the blur of his fist, then felt the slam of blin ing white pain in her jaw. She stumbled backward ont some cardboard boxes, hitting her hip hard as she fell the floor. The taste of blood was thick on her tongue. Ro was coming toward her again. She cringed, bracing for an other blow.

"Get away from her!"

Maisey opened her eyes. Ross's dark coat came in focus and then, beyond him, Julie standing on the stair Maisey tried to talk, tried to tell Julie to run, but sh couldn't move her mouth.

Julie came slowly down the stairs. Her eyes riveted c Ross, she edged past him and knelt next to Maisey.

"You're bleeding," Julie said.

"Go," Maisey whispered. "Get . . . help."

"I'm not leaving you with him."

"I'll be—"

Suddenly Julie let out a yelp as Ross jerked her to her feet. Maisey's heart was hammering. She spotted the knife near the coatrack, but she couldn't move. Something was wrong with her hip. Maybe if she could talk to him, maybe she could reason with him like she used to do when he was a boy.

But she knew he wouldn't listen. He was staring at Julie. His face was slack with astonishment, as if he were looking at a ghost. There was something else there in his eyes, something that made Maisey's stomach turn—desire.

"Julie," Ross whispered.

Julie took a step back.

"Julie," Ross said again. "God, I've missed you so much."

He held out his hands.

"Stay away from me!"

He blinked and for a moment seemed completely confused. "How can you say that to me?"

"I said it a million times before but you never heard me!"

"Julie, listen to me," Ross said. "You don't have to do this anymore. They're all gone. It's just us now."

Julie put her hands over her face. Maisey tried to use the boxes to pull herself into a sitting position. Ross's eyes darted to her, and for one second she could see something of the boy there, the needy boy who nobody needed. But then it was gone and there was just madness.

Ross started toward Julie. She backed away, frantically looking for an escape, but she was cornered by the door.

He touched the sleeve of her sweater, and she recoiled. He reached up to stroke her hair.

"Don't touch me," she said.

Maisey closed her eyes at the pain in Julie's voice.

"Julie, you know that you—"

"I said don't touch me!" she screamed.

Maisey's eyes shot open at the sound of a slap. Ross w.
glaring at Julie, hand to his cheek. Then he turned slowl
as if looking for something. He pulled Maisey's gree
plaid coat off the coatrack and held it out to Julie.

"It's very cold," Ross said. "You'd better put this on."

Julie's eyes darted to Maisey, then back to Ross.

"No."

"Put on your coat, Julie," Ross said. "We have to g
now."

"I'm not going anywhere with you," Julie said.

"Yes, you are. You're coming with me. Right now."

Julie pushed against Ross's chest and darted towar
the kitchen. He lunged after her, catching her by th
hair. She screamed and tried to fight him, but Ro
pulled her back, pinning her against his chest. Then l
slapped her.

She screamed, and he slapped her again.

He twisted her arm. "Put on the damn coat!"
shouted. "Or I'll kill both of you right here."

Julie looked down at Maisey, then slowly put on t
coat.

"Julie, no," Maisey said.

"It'll be okay, Maisey," Julie said.

Maisey tried to move, her eyes jumping down to t
knife. Ross caught her look and scooped it up.

He jerked open the door. Through the swirling sno
Maisey watched him drag Julie out onto the porch. Fo

econd, just a second, her eyes found Maisey's, then she vas gone.

The phone. She had to get to a phone.

Maisey crawled across the foyer to the phone in the arlor, knocking it from the table as she grabbed at it. Her hands were shaking so hard she couldn't hold the eceiver.

She started to dial the police but stopped and dialed the Potawatomi Hotel instead. She held her breath until he nswered.

"This is Kincaid."

"Mr. Kincaid," she said. "This is Maisey. Mr. Ross was ere . . . he's taken Julie."

"What? Taken her where?"

Maisey's mouth hurt so much she could barely speak.

"Maisey, where did he take her?"

"I don't know. I don't know. To the airport, I think."

There was a pause on the other end of the line and she ould hear him moving around.

"Mr. Kincaid—"

"Call the police, Maisey. I'll get there as fast as I can, but ou've got to hang up now and call the police."

She started to cry.

"Maisey, are you okay?"

"He hurt me, and I'm afraid he's going to hurt her."

"All right. Stay calm. I'm on my way."

Maisey hung up and for a long time just sat on the floor, rying to slow her hammering heart and the pounding in er head.

A loud crack outside, like a gunshot. Maisey jumped, er eyes shooting to the open front door. Had Ross come back? Slowly she pulled herself up to the window but couldn't see anyone on the veranda. She limped out to the foyer and looked out the open door.

A huge black limb had snapped off the oak tree in the front yard and now lay across the front steps.

She let out a painful breath and stepped out onto the veranda, leaning against the railing.

Nothing but white. And the footprints in the snow left by Ross dragging Julie away.

47

Louis ran the last hundred feet through the deepening snow, scrambled past the downed tree limb and up onto the veranda. Maisey was leaning heavily against the open front door, holding a bloody towel over her lip.

"Did Ross do that to you?" Louis demanded.

"Yes, but—"

She was shivering badly. He took her gently by the shoulders and tried to steer her back into the foyer, but she pushed against him.

"You have to go after them!"

Louis had called Rafsky, telling him to intercept Ross at the airport, although he was sure no plane was taking off in this ice storm.

"Everything's going to be okay, Maisey," he said. "Detective Rafsky is at the airport right now. He'll arrest Ross and—"

"He didn't go to the airport!" Maisey said.

"What?"

"He took Julie down the path."

"What path? What are you talking about?"

She pointed to the left. "Over there."

Louis looked in the direction Maisey was pointing. If there was a path there in the trees he couldn't see it. But he did see footprints cutting away from the house.

"Where does the path go?" Louis asked.

"Down to the main road that circles the island," Maisey said.

Louis did a quick calculation. About twenty minutes had passed since Maisey's call and Rafsky was now sitting at the airport.

"Ross has a knife," Maisey said.

Louis looked to the path. He couldn't wait for Rafsky. He had to follow Ross.

He took Maisey by the shoulders. "Go back inside and lock the door," he said. "Call the police station and tell them to radio Detective Rafsky. Tell him I'm following Ross and that Ross is headed down to the main road."

Maisey started to cry.

"Where's Cooper?" Louis asked.

Maisey shook her head. "He went to Doud's."

"Lock the door behind me," he repeated. "And then call the police."

Maisey nodded woodenly. After she closed the door Louis waited until he heard the click of the lock, then he jumped off the veranda. He followed the footprints through the snow toward the trees. As he drew closer he could see the tunneled opening of the path.

He pushed through the icy branches and trudged forward, tripping several times before he finally got the feel of the uneven ground as it sloped downhill. The chaotic footprints and drops of blood in the snow told him that Ross was dragging Julie and that she was fighting hard.

The wind grew brisker the closer he got to the lake, the icy snow like needles in the face. He drew up the hood of his parka and dipped his head, his steps slowed by the deepening drifts, his breath fast and hot.

Finally he emerged from the trees onto the road. He faced a canvas of frozen white lake and blowing snow that slithered across the horizon like chalk dust. There were no prints on the iced-over road, and he didn't know the island well enough to figure out where Ross had gone.

Then he realized he was not very far from the lodge. It was maybe a half mile up the road. But why would Ross take Julie there?

He wanted to run but couldn't manage more than a cautious trot on the icy road. He rounded a curve and spotted something moving in the distance—two dark figures standing out starkly against the vast white backdrop.

It was Ross, dragging Julie by the arm.

But Louis realized they weren't heading away from him. They were moving perpendicular. They had veered sharply left and were moving faster now.

Where the hell was he going?

Then Louis saw the line of small dark spots in the white—Christmas trees. Ross was heading out onto the ice bridge.

Louis squinted to make out the trees that formed the bridge. Some stood erect, but most were lying on their sides, blown over in the storm. He finally reached a snowy patch in the road and got some traction. By the time he reached the place where Ross had left the road, Ross had dragged Julie about fifty feet out on the lake.

He cupped his hands to his mouth. "Chapman! Stop! It's over. Let her go!"

Ross spun around. So did Julie. When she saw him, she

pulled harder to get away from Ross. He gave her a vicious yank and began dragging her farther away.

Louis peered over his shoulder through the snow at the road, but there were no flashing red lights, no buzz of snowmobiles. Where the hell were the cops?

He looked back to the lake. Ross and Julie were almost lost in the swirling white. He had to go after them.

Louis slogged through a high drift and stopped. It was hard to tell where the shore ended and the lake began, just an even blanket of snow stretching before him.

He stepped out onto the ice, cautiously at first, then, as he gained confidence in the thickness of what lay beneath him, he moved more quickly. He had gone maybe fifty feet before he was close enough to Ross to shout at him again.

"Chapman!"

Ross didn't look back this time. Julie was fighting him harder now, dropping down onto the ice in an attempt to slow him.

"Get up!" Ross screamed. He jerked her to her feet.

Louis stopped. Ross had the knife at Julie's throat. Louis was only twenty feet away, but he could see her eyes locked on his, dark with fear.

"Let her go!" Louis yelled.

"Stay away! I'll kill her!" Ross thrust the knife out at Louis.

Louis saw her move before Ross did, saw her leg come up. Ross screamed as her knee smashed into his groin. He doubled over, losing his grip on her coat and falling to the ice.

She stumbled away, crying, but found her footing and

began to run. She was running away from Ross but also away from Louis. And in her panic, she was running away from the tree path.

"Julie!" Louis shouted. "Julie!"

His eyes shot to Ross, still kneeling on the ice, then back to Julie.

"Julie! Stop!"

She was still moving away from him, stumbling now in the blowing snow. He knew she was disoriented, probably not able to see the shore. He had to go out to her.

"Julie! Stop where you are! Don't move! I'll come to you."

He looked back at Ross. He was standing, the knife at his feet. He looked in the direction where Julie had gone. Then he began to walk in the opposite direction.

Let him go. They'll get him later.

Louis looked back to Julie. She had stopped, a small blur in Maisey's green plaid coat.

"Julie! Stay where you are! I'm coming out there!"

The nearest tree marking the ice bridge was just five feet away, its silver tinsel rippling in the wind. Louis moved beyond it and started toward Julie. Five feet, ten . . . maybe twenty.

A loud crack, like a rifle shot.

Louis froze. Afraid to look down, afraid to even take a breath.

Another crack.

The world dropped.

48

Cold. Blackness. Cold, cold, cold.

As the shock of it engulfed him he gasped and water poured into his mouth. He couldn't help it, couldn't stop it. But something made him kick hard and he bobbed to the surface.

Breathe!

Oh God . . .

Breathe!

He coughed hard, trying to empty his lungs of water. His hands clawed at the edge of the ice, and it gave way with a crack, plunging him back into the water.

He kicked up again, his bare fingers grasping for a hold. He got his forearms up on solid ice and tried to be still. He could see nothing, just a swirl of white. He shook his head hard, trying to clear his brain of the panic that was streaking like acid through his body.

Breathe!

And then . . .

Breathe. Stabilize. Get out.

The four words they had taught him back at the academy. That day they had all jumped into the water to learn how to survive. But that had been a warm pool in a gymnasium. This . . .

He didn't move, afraid if he did the ice would give way again. But he was losing the feeling in his hands.

The instructor's voice was in his head.

Your uniform will act as a floatation device.

He had no uniform.

You can use your gun magazines as ice picks to pull yourself out, hand over hand.

He had no gun.

He was alone, and he was going to die. He closed his eyes. What else had they said? He couldn't remember. He could barely think.

Another voice. Was it real?

Kincaid.

Someone calling his name. And it was coming from outside his head. He opened his eyes and squinted into the whiteness.

"Kincaid!"

There, far off in the distance, a dark blur. A man, far away on the shore. A spot of red. Cooper's red wool hat.

"Cooper!"

His cry came out strangled and weak.

Through the swirl of blowing snow he saw the spot of red move toward him. Then, suddenly, it stopped. Louis blinked hard, trying to get the ice water from his eyes.

Cooper was just standing there like he was frozen. Then he started backing up.

"Cooper!"

It took every ounce of air to get it out. His lungs were burning. Everything was going blurry.

His fingers were numb and he could feel the weight of

his clothes pulling him downward. He needed something to stick into the ice, something to hold him up.

Lily's knife!

The key-ring knife she had given him the morning she left.

He thrust his hand into the water to the pocket of his jeans. He prayed the key ring was in the left pocket because he knew he didn't have the strength to try again.

He could feel the bump of it. He wedged two fingers into his jeans and finally felt the ring. Slowly, carefully, he pulled the ring out. When he got his forearm back on ice, he stopped, panting.

With shaking fingers, he worked to pull out the blade from the knife, but he couldn't work it free with just one hand and he couldn't risk losing his grip on the ice's edge. He pulled the tiny blade out with his teeth.

He reached out as far as he could and plunged the blade into the ice.

It held firm.

Kick. He was supposed to kick and pull himself out, but his legs were deadweight beneath him. He clutched the tiny knife and laid his head down on his other forearm.

Kincaid . . .

Kincaid . . .

Kincaid!

From the deep fog of his brain, he heard his name again. It took all his will to open his eyes.

A blurry spot of red.

"Kincaid! Can you hear me?"

Cooper. It was Cooper. He was on his hands and knees maybe thirty feet away.

He couldn't answer.

"Goddamn it! Hold on!"

His eyes started to close. He couldn't stop them.

"Kincaid! Listen to me! Look at me! Look at me!"

Louis forced his head up.

The red dot was closer now. It look him a second to realize Cooper was now flat on his stomach. Close . . . so close . . .

"No," Louis whispered. "Don't come."

Cooper said something, but it was drowned out by a droning noise in Louis's head. Louis felt his fingers slipping off the knife. The buzzing was alive in his brain now, like insects eating him alive, like Danny's beetles eating away at him.

No. No. I am not going to fucking die like this.

Joe . . . Lily. I am not going to leave you.

He forced himself to focus on the red dot of Cooper's hat. But the buzzing in his head didn't stop, it got louder.

Snowmobiles.

Something hit him. On the shoulder. Blurry movement now. Two men behind Cooper. And voices, but he couldn't figure out what they were saying.

Another smack of something, this time on his forearm. Bright orange. A circle. Rescue disk . . . it was a rescue disk, but he knew that if he let go of the knife to grab it he would go under.

But . . .

He had to try. He let go of the little knife and groped for the spot of orange. He touched it but he couldn't curl his fingers around it.

Falling. He was falling slowly, so very slowly, into the blackness.

Waves washing over him, around him, against him. Something hard hitting his chest. Then nothing but black.

The cold of the air hitting his lungs brought him back. He spit, coughing and gagging. So cold, but his insides were on fire.

White. But things moving within the white.

A blob of red bobbed close.

Cooper. He was in the water next to him.

Voices. It took a moment for the words to make sense.

"Got him! Pull!"

A hard tug around his chest. Then he was out, lying on the ice, his chest heaving. He tried to roll away from the hole as they had taught him but he couldn't move. Then he realized Cooper was lying there next to him, so close Louis could feel his breath warm on his face.

A pink face in a dark fur hat hovered above him.

"Chief," Louis whispered.

"I've got you. It's okay," Flowers said. "You're going to be okay."

49

A faint humming. It grew louder, building into a ball of sound rushing toward him until it exploded into a stream of words.

His name. Someone was calling to him. Saying his name over and over.

He could feel the light dancing just beneath his eyelids, but he didn't want to open his eyes. He was too tired. He was too tired to do anything, even shiver. All he wanted to do was sleep.

"Louis? Can you hear me?"

He forced himself to open his eyes. Bright lights. And pale green amoeba-like things moving around in the lights. He tried to move his hand. Something warm and soft closed over it.

"Don't move. You're okay. You're in the hospital."

He tried to nod, but his neck muscles felt as if they were rusted shut. His brain felt rusted shut.

"You fell through the ice. You might have some amnesia."

He could remember Christmas trees. He could remember seeing Joe—no, not Joe, Julie—far away out on the ice. He could remember the crack of a rifle. No, the sound of the ice breaking. After that he could remember nothing but the cold blackness covering him and seeping deep inside him.

A pinprick somewhere on his arm.

"We're getting a little warmth back in you," the voice said.

Again he tried to nod but couldn't. All he could do was feel the awful throbbing pain. It was everywhere in his body. He blinked hard and strained to look down at his left hand. It was dotted with white blisters. In his fogged mind the blisters started to balloon and he could see his fingers and toes turning black and falling off.

"Will they . . . ?"

"Your hands? The damage looks to be superficial," the voice said. "They should be okay in a week or so. Your feet, too. You were lucky."

Louis closed his eyes, a wave of exhaustion washing over him. Slowly, so very slowly, the throbbing in his body began to lessen, and he could feel warmth, wonderful warmth, flooding into his chest. He started to drift off, and he dreamed he was home, the sun hot on his face, the warm Gulf waters flowing over him.

He swam up from the deep water, resurfaced, and opened his eyes. Warm . . . he was so warm, and it felt so damn good. The sensation seemed to be coming from his gut. With difficulty he raised his head and looked. A tube was sticking out from his stomach, the line snaking up to a plastic bag suspended above his bed.

Louis stared at the bag, at the slow, syrupy drip of the fluid into the tube, at the tube going into his gut, feeding him warmth and life. She was there suddenly. They both were. Joe and Lily. They were there beside him, and he knew suddenly the warmth came from them.

Something liquid boiled up from his chest and pushed its way up his constricting throat and out his eye. He wiped away the tear.

Noises drifted to him, faint and distant, the ringing of a phone and the rattle of a cart in the hall. And the smell of something yeasty like fresh-baked bread.

Louis opened his eyes.

Someone was sitting in the chair at the foot of his bed. He blinked him into focus.

"Hey, Chief," Louis whispered.

Flowers rose and came to the edge of the bed. "How you doing?" he asked.

"Okay. At least that's what they tell me."

"You've got hypothermia."

Louis nodded. "I'm having trouble remembering some of it. I remember going after Ross and Julie on the ice bridge and falling in. I remember seeing you and Cooper."

"I was lucky I had the snowmobile," Flowers said. "I've had to pull people out before, so I had my foil blanket and hot packs. We had to cut off your clothes."

Again Louis nodded. He closed his eyes, fighting back the fatigue.

"I thought you'd want this back, though," Flowers said.

Louis opened his eyes. Flowers was holding the little souvenir knife Lily had given him. When Louis didn't move, Flowers added, "I'll just leave it here on the table."

"How long have I been here?" Louis asked.

"A little over forty-eight hours."

"I need to call Joe."

"I already did it for you." Flowers hesitated. "Was that okay?"

Louis nodded.

"I told her you were going to be fine. She wanted to come up here, but I asked her to wait until you called her." Again Flowers hesitated. "Was that okay?"

Louis nodded again. He wanted to sleep but there was too much still cluttering up his head.

"Is Julie okay?" Louis asked.

"She's fine," Flowers said. "When she saw you go in the water she tried to come back across the ice, but Clark got to her first."

"Ross Chapman?"

"It was just me, Clark, and Cooper out there," Flowers said. "While Clark was getting Julie you went under. Cooper went in after you, and it took two of us to pull you out and keep you breathing." He paused. "By the time I looked up, Chapman was this speck way out there."

"On the ice bridge?"

Flowers shook his head. "He was off the bridge heading south toward open water. I wasn't about to go after him."

"So he drowned?"

"I radioed the coast guard and they've been looking for him for two days. I think he's dead."

The memory came back sudden but clear—Chapman in his black overcoat growing smaller and smaller in the whiteness. And his own cries for him to come back echoing in the wind.

The door opened, and an aide came in carrying a tray. "You ready for some food?" she asked Louis with a smile.

Before Louis could shake his head, she hit the button to raise the bed. After propping him up with pillows she wheeled the tray in front of him, smiled again, and disappeared.

Louis stared at the cup of juice, green Jell-O, and the gray plastic cover on the plate. Flowers reached over and removed the cover.

They both grimaced at the sight of the limp cheese sandwich.

"Take it away," Louis said.

Flowers took the tray away and set a basket on the table in its place.

"What's that?"

"A present from Maisey."

When Louis lifted up the heavy linen napkin the smell rose up to him, clean and yeasty. Biscuits.

Louis started to reach for a biscuit but then saw the blisters on his hand.

"I'll do it," Flowers said. He got a knife from the tray and spread some butter on a biscuit.

Louis took one bite. It was all he could manage.

"Maybe later," Flowers said, taking the biscuit from him. He carefully broke the biscuit into small pieces and left it where Louis could reach it.

"Thanks." Louis sank back into the pillows, closing his eyes. "Thanks for everything, Jack."

50

The murmur of voices woke him up. It took Louis a moment to realize they were coming from the TV. He reached across his pillow to turn the sound down, but the remote was gone.

"You're awake."

Louis dropped his head to his left. Rafsky sat in the bedside chair, comfortably slumped down, ankle on his knee, holding the remote in one hand and a can of Vernors in the other.

"You want it up or down?" Rafsky asked.

"Down."

Rafsky muted the sound.

"What time it is?" Louis asked, looking to the dark window.

"About six," Rafsky said. "How you feeling?"

"My feet hurt."

Rafsky took a drink of the ginger ale. "I would have been out there with you on the lake, but some dumb shit sent me on a wild-goose chase to the airport."

Louis hit the button to raise the bed. "Any sign of Ross yet?"

"He's disappeared," Rafsky said.

Louis was silent, looking at the television. The screen

was full of men and microphones. The crawl identified the tall man with a shock of white hair as the Mackinac County district attorney Greg Thom. Behind him were two men Louis didn't recognize and one he almost didn't. It was Chief Flowers wearing a blue dress uniform.

"Turn that up," Louis said.

The sound came up just as Flowers stepped to the microphone. His face was serious, his mondo-grass hair gelled back.

The reporters' questions came in a salvo, and for a second Flowers looked flustered. Then he launched into a smooth recap of the investigation and a credible explanation of why Julie's existence was kept secret.

"It was a carefully calculated decision designed to protect not only the suspect Julie Chapman but also Senator Ross Chapman from a media onslaught until we were able to get a clean and complete statement," Flowers said. "There was never an attempt to cover anything up. We were in control the entire time."

"He learns fast," Rafsky said.

"Who's that bald guy behind him?" Louis asked.

"My boss, Captain Leathers," Rafsky said.

As if on cue Leathers stepped to the microphone and, after heaping more praise on Flowers, he gave a short speech about how diligently the police had worked to solve a very difficult case. Rafsky was mentioned in passing. Louis was not.

Louis looked back at Rafsky. "How come you're not there?"

"I told them I had to visit a sick friend."

"Norm, this was your case," Louis said.

Rafsky muted the sound on the TV. "Flowers needed to lead the parade, not me," he said.

"You get anything at all out of this?" Louis asked.

Rafsky took a moment to answer. "I got a bump in rank to captain. And they offered me a high-level administrative position at the training center in Lansing."

"That's great."

"I'm not going to take it."

"Why not?" Louis asked. "I thought you were getting tired of the field. That's why you were putting in your papers, right?"

"I asked to stay in the Marquette post," Rafsky said.

Louis understood. "Chloe and Ryan will like that," he said.

Rafsky didn't comment. The press conference ended, and the station switched to the weather.

"Has the DA made a decision yet on whether to charge Julie?" Louis asked.

Rafsky turned off the TV and leaned forward on his knees. "He's looking at manslaughter."

"Seems a little harsh."

"You don't think she deserves some sort of punishment?"

"I don't know."

"Look at it this way," Rafsky said. "After she hit Rhonda Grasso with that stone she had two choices. Sit there and let her bleed out or try to get help."

Rafsky was right. Julie could have gone to town to get help for Rhonda, but the truth was, she never considered it. She had covered up her crime and gone upstairs to wait for Cooper. And then there was Chester

Grasso. Didn't he—and his daughter—deserve some kind of justice?

"You think she'll be found guilty?" Louis asked.

"I don't know, and I don't care," Rafsky said. "Our job ends when they close the cell door. After that it's all up to the lawyers."

Rafsky finished his Vernors and tossed the can across the room, making a nice swish into the trash can.

He stood up. "I have to get going."

Rafsky started to hold out his hand, then drew it back when he remembered Louis's sore fingers. Instead, he picked up his coat and laid it over his arm.

"You take care of yourself," Rafsky said.

"You, too."

Rafsky turned to leave. Louis watched him, thinking about staying here all night, watching the one TV station, and eating the bland food. Joe wasn't going to get here until tomorrow, and damn it, he wanted some company. He didn't mind at all if it was Rafsky.

"You know," Louis said, "you could hang around and bring me a burger later from the Mustang."

"Can't," Rafsky said. "I have a fresh body waiting for me in Newberry."

"A new case already?"

Rafsky paused at the door to give Louis a small smile. "The dead keep us alive, right?"

And then he was gone.

51

Louis rubbed his fingers and picked up the pen again. Eight days, and although the blisters had gone down, he still had a burning sensation. The doctor assured him he would get feeling back, but some mornings it was so bad he had to have Joe button his shirt. Still, some things he had to do for himself.

He stared at the picture on the front of the postcard—Mackinac Island's Arch Rock—turned it over, and began to write.

Dear Lily,

My job here is finished. You'll be happy to know that the girl's bones went home today. Chief Flowers was on TV like a big star. He said to say hi. I'll be going home soon and

He felt Joe's hand on his shoulder and looked up at her. She read what he had written and smiled.

"You want a beer?" she asked.

He shook his head. "Something warm."

She ran a light hand over his hair and moved away. He watched her as she pulled the coffee can from the cupboard, then he went back to writing the postcard. When he was done he opened the desk drawer, looking for a stamp. His eye caught the spot of black fur at his feet.

"What do you want?" he asked.

The little black dog was sitting there looking up at him.

"Joe!"

"What?"

"It's staring at me again."

"Just ignore her."

Louis gave the dog a gentle push of his socked foot.

Except for its tail swishing on the floor, the dog didn't move. The thing hadn't been here when Louis visited over the holidays. Joe told him one of her men found the dog when he went to check up on an elderly woman who didn't show up for her job as a crossing guard. He found the lady dead in her bed of natural causes, the dog lying across her feet. Joe had agreed to take it in until someone found it a home.

Louis had laughed the first time he saw it and called it a purse dog. Joe had to remind him that her last dog was a big yellow stray named Chips who had survived a knife attack. *And besides,* she told him, *I get lonely sometimes out here by myself.*

The dog—no name yet—was still looking up at him.

"Go away," he whispered.

It didn't move. With a sigh Louis went back to looking for a stamp. Finally he gave up and rose, going to the window.

The snow was heaped high in the front yard of Joe's

cabin. This morning she had gone out and shoveled a path to her police SUV and the mailbox out by the road, but it was still coming down. It was probably worse over on the island.

Louis reached into his pocket and pulled out the get-well card that had come in the morning's mail. It was from Chief Flowers, though Louis was sure Carol had had something to do with it. He suspected the chief didn't even know she had included a short letter. In it she thanked him for saving her husband's life and told him that they were working on trying to get back together.

Louis pushed his glasses up his nose and read the rest.

> *Jack's changed. We both have. I guess that's what getting older does to you, makes you look at things different. Jack says you and your lady manage a long-distance relationship. Maybe we can do it, too. We want to try at least.*

Louis took off his glasses and slipped them into his shirt pocket along with the card. The second time Flowers had visited him in the hospital he hadn't mentioned anything about reconciling with Carol. But he had said that he wanted to stay on as the island's police chief. It was where he belonged, he said. Besides, he had made a promise to Danny Dancer.

Dancer was now in a hospital in Escanaba, thanks to a plea agreement initiated by Flowers. With some time and medication there was a good chance Dancer might return to his cabin, and Flowers had promised him that it—and all his animal skulls—would be there when he got back.

The cottage was filling up with the smell of coffee. And bacon frying. Omelets for lunch again. It was the only thing Joe could make with any reliability.

The phone rang in the kitchen, and he heard Joe answer. A moment later, she came into the living room.

"It's for you," she said.

"Who is it?"

"Mark Steele."

Louis just stood there, his brain tumbling with questions. Rafsky, he thought, Rafsky had set this up.

"You going to take it?" Joe asked softly.

Louis went into the kitchen and picked up the receiver from the counter.

"This is Kincaid."

Joe was standing in the kitchen doorway, watching him. He kept his eyes on her face as he listened to Mark Steele. He said little, offering an occasional yes or no. Finally he hung up.

"What did he want?" Joe asked.

"He said he's taking the red flag off my file," Louis said. "I'm free to work in Michigan if someone makes me an offer."

Joe raised an eyebrow.

"Rafsky must have talked to him," Louis said.

Joe hesitated. "Do you want to work here again?"

Louis held her eyes for a moment, then went to the coffeemaker on the counter. He poured himself a cup and spent a long time stirring in three packs of sugar. He couldn't get his fingers through the mug handle, so he gripped it with both hands.

"Louis?"

He turned to the window over the sink and looked out. The snow was deep and wide. Nothing but a clean white canvas stretching as far as he could see.

"Louis," Joe said. "Don't you have anything to say?"

He turned to her. "I love you."